Margie,
I hope this [book?] [brings?]
joy and ex[citement?]
Thank you so much for the supp[ort]
Kindest Regards
S. Stack 2019

BETTER THAN THIS

By

Emma Stack

Copyright © 2019 by Emma L. Stack

All rights reserved. No part of this publication may be reproduced, distributed, or transmitted in any form or by any means, including photocopying, recording, or other electronic or mechanical methods, without the prior written permission of the publisher, except in the case of brief quotations embodied in critical reviews and certain other noncommercial uses permitted by copyright law.

FIRST EDITION

ISBN 978-1-9992293-0-6 (paperback)
ISBN 978-1-9992293-1-3 (ebook)
www.emmastackauthor.com

Acknowledgments

As I sat down to write this, I wondered how I could adequately thank someone for helping me achieve such an enormous life goal, and in just a few sentences. The more I thought about it, the more I realized I couldn't thank everyone the way they deserved, but I would try my best.

This book means so much to me, and it was, undoubtedly, made better by all of you. I will do my best to give you the praise, recognition, and gratitude you all so wholly deserve.

Firstly, I need to thank someone very special to me—someone who has touched almost every aspect of this book and was my inspiration for writing it. One summer day at my family's cottage, during my adolescence, my Grandma Jane introduced me to the secret world of historical romance. And I haven't looked back since. Many years later, when I told her I was going to write a book, she was overjoyed and said she couldn't wait to read it. Well, as it turned out, life got in the way, and for the next few years, I had little time to write. As a new mom to a critically ill child, I found myself pulled in directions I never thought possible. Throughout the years, Grandma Jane would always sweetly ask how my writing was going. She would never push or rush me. She was just always there—my silent cheerleader—waiting to one day read it. When I finally finished my manuscript, I was so excited to have her read it first. After all, she was an expert on historical romance. I handed her an unedited pile of papers in a binder, and her joy in my creation pushed me to improve it as best as possible. To this day, she still says, "I can't believe you wrote all those words!" and her enthusiasm continues to encourage me into further literary endeavors.

Secondly, I would like to thank my mother, Deb, who has been a constant source of creative support during my writing process. When I would experience the worst cases of writer's block, I would call her, and she would always bring me back to reality. In addition to keeping me sane, her beautifully bizarre way of seeing the world inspired me to write with all my senses and to experience every emotion I could before putting it down on paper. Most of all, she believed in my talents so much that she forced me to believe in myself.

I would also like to thank my father, Bob, and my brother, Jim. Thank you both so much for answering my extremely random, and sometimes late-night phone calls and text messages. My father answered all my questions about blacksmithing—no matter how insignificant. My brother is and always will be my phone-a-friend lifeline, and I will forever be grateful to him. I genuinely believe he is the keeper of the world's knowledge. Thank you both for your constant support and help.

The next person I want to thank is my very talented sister-in-law, Rachael. Ray's passion for reading surpasses even my own. She is versed in numerous genres, and like me, shares a soft spot for historical romance. She has helped me with read-throughs and edits and has expressed what was lacking and what she enjoyed. Her notes and critical eye helped make my work shine. Most importantly, she lent her extraordinary artistic vision to my book's cover art and created something that is both beautiful and unique. Ray somehow managed to capture the essence of my work in one small masterpiece.

I will start this next acknowledgment by fully admitting that sometimes, I am not an easy wife. I've always had big ideas, and have always gone for the things I wanted with fervor. My husband, Greg, has stood by me and supported me through every big idea I ever threw at him. When I decided to start writing novels, I don't think either of us understood what that meant. Greg cheered me on during the long nights, the rejections, and the stress that came with the process of writing this book. It is easy to thank people who help you on a creative level, as there are concrete items to acknowledge. However, when someone supports you emotionally and believes in you even when you don't believe in yourself, it is an overwhelming feeling of indescribable gratitude. It is no surprise then that Greg has been the hardest person to thank. How do I tell someone that they make me feel safe, secure, and loved enough to fly? Greg never once attempted to stifle my dreams or pull me back down to reality. He always cheered me on and never made me feel guilty for trusting myself. Thank you, Greg, from the bottom of my heart. I love you.

My son, Will, is much too wise and too knowledgeable for his age. He has been my rock and reminded me that when I write, I write for myself and no one else. Thank you, Will, for representing everything amazing in my life. I hope you foster your creativity always; in whatever way you choose.

Lastly, I would like to say a special thank you to my fantastic editor, Tereza Racekova from EDI*TER*. Tereza helped me navigate the challenging and confusing experience of being a first-time author. She brought out the best in my work and allowed me to feel safe enough to trust her with something as personal as my first novel. I never doubted that she had anything but the best intentions for my work. Thank you so much for all your dedication, skill, and hard work.

Prologue

Philadelphia, 1741

She was fairly certain of, and almost entirely prepared for the fact that she might die. In addition to the blistering fever and radiating pain, she lay there in a constant emotional battle between wishing to die and hoping to live. At this moment, embracing death had a distinct advantage on the field. She shifted slightly, feeling the pain of her blisters worsen with the motion. Her mother was now gone, as was her younger sister who was painfully taken a mere two days before her mother's passing. She had not yet accepted the fact that they were truly dead, and that she would never again be able to look at them, hug them, or know they were close by—a comforting presence if she ever needed them. She knew, like everyone else in town, that the pox was swift and deadly. It did not discriminate and was as ruthless as it was frightening. Many people had contracted the sickness in recent months, and now it had ripped its way savagely through her own life as it had so many others. She lay on her makeshift cot in the corner of a barn that had been hastily turned into a holding pen for the sick and dying. Her mother and sister had died at home and having no one left to care for her, she had been moved to the barn to either heal or die—depending on God's will.

Her father worked for the city government, which he often stated was a thankless job full of corruption and disloyalty. She could not say exactly what position he held since whenever she'd inquire, she'd be told it was impolite for women to speak of politics and government. Furthermore, it would be beyond her comprehension even if he attempted to explain it, so she eventually just stopped asking. Her father, Thomas, had spent the past season in New York and was expected to return home to Philadelphia around the time her mother had taken ill. A tear escaped her eye, the salty wetness stinging as it hit the blisters on her face; he would not yet know. He would come home to find his wife and youngest child dead, and he would not be allowed into the barn to visit her. She had listened while family members were turned away, the sick within earshot inside the barn. No one entered this place to visit, and very few people left. She closed her eyes.

It was a few days longer, then a month when she finally walked out of the putrid-smelling barn and let the evening sun warm her pale, marred skin. She had changed into a plain, itchy and clearly previously-worn dress that hung like a monk's robe and sat too many inches above her ankles. They had taken her clothes and burned them once she had been given a cot in the sick barn—partly to help not spread the disease, and partly not expecting her to leave. She had a little less than an hour walk to her home, and judging by the state of her bare feet and weakened body, she hoped she would make it before nightfall. She had been standing for a few minutes getting her bearings back when she heard someone calling her name. She turned to the direction of the call and saw her father climbing down from his carriage which sat slightly up the road, upwind from the barn. She walked as fast as her legs would allow her, and plunged into his arms. She heard herself make a crackling sobbing sound as her father's arms came around her body and held her tight to him.

"Ada, my child. I was sure you were lost to me as well," he sniffed loudly. "I sent inquiries everyday asking about your state, then sat at home dreading the reply. The messenger came back this morning and said you would be released sometime today. You could have knocked me over with a feather." He held her at arm's length and looked at her sunken ghostly face. "I thought for sure God was calling you home to him as well." He threw his arms around her and ushered her to the carriage and toward home.

1753

She looked out the window of the carriage at the trees, so many trees. Thick, dense, impossibly tall trees by the hundreds. The packed down dirt trail the carriage traveled on was the only brown smudge in the blanket of varying colours of green. The foliage surrounding the bottom of the tree trunks was at least waist height, and seemed to wrap the bark in softness. It was truly beautiful, although the sadness in her heart could not allow her to experience the full magnitude of its beauty.

Her world was changing. She had spent twelve years at home with her father in Philadelphia. Since her mother and sister's passing, she had been alone in running his household, attending societal functions and most enjoyably, being his constant companion. It was often said that between the ages of thirteen and twenty is when a woman needs a maternal feminine influence to shape and guide her through womanhood. Ada had never wanted anything other than the life she had with her father and the relationship they shared. At twenty-five years old, it was only now while riding through this beautiful landscape and mourning her father's death that she took the time to worry about the shortcomings in her upbringing and her paternal grandmother's opinion on the matter.

 Her grandmother, Agatha, was her only living relative. She had never met her in person but had been corresponding with her at least on a yearly basis for as long as she could remember.

She had always seemed pleasant and kind in her letters, and her mother and father had both spoken fondly of her. She had been married twice and after being widowed for the second time, had never remarried. She had been running her own estate since her late husband passed. When Ada's father died earlier in the year, she had written to her grandmother to inform her of his passing. She had received a letter back stating she would be delighted to have Ada come to Acadia and live with her, adding it was not respectable for an unmarried woman of her age to be living alone. The letter concluded that she was getting in contact with someone who would see to the sale of her father's estate, and that she expected Ada to leave as soon as she was able.

After her arrival at her grandmother's house, she was able to mourn and convalesce in a somewhat peaceful manner. Her grandmother's presence was comforting, if not a little overbearing, but she was always respectful of her privacy and her need to work things through on her own. It was not until the second year of her living there that her grandmother started bringing up the merits of marriage. Ada had known it would happen soon enough. Her father had let her have all the freedom in the world to marry only if she found someone she truly wanted to be with. Her grandmother had given her time and space to mourn and explore, but now was broaching the idea of marriage as often as she could and as aggressively as possible, while still being considered polite. Ada had never disliked the idea of marriage; in fact, she had never truly thought about it at all. So, when her grandmother finally and excitedly suggested a worthy match, Ada, considering her age and station in the world, dauntlessly agreed.

Chapter 1

Acadia/Nova Scotia, September, 1753
She could hear him coming down the hallway outside her bedroom. He always walked with the same angry, purposeful step that was just slow enough to demonstrate he was important, or more accurately, arrogant. Even his walk reflected his personal attitude— He believed the world revolved completely around him and everything and everyone should wait until his arrival, no matter how slow he chose to walk. The footsteps continued past her bedroom door and down the hall to the back stairs, where they disappeared into muffled thumping caused by the dark blue carpeting that lined them. Ada sat in front of her vanity and let out the breath she had not realized she was still holding. Her reflection looked back at her, the same worried and sorrowful reflection that had been staring back at her since she had married Colin this past summer. Her recently departed grandmother had thought them a good match. Not having any other living relatives, she trusted her grandmother to look out for her wellbeing. To everyone outside their grandeur home, Colin Watershaw

was a successful businessman who was classically handsome, with a civilized and privileged upbringing. Ada had known little about Colin before they wed, other than the fact that her grandmother approved of him. She had encouraged her to settle down with a professional and accomplished man, never failing to remind her that an old maid of seven and twenty years such as herself was lucky that a man like Colin Watershaw would even consider taking her as his wife.

Ada stared at herself in the oval mirror of her oak vanity. The woman who stared back at her was not the person she had been looking at for the last twenty-seven years of her life. She looked sad, withdrawn, pale, and another emotion she couldn't quite put her finger on—most likely the look of someone who has resigned themselves to a fate they could never hope to escape. Even her hair seemed morose, and she wondered if that was even possible. She had always liked her hair; it was full, wavy and the colour of a shiny chestnut that had just fallen from its branch. Even the unruliness that came with the rainy days seemed to become her. Now, her hair hung in a truly lackluster fashion, which made her want to hide it under a hat. Ada's skin had always had a lovely tan colouring, with a sprinkling of freckles across her cheekbones that one could only see if they got too close. She was paler now, she noticed. Her eyes were the same dark blue they had always been and her lips the same soft pink. Overall, she knew she had a very pleasing face. Her grandmother had told her once that her smile was so bright, she could draw the fishermen back from the sea if she chose to stand on the shoreline. She had not genuinely smiled in a long time, and she doubted anyone would notice now if she did.

July, 1753

Ada sat waiting in the parlor of one of the biggest houses she had ever seen. The ceilings were high and white, and the windows stretched from the floor to the ceiling. Even the burgundy curtains gave off an air of wealth and splendor she was not accustomed to. Growing up in Philadelphia, her family had been upper middle class, but nothing this elaborate. The splendor of this place made her feel nervous. She was already anxious to begin with as this was the first time she would meet the man, who in a few days, would become her husband. She was trying to listen as her grandmother prattled on about the benefits of marrying well, but she was too worried about the arrival of her future husband to pay much attention. That was the first time she heard those footsteps. Back then, Ada thought they sounded proud and self-assured, but had since learned that the footsteps, like the man himself, had a very deceiving first impression. Colin Watershaw and his father strolled into the parlour where Ada and her grandmother had been waiting. Ada noticed that at a mere five foot six inches, Colin was not much taller than her. He had a slight build and fine, thin blonde hair, which added to his already aristocratic features. All of this made him appear younger than he was. Although thin in build, he seemed to have an underlying strength from which Ada could tell by the way his expensive, well-tailored clothes fit his body.

"Mr. Watershaw, sir. How very nice of you to have us in your home, and what a lovely home it is!" Ada's grandmother was clinging to Colin's father's arm as if he was the King himself. "I am so glad that our families will be joined by the union of these two fine young ones." Ada could feel herself grimace at the term 'young'. She and everyone else was well aware she was over the average marrying age. Suddenly, she felt even more self-conscious.

"Miss Jamison, may I call you Ada? It is a pleasure to meet you finally, and may I just state how excited I am for our upcoming nuptials." Colin had grabbed Ada's hand and bowed deeply over it, while her grandmother and his father were discussing everything from refreshments and today's weather, to the upcoming wedding and future grandchildren/great-grandchildren.

"Mr. Watershaw, truly the pleasure is all mine." Ada looked down toward her shoes and the lovely brocade rug under her feet. So far, Colin had been the kind of gentlemen her grandmother had promised he would be. However, something in the way he looked at her did nothing but increase her anxiety. It was as if his eyes were telling a completely different story than his gentlemanly manners and rehearsed speech.

After sitting down to tea and fresh biscuits drizzled with wild strawberry jam, they began to discuss the details of the wedding and how the day would run. Tomorrow, the day before the wedding, Ada would have all her belongings brought to the house so she could be moved in and settled before the wedding day. Colin's father's business was in England, and he lived there most of the time. He stayed in Colin's house sporadically when he was back home. The complete running of the house would fall on Ada. She was surprisingly excited to become the lady of such a fine house and aid her husband in the running of the estate. The conversation had been going on for almost an hour when Colin stood up and said, "It seems such a waste to spend a fine summer day like this inside in conversation. Perhaps Ada would like to join me for a walk while father and Mrs. Jamison continue the planning uninterrupted?"

"Capital idea, Colin. I am sure Ada would love to get to know the countryside around her new home." Colin's father stood up as Colin and Ada left the room, then resumed his planning with Ada's grandmother.

It was peaceful outside with the sound of the birds calling to each other from tree to tree. The breeze blew the smell of wood smoke softly over Ada, and she took in the beauty of the natural wildflowers and the tall trees that surrounded the back of the house by the path they had chosen to walk along.

"It really is a lovely day to walk. I have to admit, I was getting a little bored with all the talk of wedding flowers and guest lists," Ada confided with a smile, as she walked along the path of packed down earth and grass.

"I have been bored with this wedding from the beginning," Colin stated, staring Ada directly and uncomfortably in the eyes. "Much like my father had with my late mother, I need a wife to run the domestic aspect of my estate and keep up appearances when we are invited out. Other than that, I do not require or desire for that matter, to be married. I suppose that I would need a son to carry on my name, but that shouldn't be too hard to accomplish. Your hips look like they were made for bearing children."

Ada was completely floored by the tone Colin had taken and the terrible things he had just said. How could he be so gentlemanly inside the house and such a rude beast out here with her? The comment about her looking like she was made to bear children had hurt the most. Already aware of her curvaceous figure compared to other girls, Ada now felt even more shy about her physique.

"How dare you say such horrible things to me?" Ada hissed in a muted whisper in case there was anyone within earshot.

"In two days, Ada, you will be my property and therefore, I can say and do whatever I please to you. Although, I'm sure I will enjoy some of the things I must *do* to you." With that suggestive comment, Colin grabbed a handful of Ada's backside and squeezed hard. Ada shrieked and jerked away. She drew up her hand to slap him across his insolent face, but he caught her wrist in midair.

"If you ever so much as think about striking me again, I will knock your pretty teeth out of your pretty mouth. And with a body like yours, dear, you need to keep your face as attractive as you can." Colin took her trapped hand and tucked it into the crook of his arm and began to walk back. "I am not a man to be trifled with, Ada. Please try to remember that when we get back to the house."

Ada could not believe what had just transpired. She

was humiliated and hurt but beyond that, she was angry. *It will be a cold day in hell before I play the shrinking violet for him*, Ada thought, as she walked toward her future home with the husband she already hated.

Her grandmother and Colin's father were waiting for them in the parlour when they returned.

"Did you enjoy your walk, my dear?" Colin's father rose and took her hand as she entered the room.

"The countryside is beautiful, sir, and the fresh air is always refreshing," she said, smiling. *My God*, Ada thought, *he doesn't know. His father thinks him to be the gentleman everyone else thinks him to be. I will be alone in knowing the truth about him, and no one will ever believe he is anything but a good man.*

Ada and her grandmother took their leave to return home to finish packing Ada's belongings. Ada felt as though her entire existence had been turned completely around. That morning, she was an anxious but hopeful bride-to-be but now, she was an angry and hurt one. As her grandmother went on and on about the details she had discussed with Colin's father, Ada was in a daze, believing that the bonds of matrimony might as well be shackles of a jail cell, as she would be forever bound to a man who was not at all what he seemed.

Chapter 2

It was amazing how quickly the staff at the Watershaw house had unpacked all her belongings. Ada's lady's maid, who had been appointed to her upon her arrival, was a tiny mouse of a girl. Her wisps of thin blonde hair escaped her kerchief and she seemed to have a perpetual blush on the apples of her cheeks, probably because she was constantly running around cleaning, folding and washing clothes or prepping Ada's dressing table. She had introduced herself as Marie, and her tiny frame made her seem even younger than the eighteen-year-old she claimed to be. Ada sat at her vanity watching as Marie twisted pieces of her freshly washed and brushed hair into curls. She would have preferred to wear her hair down but Marie insisted she wear it piled on top of her head, with only a few tendrils coming down to frame her face.

"Madame, please. You must know it is only proper for a grown woman to wear her hair swept up on her wedding day. If I left it down, what would people think of me as your maid? *Non, non, non!* It must be up!"

Ada did not have the energy to argue with Marie, and as a stranger in the house, she doubted very much she would win even if she tried. Marie had finished her hair by adding two white flowers she had picked fresh from the garden. Ada had to admit that her face suited this hairstyle and the flowers made her feel young and pretty. She stood up to take a final look at herself. Her dress was lovely. She had chosen it a few months ago, hoping to wear it on a happier wedding day. Back then, she never thought she would be marrying someone who could say such cruel things to her with no provocation. She swished her skirt back and forth, enjoying the sound of the silk and linen. It was a pale pink linen dress, with small white flowers embroidered along the hem at the bottom of the skirt. The silk sleeves were fitted to just above the elbow and gave way to white lace that finished the sleeve down to her wrist. She had a square neckline that showed the tops of her breasts which moved when she breathed. Her favorite part of the dress was the triangle of cream coloured silk that ran from under her neckline to a point at her waist. She thought the dress was very becoming on her, showing off an appropriate amount of décolletage while allowing her larger waist to be cinched in and her hips and bottom to be hidden within the blooming skirt. She attached her grandmother's pearls around her neck and pinching her cheeks for a final touch, squared her shoulders and grabbed the door handle to go downstairs and face her fiancé and guests.

"He may not love me but I will be damned if I will be bullied into looking forlorn and woe begotten on my wedding day." Ada spoke to her reflection, her hand still on the door latch.

"Pardon, madam?" Marie popped her head out from the armoire where she had been putting away Ada's dresses.

"Nothing, Marie. Thank you for your help with my toilette."

"It is my pleasure, madam! Now, go before you are late for your own wedding." Marie ushered her down the stairs and out to the garden where her groom and guests were waiting for her.

As far as weddings go, the ceremony had been uneventful. The guests had retired to the tables set up in the garden to enjoy the lavish dinner that had been prepared to follow the ceremony. Ada sat at a table with her new husband, her father-in-law and her grandmother. She had to admit that her grandmother and father-in-law had done a wonderful job with the details of the wedding. The servants had made the tables and garden look lovely. There were lace tablecloths with fresh flowers in the centre of each table and the plates and crystal drinkware matched flawlessly. Had she married someone she loved, this would have been the perfect day. However, now she sat next to Colin eating roasted chicken in complete silence. When they had finished their main course and the dessert was brought out, Colin leaned close to her ear and whispered, "Normally, I would not suggest that someone with your figure eat such a large meal and then indulge in desserts as well, but I expect you're going to need all the energy you can get when we retire to our bedroom." He laughed rudely and then turned to speak to his father about something regarding the livestock.

In all the events of the past few days—meeting Colin for the first time, moving into his home and the wedding itself, not to mention the emotional drain of realizing what her future might hold—Ada had not spared a minute to consider her wedding night. Colin's comment, like a slap in the face, had shocked her into recalling he would expect her to consummate their horrible marriage.

Well, she thought, *they can lead a horse to water but they cannot make it drink. There is no way I will be sharing my bed with a man as crass and heartless as him. I may have been obliged to marry Colin, but allowing him to take my innocence is an entirely different matter.*

Colin had started drinking before the wedding ceremony that morning, and had not stopped since. With his back to the door, he was now standing at the shelves in his office staring at the rows of books with a whisky in his hand. A shadow quickly fell across the floor, shading the light of the candle sconces in the hallway. Colin whirled around, wondering who would dare linger near the doorway of his office.

"Oh, it's you." Colin relaxed as he saw his father enter the dimly lit room.

"A fine greeting to give your father," he replied, "and after I found you a wife whose only living family, fortunately, has not heard of your escapades with the serving woman down at the inn." He walked over to fill himself a glass of whisky and looked at his son. "You should be glad that anyone would wed you at all!"

"Honestly father, the woman in the inn was nothing but a common servant. I can do with her as I please, and it pleased me to teach her to never disrespect me with refusal ever again." The conversation with his father was beginning to diminish the effect of his fine aged whisky. "I am tired of this conversation, father. I am going to bed while I am still drunk enough to pretend you married me to a woman who has any attractive attributes at all."

With that, Colin downed the remains of his drink, hissing as the heat hit the back of his throat. He placed the crystal glass on his desk and walked toward the staircase. If only Ada looked like that tavern maid he had beaten. He remembered how her thin and frail frame had turned him on before she had refused him and had to be punished. His wife—he wanted to spit at the word wife—was everything he hated in a woman. Perhaps, it was because Ada reminded him of his older cousin whom he had longed for growing up, until he tried to kiss her at the age of twelve and she had mocked him and called him a little boy in front of a group of their friends and family members. Colin shook his head feeling slightly dizzy.

God, why am I thinking about that? Colin grimaced. He did not know whether it was the marriage, the whisky, or a combination of both that had thrown him into his unhappy memories.

He had reached the door to the bedroom he had selected for Ada. He knew she was in there because the light from the hearth peeked out from beneath the door. He sighed sharply. There was no help for it; he would have to go in and make this marriage legal if he ever hoped to gain a son and heir. Besides, the whisky had made him crave a woman, even if it was his undesirable wife.

Ada saw the shadow of her husband's feet darken the light from under the door. She had, much to Marie's confusion, worn the thickest and most concealing night dress she owned, and had sat down in the chair in front of the fire to read. She did so purposefully to be nowhere near the bed when Colin came in, lest she gave him any ideas. He threw open the bedroom door without as much as a knock or call to let her know he was entering.

"You should have knocked, I could have been indisposed," Ada muttered as he began to kick off his boots.

"Knock, it's my house! I sincerely hope that was a failed attempt at humour, Ada. Or, are you actually that unintelligent? snapped Colin.

"I was merely suggesting that perhaps you show me a little respect. I am your wife now, regardless of how much we both dislike that fact."

"My wife will respect *me*; I have no need to respect her. I am not asking for your respect, Ada. I am telling you that you will give it to me." Colin had taken off his overcoat and was now standing in his shirt and vest, breeches, and silk stockings. Had he not been such an overall loathsome individual, Ada would have admired the fine quality and tailoring of his wedding ensemble. Instead, she stood staring at him as if he was wearing ladies' undergarments, a mocking glare in her eye, which seemed to be going unnoticed by Colin.

"On that note then, I will wish you a very respectful goodnight, husband." Ada's words were full of sarcasm.

"I do hope that the morning will find you in a much better temper than the one you are in this evening."

Ada rose and moved toward the door to show Colin out, finally allowing herself to get some sleep and hopefully recuperate from the last few days. She made it less than three steps before Colin stepped in front of her. They were so close in height that she looked almost directly into his eyes and what she saw made her take a hasty step back. Colin's eyes were afire with rage and she thought she noticed a fleeting moment of revenge, although she could not imagine what she could have done to make him vengeful. She took two more steps back and Colin matched her steps until her back hit the wooden wall behind her. She looked to her left and to her right, but Colin had placed both of his hands flat on the wall on either side of her head.

"Did you think I would be leaving so soon, Mrs. Watershaw?" Colin hissed.

Ada was more than a little afraid. She had assumed that if she stood her ground, Colin would have given up, stormed out and would have found another bed for the night. She now cursed herself for not thinking of the possibility that he would force himself on her. Good men from good families do not behave this way... but then it truly hit her: Colin Watershaw was not a good man. His coarse behavior was not all talk, he had the capacity to do unimaginable things, and he meant to do them to her.

"Get out!" Ada spoke as authoritatively as she could muster but before she could say anymore, Colin had forced his tongue into her mouth and was kissing her hard. He tasted of whisky, and she had to fight the urge to throw up from both fear and disgust. She brought her hand up and slapped him across his cheek as hard as she could. He had shut his eyes during the kiss and was taken completely off guard. His eyes shot open and he looked directly into Ada's face.

"That was a mistake, bitch." He took his left hand off the wall and grabbed a handful of hair at the base of Ada's skull. He pulled her head back hard, making her eyes water and her neck ache from the sudden jerking movement.

"What did I tell you about respect? Do you think you are the first woman I have had to teach this lesson to? You whores are all the same, believing you can have the upper hand with men. I'll prove you very wrong, Ada." With that snarled comment, Colin released her hair, raised his left hand and backhanded Ada across the cheek. She didn't even have time to cry out before her knees hit the floor with her hands following.

Supported by her hands and knees, she spat on the floor. She could taste the metallic taste of blood mingled with the whisky from Colin's earlier kiss. She spat again, trying to clear the taste from her mouth. Her face burned ferociously and although the pain was not unbearable, she knew it would feel a lot worse come morning. She turned her reddened face toward Colin

"How dare you?" she spat again but this time toward his shoes. "You intolerable bastard, I cannot…"

Before she could finish her sentence, his rough hand was back in her hair and he was dragging her into a standing position. With a grunt, he hauled her to her feet and pushed her, face first, onto the bed. She could feel the bed sheets against her cheek and she noticed that her lip had left a streak of blood across the cream coloured linen. She threw herself onto her back and kicked madly. There was no doubt in her mind of what Colin intended to do, but she was not going to make it easy for him. She saw him pull back his hand, then she felt it come down hard against her face. She tried to reach up and grab a hold of his hair but as she rose, Colin smashed his forehead into hers with such a force that she saw flashing lights and fell back onto the bed. He took this moment of forced docility to rip at the front of her robe and night dress. Through her haziness, she thought she could hear ripping fabric and then her breasts were exposed. She could feel his hot breath against her face and drops of sweat raining onto her chest. She felt sick from the blow to the head and moved her body to the side and moaned, thinking she might vomit. Colin put his hand around her neck.

"Moan like that again, wife," he whispered into her ear. She could feel his manhood pressing against her thighs but the tighter she pressed her legs together, the harder he squeezed her throat. She was becoming dizzy and she did not have the strength left to fight. She needed to survive and right now, she was not completely sure Colin would let her live. She did not resist as Colin used his knee to pry apart her legs. She shut her eyes, attempting to block out any sensations she could. She could feel Colin prodding around looking for her entrance. He found his way and her entire body stiffened as he thrust deep inside her. She shrieked, and with resumed fear and strength, tried to kick him off her. The hand that was on her throat moved up to cover her mouth. Tears streamed down the sides of her cheeks and she looked up at him. His cold eyes were laughing at her. He continued his penetrating assault. Thrust after thrust he pounded against her, muffling her whines with his hand. Then, his body went rigid and he grunted—a more disgusting sound Ada had never heard. He looked down at her face.

"Ada, Ada, Ada… you are going to be a sight tomorrow. At least you will not be leaving the house. Besides, it's not like I ruined that beautiful of a face, is it?"

With that, Colin pulled himself abruptly from her, making her wince. He pulled up his pants with one hand, strode to her dressing table, picked up the mirror her grandmother had given her as a wedding present and looked briefly at his face. Running a practiced hand through his now disheveled hair, he put the mirror down, opened the door and left. She could hear his footsteps walking arrogantly down the hall to his bedroom. Ada curled up into herself, pulled the ripped pieces of her night robe together and sobbed relentlessly until she drifted into a disturbed sleep.

Chapter 3

Ada awoke the next morning still curled in the same position she had put herself in the night before. She cracked one eyelid open but soon realized it hurt to try and open it any wider. She pushed herself into a sitting position to take a better look at the room around her. She was glad to see that Marie had not yet been in. Her wedding night was too humiliating and painful for even herself to think about. What would Marie think when she saw the room and her face? The thought of her face forced her to stand up. Stifling a groan, she limped over to the dressing table and picked up the small mirror. She took a deep, steadying breath and looked at her reflection. She slammed the mirror back down on the table in disgust. Cautiously picking it up again, she saw that her bottom lip was split by the corner of her mouth. She touched the cut with her tongue and tasted the coppery taste of dried blood. The right side of her face was slightly swollen; she had bitten the inside of her cheek when Colin had slapped her. When she tentatively put up her fingers to investigate the swelling, her skin felt warm and tight to the touch. Her right eye looked the worst. It was visibly swollen and painted with countless shades of red and purple that it was almost artistic. As far as she could tell, her vision seemed to be normal because she could see clearly through the swelling.

First things first, she needed a bath badly. She could smell fear on her body from the night before, but much worse was that she could smell him. A musky odour that she had never smelled before and frankly, would love to never smell again. There was no need to lift the hem of her nightgown to check, she knew there was blood and Colin's seed on the inside of her thighs. Before she could continue her personal examination, Marie bustled into the room with a pot of tea and some toast with honey.

"Good morning, madam!" Marie set the breakfast down on the dressing table and turned to look at Ada. "*Tsk*." She took a delicate finger and traced it down the side of Ada's face. "I knew he was an angry man, but I never thought he would leave such marks. He usually tries to hide his aggression from the world. Now, you are a glaring sign for anyone who wishes to speculate."

Ada remained still while Marie turned her toward the window to examine her face in the morning light. "It is alright, madam. Your face will not be permanently damaged, just sore for a while and I'm afraid you will be a fright to look at until those bruises clear. Are you much hurt elsewhere?" Marie glanced toward the bloodstains on the bed sheets as well as the stains on her night robe.

"No, I am fine. Thank you, Marie." Ada was trying to keep herself composed. Even though she liked Marie, she was still a stranger to her— a stranger that did not seem at all surprised to see her in this state.

"Please call for a bathing tub and water to be brought up. I would like to take a bath. You do not have to stay, Marie. Thank you. You can come back for the linen and my clothing a little later. I would like to be by myself just now." Ada took the cup of tea and sat down on the chair at the dressing table. She wrapped her hands around the hot teacup and let the warmth soak into her chilled hands. The toast smelled enticing but she had no appetite.

The tub had been brought up, and a quarter of an hour later when enough water had been poured, she ushered everyone out of her room, discarded her soiled clothes and sat down in the hot water. She let the water calm her, then picked up the sponge Marie had provided for her and began to scrub herself clean. Tears silently rolled down her cheeks and disappeared into the bath water. She should be angrier, she should be deeply hurt, she should mourn the loss of her old life and mourn the beginning of this new life. Instead, she felt numb. She thought that maybe this numbness was a blessing, because she would rather feel nothing at all then relive any of the emotions she had felt last night. She rose from the tub only when the water began to cool. No longer in the sanctuary of the hot calming water, she quickly dried herself with a large drying cloth and got dressed in a simple but pretty pale blue dress. She would need to leave her bedroom eventually, so this was probably as good a time as any.

She walked toward the staircase and passed Marie who was on her way back upstairs. "Are you much revived, madam?" she asked. "Is there anything else you need? They are serving luncheon shortly in the dining room."

"Please see that my room is set back to rights, Marie. Also, is my husband downstairs?" She tried to sound calm but thought she heard her voice catch on the word husband.

"No, madam, he was out in the stables this morning with *les chevaux*."

Ada relaxed slightly. She had worn her hair long to try and shadow some of the bruising on her face, no doubt Marie had probably already informed the staff about her appearance but she still could not face seeing everyone with her hair pinned back and face on display. She descended the stairs into the foyer and slowly walked down the carpeted hall into the dining room. The room was large and pretty. The long table and matching chairs were the focal point of the room and the place settings for luncheon were beautifully painted with intricate flowers. She sat down in one of the dining chairs by the window. It was open and she liked to smell the scents of the meadow that blew over her with the strong and gusty summer breeze that came through the window. She closed her eyes and breathed deeply. She could almost imagine herself elsewhere to when she was younger, lying in the fields by her parent's house while reading and feeling the warmth of the sun on her cheeks. She heard someone clear their throat and she opened her eyes. A butler. She remembered meeting him briefly on the day she visited with her grandmother.

He was now standing in the doorway to the dining room, observing her with a carefully blank expression.

"Good day, ma'am. It is a pleasure seeing you again. My name is Robertson. Shall I bring you some water, or perhaps a cup of tea to sip on while we await Mr. Watershaw's return from the stables? He has asked me to serve lunch upon his arrival."

Ada refrained from sighing aloud. Obviously, he would be coming home. It was his house too and she could not expect to avoid him indefinitely. She wished, however, that she could have had a little more time to prepare herself.

"Some water would be lovely, thank you," she replied. As he left the room, she was glad he had not had any reaction to her face. She smiled to herself. It was odd to be relieved that someone could completely ignore such a blatant sign of mistreatment, but perhaps it was even stranger for her to be both relieved and happy about such ignorance.

Ada sipped her water and waited. She heard the front door close and Colin entered the dining room. As soon as Colin sat down, Robertson appeared carrying steaming bowls of something that smelled delicious with thick pieces of home baked bread. Ada was starving, she had not had the appetite to eat her toast that morning, and had only consumed a cup of tea and her current glass of water. Upon it being placed in front of her, Ada noticed that the steaming bowls were full of a very thick soup. She glanced at Colin, and seeing he had already begun to eat, she eagerly picked up her spoon.

Colin glared at her as she spooned the hot soup

carefully into her mouth, trying unsuccessfully to avoid the cuts on her lip.

"I hope you understand you obviously cannot leave the property looking like you do. I will not have people thinking my wife is such a terror that I must go to such lengths to keep her reigned in. It would look terrible for my reputation." He chewed his bread industriously before continuing. "You may stay in the main house, help in the gardens, or even venture to the stables. You must not ride out anywhere until your face has healed." He brushed at crumbs on his vest.

"You will allow me to go to the stables?" Ada was surprised. She had doubted that Colin would let her outside at all, let alone in the barn where he kept his fine sale and breeding horses.

"I would love to lock you inside all day to save me the embarrassment of having people see what I was forced to marry but I fear it would cause more speculation and gossip then allowing you out."

Ada glanced down into her lap and pulled at her dress, trying to smooth the material around the midsection which now seemed too tight and uncomfortable.

"Is there a horse I could ride around the grounds, Colin?" she asked, already expecting to be disappointed by the answer. She loved to ride but after her treatment last night and before the wedding, she had never expected to be allowed to enjoy that pastime again.

"There is a mare in the back stall I was going to sell to the butcher. She is too old to produce anymore good offspring and she has always been terrible to look at— you two should have a lot in common." Colin stood up and put his napkin on the table. "Robertson, I will not be eating dinner here tonight, and tell the cook to make the bread a little fresher next time, I may as well have chewed on the table leg." With that, Colin left the dining room without so much as a backward glance at Ada.

As she rose from the table, Ada still could not believe Colin had granted her access to one of the horses. If she could not go into town for a few weeks, she could at least get fresh air and acquainted with her new mount.

Thirty minutes later, Ada had retrieved her long navy-blue cloak, had asked Marie to pin her hair up and managed to beg an old withered apple from the kitchen maid. With her hood pulled up to hide her face, she set off toward the barn at the edge of the property. It was windy but warm, and although she was hot in her cloak, she was glad to be wearing it because the hood hid her face. She quickened her step and grabbed the wooden latch and pushed up, blowing herself and the warm air into the barn with a whoosh. She re-latched the door and stood with her back against the heavy wood, letting her eyes adjust to the dim light the windows let in. She always thought the smell of barns was relaxing. She looked around and noticed it was a very grand barn. Colin obviously loved his horses. *Probably because they made him money in stud fees and offspring,* she thought angrily. She pushed the thought of her husband aside, not wanting to sully her decent mood with her disgust toward him. She walked down the aisle of stalls looking at all the shiny noses when a very large man stepped out of a stall door in front of her. She jumped back and let out a yelp, making the horses closest to her shy back into their stalls and snort at her. When she leapt back, her hood had fallen off her head and she quickly grabbed it and pulled it back up and low over her forehead.

The man spoke, "I am sorry, miss. I thought ye were Mr. Watershaw back again. I dinna mean to startle ye." His deep Scottish voice sounded as surprised to see her as she was to see him. She had seen him quickly glance at her face before she pulled her cloak back up and could have sworn she saw an expression of angry pity before he guarded it with a polite smile. "I'd best be getting back to work. My apologies again, miss." He turned and walked back into the stall with one of Colin's stallions and began to rasp the horse's hoof industrially.

She wondered whether he worked at the house. He was probably a stable man Colin had forgotten to mention when he was introducing her to the staff during her visit in the days prior to their wedding. She found the stall at the back of the barn where a plain bay mare was concentrating on chewing the scraps of hay she found in her manger. The mare looked up as Ada unlatched the stall and snorted a greeting before going back to what was left of her dinner. It was true that this mare was not much to look at—she had a dull brown coat, which looked dusty and ill-kept, and her black mane was missing chunks where she had obviously caught it on a fence or her stall and pulled it out. Her tail looked as if it had had the hair chewed off by a passing goat, and her ears seemed slightly too big and droopy for her head. Ada loved her right away. She knew that whatever this mare looked like, it had been a direct result of the horse no longer being part of the breeding operation and being therefore disposable and unworthy of time that could be spent otherwise on the more profitable horses. Ada held out the apple she had gotten from the kitchen and the homely horse raised her head and walked daintily over to her to accept the gift. She nuzzled Ada's palm once she had consumed her present and looked into Ada's eyes as though she knew life was not perfect for her either. Not knowing whether she already had a name, Ada decided to call her Gypsy as she could see this horse knew her already.

Chapter 4

Grant watched as the young woman finished feeding the mare an apple. He did so not in an obvious manner to be sure, but from the stall where he was working, half hidden by the valuable stallion he was trimming. It amused him to hear her speaking to the ugly horse as though it was a prizewinning broodmare. He assumed anyone working in the Watershaw household would only have eyes for things of high quality and that mare had not been considered high quality for some years now. He had heard that Colin Watershaw had taken a wife. He felt sorry for the woman already. Although Colin had most people believing he was a gentleman, Grant saw how Colin's eyes changed when he talked about women. Moreover, he had heard rumors in the tavern at the inn that Colin had something to do with the abuse of one of the serving girls.

The sound of soft talking brought him back to the present. He laughed to himself as he listened to the conversation between the woman and the horse. This woman must be under the service of the new Mistress

Watershaw, and it seemed she had gotten on the wrong side of someone recently. Perhaps Mrs. Watershaw beat her servants for bad behavior. It was not an uncommon practice, and if that was the case, maybe Mr. Watershaw and his new wife were well suited after all. He realized that he was still watching the woman as she brushed the burrs out of the mare's coat. *You're acting like a thirteen-year-old lad,* he scolded himself. *Ye still have three horses to trim for Mr. Watershaw and it's already well past noontime.* Grant sighed and went back to work although he would much rather continue enjoying the view.

Three weeks had passed and this morning was the first where Ada could see no sign of bruises on her face when she looked in the mirror. It was a good thing too because she had overheard Colin speaking to his father about the talk he had heard while in town working. People were wondering why they never saw the new Mrs. Watershaw and why Colin kept her hidden away. Some ladies had speculated that she must have some disfigurement Colin was ashamed of, and some of the bawdier gentlemen had nudged each other in the ribs and hinted that Colin must be keeping her too busy during the night to want to venture out the next day. Regardless of the reason, Colin hated gossip and Ada knew that his increasingly foul mood was a result of her bruises remaining longer than he thought they should have. Therefore, this made it impossible for him to go out in public with his wife and silence the townspeople's wagging jaws. During this time, Colin had not spoken to Ada unless it was absolutely necessary. He had, however, visited her bedchamber half a dozen times to copulate with her. She refused to call it making love because there was nothing remotely tender or loving about it. After the beating she had received on her wedding night, she was too terrified to try and fight back, though it seemed Colin wanted her to—he liked the power and dominance it gave him. Instead, she would lie down and silently concede with any demand he made. Most of the time, his demands were demeaning and painful, but it was a lot better than spitting blood on the floor.

Marie was dressing Ada for the day when the bedchamber door slammed open. Colin walked over to Ada, pretending Marie did not exist, and grabbed her chin roughly. "It's about time you looked bloody normal again." He released her chin and stepped back.

"The men in my circle are going fishing today and you will be attending a picnic lunch with the wives. Try to find a dress to wear that flatters some part of your figure, won't you?" On that uncomplimentary note, Colin turned on his heel and strolled out of the room, then quickly turned back to say, "Eleven o'clock and no later, understand?"

Before Ada could answer, the door was shut with a bang and the footsteps abated.

Although Ada was commanded to attend the picnic, she could not help but feel excited at the thought of being social again and getting to speak to someone other than Colin, Marie, the other servants and Gypsy.

The buggy clattered down the driveway at five minutes past eleven. Their contribution to the picnic—or more accurately, the cook's contribution to the picnic—sat in a wicker basket behind Ada's seat. The food smelled delicious. She wondered what the cook had packed for her but was reluctant to ask in Colin's presence, as she couldn't risk receiving another comment about her figure. Her self-esteem had never been lower since she married Colin and even today, it took Ada over thirty minutes to choose an outfit she felt comfortable wearing. These women were her new peers and potential new friends, so she wanted to look her best. She ended up choosing a white day gown with a small pattern of blue daisies embroidered all over the material. She had also chosen a straw sun hat with a blue ribbon that matched the colour of the daisies. She hoped she looked good enough. She was still thinking about her attire when Colin finally spoke to her. They were sitting side by side on the front bench of the buggy and although he had helped her into the seat, Colin had said nothing to her as the buggy drove through the town and finally into the countryside by the shore. "We are almost there, do not do anything to draw attention to yourself, and try not embarrass either of us in anyway. Is that understood?" Colin seemed nervous. She supposed he was worried she would tell the ladies how he had been treating her and as a result, stain his image.

"I will be on my best behavior, Colin," Ada replied more sarcastically than she intended to and saw Colin's head turn sharply toward her.

"Careful, wife. I am only gone for the afternoon and I would not want to give you another reason to keep your face hidden for another three weeks."

Ada's belly clenched and she wisely said nothing. Her bruises had just faded and the taste of freedom was enough to make her swallow her pride and make no reply to Colin. She concentrated on the smell of the summer breeze that was lightly tickling the trees into a slow dance. It was a beautiful place. If only her heart was as calm as the countryside seemed to be.

They arrived at the area where the ladies would set up their picnic and the men would collect their fishing equipment and head down the hillside to the small boat on the shore. There were already four couples there and another carriage was coming down the path behind their own. Colin hopped down from the driver's seat and walked over to Ada's side of the buggy, then put his hands around her waist and lifted her down. She was very conscious of everyone watching their interaction and no doubt Colin was aware as well—nothing else would have made him help her down. He grabbed the picnic basket from the back of the seat, offered Ada his arm and set off toward the large blankets that were already spread out over the grass. Ada had to stop herself from rolling her eyes—surely someone could see through this doting husband act that Colin was playing so well. He delivered her to the small group of women, placed the picnic basket down on the blanket and gallantly bowed over Ada's hand, brushing his lips across her knuckles. With a smile—that on anyone else would have been dazzling—he turned and strode over to the group of men.

"Oh, for God's sake," Ada muttered, then plastered on a smile and turned to meet the throng of ladies who had watched the entire charade with doe-eyed enthusiasm.

A pretty brunette was the first one to approach her. She grabbed Ada's hand in her delicate, satin gloved-hand.

"Mrs. Watershaw! I cannot tell you how good it is to finally meet you! Anyone who did not attend your wedding was beginning to believe you did not exist… of course, I never listened to a word of that gossip. I knew you must just be getting settled into your new home, and getting to know your new husband, I am sure. Oh, gracious! My manners are deplorable, do forgive me, please. My name is Ruth, Ruth Margaret Banks O'Dell. My maiden name is Banks of course, but my husband's family is originally from Ireland, hence the O'Dell."

Ada could hardly believe that this woman had not taken a breath. She nodded politely and smiled while she watched Ruth talk. She still had a hold of her hand and her tiny fingers kept shaking Ada's larger hand up and down for emphasis on whatever she was saying. *Ruth was truly beautiful—very petite and almost doll-like*, Ada thought while staring at her perfect skin and large expressive eyes. She only went up to Ada's shoulders and she was certain that Ruth's waist was about as big around as one of Ada's legs. Not quite realizing the conversation was finished, Ada noticed she was being led, by her imprisoned hand, over to the rest of the ladies who were lounging on blankets under a large willow tree. Ruth introduced Ada to all of them and finally released Ada's hand so they could sit down and commence eating their picnic.

Ada looked around the circle of women. Although no one was outwardly inhospitable to her, she could feel a few of them eyeing her with curiosity. She had tried to commit all the names to memory upon being introduced to them and felt proud for having recollected them all. As the others were chatting, she went around the circle saying the ladies' names in her head, hoping to permanently retain them. Ruth O'Dell was the one aimlessly chatting about nothing in particular to anyone who would listen; Anne Cumberland was the regal-looking lady to Ruth's left, who was perhaps five years older than Ada herself. Next, was Louise Davaneaux, whose very French giggle and endearing smile made Ada like her already. Then, there was Mary Smithson, who was almost as plain as her name made her seem—poor thing; and finally, the last woman was Amy, who seemed to be industriously shoving everything she could find in her pouting mouth, and who was so far advanced in her pregnancy that it made Ada nervous she could give birth any minute at this picnic. Ada took a bite of her apple, chewing methodically. *No, her name was not Amy, it was… Emilie. Yes, Emilie Jacqueline Brigitte DuPont.*

"Are you alright, Ada?"

Ada swallowed her apple and looked around the blanket. All the women were looking at her with concerned looks on their faces except for Emilie who was too busy devouring her slice of cheese to notice anything. Embarrassed and realizing it was Louise who had spoken, she quickly nodded her head.

"I am very sorry, Louise. I must admit that my mind was in another place. I am terribly rude and I do beg your pardon, ladies." Ada could feel her cheeks getting red. Could she not just get through one lunch without doing something foolish?

"No matter at all, love." Anne laid a reassuring hand on Ada's shoulder. "I merely inquired as to how you are finding your new marriage? Your husband must have been keeping you quite occupied these past weeks, since no one has seen you." Anne smiled.

"I have been busy adjusting to my new home and setting things up the way I like them. So far, Mr. Watershaw and I are enjoying each other's company very much," Ada lied.

"I bet you are!" Emilie piped in, dabbing crumbs off her protruding belly with a moistened fingertip. "I enjoyed my Stephen's company very much as well and look where it got me!" Emilie smiled and patted her fidgeting bulge. A chorus of giggles erupted and Ada found herself laughing in earnest. This was the first time she had laughed in over a month, and it felt good.

"Well, perhaps that is why I am not yet with child," Mary chimed in, "because most of the time, I do not enjoy Harold's company at all!" Another wave of laughter broke out. Maybe it was the relaxing day or the often contagious chatter and giggling, but Ada and the rest of the women soon found themselves hooting with laughter and making no real effort to demurely cover their mouths.

"More often than not, I think men enjoy their own company just as much as they enjoy ours! Just the other day, I was composing a letter to my sister, and when I went to get a new quill from Allain's desk, I found a booklet with lewdly dressed women's images inside the top drawer." She laughed good-naturedly. "It is a little wonder why Allain spends so much time alone in his study." Louise had been married to Allain Davaneaux for two years. He was very tall and very thin, which seemed to be the perfect match to Louise's lithe figure. Ada had met the couple previously at her wedding and liked them both instantly. Louise had looked at her husband with a spark that showed that two years of marriage had only increased the feelings between the couple.

"I cannot for a minute understand why a man would need a book of scantily-dressed females when he has a flesh and blood wife just in the next room," Ruth huffed.

"It's just human nature, Ruthie," Louise responded. "Wouldn't you look at a book of handsome men wearing very little clothing? Even just to peek?" Louise laughed as Ruth's face gave away her answer with a tell-tale blush.

"The other day while I was still in bed, I opened my eyes to see Charles standing over me naked as the day God made him! I have been married over five years, and looking at him like that still gives me flutters in my stomach." Anne smiled at Ada.

"Why would he just be standing there naked? Was he not cold?" Mary perked a pretty brow up questioningly.

"Not for long," Anne answered seductively and once again, the ladies whooped with laughter.

Ada nibbled her crackers and cheese as she listened to the conversation with fascination. These women, except for Mary whose husband was at least thirty years her senior, seemed to enjoy marital relations with their husbands. As the talking continued, Ada could not help but feel ashamed and sad that her marriage would never hold the special romance of waking up to find your lover gloriously naked and wanting to make love before breakfast. Colin had once taken Ada in the morning. She had woken up to find him on top of her thrusting away like a stray dog. She opened her eyes to have him promptly tell her to shut them again so he did not have to see her look at him. Ada knew that the women were likely embellishing their stories just like men did when they spoke of fishing or business prowess. It was not possible to truly enjoy such an uncomfortable and demoralizing act as much as these ladies were letting on.

    The conversation switched from bedroom activities to babies as Emilie's belly had undergone a series of very prominent movements. The ladies discussed the impending delivery and how lucky it was that Louise's lady's maid, Martha, was an excellent healer and midwife. Ada listened intently—she had always wanted children, but being married to Colin had made her pray for barrenness.

    Two hours had passed in companionable chatter when the men could be heard walking back from the shore. They were chatting loudly and laughing amongst themselves. They all had at least two large fish hanging from the lines in their hands. As they reached the top of the hill, Charles held up his line of fish and the ladies clapped enthusiastically, looking at each other and giggling about their earlier conversations.

Chapter 5

One week after the picnic, Ada received a message from Louise Davaneaux. It had been waiting on a silver tray at her place setting when she came down for breakfast. She opened the small folded paper and read the note while she sipped her tea.

My Dearest Mrs. Watershaw,

I do hope this note finds you in good health. I so much enjoyed getting the chance to speak to you again at last week's picnic and was wondering whether you might be interested in attending afternoon tea at my home at three o'clock today. I am very sorry for the short notice, please excuse my ill-manners; however, my day trip out of town was canceled and I would love to use my newly acquired and much longed for spare afternoon by getting to know you better. Please feel free to send your response back with my messenger.

With Kindness and Regards,

Mrs. L. Davaneaux

Ada placed the card down on the silver tray. "Robertson!" The butler's bald head appeared at the edge of the doorway. Smiling at the thought that he never seemed to be more than one step away, she asked,

"Is the messenger who carried this message still in the house?"

"I gave him some refreshments and he is awaiting your reply in the kitchen, madam. Would you like me to fetch him for you? Or would you prefer to write a note and I will deliver it to him myself?" Robertson looked as though he preferred the latter so the messenger would not come up to the dining room and risk putting road dust on the freshly beaten rugs.

"Send him up please, Robertson. No sense in wasting paper when I can speak to the man myself."

To Robertson's credit, he refrained from rolling his eyes or sighing outright, and proceeded to the kitchens to fetch the messenger. Five minutes later, a boy of about eleven years old was basically shoved into the dining room by a red-faced Robertson. "Good morning to you, ma'am." He bowed deeply and smiled shyly at Ada.

"Good morning. May I ask your name?"

The child looked startled that anyone should want to know his name. Perhaps no one had ever asked him. "It's Andrew, ma'am."

"Well, Andrew. Would you please tell Mrs. Davaneaux that I would be happy to attend tea with her this afternoon at three o'clock?"

"Absolutely, ma'am, at once. Thank you very much." He bowed again and turned on his heel and all but marched to the front door with Robertson nipping at his tiny heels. Ada smiled to herself. She wished she had the same level of pride that Andrew seemed to have in his job of delivering messages for Louise Davaneaux.

"Who was that?" Ada had been watching Andrew leave and therefore had not seen Colin come in from the door on the other side of the dining room. She nearly jumped out of her skin when he spoke.

"It was Louise Davaneaux's messenger boy, Andrew. She has invited me to tea this afternoon and I have just sent back my reply saying I would attend."

"You think it is acceptable to make social plans without asking my permission first?" Colin watched Ada calmly as he sipped his coffee.

"I did not think I needed your permission. I assumed you would be out of the house all day working. Was I mistaken?"

"Yes, Ada, you were mistaken. There is nothing in your life now that you do not need my permission to do. I thought that would have been clear by now. Perhaps it is my own fault for being too easy on you, and therefore allowing you to think you can take liberties." He rose. "I am, as you said, working this afternoon but I will be having an associate over to the house for a meeting. In fact, I would rather you be gone so I do not have to introduce you or make excuses for your obvious dishevelment." He waved a hand at her hair which had been fine when she dressed not even an hour ago. He watched as she put up a hand to smooth it back into place.

"So, I may attend then?" she asked.

"Yes." He strode past her carrying his cup of coffee and grabbed a handful of her behind as he walked by—much too hard to be considered flirtatious. Ada knew it was a warning.

It was ten minutes to three as Ada's buggy rattled down the road toward the driveway at the Davaneaux house. It was a gorgeous white house with black trimming around all the windows and an extensive wrap-around deck that overlooked the wonderful gardens beside it. She adjusted herself in the carriage seat, craning her neck for a better look as the house came into view. Initially, Ada had wanted to ride Gypsy over to Louise's but decided against it. She had realized she had never been, and she did not want to risk getting lost, possibly making herself late for tea. Instead, she had demanded—to much of the driver's chagrin—that Gypsy would pull the cart rather than one of Colin's fancy horses. Gypsy needed to get off the property as much as Ada did, and she trusted Gypsy and enjoyed her company. She was sure she would pay for it later when Colin found out she had been seen in public with Gypsy pulling his buggy. He would no doubt be embarrassed of people's assumptions that he made his wife ride around with less than magnificent carriage horses. Nonetheless, she would cross that miserable bridge when she came to it.

They turned up the driveway and began to slow down. *Too slow,* Ada thought worriedly. She rose in her seat, put her hand through the front window and tapped the driver on the shoulder.

"Is something the matter, Henry?"

"This disgraceful mare has thrown a shoe. Obviously, she has not had new shoes for a long while. We were barely going at a fast walk." He clucked and snapped the driving lines, trying to get Gypsy to trot up the laneway.

"Stop this minute and unhook her," Ada said. "I can easily walk up the driveway. I do not want her going lame trying to pull this carriage up the lane, missing a shoe and walking on uneven footing."

"Mr. Watershaw would not approve of this one bit, madam!" Henry was obviously torn between Ada's request and Colin's wrath—not to say she blamed him one bit.

"It's okay, Henry. Take Gypsy to the stable and I will ask Mrs. Davaneaux to send a groom for the smith. I am sure there is one close by." Without looking back, Ada strode off to the house, reaching the front porch. The door swung open before Ada had finished the three front steps.

"Are you well, Ada? Where is your carriage and driver?" Louise's concerned face was peering beyond her down the laneway.

"My horse, Gypsy, threw her shoe. I did not want her to go lame by pulling the cart, myself and my driver up the driveway. I hope you do not mind I had Henry pull the carriage to the side of the driveway and unhook her. He is bringing her up to your stables. Would it be a tremendous amount of trouble for your groom to go for the blacksmith? I would like to be able to take my own carriage home when the time comes."

"Oh, to be sure!" Louise turned to a man who has waiting just behind the door and asked him to send someone to fetch the smith.

"Please excuse the interruption, but would it be possible to speak to the blacksmith upon his arrival?" Ada inquired.

Both Louise's and the butler's heads turned to look at her with mouths agape.

"My dear, please do not trouble yourself. I assure you my groom is entirely capable. You should not have to concern yourself with such matters." Louise had scrunched up her face at the word 'matters'. Obviously, she thought this to be a servant's job or at most, a man's job but certainly not a lady's job.

"I just have a few questions about my horse I need answered, if it is not too much trouble." Ada was appealing to Louise's duty to keep her guest happy. A cheap trick but Gypsy was worth it.

"Of course, Mrs. Watershaw! If that is what you want, I will tell them to inform us at once of the smith's arrival. Shall we have some tea and biscuits while we wait?"

"I could think of nothing I would like more, and please call me Ada."

Louise smiled and took Ada's hand in hers and led her to the parlour where fresh biscuits with butter, honey, and strawberry jam were being set out by a rather stoutly maid. A fresh pot of tea was being carried in by another kitchen maid who looked only at the ground before depositing the tea pot and walking out.

"This all looks wonderful, Mrs. Davaneaux." Ada breathed in the smell of the fresh biscuits.

"Louise, please. Mrs. Davaneaux still sounds too much like my husband's late mother!" She smiled and laughed.

While Louise was serving Ada her tea, Ada helped herself to a warm tea biscuit. It was freshly buttered and she selected the honey to drizzle over top. She could smell the honey mingling with the freshly baked biscuit and her mouth was watering in anticipation.

"Sugar?" Louise was holding a spoon of sugar above Ada's soft pink teacup.

"One, please. Thank you very much. These biscuits are truly delicious." Ada licked a dab of runaway honey off the tip of her finger and accepted her tea from Louise's outstretched hand.

"So, Ada, how are you enjoying your new home? I am told you are from America; do you find it much different?"

"It is different, yes. It seems to be a slower life than I was used to in Philadelphia but when my parents passed away, I had no reason to stay down there as my only family was my grandmother—and she is from here. I really enjoy the country though. It's beautiful and much more rural, which seems to suit me well." Ada finished and popped the last bit of her biscuit in her mouth.

"I am so glad you are enjoying it here. I feared you might find all of us a trifle boring compared to those in your past city life. Sometimes, I find it dreadfully boring around here—talking with the same people, doing the same needlework, managing the same household day in and day out. Oh, my goodness! I sound so rude, please do not think me a complainer but sometimes, I just feel very humdrum." Louise seemed uncomfortable with what she had just said as two spots of red on her cheekbones appeared.

"Is Mr. Davaneaux often away, or does he spend a lot of time at home?" Ada inquired.

"He is away a good deal of the time. I think that I would feel much more purpose if he were at home more to see the fruits of my day-to-day efforts. It is silly to need approval but it's certainly nice to get it!" Louise laughed. "Is Mr. Watershaw home more than he is away, or the contrary?"

"He is gone during the days but mostly returns in the evenings." Ada was hoping to avoid talking about Colin. She was worried someone might see through her lies and find out the humiliating truth. Ada quickly changed the conversation to ask Louise about her beautiful furnishings. This led to a tour of the house, which was elegant from top to bottom. The pair eventually sat back down and resumed their conversation over a second cup of tea. Louise opened her mouth to follow up with another question when her butler entered the room.

"Very sorry to interrupt you, madam, but the smith has arrived. He is in the stables with Mrs. Watershaw's mare. Should I have him come up to the house when he is finished?"

Ada was already standing up. "I would much prefer to speak to him while he is with my horse, you know, for clarity's sake." She waved her hand vaguely in the direction of the barns. "If I have questions about the wellbeing of my horse, it would most likely be better if he could explain it to me with Gypsy on hand, in case I need a physical demonstration."

Louise nodded knowingly. "Of course, Ada. If you wish to look over your mare, please feel free to go down to the stables. Hughes will escort you personally."

She gestured at her butler who nodded but looked less then pleased to be traipsing to the barn in his finery to pacify what he thought was a silly woman's fancy.

Regardless, Hughes had fetched Ada's wrap and they were headed down toward the stables, waving to Louise who was standing on the front porch. Louise had insisted on staying inside the house to ensure Ada had a cup of fresh hot tea ready for her upon her return.

Chapter 6

Grant was fetching his wooden tool box and his smallest anvil from the cart that the Davaneaux's groom had picked him up in. He was happy to get away from the drudgery of a slow day in his barn, and the buggy ride over had been a refreshing change from the heat of the forge. He had already been in the barn to look at the Watershaw mare who had thrown her shoe. Had he not been informed that this horse belonged to Colin Watershaw, he would never have believed it. He had not seen this horse since nearly four weeks ago when he had watched that attractive servant lass feeding her apples and brushing her mane. Why in the name of God almighty would Colin not take one of his prized horses out to pull the buggy? Even if his wife had been visiting the Davaneauxs, surely she would have wanted to take a flashy expensive-looking mare. As he carried his tools on his way back to the barn, he gazed toward the house to see a butler and a woman heading toward the stables. Perhaps it was Lady Davaneaux but she was too far to recognize, and he had never seen her near a barn in his three years working in the area. He went inside the barn and put his tools and anvil down in the aisle by the stall where the elderly mare was happily munching on fresh hay. He patted her solidly on the neck. "How is it then, lassie?" The horse eyed him warily, looking at him, then back at her hay trying to decide whether he intended to lead her away from her snack.

"Enjoy your hay in peace, I have to talk to our visitors first anyway." He could hear the woman telling the butler to return to the house, assuring him that he need not wait and that she would be perfectly fine walking back up to the house on her own. Intrigued, he latched the stall door and walked back toward the barn door to meet her.

He swung the door open just as she had grasped for the latch herself. Startled, she looked up at him from his chest upwards, with her hand hanging in the air still reaching for the door.

"We seem to be in a habit of startling one another." Grant, recovering first, opened the door wide and waved her into the stables.

Ada looked down at the dirt floor feeling flustered. "Are you the blacksmith? I am sorry I did not ask you last time we met. I assumed you must have been a servant or a groom of Mr. Watershaw's." Ada was intimidated by the size of him. His arms were as big around as her leg and he must have had seven or eight inches on her height wise.

"It's not a problem, miss. As I recall, your mind was probably busy with many other things that day." His eyes looked over her face.

Ada could feel herself turning scarlet. She had sensed he had seen her bruises that day but to know for certain, was much more humiliating.

"Have you looked at my Gypsy yet? I am worried about her; she really is a dear companion." Ada needed to change the subject to hide her embarrassment. Grant gazed at the mare and back at Ada, his eyes were curious. They were also very green, she noticed, and not hard and cold like Colin's.

"Aye, miss. I have looked at her feet. She is long overdue for new shoes; the heads have worn clear off the nails on the ones she's wearing and I am surprised she hasna thrown more than just the one shoe by this point. Ye need to tell Mr. Watershaw or your mistress that I could have done this mare while I was trimming the others a few weeks ago. I had no idea he was planning on driving her." Grant realized that Mr. Watershaw was not the type of man who would take kindly to one of his servant girls telling him how to manage his livestock. "Never mind, lass. The fault is mine. I should have inquired as to whether there were any other horses needing shoes, perhaps he just forgot."

"He did not forget," Ada declared angrily. "My husband has the unfortunate view that if something is not making him money or earning him respect, then it is not worthy of his time or resources. He was planning on sending Gypsy to the butcher, so even if you had asked him, he never would have told you to replace her shoes." Ada looked sadly at Gypsy munching away in her stall.

"Your husband," Grant asked, "is Mr. Watershaw?"

"Yes and yes." Confused, Ada looked up at him. Had he not known? Grant pushed his hands through his hair on each side of his head above his ears.

"Holy God, Mrs. Watershaw. I am so sorry for treating you so familiar. I thought you were a chamber maid for the new mistress or perhaps a new house servant. Not that ye look like ye would be a servant. I just assumed… I dinna know …" He trailed off, completely ashamed.

Ada started to laugh. She looked up at the smith who was obviously discomposed and remembered how embarrassed she had been just a few minutes before. She could not help it. The laughter continued to bubble and she hiccupped and finally got herself under control, blushing slightly. She looked at the smith who was eyeing her with a look of embarrassment mixed with caution.

"I am so sorry, I don't mean to laugh at you," Ada hiccupped again, "but you look so worried and I cannot even imagine anyone ever being worried of what I might do or how I might react."

"Well, this isna the way I thought you would react to be sure. I do truly feel bad about assuming ye were a servant. Your husband will be most displeased when he finds out. It is an insult to his wife." Grant frowned.

"I am certain it will bother him less than you think. It is more likely my fault anyway for not making proper introductions the first time we met." Ada looked away. The merriment he had seen in her eyes only moments ago, faded into nothing. "Will you show me what you plan on doing for Gypsy? Mr.…?"

"My name is Grant Ross, ma'am, your humble and unforgivable servant," he said as he bowed quickly before they started making their way toward the stall.

Grant could not believe his stupidity. He had

insulted, although accidentally, the wife of Colin Watershaw. He was concerned Colin would be angry with him, but he was more concerned about losing his business should he enrage him. Mr. Watershaw had influential friends and although he was the only smith within fifty miles, he would not put it past that conniving bastard to ruin his reputation all the way back to the British Isles. He glanced at Mrs. Watershaw walking in front of him toward Gypsy's stall and found himself staring at her hips. They were round and lovely—well, the entire package was lovely. That should have tipped him off at once to her status. He had never seen a serving girl who looked like she did. Her hair was smooth and thick and was pinned up in a pile on top of her head. As much as he would have loved to have seen it tumble down to her bare shoulders, he appreciated the expanse of neck it showed—neck that went right down to her chest where her gown was cut low. God, he had never seen a woman whose body was so inviting he wanted to run his hands down every bit of it. He imagined he was resting his hands on her ample hips, letting one hand feel its way up the side of her body till he could almost cup the side of one of her rather squeezable looking…

"Mr. Ross, are you quite all right?"

His vision cleared and he saw Mrs. Watershaw standing in front of him. He had no notion of when they reached Gypsy's stall, or how long he had been staring into oblivion like a buffoon. She was looking at him with an expression of concern mixed with confusion, which caused her pretty brows to draw together in the middle of her forehead. That simple gesture made him want to take her face gently between his hands and place a kiss right in that spot. *Mary Mother of Christ, pull yourself together!* He thought angrily, shaking his head. "I'm fine, I was just debating how best to go about Gypsy's shoe," he lied.

"What do you think you will do, Mr. Ross?"

He wished she would stop looking at him, or saying his name, or standing close enough for him to smell the clean scent of soap mixed with the dung smell of the stables. "I am going to attempt to re-shape the shoe enough to tack it back onto her hoof with some new nails. This will not last but at least it should be sound enough to get ye back home, Mrs. Watershaw," he said and wondered what her first name was. "Once you get there, just make sure she isna worked until I am able to come out and put a new set of shoes on her. Her feet are long overdue and I would like to see her properly done for your safety, ma'am." He smiled and kept looking at her, probably for longer than he should have... "Shall I start?" he asked.

"Oh! By all means, thank you so much, Mr. Ross. My Gypsy seems to be in very capable hands." She brushed some dust off the skirt of her dress.

"I thank ye for your kind words, ma'am. Would the day after tomorrow be acceptable for me to come out and do her shoes? I would come tomorrow but I have two other homesteads I have already agreed to do."

"The day after tomorrow sounds lovely. Thank you again, and your willingness to come on such short notice will not be forgotten." Her eyes went wide as if she had just remembered something important. "I will have to compensate you when you come to do her new shoes. I am embarrassed to say I just came for afternoon tea with Mrs. Davaneaux and did not bring a speck of coin with me. Will that be all right?"

Grant thought it would be all right if he never got paid again as long as he could keep looking at her.

"Aye, ma'am, dinna fash, it will be included in the price of the shoes." He opened the stall door and began to lead Gypsy out toward the ties in the long hallway of the stables. "I'd best get started, Mrs. Watershaw. Ye will want to be leaving before long and this lassie's not much good to ye with only three shoes." He smiled brilliantly at her as he tied Gypsy.

Ada began to walk toward the barn door, then turned back to him, smiled and said, "Ada, Mr. Ross." With that, she was out the door and he could hear the latch fall behind her.

He patted Gypsy's silken nose. "Her name suits her well," he said quietly to the horse. Gypsy pawed the ground in agitation and Grant rolled his eyes. "Aye lass, give us your foot then."

Ada picked her way across the grass from the stables to the house. She did not want to step in mud or scuff her shoes on a stone before returning to finish her visit with Louise. Her mind travelled easily back to the smith working in the barn. So, Grant Ross was not a groom or horse master for Colin like she assumed on the day of their first meeting. She did not understand why but she had felt a lifting of her spirits when she realized he was not directly under Colin's employ. She put this down to the fact that she would not wish Colin's company on a condemned criminal, lest a seemingly nice man like Mr. Ross. She giggled at the thought of the poor man's face when he realized who she was. Personally, she had not thought anything of it but was sure many of her peers would not have reacted the same way she did, so it was quite understandable he was nervous. She slowed her pace slightly as the afternoon sun beat down on her and made sweat tickle down her back. She did not pity Mr. Ross doing physical work inside the hot barn. In fact, she had found it odd that Mr. Ross had kept his sleeves rolled all the way down and fastened, and his collar done up right to the top button. With his heavy leather apron, he must have been sweltering. Most of the men she knew growing up would roll their shirtsleeves up while working to keep their shirts clean and keep themselves cool. It was odd, but maybe he did not feel the heat as much as she.

As she reached the front porch, the door swung open and she was ushered in, this time by the butler who had escorted her down to the barn. Louise was in the parlour reading a book when Ada returned. Upon seeing her, Louise stood up. "Oh, you're back! You must be thirsty. It is so terribly hot in here, let alone outside in the baking sun. I took the liberty of having some lemonade brought up in addition to the tea in case you fancied something cooler."

Ada took the lemonade gratefully; she was still hot and slightly red-faced from the walk back to the house.

"Everything is suitable with the smith?" Louise took a sip from her own lemonade and sighed, blissfully savoring the tart flavor as it filled her mouth.

"Yes, thank you very much for sending for him. I was lucky he could come on such short notice." Ada tried hard not to gulp her lemonade but it was refreshing and delicious and she was thirsty.

The two women passed the next three quarters of an hour in conversation. Ada found herself very relaxed around Louise and was surprised when the butler appeared at the parlor door with Henry—Ada's driver.

"What can I do for you gentlemen?" Louise inquired, raising one eyebrow delicately.

"The mare's shoe has been tacked back on, ma'am, and I have hitched her back up to the cart." Henry looked down at the ground, flushing slightly. "I am terribly sorry to have interrupted you, ma'am, but Mr. Watershaw said I must have you home by no later than half past five." He looked as though he would like nothing better than to crawl under the rug that lay at the front door.

"It's fine, Henry. Thank you for letting me know, we were just concluding our conversation anyway. You may wait for me outside and I will be with you momentarily." Ada nodded at him and smiled as a look of relief spread over his thin features.

After Henry and the butler had left, Ada grasped Louise by both hands. "Thank you so much for such a lovely day. It means so much to me to be able to have a friend that I can call on from time to time." She squeezed her hands and released them to tie on her hat.

"I do hope we will see more of each other very soon, Ada. Are you and Mr. Watershaw planning to attend Mr. and Mrs. O'Dell's dinner? The ladies will be there and we can catch up more after dinner when the men are off smoking pipes and drinking." She dismissed the men's activities with a wave of her hand.

"I certainly hope to, but I have not heard from Colin yet as to whether we are going. I must go, I can feel poor Henry's anxiousness all the way in here. Thank you again."

As Ada appeared on the front porch, Henry's sigh of relief was almost audible. She could not say she blamed him as she knew what the penalty would be for her if she were late, and she could only imagine what Colin would do to poor Henry.

Chapter 7

Dinner that evening had passed in silence, as most of the dinners at the Watershaw residence tended to—with Colin and Ada politely eating without as much as a 'please pass the salt' spoken between them. Ada preferred it that way. She had nothing to say to Colin, not that he would want to listen even if she did, and anything Colin said to her was always scolding or demeaning and she could do well without both of those things. Still, it was lonely having night after night of silence, only hearing the scraping of the cutlery on the china plates. Ada finished up the last bite of her roast beef with a swish through the gravy on her plate and wiped her mouth delicately on the corner of the napkin.

"May I be excused, please? I would like to retire to my room and read." She almost whispered it, her regular voice sounding too loud after such a long period of silence.

"Yes, I will attend to you directly after I have dealt with a few tasks down here." Colin did not even look at her but continued to butter a dinner roll.

Attend to her directly? What the hell had he meant by that? Ada walked up the stairs leading to their rooms. Thankfully, Colin had taken a separate bedroom from Ada's. He only came in to perform his marital duties, then leave and retire to his own room. He could not have meant sex—he always just barged into her room without a word of warning if that was what he wanted, he never told her beforehand. This must be about something different. He was most likely angry about something she had not realized she had done.

About thirty minutes later, her door was pushed open and Colin sauntered in. Ada put her book down on the arm of the chair she was reading in and looked up at Colin.

"What can I do for you, Colin?" She thought perhaps that addressing him calmly might soften whatever ire he was about to unleash on her.

"Oh, most likely nothing, as per usual." He pulled the chair from her dressing table and sat down opposite her. He crossed his legs at the ankles and examined the fingernails on his left hand. "What did I tell you this morning when you *informed* me that you were going to tea at the Davaneaux house?" He looked up from his nails at Ada's face.

"You said you were having a meeting at the house and that you would have rather have me gone so I would not bother you." Ada answered politely but she suddenly knew where this conversation was headed; he had found out she had taken Gypsy. Her stomach clenched a little as his eyes darkened.

"No, Ada. I had thought that I made it clear enough that you do not make any decisions without my consent, did I not?"

"Well, yes you did, but…"

"Then explain to me why I was informed by Henry that you forced him to drive that ugly mare instead of one of my horses?" He was getting angry now. He stood up, knocking the wooden chair over as he stood. "How do you think it looks for my wife to be driving around the village with that hideous nag pulling the carriage? I breed and sell horses, Ada! For Christ's sake, how does it look that my carriage is not being driven by the same horses I charge people an exorbitant amount of money to purchase for their own buggies!" By this time, a flush of red was creeping up Colin's neck into his face. "If that was not already enough, Henry also informs me that the horse threw a shoe and the smith had to come see to her at the Davaneauxs!" He took a deep breath, clearly not for calming purposes. "Furthermore, I have also been told that Mr. Ross will be coming the day after tomorrow to put new shoes on her! Who the fuck is paying for that, Ada?" He took a step toward her. She jumped up from the chair and quickly ran around, putting the high back chair between them.

"I am sorry, Colin. I thought you would not mind because you are always ensuring that your horses have the best care." She was trying to calm him down by talking about his other horses but this seemed to enrage him even more. Ada kept a grip on the chair for dear life and continued, "If it is too expensive, I can…" He interrupted as if she hadn't been speaking at all.

"Do you think me stupid, Ada?" He was screaming and his face had fully taken on the reddish hue that was previously on his neck. "I do not give a sweet damn about the cost of putting shoes on that mare! I still will not be paying for it, however. *You* cannot make decisions! If you are too stupid to understand our previous conversation, think of it like this: your ugly mare is my property, she does what I say when I say it and she damn well better do it to my satisfaction. I feed her, I shelter her and I decide when and *if* she needs care. She does not make decisions on her own, she does not speak back to me, and she knows her place. Now, the next time you look in the mirror and consider making a decision about anything in your life, I need you to think of yourself as that mare and decide whether to shut up and eat the hay or speak up and be whipped."

"You are an indescribable bastard!" Ada screamed back at him, tears of rage and humiliation ran down both her cheeks. No one had ever spoken to her with such hate and vehemence before.

Colin moved before she could even register what had happened—he had taken the chair she was holding and threw it against the wall. He had shoved her into the wall and put one hand around her throat, while the other hand gripped her forearm hard enough to force it down by her side. She struggled against him using her free arm, then grabbed the arm that was choking her and pulled on his sleeve with all her strength, desperately trying to pull his hand off her throat to get a single wisp of air. He just squeezed harder and she could feel his fingertips on the sides of her neck. She was starting to become dizzy and could hazily see she had scratched his arm with her fingernails while trying to pry his hand off her neck. The small bloody lacerations were the last thing she saw as lights started to flicker behind her eyes.

She felt her legs sliding to the floor, then, she felt nothing.

Chapter 8

"Madam, madam! She could hear a small French voice floating somewhere around her. She would have rather ignored it and stayed in her state of nothingness but it was too late as in addition to the voice, she could also feel hands frantically shaking her shoulders.

"Madam, please open your eyes!" Marie sounded very worried, which was odd because Ada felt quite calm. She opened one eye a slit. "Oh, thank the lord you have awoken. Just sit for a moment and I will have your bed ready for you *le plus vite que possible!*" With that, Ada watched Marie disappear in a flurry of skirts. She could hear her pulling on the bedding and fluffing her pillows, and she desperately hoped Marie had added a warming pan to the bed as well. Even though it was summer, Ada felt suddenly very cold. Marie was still muttering to herself in French when she came back over to Ada.

"Do you feel well enough to walk to the bed, madam, with my help of course? I can fetch one of the houseboys to aid us, it would be no trouble at all." Marie looked at her worriedly.

"I am sure..." Ada had wanted to communicate that she was sure she could manage, but all she could croak out before she began to cough and choke was, 'I'm sure.' She walked the few steps to the bed, still choking all the way until she finally sat and eagerly accepted the glass of water Marie had been desperately trying to hand her. She took a cautious sip between hacking coughs, which seemed to help slightly. The spasm loosened its tight hold on her throat and she was able to drink a bit more water. She reached her hand up gingerly to her throat—it felt sore and swollen on the inside as well as painful on the outside where she knew the bruises would appear. She took another sip of water.

"Marie," she managed in the softest of whispers. "How long was I unconscious?" Even that small bit of talking made her want to choke again, so she sipped more water.

Marie pursed her lips in thought, "I came up here at around ten this evening to dress you for bed. I had assumed you were reading in your room. I saw Mr. Watershaw come back downstairs after he went up to you. We had heard a crash but when we asked him, he assured us nothing was amiss and mentioned you would like to be alone to read. I did not know, madam. *Je suis désolée,* so very sorry."

"There would have been nothing you could have done if you had come sooner," Ada whispered. She pulled the covers up over her chest. "I think I need to sleep, Marie. I am suddenly very tired."

"*Oui, madame, certainement.*" Marie efficiently

went about the room righting the tipped chairs and picking up discarded clothing. She stopped to blow out the last candle by the door with her small hand cupped behind the flame.

"Marie?" Ada whispered from the bed, "Mr. Watershaw, is he still here?"

Marie came over to the bed and placed a small hand on Ada's thigh. "He left for the evening, madam." Marie's small hand patted her comfortingly. "Sleep well with that knowledge."

Ada waited for the latch on the door to click closed. She was in complete darkness; Marie had obviously closed the shutters. She was glad for it tonight and thankful for Marie's ability to do what needed to be done without asking questions or coddling. But even with Marie around, Ada felt very alone. Tears slid down her cheeks and she closed her eyes and hoped to dream of better days.

Ada spent the entire next day in bed. Marie kept bringing her teas, tonics, soups, lemon waters and something mysteriously alcoholic that the little maid had simply called a restorative. Whether it was the refreshing feeling of just having finished her twentieth trip to the chamber pot or the magic of Marie's elixirs, but she had started to feel a little better by mid-afternoon. The cold and tired feeling had left her. Although the pain in her throat had subsided to an ache when she talked or swallowed, she felt nothing when she was still and silent. Her voice still sounded hoarse, and she was obliged to clear her throat gently before speaking. Overall, it was maybe not as bad as she thought. She had decided she would sit by the fireplace in her bedroom this evening instead of lying down. She had managed a bit of the diluted beef broth that Marie had provided her and it felt warm and comforting in her stomach. She read for about an hour but found herself weary from emotion and a restless night and went back to sleep hoping she would wake up in a different state of mind the next day.

Ada woke up in the morning to Marie knocking on her door. She cleared her throat, finding it much improved. "Come in, Marie!" she said, surprised to find herself sounding less hoarse than yesterday.

"Madam, you look much improved today!" Marie beamed at her. Ada knew that at least half of that smile was Marie congratulating herself on the obvious success of her many drinks and medicinals. Ada smiled back.

"I suppose, although the markings on my neck are most likely worse."

Marie looked down.

"Please hand me the mirror, Marie. We may as well get this over with." Ada had not wanted to look in the mirror yesterday, trying instead to concentrate on just feeling well again. She picked up the mirror and examined her neck. She had four purple and blue tinged bruises on the left side of her neck. They were perfect imprints of Colin's fingers and they spanned from just below her ear to the base of her neck. The right side had a very large purple splotch where his thumb had been and a scratch where his nail must have cut her when his thumb slipped slightly. Ada sighed. "Not much disguising what this is, is there? Perhaps I should just have one of the house servants paint me a sign to hang around my neck that reads 'I've been strangled'." Ada laughed bitterly.

"Madam, you must not jest like that! It is a terrible thing Mr. Watershaw did to you." Marie looked over her shoulder at the bedroom door as if to double check Colin had not heard her. Frankly, Ada wanted to do the same thing.

"Oh well, what is done is done. Marie. There is not much I can do about it now, is there? At least no one will see me up close other than the house servants."

Before Ada finished her thought, there was a brisk knock on her door. Both Marie and Ada jumped instinctively, then Ada relaxed knowing Colin would never knock. Robertson's voice boomed from outside the wooden door.

"I am sorry to interrupt you so early, ma'am, but Henry has informed me that the smith has arrived. Mr. Ross seems to think he is putting shoes on a horse for you!" Ada could practically hear the scoff in Robertson's voice. "Shall I inform Henry to inform Mr. Ross that this is indeed absurd. I would not bother coming to you with this nonsense but Mr. Watershaw is still away and I was not sure what to do."

Ada rolled her eyes. "I have just about had my fill of men," she whispered to Marie, who giggled silently. She cleared her throat. "I will be down presently; the smith is *indeed* here to put shoes on *my* mare. Please offer Mr. Ross some refreshments and tell him that I will meet him in the stables."

Ada knew Robertson's mouth was impolitely hanging open on the other side of the door as she could hear nothing. "Did you hear me, Robertson?"

"Yes, madam," he replied, not bothering to remove

the disdain from his voice. She heard his footsteps as he walked away.

Ada had Marie dress her and arrange her hair as quickly as possible. She chose a simple blue dress with darker blue pinstripes on it. Her hair was tied in a long simple braid down her back, easy and quick. She was running down the stairs when she remembered the bruises. She should have tied a scarf around her neck or perhaps wore a dress with a higher collar. She shrugged, there was no help or time for it now. She had kept Mr. Ross waiting long enough already and Gypsy needed her shoes more than Ada needed her pride. She swallowed and continued out to the barn.

Mr. Ross had been offered refreshments and upon declining, had opted to wait at the barn for Mrs. Watershaw. He felt bad about declining her hospitality but the thought of sitting and sipping lemonade while that bald-headed tub of a man Robertson stared at him with his permanent look of disapproval was enough for Grant to risk being branded as rude for turning down a drink. So, he sat on the fence, watching the dark stallion graze in the field. The big horse suddenly lifted his head and sniffed the air, turning his face toward the main house. His glossy mane shone brightly in the sun, rippling with each movement. Grant could hear footsteps coming down the gravel path behind him. He turned his body, lifted his leg over the top rail and hopped down. It was Mrs. Watershaw, she looked as though she had been hurrying.

"Good morning to ye, ma'am. I hope the day has found ye well so far." He ducked his head in greeting. God, he could watch her walk for hours. The way her hips moved under her skirt, he was beginning to regret the path from the house to the barn was so short.

She waved happily, "The day finds me very well, Mr. Ross, thank you. I must apologize, however, as I have overslept and kept you waiting." She smiled as she walked up to him.

"No matter, ma'am. The day is verra fine and I love to watch yon man over there." He shaded his eyes from the sun with one hand and looked at the graceful stallion. "He truly is a beauty, aye?"

"He is wonderful. I believe Mr. Watershaw said he sired foals with my Gypsy, in her younger years that is." She walked over to the fence, put her arms over the top rail and linked her hands. Grant had been standing near the fence and with her apparent intention of watching the big horse, he leaned his right side against the fence so he could watch the horse, and her as well.

"Is that your horse tied up in the laneway? He is lovely." She had stroked the horse's soft white nose as she passed him on the way down to the barn.

"Oh aye, he's mine. His name is Duff. He's none so fine as your horses, ma'am." He gestured toward the stables.

"Gypsy is my horse; all the rest are Mr. Watershaw's and I daresay Duff is just as fine as Gypsy is." She laughed softly. "The poor old thing, she is not much to look at but she has a wonderful heart."

"That is all any of us can hope for, ma'am." He looked at Mrs. Watershaw. She had turned her head sideways to follow the stallion as he trotted to a new place in the field. The sunlight shone on her white skin and his eyes had been immediately drawn to the angry purple bruises on the side of her neck. Anger rose in his body like waves in a storm. If he had any doubt from the first time they met, this only confirmed that her cowardly prick of a husband had done this. Nothing else could leave fingerprint-shaped bruises on someone's neck. Before he could say anything, she was speaking.

"I fear you may have wasted your time in coming all the way out here today," she looked sad and embarrassed. "Colin… I mean Mr. Watershaw has informed me that he will not be paying for Gypsy to get new shoes. You see, she is not a worthy investment to him any longer and therefore, he is of the mind that no money should be spent on her. I do, however, have money to pay you for the job you did tacking her shoe back on at the Davaneaux house." She took her arm off the fence and reached into the pocket of her gown.

Before Grant realized what he was doing, he put his hand on her forearm to stop her from rummaging in her pocket for his pay. She looked from his hand up at his face, startled. He should have taken his hand away, he should have probably taken a few steps back, packed up his tools and left but instead, he gripped her arm harder. "Your horse will be getting new shoes, ma'am." He was looking directly at her face.

"But I cannot pay you!" she pleaded. "I only have enough to cover the work you have already done."

"Ye willna be paying me for the work I have already done or for the work I will be doing. You have a good mare, ma'am, and she deserves better." He released her arm and walked into the barn. Hesitantly, he turned back to the door and looked at her, "Ye both do. Are ye coming in?"

Ada could barely breathe. She knew Mr. Ross had seen her neck. Was he doing this for her out of pity? Look at the poor woman whose husband beats her. She could not bear to have him pity her. He was so kind and good natured. Although, it could not be anything but pity. Mr. Ross was a very appealing man and as Colin had told her many times, she was not the kind of woman men would do things for because of the way she looked. Perhaps, he was just being kind and, in that case, it would be rude for Ada to turn down his wonderful gesture. Besides, Gypsy desperately needed her feet taken care of. Well, it was decided then. She gathered her skirt in one hand and headed toward the barn door that Mr. Ross had left open for her.

Once inside, she walked toward the stall that belonged to Gypsy. Mr. Ross was already inside with the little horse putting on her ancient halter that looked as though it would fall apart if the poor girl moved her head at all. He walked her out of her stall and hooked her to one of the leather straps that hung on the wall of the aisle. "Ye needn't stay, ma'am. I promise to take care of her and I am sure ye have plenty of important things that require your attention." He picked up Gypsy's front foot and started to clip off the nails from her old shoe.

"If you do not mind, I have nothing else to do that is not tediously boring, and I enjoy watching her. Will it bother your work if I'm here?" she asked.

"Not one bit." He looked at her. "It's nice for her to have another familiar face around."

As Ada sat on an upturned bucket and watched Mr. Ross work on Gypsy's shoes, she could not help but notice he was beautifully made. He was very large—his legs, his arms, his shoulders, everything just seemed massive with only Colin's aristocratic form to compare it to. He had his dark brown hair tied back in a leather thong but strands kept escaping and he would constantly tuck them behind his ears as they fell onto his face as he was working. He had a larger nose and brow but it fit his face very well. His hands were filthy and they looked calloused but warm. Of course, with a profession like this, his hands must take a beating almost daily. Ada found herself wanting to wash his hands and soothe them with the mint grease that Marie had made her. She cut off that train of thought as quickly as it came. *For heaven's sake, Ada. You are a married woman and look at the man, even if you were not taken, he would obviously prefer some petite blonde with large eyes and long eyelashes.* She continued to watch him and suddenly realized the barn was as hot as the devil himself and she had not offered him a single refreshing beverage.

"Mr. Ross, can I offer you some water or lemonade? It is terribly hot in here and you are working very hard." She could see the beads of sweat running down his face and wondered again why he would not roll up his shirtsleeves to be cooler.

"I would take some water, ma'am, if there is some at hand." He stood up straight with a groan and wiped his forearm across his sweating forehead. Grant moved toward the door to get some water.

"I've just been sitting here, please let me be useful and get the water. There is a well just around the side of the barn. I will be back momentarily." She got off her stool and disappeared out the door.

When Ada returned with the water, Grant was sitting on a bale of hay in the aisle. He wondered why he felt so relaxed with her. He would not have dared to sit down in the presence of Mr. Watershaw. Perhaps it was disrespectful, he began to rise.

"No, no, sit and enjoy the water. Gypsy will wait." Ada looked over at Gypsy who looked as if she was asleep in the aisle. No need to hurry on her account. "How did you come to be in Acadia, Mr. Ross?" Ada inquired while sipping from her own ladle of water.

"I was injured badly at the battle of Culloden and my friends found me a place on a boat and sent me here." He looked down at his hands—that was close enough to the truth.

"That sounds terrible. Excuse my ignorance please, but what is the battle of Culloden?"

"A slaughter." His eyes darkened with the memories. "The English army completely massacred the Highland clans on a place called Drumossie Moor. I dinna like to speak about it much, many of my kin and friends died that day and it fills me with guilt that I did not go with them." He realized he had spoken that last bit aloud and hung his head lower to hide his embarrassment.

"I am so sorry. I should never have brought it up. We will not speak of it anymore. It is obvious that your injury has healed well because you seem quite able-bodied." She looked at him sitting on the bale, then realized what she had said and flushed terribly.

Grant chuckled sensing her embarrassment, a low sultry sound. "I thank ye for your compliment, ma'am. It is obvious ye mean that the nature of my work would make a prolonged injury impossible to bear, aye? And yes, I am quite healed."

"Yes." Ada was flustered. "I am very glad to hear it."

"What about yourself? If I could be so bold as to ask, ma'am, you dinna seem like you're from around here either."

"I am originally from Philadelphia but when my family passed, I moved up here to be with my grandmother as she is the only family I have left."

He noticed she had not listed Mr. Watershaw in her remaining family. Grant shook his head. "I'm verra sorry to hear about your family. Are you close to your Gran?" he asked, taking another sip from his ladle.

"I suppose so. To be honest, I had never met her growing up, most likely because she lived so far from us. I did get letters from her but that was about the extent of it. We became closer when I came to live up here with her."

"Did she choose Mr. Watershaw for you?" Grant asked bluntly. In a different situation, he would have been very concerned with his lack of verbal filter but he felt like he had to know the answer to this question, and hear it from Mrs. Watershaw herself.

She looked at him, her lips curved up in a half-smile. "Between you and I, Mr. Ross, I sure as hell did not pick him myself."

Grant's eyes widened and his brows rose. He

whooped with laughter. "I sure as hell dinna pick him myself." He was still laughing, he pressed his hand to his middle and leaned back on the hay bale to rest his upper back and head against the stall behind him. He wheezed, "My God, Mrs. Watershaw, I would never have expected that from a lady. However, you need to make sure you dinna say things like that in the earshot of your husband or anyone who is loyal to him." He glanced again at her neck, "but perhaps you know that better than I do."

"Are you not loyal to my husband? I mean, you work for him. Should I worry about what I say in front of you, Mr. Ross?" Ada's hand had automatically gone to her neck when Mr. Ross had glanced there, and she massaged the bruises softly with her fingers.

"Well, to start, I do not work *for* your husband, I occasionally do his horses for him but I am not under his employ. There is a difference, ken?" He winked. "As for whether ye need to watch your words in front of me, I think we have both said too much that could get us in trouble. I propose we make a pact, of sorts." He smiled mischievously at her.

When he had winked at her, Ada had almost fallen off the bucket she was using as a stool. My God, he was handsome. He had a playful air about him that she had never seen in Colin, or her father come to think of it. She knew he was just being kind to her, but she couldn't help but wonder whether he liked her a tiny bit too. She pushed that thought far from her mind, but it crept back. At least he could give her something to think about at night when she was alone. She blushed furiously at that thought. She cleared her throat. "A pact, Mr. Ross?"

He had noticed the blush; she was so alluring it was all he could do to keep himself on the bale where he was sitting. This woman did not act like other attractive women though—women who use their assets to get what they want. It was almost as if Mrs. Watershaw did not know about her own appeal. He scoffed at the thought. If she owned a mirror, she knew she was attractive. "Yes, ma'am. I propose that ye may speak to me however ye want, whenever ye want and I will listen and not hand ye over to your husband or the local law for being a hateful gossip, or a foul tongued wretch, or a woman of lewd speech. Ye know, anything of that nature…" He laughed as she raised her brows.

She laughed, "Woman of lewd speech? Just what is it that you think I will be saying to you, Mr. Ross?" She feigned shocked affrontedness.

He laughed, "Well, according to the pact, Mrs. Watershaw… Anything ye want."

"Well then, Mr. Ross, you have yourself a pact. Shall we shake on it?" She stuck out her hand absurdly in front of her. "I mean, it makes it very official, don't you think?" she giggled.

Her giggling made him feel reckless. Wiping his filthy hands on his breeches, he grabbed her outstretched hand and shook it. "Oh, to be sure," he retorted. Instead of letting her hand go, he flipped her hand over and placed a small kiss on the back before letting his own hand fall away. "Now, get out of here, aye? You are verra distracting."

She smiled and left without saying another word. As she walked back up to the house, she realized she was holding the hand Mr. Ross had kissed in her other hand, pressed against her chest. "Well, that was interesting," she murmured and walked into the house smiling.

Chapter 9

Three weeks had passed since Ada's conversation in the barn with Mr. Ross had taken place. She had wanted to talk to him again, but he had not been around and there was no way she could go without looking like she wasn't going specifically to talk to him—and she obviously could not have that. Today, however, she had overheard Colin talking to one of his business partners about two horses needing new shoes put on before they were sent to their new owners, meaning Mr. Ross would be coming today. She had decided to take her morning tea on the wooden swing that sat on the front porch. It was a beautiful morning with a cool breeze, but with the promise of a very hot afternoon to come. Her excuse to take tea outside to enjoy the weather was believable but she secretly hoped to see Mr. Ross as he came up the lane, then find some excuse to sneak to the barn and speak with him again. She laughed at herself. *You would think I was a young and infatuated girl.* She smiled into her teacup.

She could still hear the voices of Colin and his associate Bernard drifting through the open window, arguing about nothing no doubt. Colin had been in a foul mood for the past week as Henry had fallen from a horse he was training and badly injured his knee. The doctor had said he needed to be in bed for at least two weeks. Following the bed rest, he would only have limited mobility, with no heavy work for two to three weeks thereafter. Ada had asked the kitchen to bake a sweet loaf and she had brought it to him in bed with some butter and lemonade. Henry had told her he was afraid Mr. Watershaw would fire him because he could not work for over a month. "Who will train the horses, ma'am? Who will drive you around?" Henry looked pale—whether it was from the pain or the fear, she couldn't tell. She had tried to reassure him everything would be fine but she could only hope so herself as she never knew how Colin would react.

A buggy bumped off the road and into the laneway and Ada's heart jumped, surprising her. As soon as the cart came a little closer, Ada could see that it was not Mr. Ross—this man was much shorter and older, his grey hair visible against the sunlight even at a distance. Colin and Bernard had heard the horse coming up the lane and most likely sharing Ada's assumption, had come out on the front porch to greet Mr. Ross. The old man pulled up in front of the house and appeared seemingly oblivious to the four of them standing there, as Robertson had also joined them. He climbed down from his buggy, beat the dust from his worn but still serviceable suit and produced an envelope. "I have special correspondence for a Mrs. Ada Watershaw, formerly Jamison."

Ada looked up from the porch boards, "I'm Mrs. Watershaw." She was instantly concerned as she never received mail by a personalized messenger like this. Before she had the chance to hold out her hand for the envelope, Colin had taken the letter from the man's hands. "I am Mr. Watershaw, so obviously, I will be accepting this on behalf of my wife." He handed the man a coin and the messenger happily climbed back onto his cart and departed.

"Whatever could this be, Ada? No one sends you anything." He did not bother to hide the mocking in his tone. Bernard was one of the few friends and associates who knew Colin for who he truly was. He opened the letter carelessly and stuffed the envelope at Ada, who took it begrudgingly. He unfolded the letter and began to read:

Dear Mrs. Watershaw,
My name is Minerva Potts, perhaps you remember your grandmother talking about me…"

Colin sighed impatiently. "Get on with it woman!" He scanned the rest of the letter, reading it to himself instead of aloud.

As Colin read, another buggy appeared in the drive and Ada could see it was Mr. Ross due to his immense size. Mr. Ross pulled his cart up to the barn, gracefully hoped down and began to walk toward the crowd on the front porch. *How could such a big man move with such grace?* Ada wondered.

By this time, Colin had finished the letter and looked up at the smith. "Oh, good. He's here. Let's get the shoes on these sale horses, Bernard." Colin clapped his friend on the shoulder and started down the porch steps to the barn, then paused as if remembering Ada standing there. "Oh, right," he looked directly into her eyes, "your grandmother is dead." He threw the letter down at Ada's feet and strode away, chatting happily with Bernard.

Ada stood very still. Did she hear him correctly? Was her grandmother dead? She bent slowly and retrieved the letter that spiraled to a landing about a foot away from her. She unfolded the letter and read.

Twenty-Fourth of August, 1753

Dear Mrs. Watershaw,

My name is Minerva Potts, perhaps you remember your grandmother talking about me. I am very sad to have to write this letter but last week, your grandmother took sick with a fever. She was put to bed and unfortunately, the fever worsened and there was little the physician could do. Despite trying many tonics and bleeding her regularly, she passed away only four days later. Please accept my heartfelt condolences and know that although you will not be able to travel out here in time for her funeral service, she will be buried with her friends watching over her. Please do come when you can to see to her estate. She made it clear you were to have final say in everything, being her only remaining family.

Put your grief and trust in God.
Your humble and grieving friend,
Mrs. Minerva Potts

Ada felt the warm tears slide down her cheeks as she read the letter. Her grandmother had passed and she had not been able to be there for her. She re-folded the letter, put it into the pocket of her dress, and opened the front door of the house. She must start packing her things. Having read the letter, Colin obviously knew she intended to leave and settle her grandmother's estate. He would either be very happy to have her out of his sight, or very angry that her grandmother's death had inconvenienced him in some way. She swiped bitterly at the tears that were still flowing. She could not worry about Colin now, she had far more important things to deal with. Once she reached her bedroom, she called for Marie, shut the door, sat down in her chair abruptly and started to cry in earnest—such huge racking sobs, she was certain, were for more than just her grandmother.

Grant walked to the barn with Mr. Watershaw and his business partner, Bernard-something. He did not care to remember the man's last name. They were laughing and joking about something he was not paying attention to; his mind was on the scene that had just played out on the front porch. What did the paper Mr. Watershaw had thrown at his wife say? She had not looked happy at all. His mind also kept wandering to thoughts about how quickly he could beat the holy hell out of Mr. Watershaw in a fist fight. He was surprised they had already arrived at the barn. He excused himself to fetch his tools from his buggy while the two men went inside.

When he entered the barn, the men had already pulled out one of the geldings he was scheduled to shoe. The horse snorted and tossed his head in greeting when he saw Grant, and the men looked up at his arrival.

"This is the first one we need done, Mr. Ross." Bernard stated.

"Alright, I will start with this lad, if that's what ye wish." It did not matter to Grant whom he shod first. He just agreed readily in hopes these idiots would leave him to his business and go find someone else to piss off. No such luck today, though. Mr. Watershaw and Bernard Whatever-His-Name-Is sat down on the bench just outside the open double doors and began to smoke their pipes and talk. Grant had absolutely no interest in what they were saying until he heard Colin spit out Ada's name like it was a sip of bad liquor.

"And now, that old bitty grandmother of hers is dead and I am expected to just let Ada traipse all the way to her grandmother's estate to clean things up? Seriously, I sometimes wonder if that woman was put on earth to cause me stress." Colin spat in the dirt. Grant could hear it smack on the packed dirt walkway.

"Maybe the old lady left Ada money?" suggested Bernard. "That way, Ada's trip could be doubly advantageous for you. Did you ever think of that?"

"Where does the double come in?" Colin inquired, obviously intrigued.

"Well, Ada will be gone to her grandmother's house, possibly making you more money. And while the pussy is away, the mouse will play—if you take my meaning, man." Bernard chortled, stopped, then hacked and spat as well. "I know you have had your eye on that little piece at the market, why not invite her to see your new foals?"

"My, Bernard, aren't you the clever one? I think I might do just that." The bench creaked as Colin readjusted his position. "Shit! That goddamn Henry has injured himself. I will have to pay a fortune to bring in someone, especially to escort Ada on her journey. However, I'm not saying it would not be worth having her out of my sight for a few weeks. I would much rather look at that young petite Lucy from the market than my cow of a wife." Both men laughed.

"I will take her." Both men's heads shot upwards at the smith standing in the doorway of the barn.

"What?" Colin said, rising from the bench.

"It has been a slow season for me. I would be happy for some extra income. I willna charge ye nearly as much as the driver's for hire that ye'll find in town, and I'll be sure to see Mrs. Watershaw safely there and back." This, however, was false. He had been busier than ever lately and would have to cancel some of his clients to undertake this trip. Grant was sweating, and not just from the heat of the day or the fire. Where in the name of the Virgin Mother did he get off offering a thing like that? Mr. Watershaw will surely see right through him and have his balls for luncheon.

"That's a decent offer, Colin," Bernard said as he elbowed his friend in the ribs. "Look at the size of the man, no harm will come to Ada. Plus, it will save you money and free you up for your previously discussed social activities." He winked at Colin.

It took everything Grant had not to smash both of their heads in with the horseshoe he was holding. He just shrugged and smiled, "Just thought I'd make my offer, sir. I'll be back to work now if you have need of me." He turned to walk into the barn.

"Wait... Mr. Ross." Colin called him back. "You have yourself a deal. She will leave tomorrow at nine in the morning. Does that suit you?" He stuck out his hand.

"I thank ye very much, sir. At nine then." He grasped Colin's hand in his own and shook it. He gripped it a little harder than necessary but Colin did not seem to notice. Grant had always wondered what it would be like to shake hands with the devil, and in that moment, he thought he just did.

That evening, Ada had declined to come down to dinner. She picked at her tray of food in her room as she watched the flames from the fire lick the unburned log that sat in the centre. She missed her grandmother terribly but more than anything, she had never felt this alone. She now had no remaining family and the closest thing to family she did have was Colin, and that thought drove her deeper into grief than anything.

Marie had just left with her food tray when her bedroom door opened again. Colin entered, shut the door behind him, walked over and sat down on her bed. She turned to look at him. She knew what she looked like and she did not care. Her eyes were swollen from crying and her nose was red and puffy from her handkerchief. Her trunk and her carrying bag were ready and waiting by the door. Colin glanced at these and gestured for her to come and sit by him on the bed. She got up. She was numb with emotion; she did not care what he wanted with her as long as he left her alone afterwards.

"Mr. Ross, the blacksmith, will be escorting you on your trip," Colin said without preamble.

Ada did not expect to hear this. She looked up at him and felt a tiny sparkle of light shine on her shadowed heart at the mention of Mr. Ross's name. "Mr. Ross?"

"Did I stutter? Yes, Ada. Mr. Ross. Henry obviously cannot take you in his state and I did not want to hire a special driver for you, so when Mr. Ross offered, I accepted. You leave at nine in the morning," Colin finished.

Did Colin just say Mr. Ross had offered to take her? The tiny sparkle of light inside her became a bit brighter. "Thank you, Colin. I appreciate your allowing me to go and take care of my grandmother's final wishes. It is important to me."

"Yes, it's all fine. I will be able to get a lot of work done with you gone. Now, lie down." Colin stood up and began to unbutton his pants and after rolling down his stockings, he kicked them and his shoes off and stood in his bare feet.

Ada sighed. She thought he might leave her alone this evening and go away without abusing her. He clearly had another idea. She lay down backwards on the bed and began to squirm back to allow room for him. She had learned long ago that just allowing him to have her resulted in not getting beaten by him, and she preferred the emotional bruises to the physical ones.

"Are you mad, Ada? Have you seen yourself? You are unsightly this evening, even more so than usual. Roll onto your stomach."

Confused, Ada rolled over. Colin grabbed her hips and pulled her back with a grunt so that her feet were on the ground, her body was pressed into the bed and her rump was high in the air. She felt exposed, even more so than usual. She tried to wriggle back over onto her back but Colin put a hand flat in the centre of her back and smashed her into the feather mattress. She felt his knee jam in between her thighs to spread them even wider apart. She heard him spit into his hand and he roughly rubbed it on her entrance. She tried to relax and tell herself it would soon be over, it always was. He grabbed a handful of hip and entered her hard. She gasped and closed her eyes, waiting. True to form, Colin thrust maybe half a dozen times, each one harder than the last, then made an inhuman groaning noise. Ada could feel his warm seed trickle down her leg as he pulled free of her.

    She felt something land on the bed by her face. She opened her eyes and saw a leather purse. Confused, she turned her head toward Colin. He had already re-buttoned his pants and had his shoes and stockings in his hand. He nodded toward the leather bag. "You always pay a whore, my dear, not matter how bad they look and how mediocre the fuck." He laughed at his own joke and strode confidently out of the room, leaving Ada to clean herself off and contemplate the purse.

Chapter 10

Ada sat looking herself over in her oval dressing table mirror. She looked weary. She tried to pinch her cheeks a little to help give her some colour but that only succeeded in making the red that outlined her grieving eyes more pronounced. She wore a loose black travelling gown. Although it was still very warm in the daytime, it was mid-September and the evenings could get chilly, so she grabbed a black woolen shawl from the peg behind the door. It was a quarter to nine in the morning and Mr. Ross was arriving to pick her up at nine. Her grandmother's house was only a two-day carriage ride away but she hoped Marie had packed extra clothes to protect against the rain, just in case. She walked silently down the main stairway and politely acknowledged the servants who were giving her their condolences. By the time she reached the front door, Mr. Ross had already loaded her luggage and was at the bottom of the porch steps waiting with the carriage. Not to her surprise, Colin was nowhere to be seen. She approached the carriage and Mr. Ross took her hand in his to help her into the back. His hand was very large, very warm and reassuring. He gently closed the door and gave her a sympathetic smile. She felt the carriage shift under his weight as he climbed onto the driver's bench at the front and she gladly sank back against the seat as Mr. Ross clucked the horses forward.

 She waited until they had been on the road for approximately an hour before she banged her hand on the ceiling of the carriage and yelled for Mr. Ross to stop. He reined the horses in and hopped elegantly down to the ground. The carriage door swung open and Mr. Ross' anxious face shoved itself inside.
 "Are ye all right? Is ought amiss?" He looked around in the carriage as if expecting villains to materialize out of the upholstered seats. Ada bit her lip to hide a laugh, she felt better already. Although she missed her grandmother, that overwhelming sense of total solitude she had been feeling at home was already lifting.
 "I'm sorry to have alarmed you, Mr. Ross. I only wondered if you would think it too outrageous for me to come join you on the driver's bench." He cocked an eyebrow but she bravely continued. "It is frighteningly dull back here alone and I get enough silence every other day of my life, so I fully intend to have some conversation on this trip!" She finished triumphantly, pleased with herself as she met his eyes.
 "I am but yer lowly driver, ma'am," he said as he smiled playfully. "Although I am certain no one would approve of this, who am I to stop ye from sitting yer pretty arse wherever you want." He laughed and extended a hand to help her from the carriage.
 She was aware her mouth was hanging open, most unladylike, and promptly closed it. Well, she could see

Mr. Ross had taken their pact to heart. She accepted his hand and help from the back of the carriage and up onto the bench, then he went around the buggy and hopped up beside her. Whether it was grief or the sheer giddiness of being away from Colin and her miserable existence at Watershaw house, she felt free. She waited for Mr. Ross to be settled, then pretending to look at something, scooted her previously discussed body part up against his leg. She thought she saw him smile.

Dear Lord, please give me strength to endure this situation that I have brought upon myself, Grant prayed in his head, then shifted in his seat. Had she just pressed her prominent arse onto his leg? So many images were running through his head. She looked so lovely, even the black of her mourning dress brought out the dark blue in her eyes and made him want to count each one of the freckles that stood out along her nose. He wished she was not wearing that ridiculous straw hat with the black ribbon, he wanted to see her chestnut hair being picked up by the wind as the carriage drove. *For God's sake, get a grip!* he chided himself. There was nothing wrong with a little bit of harmless flirtation amongst friends, well in fact, there was a lot wrong with this flirtation. One, she was married. Two, she was married to someone who had hired him. Three, she was way above him in social standing. Finally, she was like dry grass to him—one spark and there would be no way to stop the fire that sprang up everywhere.

Some time had passed in silence and he could see Mrs. Watershaw was deep into her own thoughts, so he searched for something to start a conversation with.

"So, ma'am, I never did tell ye how verra sorry I was to hear about your Gran." He chanced a glance at her. She was looking at her hands again. Why does she always look down? In fact, he could not remember seeing her look anyone in the eye for more than a few seconds.

"Thank you, Mr. Ross. It is very distressing but I feel that I did not know my grandmother as well as I could have and that may be lessening my grief slightly. Is that terrible of me?"

She looked up at him, her large round eyes looked so lost. Once again, the urge to punch Colin Watershaw rose in him. What had he done to this woman?

"I think ye could tell me that ye murdered fifty people just for sport and I would not think ye terrible, lass." He reached his arm across and platonically patted her leg with his hand. He tried to remove his hand as quickly and quietly as he placed it there but her hand shot out and grabbed onto him.

She held tightly onto his hand and he could feel her wee nails digging into his palm. When he looked down at her, he saw tears rolling over her cheeks and landing on the black material in her lap. "Are you overwhelmed, ma'am? Should we stop for a bit?" he asked, stopping the carriage. He would have done anything to have her stop looking so utterly miserable.

She suddenly let go of the hand she had been holding and grabbed onto the front of his jacket with both hands, then lifted her face up and glared at him directly in the eyes. Tears still spilled down her face. "Why are you being so nice to me?" she screamed, as she shook him by the jacket. "I know I do not deserve it! Do not tease me! My husband has made me well aware that I deserve whatever misery this world gives me and lately I have been having a hard time finding reasons not to believe him. What kind of person allows someone to treat them so poorly? Someone who has been made to believe she is old, unattractive and has no other options! All of that is true. Can you not see that?" By now, she was sobbing and gasping while still attempting to shake the gizzards out of him.

Grant attempted to respond, saying, "Ma'am, I…"

"Do not call me ma'am! My servants call me ma'am, and my husband calls me many other things but never that. Please, just call me Ada, please… please just call me Ada..." She had stopped shaking him and put her forehead on this chest and continued to sob in earnest, hiccupping occasionally.

"Ada it is. Would you call me Grant?" He asked her softly, stroking her back like a skittish horse. He felt a small nod of assent against his chest and smiled despite her misery.

"I'm sorry, Mr... Grant. You have been the only one in my life in a long time who has treated me with any kindness. You even care about my opinion, and that is something I have never had— not even as a child." She was speaking muffled from his shirt. "Now, I have yelled at you and shaken you and made a complete ass out of myself. I guess I am asking that you please not stop being my friend, because you are the only one I have, and I could not bear it."

She sniffed and lifted her head off his chest to look at him. She looked so lovely, wild and vulnerable. He wanted so badly to press her against his body and kiss her until she forgot her miserable life but that is not what she needed, and he knew that. He took her hand, placed a soft chaste kiss on the back of it and whispered, "Do ye really think ye can be rid of me that easily?" She smiled, placed her head on his shoulder and was asleep before he could get the carriage moving again.

Grant shook Ada softly. She cracked an eye open and upon realizing she had been sleeping on his shoulder, she opened both eyes and quickly sat up. She noticed he had one hand holding the reins and one arm around her to keep her from jostling in her sleep as the wagon bounced down the road. She rubbed her eyes sleepily "What time is it?" she asked.

"Just past midday according to the noise my stomach is making. Should we stop for a wee bite?" Grant inquired, already slowing the horses down.

"Oh, yes, please. I'm famished," Ada eagerly replied, anticipating the delicious lunch the cook would have packed for them.

Grant pulled the wagon off the road, allowed the horses to graze and came back to sit on the grass where Ada had spread out a tantalizing packed lunch from a cloth sack. He was crunching his dilled cucumber slice when he looked around at the scenery, the wonderful lunch, and Ada chewing delicately on a piece of buttered bread. He tried to remember the last time he had been this content. It would have been before Culloden, when he was a young boy with nothing to worry about. In his mind, he wished he could eat like this with Ada every day of the summer. For a moment, he almost forgot she was taken, not to mention too good for him.

"I've just realized that I have never even asked you whether you have a family, Grant. A wife, perhaps?" Ada thought about the flirtatious behavior that had already gone on between them and felt ashamed she had not thought to ask earlier, but then again, she had a husband and it didn't seem to matter that much.

"No wife, no family, it's just myself. I have a brother somewhere back in Scotland, or I did, I havena had the opportunity to speak to him in many years. I do not even know if he's still alive." Grant grabbed a slice of cheese.

"I'm sorry to hear that. I know what it's like to have no family." Ada nodded in sympathy. "My mother and sister died of smallpox when I was younger. I contracted the illness too but I obviously survived. My father died more recently." She took off her straw hat to let her hair catch the whisper of a breeze that was blowing through.

"I am sorry for ye, lass," Grant said softly. Grant's breath caught in his throat as the sun ricocheted off the reddish-brown hair that had been released from her straw hat. Unfortunately, so did the piece of bread he was eating. He choked explosively, cough after embarrassing cough, his eyes were streaming and he was gratefully accepting Ada's pats on the back and attempts to give him water. He was still hacking when Ada reached for the top two buttons of his collar, no doubt to give him some air. His hand caught hers, perhaps harder than he intended and she pulled her hand back with a confused look.

"I'm sorry, I was only trying to help." She sat back on the grass with her hands wrapped around her knees as he brought his choking under control with sips of water.

"I'm sorry, you startled me and I…" he trailed off looking upset. Even still, he was checking to make sure the buttons had remained fastened.

"Shall we continue?" Ada asked politely. "We would like to make it to the inn before it gets too dark this evening, and there is a lot more ground to cover." She stood up, swished her hands over her skirt to dislodge bits of grass and straggling crumbs and began to pack up the remains of the lunch in the cloth sack.

"I'll see to the horses." Grant stalked off in the direction of the horses and carriage.

Ada watched him go. She was puzzled about his behavior. He had almost seemed scared to let her open his top buttons to allow his neck more room and movement. Maybe she had just startled him. She was enjoying herself again and did not want to read too much into it. She picked up the cloth bag and set off toward the carriage with a renewed sense of curiosity about Mr. Grant Ross.

Just after it became dark, they rolled into a small hamlet that boasted a tavern with rooms above to rent. Grant had Ada stay in the back of the carriage while he went inside and acquired rooms for them both. He was gone less than ten minutes when the carriage door opened and Grant hopped into the back with her.

"That didn't take you long!" she said into the darkness in front of her.

"It's not the nicest place, Ada. I inquired about rooms and they said they had one available. I was going to just let ye take it and I would sleep in the carriage or on the floor in the hallway but I worry for yer safety alone up there. I have a suggestion but I dinna want ye to think it unseemly of me."

"Go on, please…" Ada was desperately tired and just wanted to lie down and sleep.

"I have told the owner that my wife and I require the room. You will, of course, have the bed and I will sleep on a pallet on the floor but this way, no one will venture into yer room at night while I'm there, aye?"

"Well, you are rather large," she said jokingly. "Thank you, your plan makes me feel quite at ease. Shall we?"

Surprised at her quick acquiescence, Grant nodded. "Oh, aye, come along then, Mrs. Ross." They were both laughing as they entered the tavern and climbed the stairs to the room they were to share.

"I'll go down and fetch myself a wee dram while ye get yourself settled and have some privacy. I willna be back up for at least an hour. Does that give ye enough time?"

"Plenty, thank you very much, Grant," she touched his arm in farewell, "for everything."

Before he turned to leave, she looked up at him. Her freckles were standing out like tiny ink dots in the candlelight of the room. He heard her sigh. She did feel safe, and he was happy. Before he could change his mind, he brushed a small lock of hair back behind her ear. He looked at her face trying to find some sign of what it was she was thinking. She reached a cold hand up to his cheek, brushed his face softly with her thumb and standing on tiptoes, kissed his lips with ethereal softness. He peered down at her but her eyes were closed, revealing nothing. As quickly as she had kissed him, she had ceased and giving his hand a final squeeze, closed the door.

Grant walked down the creaky stairs to the tavern below. He made sure to take a seat at the table closest to the stairs so he could watch anyone who ventured up or down and thus, keep an eye on the room he would share with Ada. His mind immediately went back to that kiss—she had kissed him. He adjusted his seat as he thought about it to allow for extra room in the crotch of his trousers. Thank the Lord he had already made an excuse to leave the room. He could not have stayed in there while she did simple things like wash her face, or pull back the bed linens. God, he could not even think about her doing anything at all without heat coursing through his entire body. Her bright face freshly scrubbed leaning over the bed to turn down the linens with her arse up in the air covered only by her night robe.

"What can I bring you, SIR?" the serving woman asked Grant for what he was sure was not the first time. How long had she been standing there watching him daydream like a fool?

He lifted his head and cleared his throat. "Ale, please. My apologies, my mind is somewhere else." *So is every other part of my anatomy,* Grant thought painfully, shifting his position yet again.

The serving woman looked at him. "I'd like it better if your mind was on me," she purred and reached a practiced hand up to his cheek.

He moved his head away and she let her hand fall. "Just the ale if you please, miss. I have a wife and a bed upstairs and I am eager to get back to both." The woman pouted and flounced away. When she returned with his ale, she plunked it onto the table, spilling some of it and without a word, marched away looking sullen. Grant sipped the ale and chuckled softly to himself.

When the hour he promised Ada had finally passed, he walked up the wooden stairs, which creaked alarmingly under his weight, and knocked softly on the door to their room. "Are ye decent, Ada? Should I go back down for a wee bit longer?" He hoped she was decent because he was desperately tired and wanted to sleep.

"Please, come in, Grant." A muffled voice from across the room spoke through the door.

He entered the room. She had left the candles burning for him and was tucked up in the bed with the sheet pulled up to her chest. He tried not to look at her. Instead, he sat down on the wooden chair and began to take his boots off. She had laid a pallet out for him on the floor and by the looks of it, had given him most of the decent blankets.

"Ada, ye must take more of these quilts back, ye'll catch yer death with only the one blanket ye have there." He bent down to scoop up one of the top quilts and grabbing it, he brought it over to her on the bed. He handed it to her. "I sleep warm, lass. Please, it would make me feel better if ye'd take it."

She took the quilt from Grant and spread it out over her. "Thank you, I'm sure I will be just fine." She looked directly into his eyes. The candlelight made them look like dark pools on his face, with no distinguishable colour.

Her eyes connected with his like wildfire. He started to lean closer to her and quite suddenly, stopped. "Goodnight, Ada. Sleep well. I best be retiring to my pallet now before something happens that we canna take back." He stood up and walked over to the candles and began to blow them out one by one, then with only the candle beside his pallet remaining, he lay down on his pile of blankets.

"I'll give you some privacy if you want to change for bed." Ada rolled onto her side with her back toward Grant.

"Thank ye kindly, but I'm fine as I am. I'll see you in the morning, goodnight." Grant blew out the remaining candle.

Ada lay in the dark facing the wooden wall feeling ridiculous. Of course, he did not want her. No one would. She acted shamelessly and her wanton behavior had now embarrassed them both. What was she thinking? She had never in all her life behaved in such a fashion. She flashed back to the kiss she had given him at the door. He must think her a very forward woman. She heaved over onto her back and sighed. There was no help for it, she must throw herself on her sword and apologize for her conduct. Besides, what is a little more humiliation on top of the heap she had already shoveled for herself. "Grant…?" she whispered.

All she heard from the pallet on the floor was the deep steady breathing of an exhausted sleep. Tomorrow she would set it right.

She woke the next morning to the sun shining directly onto her pillow through the only window in the room. It was still early and when she sat up, Grant was already gone, no doubt to check the horses. His pallet was cleaned up and sat folded on the wooden chair. She quickly took the moment of solitude to use the chamber pot and attempt to freshen herself up as best she could with what Marie had packed for her. She was pinning up the last of her stray wisps of hair when there was a soft rap at the door. She was so used to Colin just barging in regardless of what she was doing, she was startled by the soft knock more so than she would have been by a swinging door banging against the wall.

"It's me, Grant. I've brought ye some toast and water," the door said to her.

She immediately got up and ran over to open it. "Thank you so much, you really did not need to fetch me anything. I should be the one fetching your breakfast after how I behaved yesterday." She looked down at the floor. *Well, it's now or never*, she thought.

"Och, well, I wish they had something better then honeyed toast and water. I mean, jailers are served better meals than this... Wait, what did ye say?" Grant had obviously been paying more attention to the lack of proper breakfast essentials than what Ada had said.

"I was simply saying that how I acted yesterday is in no way a representation of my normal conduct or character. I do not know what came over me, it was possibly the grief over my grandmother or the sense of freedom I have from being away from Colin... Oh, dear. I should not have said that. That sounded terribly rude. Now, I am crass as well as lewd. Please, forgive me. I understand I have nothing to offer a man beyond kindness and ladylike charms and I am afraid that I did not exhibit any of those attributes yesterday. Please, accept my truest and most sincere apologies." Ada finished triumphantly, proud to have gotten the entire apology out without blundering it too much.

Grant had stood stock still through Ada's entire speech. Did she truly think such terrible things about herself? He had put a stop to everything last night because he was so much beneath her that once she was back in a stable frame of mind, she would realize she had made a terrible mistake. He did not want to be her lifelong regret. He placed the toast down on the tiny rickety table by the door.

"I stopped ye because if I dinna stop it, then I never would have." He stared at the top of her chestnut head. She was looking at the floor again.

"You needn't say these things to save my pride, Grant. I understand what I am, and what I am not," she said softly.

"Oh, aye, and did yer husband tell ye what ye are?" Violence dripped from the word husband and she flinched slightly.

"In a way, I suppose, yes. He has informed me of what men admire and lust after in women. I am astute enough to realize whether I have those qualities."

"Perhaps yer nay as clever as ye think, Ada." Grant put his fingers gently under her chin and lifted it so she was looking at him in the face. "If ye were more astute ye would realize that I have wanted ye since I scairt ye in the barn the first time I saw ye. I watch yer arse and hips sway every time ye walk and I need to remember to let out the breath that I never realize I am holding. Ye look at me with eyes that are sad and alone and all I want to do is make ye feel safe and cared for. My God,

Ada, ye have put me in a trance for months." He finished speaking but did not take his hand from her chin.

She tried to move her head back down to the floor. This could not be true. She could not make a man feel this way, she did not have the capabilities. "Thank you, Grant. It was very nice of you to try and lift my spirits…"

He cut her off, "Do ye no believe me? Do ye think I go about saying things like that to any lassie I meet down at the market. I have never said anything like that before, because I have never meant anything like that before." He was breathing faster, trying by sheer force of will to make her believe what he knew to be true about her.

She tried to move away. "Perhaps it is about time we depart; we do not want to lose anymore daylight."

If she would not believe his words then by God, he'd make her believe his feelings, by feeling them herself. He put both of his hands on her cheeks and pressed his lips down onto hers. He thought he heard her gasp slightly but he did not care, he was already damned for saying what he did and he may as well be damned for showing her the truth of it. He removed one hand from her cheek and slid it down to the small of her back, pressing her against him. He continued to kiss her, willing her to understand her appeal, willing her to understand what she did to him. He stopped the kiss and placed a kiss on her forehead.

"Can ye truly not see, lass?" he whispered. He almost looked saddened by her refusal to see herself the way he described her.

She had never felt anything like that. Her body was vibrating as though a strange current was running through them both at the same time. She had kissed other men before Colin and even though she had felt excitement before, she never felt this feeling. She wondered, *Is this passion?*

"Show me again," she whispered back and put a hand on his warm chest, leaning up to him.

He needed no other signal. Her invitation had melted him and he crashed down onto her mouth and pulled her hard against the length of him, wanting to use sheer force to meld them together. He kissed her in earnest for what seemed like days but in reality, had only been moments. Then, he softly broke away.

"We need to go, Ada. As right as this seems, it isna the right time, nor the right place. Ye have your Gran's estate to see to and I should like to get ye there before sunset this evening." He grabbed her hand and held on for dear life. "What have ye done to me, Ada?" he asked, looking down at her.

"What have we done to each other?" she replied. She grabbed her shawl and turned toward the door. Still holding his hand, she asked, "Are you coming, Mr. Ross?"

He laughed, relieved and pleasantly surprised by her jaunty mood. "Mrs. Watershaw, I told ye, ye canna be rid of me that easily." They closed the door behind them and paid the tavern owner for the room. The toast and honey sat untouched on the table.

Chapter 11

They drove down the laneway of Ada's grandmother's country estate just as the final glimpse of the sun disappeared underneath the horizon line. Grant dropped Ada at the large front doors and proceeded to the barn to unhook and brush down the pair of geldings.

Ada opened the huge wooden doors and walked into the large foyer like she had so many times before, but it was different this time. The house looked empty and there were only a few servants bustling around. Ada guessed that many of them would have found new employment by now. A lot of her grandmother's bits and pieces had been packed up in crates with the lids left unnailed so Ada could see what was inside. They sat stacked by the foot of the staircase, kept clean and dusted by the remaining servants.

"Hello?" Ada called softly, wondering if she knew anyone who was still employed there.

A tall, thin man poked his head over the railing from the landing at the top of the stairs.

"Carmady!" Ada squealed, delighted that her grandmother's butler—even more so, her grandmother's dear friend—was still there. Ada ran toward the older man who was running as fast as he could down the flight of stairs. She reached him when he hit the bottom step and they embraced, cried and laughed at each other for their reactions.

Carmady wiped a wrinkled hand over his streaming eyes. "I'm so glad you're here, Ada. I hoped and prayed to see you again before I went to live with my son in New York." He held both of her hands tightly. "How was the travel, my girl?"

Ada had always considered Joseph Carmady somewhat of an adopted grandfather. Her grandmother had never frowned on her being so close with Carmady because secretly, she thought her grandmother was a lot closer to him then she allowed her friends and other society members to believe.

"The travel was wonderful; it was so nice to be out of the house and to have some freedom and fresh air."

"Good to be out of the house?" He crooked a white eyebrow. "Are you not happy in your new marriage, Ada?" Carmady asked, but Ada knew he could see the answer just by looking at her face. He could always read her expressions, and it was one of the reasons she liked him so much.

"He is not the man I expected, Carmady. It's just a different life than I had envisioned myself having." Ada was not going to tell him anything more than that. She would not have him worrying about her when there was nothing he or anyone could do to change it.

"Do you know if there is a room ready for me? I would like to try and wash some of this road dust off before we eat supper." Ada had deliberately changed the subject before Carmady could whittle more information out of her about Colin and their marriage.

"I had your old room set up upstairs. I knew you would come once you received Mrs. Potts letter." He smiled thankfully at Ada. "Do you need a room set up in the servant's quarters for your driver?"

"My regular driver had an accident that prevented him from accompanying me, so Mr. Ross, a friend of mine, gallantly agreed to be my escort. I would much prefer if he stayed in a guest room upstairs, please."

Carmady quirked one side of his clean-shaven mouth but said nothing, bless his heart. "Absolutely, let me just get one of the remaining maids to help make up a room at once, then I shall return down here and wait for him to come in and I'll show him to his room. You go relax and get freshened up, my dear." He smiled and kissed Ada on the cheek, then turned and scuttled away in search of a maid.

One he finished in the barn, Grant walked up to the huge wooden doors and placing Ada's bags on the porch, knocked loudly. Before he had time to pull his fist down, the door opened wide and an elderly man with a kind face ushered him inside. His butler livery was clean and crisp and slightly too big on his stick-thin frame.

"You must be Mr. Ross, Ada's escort. Come in, come in and let me take those bags from you, sir." The elderly man reached for Ada's luggage.

Startled, Grant handed over the bags. "I am Grant Ross, sir. It's verra good to make your acquaintance. I was just dropping Mrs. Watershaw's baggage off to her and I will be going to find my own bed in the stables.

Not to worry." Grant was used to the way butlers treated him, like a stain they were desperately trying to remove before more company came. Although this gentleman seemed kind, he did not want to push his luck.

"In the stables? No, no, lad. Mrs. Watershaw has insisted that her friend, Mr. Ross, be given a guest room upstairs and we are very happy to oblige you, sir."

Grant was aware that his mouth was hanging open and he quickly closed it. Ada had obviously embellished his station slightly or there was no chance he would be offered a room in the main house. "I think there is a miscommunication, Mr...?"

"Carmady, sir. Joseph Carmady," the man said and smiled patiently.

"Mr. Carmady, as I was saying, there must be a mistake. I have been employed by Mr. Watershaw to escort his wife. I am just the blacksmith, sir," he finished badly.

"A noble profession to be sure. I am a butler, sir, so follow me upstairs, please." Carmady winked a creased eye at Grant and set off up the stairs.

Grant sighed, picked up the one remaining bag and followed the sprightly butler up the flight of stairs. They arrived in a room with more furniture than Grant had ever owned in his entire life. There was a fireplace, a writing desk and chair, an overly large bed with what looked like a feather mattress and even a large upholstered chair to enjoy reading beside the fire. Grant looked around, then back at Carmady.

"Thank ye, sir. This is a room fit for better people than the likes of me."

Carmady patted Grant on the shoulder. "Enjoy it, Mr. Ross. Dinner will be in a few hours; you will find water in the ewer on the dressing table. Until then, I'll bid you farewell." Carmady closed the door quietly behind him, leaving Grant standing in the biggest bedroom he had ever seen. He wondered where Ada's room was located. No, he should not think like that, she was married and for now, that was all that mattered.

    Hours later, Grant lay sprawled across his giant feather bed. His arms and legs outstretched with his boots sticking out over the end of the mattress. Dinner had been delicious. He could not remember when he had had such a huge amount of fish, roasted chicken, boiled vegetables, bread and pie… the pie. Grant had eaten two slices of the best cherry pie he had ever tasted. He would have had three, and damn the good manners, but he feared he would literally explode if he forced another bite past his lips. He was still lying there blissfully full and drowsy when he heard a soft rap on the door. He could not summon the energy to get off the bed and open the door but he didn't think the old butler would mind.

    "Come in, Carmady! I fear the dinner has got the best of me!" He laughed jokingly as the door opened.

    "Grant? It is only me." Ada stuck her head through the crack in the door she had just opened. "I brought you a book from my grandmother's library. I did not know whether you packed yourself one and there are plenty of novels on the American West, you know, horses, Indians, traders and the like. I thought you might be interested. My grandmother added them to the library for Carmady—he loves them." Ada held out the book to him.

Grant had stood up from bed the moment he realized that it was Ada and not Carmady at his bedroom door. Suddenly, he did not feel as tired as before. Her hair was in a long plait for bedtime and Grant could see a slight flush on her face, perhaps from being in his room or from her walk down the long hallway. She still wore the black dress she had worn to dinner but she had removed her shoes and was standing in just her stockings on the rug in his room. He looked down at her feet, then back up to her face.

"Thank ye, I am sure I will find this book a great entertainment. It was nice of ye to think of me, Ada." He took the book from her hand, walked over and placed it on the pillow of his bed. He took a step toward her. "Ye look verra lovely, with the colour on yer cheeks and your stocking feet against the rug." He laughed softly.

She looked suddenly down at her feet, aghast. She had kicked off her pinching black dinner slippers the minute she went back to her room. Then, she remembered the library and hurried out to select a book for herself to read that night. Upon seeing the Colonial West books, she immediately thought of Grant and decided to bring him a book too, forgetting about her shoeless feet. She shrugged her shoulders. "Well, it's not like I have much of a refined lady reputation to keep up with you, do I?" She laughed. "I think that ship has long since sailed."

Grant laughed. "Oh, aye. Ye are right back to the servant that I originally thought ye were!" He laughed as she playfully swatted at him. "Not that I'm saying it's a bad thing, of course." He caught the hand she had swatted him with and held it in his own rough hand. It seemed so delicate and smooth. Although he would not describe Ada's hand as dainty, it was pale and feminine and beautiful. He wanted to protect it with his own coarse and battered hands, like a metaphor for her whole body.

With that thought in mind, Grant released her hand. "Ye need to go back to yer own room now, lass."

"But I thought..." Ada looked up at him with confusion in her beautiful dark blue eyes. She liked the feeling of her hand in his; she liked the way it made the rest of her body feel.

"Ada, ye know how much I would love to have ye stay but there are still some servants about the house. I know you trust Carmady but can ye trust the others as well? People talk, Ada. I will not allow you to be hurt because one of the servants sees ye in my room and makes a speculation. It's nay that far back to Watershaw house, aye? And word travels faster than ye'd think." Grant reached up and lifted the braid off her shoulder, letting it run through his hand. "Goodnight, lass." He followed her to the door as she walked out and closed it behind her.

How could she have been so utterly brainless? Of course, she did not trust the other servants. What would have happened if Grant had not sent her to bed? Thank God he had. If word had gotten back to anyone at Watershaw house that she had spent the night, or even just a few hours, in Grant Ross's bedroom, Colin would surely kill her. She shivered at the thought. She berated herself for not having thought of the consequences. It was times like these that she truly felt the naivety of her upbringing. What had gotten into her recently? Never in her life had she acted so heedlessly of her own safety, and Grant's for that matter. She shut the door to her own bedroom perhaps a trifle too hard, and plopped down on the bed. Within minutes, she ceased her thoughts with the promise of a good night's sleep.

She spent the next few weeks packing what would be sold or donated to the church, which would then be distributed to people in need. She felt a sense of accomplishment at overseeing a task as important as this. Although she missed her grandmother terribly, it was not especially hard to part with her things as Ada felt her grandmother was with her and not with the belongings she was giving away. The last few days saw her saying goodbye to all the remaining servants who were starting employment elsewhere and by the last day, Carmady was the only one left. He would soon depart as well; he was only staying to oversee the sale of the house and to ensure the money was put into an account in Ada's name at the local bank.

The friendship between her and Grant had grown over the two weeks and although there were often accidental unchecked glances, nothing happened that would give anyone anything to suspect or talk about behind their backs. She had resigned herself to understanding that her life was as it is. She was married to Colin Watershaw and she lived the life that came with that fact. However, she found hope and happiness in her new friendship with Grant—joking with him as he hauled and stacked crates of goods, and generally helped her with this entire endeavor. Still, there was a tiny piece of her somewhere in the very back of her brain, that was sad and almost angry. She could picture her life with Grant. She often did when she went back to her room at night. She thought about the easy conversation, the novelty of being looked at as if she was beautiful, and the fact that he seemed to respect her input and opinions. There were so many more things about him and about them both together, that she had to push out of her mind for fear of becoming too involved. She realized that the more she grew to respect and adore Grant Ross, the more she despised her husband. This was becoming very dangerous indeed.

Chapter 12

The weather was miserable for the two-day trip home. Grant had insisted she ride in the carriage and out of the cold driving rain. Although she desperately missed the conversation, not to mention being close enough to 'accidentally' rub against him when they hit a bump, she was thankful she was dry and somewhat warm in her cloak. Poor Grant was probably soaked through and freezing. She had been glad when he accepted the offer of the wool blanket she had given him from inside the carriage seat.

The scenery that jostled by was becoming recognizable to Ada, and she knew they must be approaching the town. The town was only a half of an hour's ride to Watershaw house. Ada's spirits sank. She would soon be back to her solitary silent life, with the occasional rape and beating to keep her company. She had half a mind to beat on the carriage roof and beg Grant to keep on driving. Instead, she sat there, hands folded in her lap, watching the sights become more and more familiar and her heart become more hardened.

Grant stopped the carriage at the front steps of her house. She waited while he ran around to open the carriage door and help her down. The rain had subsided to an annoying drizzle but the wind still had a harsh bite.

"Home safe, Mrs. Watershaw." Grant smiled warmly at her as he opened the carriage door.

"Those two words do not fit together well in this house, Mr. Ross." Ada tried to smile reassuringly. It was not a surprise that no one was waiting for her on the porch. Ada doubted if anyone in this house, with perhaps the exception of Marie, would be curious or would even care if she came back at all.

"Listen to me, Ada." Grant spoke quickly into her ear. "If ye have need of me, send word and I will come and be damned the consequences. Ye willna be mistreated if I can help ye in anyway. Do ye understand?"

She nodded softly, hopped down from the carriage and walked up the steps of her front porch. Grant was fetching her bags and bringing them up the stairs behind her. "Thank you for everything, Grant. I mean it." She reached out for him and the front door swung open.

She dropped her hand back down to her side as if she had touched fire, then whirled toward the front door to see Colin standing there.

He, as usual, ignored her. "Mr. Ross, I do hope your trip was not too troublesome. The weather has been just ghastly these past few days. I have your pay here and I hoped to speak to you before you left about getting a couple horses done in the next few days. I have a sale coming up and…" He seemed to have just noticed

Ada's presence. "What the devil are you still doing out here?" He shooed her with a flick of his hand and continued talking to Grant. She nodded a subtle goodbye to Grant from behind Colin's shoulder, then went inside closing the door behind her.

She was ascending the stairs to her bedroom when she ran into Marie.

"Madam, you are home! Why did no one tell me?" Marie's pretty young faced scrunched up in a frown. "I would have had a bath ready for you in your room. *Tsk* not to worry, I will have one brought up *tout de suite.*" Marie was ready to skitter off like a tiny field mouse.

"Thank you, Marie. I would love a bath and then my bed. I fear I am too tired to even eat any dinner this evening." What she really wanted was to be in bed and faking sleep before Colin came back upstairs from his business with Grant and his own supper. Not that it would make much difference to him whether she was sleeping or not.

Ada changed into her dressing gown and waited as buckets of steaming water were brought up and dumped into her bathing tub. She could hear Marie yelling in French at some poor kitchen boy who spilled some of the hot water while carrying a heavy bucket up the stairs. She laughed to herself. Marie was so petite but she would tell off the King himself if she felt the need. Ada used to believe she had that strength but lately, she was not so sure.

Thirty minutes later, Ada had finished soaking in her bath and was waiting for Marie to hand her a drying blanket. The bath had done a great deal to restore her but she was still bone tired from the grief, hard work and emotion of the past two weeks and wanted nothing more now than to go to bed. She reached out to Marie who had the blanket held up in her outstretched arms. The little maid had her sleeves rolled up to protect her clothes from the bath water and Ada noticed tiny circular bruises on Marie's arm, much like those on Ada's neck.

"Marie, what happened to your arm?" There was no point in beating around the bush. Ada had an idea who had put the bruises there but what she did not know yet was why.

Marie looked down at her arm and quickly rolled down her sleeves. "Oh, it is nothing, madam. I slipped going down the stairs while I was carrying some of the household laundry and one of the house boys grabbed my arm to catch me. I was quite lucky he was there, actually." Marie was a terrible liar. She transferred her weight from one foot to the other and stared at the bathwater, desperately trying to not look Ada in the face.

"Marie, you will tell me the whole truth this instant or I will ask every servant in this house until I find it." Servants gossiped worse than pupils in a school house.

"It's not that I don't want to tell you, madam, it is just that you have the O'Dell dinner engagement tomorrow and I did not want to upset you. You look so tired and I was only trying to save you from anymore distress." Marie honestly looked as if she would run out of the room if Ada's glare was not holding her to the spot.

"That is kind of you, Marie. I had quite forgotten about the O'Dell's party but I need to know the truth of how those marks got on your arm, please." Ada gestured for her to take a seat in the big reading chair by the fire and pulled up the wooden chair to sit across from her. Suddenly, the night when Colin had strangled her sprung to mind and she decided to sit on the bedside instead of across from Marie in the wooden chair.

Seeing no help for it and no escape, Marie began to speak tentatively. "Well, when you were gone, madam, *Monsieur* Watershaw spent the first few nights away from the house, no doubt he was gaming or drinking in the town." Marie looked nervous. She looked swiftly at the door.

"It is all right, Marie. Please, keep going," Ada said encouragingly.

"Each night, while Robertson extinguishes the lamps downstairs, I walk around to all the rooms on the upper floor and make certain the candles and lamps had been put out up here too. *Monsieur* Watershaw usually leaves the lamps burning in his room after Robertson dresses him for his departure. So, the night I got these…" she touched her arm lightly through her sleeve, "I had opened his bedroom door and walked in to extinguish the lamps." Her face flamed red.

"But he was there…" Ada chimed in, non-pulsed.

"*Oui,* madam!" Marie nodded furiously, her blond hair bouncing. "What is worse, madam, is he was not alone—there was *une fille* in there with him. They were in bed together, madam. I am very sorry." She hung her head. "I must have looked shocked or angry, because I certainly felt both. I turned to leave quickly but *Monsieur* Watershaw had already leapt from the bed. He grabbed my arm and turned me around to face him. He told me I was a stupid girl for waltzing in there without so much as a knock. I tried to explain that I was just turning the lamps down but he slapped me across my mouth before I could finish. He had a firm grip on my arm, and I knew it would bruise. He told me that if I told anyone what I saw he would beat me senseless and dismiss me from service. I am sorry, madam. I have nowhere else to go."

Tears ran slowly down Marie's flushed cheeks. Ada got up from the bed and went over and knelt in front of her. "Colin will never know you have spoken of this, Marie. You have my word." She handed the girl a handkerchief from the bedside table. "Keep your sleeves rolled down so no one else notices, and trust that both your secret and you are safe as far as I'm concerned. Now, go find your bed. I will not need you for the rest of the night." Ada reached a hand up to pat Marie on the shoulder. Oddly, she was not at all surprised by this news.

Marie met her eyes with a look of such overwhelming relief that Ada felt tears prick the sides of her eyes. "*Merci*, madam. Thank you so much." She stood up and walked out the door, closing it softly behind her.

Ada lay down in her bed shortly afterwards. She had always suspected Colin slept with other women, but to know for certain did not seem to upset her nearly as much as it should have—perhaps if he was sleeping with other women, he would not force himself on her as much. She let the thought of sweet interrupted sleep lull her into darkness.

O'Dell Residence

Ruth O'Dell certainly hosted a wonderful dinner party. From the moment they arrived, Colin and Ada were given a seemingly unending array of beverages and appetizers—mere glimpses into the culinary delights that dinner would hold. Now, seated around the O'Dell's long wooden dining room table, Ada could not even remember if she had ever eaten food this delicious in her entire life. She sipped her wine and let the flavor swill through her mouth before swallowing—even the wine tasted exquisite. Everyone was chatting happily amongst themselves, and Colin even seemed to be having a good time. She had yet to see him in a social situation where he truly enjoyed himself, but this was a start. Whatever Colin was feeling was of no importance to her because she was having a fabulous time. She enjoyed every chance she got to talk with the other guests and engage in discussions with them; it was so different from what she normally experienced at home. She loved gossiping aimlessly with the women and exchanging pleasantries with the men. However, it was somewhere between the clam chowder and the main dish that the conversation shifted, making Ada pay absolute attention.

"I was so very sorry to hear about your grandmother's passing, Ada," Emilie voiced from three chairs down.

"Thank you, it came very much as a shock," Ada replied. Emilie smiled sympathetically at her. Emilie's pretty face looked almost gaunt in comparison to the last time she saw her at the picnic, with plumpness radiating across her pregnant face.

"Congratulations on the birth of your son," Colin piped in. "I hope you will excuse the lack of a note in the mail but Ada has been away and she normally handles those sorts of things." He looked sidelong at Ada.

Emilie waved Colin's apology off with a twist of her hand. "I'll not hear a word of it, Mr. Watershaw. You and Ada have obviously had much more emotional and important things to deal with yourselves. There would be no need for you two to be thinking about us in your difficult time."

Ada opened her mouth to explain how terrible she felt about not sending a note of congratulations when she was pre-emptively cut off by a male voice from further down the table.

Anne's husband, Charles, turned toward Ada and said, "I hope the travel was tolerable for you, Mrs. Watershaw." Before she could reply, his gaze turned to Colin. "How did you make out hiring a driver from town? Was it ghastly expensive?" Colin had obviously informed them that Henry had been injured and therefore unable to escort her.

"Oddly enough, I ended up hiring Mr. Ross." Colin sipped his wine.

Charles put down his own glass and raised his eyebrows. Chuckling, he said, "The smith? Is he in transport now too?"

"He informed me he wanted some extra money and would be happy to pick up the work." On the word 'work' he looked over at Ada so she could see he was implying she was the terrible task. "Worked out quite well, actually. I paid him a lot less than anyone in town would have charged for the task."

Mary spoke up from the far side of the table, a concerned frown on her young brow. "Were you not timid going with someone other than your usual driver, Ada? I would be frightfully concerned myself."

Ada thought Mary would be frightfully concerned about anything from a poor fashion choice to a sour tasting pie but not wanting to offend anyone she just shook her head politely.

"Ada knows Mr. Ross, do you not, Ada?" It was her friend Louise Davaneaux's turn to speak up. "She spoke to him at length about her mare while she was at tea. Did you not say he was fantastic with your horse, Ada?"

Ada could feel Colin's anger seething from him in the seat next to her. Poor Louise had no idea what she had just done.

"Well, I would not say that I knew him well, I am obviously better acquainted with him now after the trip but he does have a wonderful hand with the horses. Clearly that is why my husband hired him because Colin knows good quality when he sees it." She was trying her best to play to Colin's need for respect and public admiration. She already knew what would be in store for her when they returned to the house.

Ada dared a quick glance at Colin. His cold eyes and rigid posture emphasized to her that her attempts at flattery did not remain noticed in his present emotional state.

"I heard there is something strange about Mr. Ross." Ruth, the relentless gossip had not spoken in over five minutes. *So, it was obviously time for her to chime in*, Ada thought maliciously.

"My dear, whatever are you talking about?" Mr. O'Dell inquired.

"Well, when I was volunteering at the church—oh it would have been a few months' past—I overheard, by no fault of my own, I assure you!" Ruth giggled.

It took most of Ada's strength to refrain from yelling, "Just get on with it, woman!" Instead, she nodded her head encouragingly at Ruth to help move the story along with her apparent eagerness and rapt attention.

"Where was I? Oh, yes. I overheard some women speaking about their husbands who were returning from fishing and saw Mr. Ross bathing in the water by the shore. Their husbands said he had disfiguring scars all over his body!" Ruth was flushed with excitement.

Ada realized her wine glass had been frozen in midair since Ruth had explained what the men had seen. She hastily took a sip, and tried to look nonchalant. *Scars,* she thought. *What kind of scars? From what? Poor Grant.* Thoughts raced through her mind, she took another gulp of wine.

"Scars, you say?" Allain Davaneaux chimed in. "That is very curious, indeed."

"No doubt obtained in some lower-class tavern brawl." Colin had calmed enough to speak again. "I am fond of Mr. Ross but I can hardly be surprised he has some kind of dangerous past, I mean look at the man, he hasn't a refined bone in his oversized body." Colin chuckled as did the others at the table.

"Apparently, the scars are much worse than what one might obtain in a bar fight." Heads turned back to look at Ruth. "Well, from what I overheard, they were noticeable at quite a distance. Did you notice anything off about Mr. Ross during your travels, Ada?" Ruth was panting at the chance for more gossip to add to her repertoire.

"Not in the least, but in all honesty, we were both working very hard and saw little of each other while we were there. Besides, I would hardly have an occasion to see any scaring, how inappropriate!" She hoped her tone would put an end to Ruth's questions and the present line of conversation.

It seemed to have worked as Mary's husband Harold brought up an old companion, he had that became terribly scarred by a farming accident—something about a runaway horse still attached to the plow. Ada was not paying any attention. She was deep in her own thoughts about Grant and this new information. When she finally looked around again, she saw Colin staring at her with a look she knew she would regret.

Chapter 13

With Henry injured, Colin had decided to drive the carriage himself to the dinner party so he would not have to spend money on hiring someone else from the town. Ada had never been more thankful that her husband was cheap. She sat alone in the back of the carriage. The air was unseasonably frigid and it was pelting down rain as though Mother Nature was as angry as Colin appeared to be. She was thankful to be in the carriage protected from the rain but more so protected from Colin—for now. She could see in his demeanor that Colin had been furious with the comments at dinner. She was sick to her stomach with fear of what he would do to her when they arrived back at the house. She wrung her hands together on her lap. She was freezing partly due to the cold, but mostly from terror. She felt terrible about feeling relieved that Henry was still injured. If he had been well, Colin would be back here with her right now, no doubt screaming at her. He usually saved the violence for behind closed doors at Watershaw house.

It was very dark outside and with the rain, it was terribly hard to discern through the tiny coach window where she was. They should be home anytime now; she had anticipated the possibility of slowing down due to inclement weather and darkness. With such an allowance, the journey should nevertheless have only taken three quarters of an hour to reach home, and they had been travelling for at least that.

As if reading her thoughts, the carriage turned abruptly and bumped into the lane to Watershaw house. Ada could make out the tiny painted sign at the end of the laneway before the carriage surged forward. After jostling up the lane, Ada gathered her handbag and pulled her cloak tight in preparation to get let off at the front porch. Perhaps if she ran upstairs and quickly got into bed, Colin would go get drunk and take his anger out on her tomorrow instead. Ada snorted to herself. Who was she trying to fool? He was much too angry to be put off.

Ada saw the lights from the windows of the house whir by her, the carriage was not stopping. Confused, Ada sat bolt upright. He was headed straight to the barn. *No doubt Colin wants to get directly out of the rain*, Ada mused to herself. *He will probably make me walk back to the house as part of my punishment. It could be a lot worse than wet clothes and soggy shoes*, Ada thought.

Someone had opened the barn doors on the carriage side for Colin, most likely knowing his approximate time of arrival back home. He drove the carriage and the horse team neatly into the huge wooden doors and pulled up on the reins to halt the horses. Ada heard him jump down from the driver's side, his boots crunching the dirt floor as he walked to the carriage door to open it for her. But instead of opening it, he bolted the door from the outside.

"Colin! What are you doing? Let me out, please!" Ada banged on the inside of the carriage door until the heel of her hand stung badly.

Colin did not pay any attention to her shouts or the persistent banging on the door. By the sounds of it, he was preparing to unhook the horse team. There was a door in the middle of the carriage room that led to the stables, toward where she could see Colin heading. Once he disappeared, lantern light washed through the door, suddenly illuminating both sides of the barn. He took the first horse over to the stables; he was gone not even five minutes when he returned for the other one.

"Please, Colin. You cannot keep me locked in here! It's freezing!" Ada was becoming frantic; how long could he keep her trapped in the backseat? With Henry still on limited chores, no one would come looking for the carriage until Colin himself needed to go somewhere, and who knows how long that would be?

She sat quietly listening as hard as she could, trying to figure out what Colin was doing in the stables. She could hear the soft rasp of a brush as he quickly brushed the sweat and rain off the two horses and undoubtedly covered them in their blankets to ward off the chill. It seemed that his prize horses were the only things Colin was capable of nurturing.

After what seemed like an eternity, Colin came back through the door into the carriage house, his lank body casting a tall eerie shadow on the dirt floor as he walked through the doorway. She heard him pick up the harness and hang it on the hooks on the wall—someone would clean it for him tomorrow. She could hear his footsteps coming closer to the carriage door, then heard him slide the bolt back and the door swung open. She sighed in relief.

Ada swallowed the urge to throw herself from the carriage lest he decide to lock her in again. Instead, she stood up, hunched over and walked close to the doorway, prepared to step down in a ladylike fashion as if being held captive in the backseat had had no effect on her. However, she did not get that chance. Colin immediately reached into the carriage and grabbed a fistful of Ada's hair. He pulled hard and jerked Ada out of the backseat and she landed in a heap on the dirt floor just under the carriage door.

"Get up now, or you will regret it," Colin said in an unnervingly calm tone.

Ada had bashed her shins against the mounting stairs of the carriage during her fall, and her scalp was still stinging from having her hair pulled from her head. She made a small groaning noise and tried to stand up, still pressing a hand to her head.

"I said NOW." Colin took a riding crop he had taken from the stables and brought it down hard against Ada's back.

She screamed and tried to crawl toward the stables and away from the biting lash. Colin managed to hit her with two more excruciating blows before she was up and running, staggering slightly, toward the other side of the barn. Her back felt as though it were on fire, with the stinging sensation in her shins having been superseded by this new, more savage pain on her back. She felt Colin grab her arm just below the elbow and whirl her around.

"Colin, please! My God, stop! Please!" She was begging, but saw nothing in his eyes apart from cold rage. She felt icy terror ripple down her spine which seemed to slightly cool her burning back. She struggled against his arm, trying to run. There was no doubt in her mind that he had gone mad with rage.

He no longer spoke; just glared with ruthless intention. He drew his free arm back and punched her in the stomach. She crumpled to the floor with her hands pressed to her middle, waiting for air to return to her lungs. Colin snorted and ran his hand through his sweaty, rain-drenched hair. Sweet tendrils of air began to flow into and out of her mouth. She began to wheeze and promptly threw up on the dirt floor by Colin's feet. He jumped back, startled.

"You disgusting creature!" He spat at her and she felt it land on the ground by her hand. He advanced toward her and she tried to scoot herself backwards, pulling herself along on her elbows.

Like an extinguished flame, Colin became calm. She heard a swishing noise that she could not quite place, then something shiny drew her eyes to Colin's hand. He had pulled a knife from his pocket and was walking toward her with it hanging in his hand by his side.

"I am so sorry, Colin, I never meant to make you angry. I cannot possibly control what people talk about! Please, I'll do whatever you want. Please, don't." There was no doubt in Ada's mind that Colin was going to kill her—she had known he was capable of it since he strangled her in her bedroom. She was still begging and crab-walking quickly and clumsily away from him, until she felt her hand hit something hard. Colin squatted down over her.

"You have been nothing but a disappointment to me since I met you. I should have drowned you in the river on our walk that first day and it would have saved both of us a lot of trouble." He raised the knife and began to toy with it, moving it from his right hand to his left and back again, trying to intimidate her. It was working.

There was nowhere left for her to crawl. Ada slid her hand back over the hard object and felt an arch and the tiny indents for nails. She said a quick prayer of thanks and mercy and without hesitation, swung the horseshoe into Colin's leering face.

She watched him fall back from his crouched position onto his back and grip his blood covered face. He was yelling in pain and trying, somewhat successfully, to sit back up. She wasted no time in springing to her feet. She swung her arm back, and with as much force as she could, swung the horseshoe again, this time connecting with the side of his head by his left ear. He dropped like a bag of rocks in a pond.

Ada staggered backwards. The reverberation of the last blow made her arm go numb and the horseshoe fell from her nerveless fingers. She looked down at Colin; he was very still. She kicked his knife away and nudged him with her shoe. He did not move. She nudged him harder. He had fallen the second time on his side and had rolled lifeless onto his back, with one forearm covering his face. The second nudge caused this forearm to fall away. Ada could see his face clearly. There was blood running from the side of his head. His nose was moved out of place, with both his eyes already swelling shut; yet what she noticed most was how pale and still he was.

"Oh, my God," Ada whispered, bringing her hand up to cover her lips. "What have I done?"

It was not that she felt especially bad for Colin, rather she never thought herself capable of such violence. She could feel her heart beating frantically under her dress. She turned around and vomited again, her bile spraying the dirt floor. She could see lights still on in the house. People would soon begin to wonder why neither one of them had come inside yet. Robertson would have seen the carriage drive up the lane; he never missed anything. Someone would be coming—and soon.

There was no longer a choice. Ada took one final look at Colin's body lying in the bloody mess on the dirt floor, then took off running for Gypsy's stall.

The horses had all been spooked by the struggle and noise in the barn, and Gypsy was no exception. The mare danced and pawed the ground viciously while Ada struggled to tack her up with shaking, cold fingers. She started to feel numb, and all the throbbing that had temporarily vanished because of the adrenaline, began to resurface.

With Robertson's relentless vigilance in mind, Ada took Gypsy to the back door of the barn where she would not be seen from the front of the house. She mounted the anxious horse and they ran off before Ada could even get her other foot in the stirrup. The cold wind whipped her hair against her face, and Gypsy's mane beat hard against the open neck of her gown as she leaned low over the little mare's neck.

"Run, girl—run for both of us," she commanded, as she shut her eyes and held on.

Chapter 14

Gypsy ran as though an evil spirit was following her. Oddly enough, Ada felt similarly. After some distance, she was able to slow Gypsy into a trot. She still found herself looking over her shoulder every two minutes but so far, she had seen nothing but the mud flying from the horse's hooves. She tried to burrow farther into her soaking wet cloak. Having taken the carriage to the dinner party, she had worn her lighter but prettier cloak thinking she would not need protection from the rain. It was a heavy, cold rain and the wind off the ocean made her shiver uncontrollably. They were obviously nearing the shoreline, the air was more biting and Ada could smell the tang of fish, mud and seaweed even over the scent of the rain.

Once she reached the shoreline, she began to follow it. She knew that following the beach to the west would take her farther and farther from Watershaw house and closer to her hopeful destination.

She needed to find somewhere to stop, and quickly. Her shaking was getting worse and she was aching all over from her encounter with Colin.

"God, was he dead?" she whispered to herself, her breath forming a small white cloud in front of her mouth.

Gypsy snorted and formed a similar cloud. "I know girl, we can stop soon. Please, God, help us find the house."

She had already been in the saddle for about an hour and considering the speed they started out at, she should have been there by now. Ada started to feel panic rising in her belly. *What if I came the wrong way?* Tears began to run down her face, camouflaging with raindrops.

Within five minutes, she saw it: a dull light flickering from inside a tiny window. Ada gently kicked Gypsy to pick up speed, wincing as her battered shin throbbed with the small movement. As if sensing a roof and a meal, Gypsy took off toward the tiny light that shone like a beacon of hope for them both.

Ada halted the mare outside the front door and had to work to open her fingers from the reins as they were frozen and stiff. She managed to dismount slowly but stumbled and fell onto the muddy ground of the path. She was pulling herself up with the help of a makeshift hitching post when the front door swung open.

"What in Christ's name…?"

She lifted her mud-splattered face and climbed to her feet, holding onto the post in fear that if she didn't, she would end up back in the mud. "Grant, I…"

"Ada?" Grants face underwent a bizarre series of facial expressions. "My God, lass!" He grabbed her, put a large arm around her waist and dragged her inside.

"Grant, I did not know where else to go, please you have to help me." Her teeth were chattering so loudly she could barely push words past her lips, let alone get proper breath in. "Gypsy needs food and a blanket. Colin... I..." She began to feel weak and dizzy, she knew she was breathing much too fast.

"It's all right, sit down in this chair by the fire. I'm going to git ye a blanket." Grant grabbed a ragged wool blanket from the bed and put it around her shoulders. He also handed her a small wooden cup with something in it that smelled like wood and fire. "Drink, lass. It will help wi' the chill. Slowly though..."

Ada accepted the cup and sipped gingerly. The liquid tasted just as it smelled and burned her throat on the way to her belly. She sighed, enjoying the momentary warmth in her throat. She looked over as Grant was pulling clothing out of a wooden trunk at the end of his bed.

"I am going outside to tend to the mare, dinna worry for her, I willna be back till she's brushed, fed and stabled. By the looks of her, she seems like she could use a dram too, aye? Put those clothes on," he said, gesturing to the clothes he had thrown on the bed. "Ye will catch an ague in yer sopping things." He put on a cloak and headed toward the front door, then turned just before he went out and looked back at Ada. "We will talk when I get back. You're safe here, lass." He smiled sympathetically and walked out into the rain.

Ada had shed her shift and gown. She had thankfully been wearing a gown that laced at the front with a stomacher and was therefore able to disrobe without assistance. She had already changed into an old pair of Grant's breeches that were slightly too big and had wooden buttons on the knees, as well as a thick woolen shirt that was itchy but deliriously warm when Grant came back in from stabling Gypsy. She had wrapped the blanket around herself and was beginning to thaw in front of the warm fire. She looked apprehensively at him when he came in.

"Aye, she's fine now," Grant answered as if divining the meaning of her anxious look. "She was a wee bit chilly but nothing a belly full o' hay and a good rubdown canna cure." He pulled a wooden stool from under a table in the corner of the room and came to warm himself by the fire as well. "Now, you'll tell me what's amiss." He gently took Ada's cold hands in his warm ones. Raindrops dripped from his hair onto the wooden floor.

Ada began to speak, haltingly at first but as the story progressed, it just flowed out of her as if it wanted to be told. She needed to say it out loud. After drinking the last of the second glass of whisky that Grant had handed her, she finally finished speaking. Grant had said nothing during her telling, just held her hands and listened, his face giving away only slight emotions at certain parts.

"Are ye sure yer all right now, Ada? Nothing is seriously damaged?" He looked her over quickly, his eyes searching for any sign that she might die on the spot.

"No, truly I'm fine, just bruised and a little sore." She stopped herself before she said, "I've had worse." Grant did not need to hear her entire sorted past.

"Well, right then." Grant stood up suddenly and began to put on his wringing wet cloak that was hanging by the fire to dry.

"What?" Ada looked around at his abrupt motion, clearly surprised. "Wherever are you going?"

"Is it not obvious? I'm going to check whether ye did kill that bastard Watershaw, and if ye dinna, I am going to kill him myself." He turned to walk out.

Ada stood up quickly, the wool blanket falling off her shoulders. He was surely joking. He cannot do this! Ada grabbed a hold of his arm.

"Grant, no, please! Someone will have already gone to look for us in the barn. They will have seen Colin and they will know I fled. Please, stay with me. I'm scared." Her dark blue eyes looked pleadingly into his. "What are they going to do to me?"

Grant turned to face her. He pulled her damp head onto his chest and allowed his warm arms to encircle her. "They will never find ye, lass. Ye'll stay here with me and I'll make sure of it." Grant breathed in deeply. He could smell the sweet scent of her through the smell of wool, horse and rain. "May God help us both," he prayed softly into the top of her wet head.

Having spoken for a while longer by the fire, it had been decided that Grant would travel to Ada's house on the morrow. He would claim he was trimming one of Colin's stud horses. If Colin was in fact dead, then Grant would beg his sympathies and leave to return home. If he was alive, he presumably would not be in any condition to tell anyone he wasn't expecting the smith or he might have simply forgotten about the trimming with such a severe injury to the head. With that settled, Ada at least seemed more outwardly calm. She was aware there was nothing she could do tonight and would need to wait till tomorrow when everything would be revealed.

She climbed into Grant's bed. She was so tired that his plain straw mattress felt like the softest, most comfortable thing she had ever slept on. He had, of course, insisted on sleeping on a pallet by the fire—just like he had in the inn on the way to her grandmother's estate. Too tired to argue, and knowing she would not win, she thankfully accepted the bed. She was asleep by the time she rolled over. The terrible and draining events of the night mixed with the calming effects of the whisky had carried her away before she even said goodnight.

She was running. She knew Colin was behind her with the riding crop because she could feel leather tearing strips off her back. She fell hard, scraping her hands and knees on the barn floor. Something big kicked her and she doubled over. It kicked her again and again. She screamed. Colin laughed and hit her with the crop again. She kept screaming—screaming for someone, for anyone to help her. The lash landed across her cheek and she tried to fight…

"Ada, Ada, it's only me. You're having a dream, wake up, lass! It's only me." Grant was sitting on the edge of the bed trying to grasp Ada's flailing form before she hurt herself. He had been awoken to terrible screaming. His initial thought was that someone had broken into his house but when he glanced at the bed, he only saw Ada's silhouette, blankets thrown onto the floor, thrashing and screaming like a banshee.

"Yer all right now, wake up." Gently, he shook her shoulders harder to try and bring her back from her terror.

She came awake suddenly, looking around madly trying to place herself and make certain that it was all a dream. Finally, her eyes focused on Grant. "Grant?... It was terrible." Tears welled up in her tired eyes.

"Do ye want to tell me of it? Do you think it will help?" he asked softly.

"I was being attacked. It was similar to what actually happened but much worse. I could not get away. Colin was back, he was beating me." She felt the welled-up tears escape over her eyelids and slip down her cheeks. She shuddered involuntarily.

Grant immediately bent to retrieve the blankets that had fallen during her struggling, the light from the window hit him and she realized he was still wearing his shirt and breeches. His face looked flushed and hot from sleeping so close to the hearth, yet he was still fully dressed. Was it her modesty that he was protecting or was there perhaps some truth to Ruth O'Dell's childish gossip?

"Here ye are." Grant covered Ada back up as if she was an injured child, smoothing the hair from her face. "It's over now, lass. It was all in yer mind. I'm right there if ye need me." He gestured to the pallet by the fire and stood up to walk away.

"No, please!" Ada yelled out before she could stop herself. "I'm scared to be alone, please come back."

Grant immediately turned around and was at her side, sitting on the bed with her.

"Will you sleep here tonight? Please." She patted the bed beside her. "It would make me feel much safer to have you here."

"Sleep in the bed wit' ye? I canna do that, Ada. Think about your reputation…" Realizing what he had just said, he went red and looked down at the blanket.

Ada began to giggle; her giggling grew until it was full hearty laughter. "Oh, you are quite right, Grant. What *will* society think…"

Grant began to laugh as well. After what Ada had been through that night, having someone sleep in her bed was the last thing she needed to worry about. "Aye, lass, move over. I'll keep you safe."

She scooted on her side as close as she could to the wooden wall until her back was pressed against it, allowing room for Grant to climb in bed beside her. She closed her eyes and sighed, feeling instantaneously better that Grant was close to her.

Ten minutes or so had passed since Grant had stopped moving around and she could hear his steady regular breathing. She opened her eyes to stare at the handsome face beside her on the pillow. He was turned toward her with his eyes closed—he seemed relaxed and content. His soft brown hair fell around his face; he had obviously taken off the leather that had been binding it back earlier when he went to sleep. He had kicked the blanket off and was lying in his full clothing with his knees curled under him. She looked down as his massive forearms. He had undone the buttons at the wrist of his shirt, obviously while he was sleeping on the pallet. One of the billowy sleeves had been pushed upwards and revealed his well-built, but terribly scarred forearm.

"It is true then," she said softly to herself. She laid her hand gently on his forearm and looked back up toward the pillow. Two open eyes stared back at her, they looked almost black in the darkness.

She almost drew her hand back instinctively but could not help but notice how right it felt lying there, touching him.

"So, ye'll have heard then, aye? About the scars, I mean," he whispered to her, not moving.

"Yes, I did not know whether it was true or not until right now," she said bluntly. There was no point in lying to him, nor did she want to.

"I'm sorry if it offends ye, should I go back to the pallet then?" He made a move to rise. He looked sad, like he expected rejection or disgust.

She sat up and put a hand in the middle of his chest. "Stay, you're just as appealing now, as when I saw you for the first time… perhaps even more so." She spoke gently, thinking about how he had taken care of her tonight.

"Ye dinna need to say that, lass. I'm used to how it makes people react. How they feel when they look at it. It shows in their eyes."

He was lying on his back now. She pushed herself up on her elbow and brought her face right up over his so she was only an inch from his eyes. She leaned down and softly kissed him.

Grant closed his eyes as Ada's lips touched down on his. She had kissed him once before but that kiss felt almost chaste compared to the way she was kissing him now—gently but full of intention. He had skimmed one hand up her back onto the base of her neck underneath her hair, then pulled her closer to him, deepening the kiss.

Her free hand was on his chest. He felt too hot through his cotton shirt from lying by the hearth and now from being here with her. She broke the kiss and sat up in the small bed. "Sit up," she said to Grant.

He did as she said, his eyes intensely held her gaze but he said nothing. She reached both hands for the hem of his shirt and pulled it straight up and over his head, tossing it to the foot of the bed. He sighed, and kept watching her.

When Ruth had said his scars were noticeable at a distance, Ada could now see that that was a vast understatement. Even in the dark room, lit only by the smoldering fire in the hearth, Ada could see that Grant's entire chest and stomach—from one shoulder to the other—were completely covered with scars. His skin was shinier than normal but not smooth, it was puckered in some areas and pulled tight in others. From what she could see even in the darkness, his skin was darker in some parts and light in others. However, his right arm and the right side of his torso over the ribs seemed to have been saved from the terrible scars.

Ada looked up from his body to his eyes. She could tell he was waiting for her reaction.

"Your back as well?" she asked softly, although she could already deduce the answer.

"Aye, on the one side," he nodded, "and all of my left leg and foot too." He didn't dare reach out for her. He knew he was shocking to behold and he had to give her time to absorb it. Perhaps she couldn't, but he did not want to think of that. He couldn't bear to lose her now.

He sat waiting for what felt like an eternity. She was looking closely at him as if she was not sure what to say. He watched as she brought her hands down to the bottom of her own shirt and pulled it up over her head, letting her hair cascade down around her shoulders in the process.

Grant was certainly not expecting that. He looked at her with astonishment, which quickly turned into a look of seductive approval.

"Fair's fair, I guess," Ada shrugged and blushed slightly because he was still staring at her. She had a sudden thought of Colin consistently complaining about her size and her unattractiveness and she hastily pulled the blanket up under her arms.

Grant spoke and brought her back to the present moment. She pushed Colin firmly out of her mind, angry that she had even let him in to begin with. Not in this moment and not with him. She looked at Grant.

"I'm sorry, what did you say?" Ada asked.

"I said, my God, you're beautiful."

She was possibly the most magnificent thing he had ever seen. Her skin was smooth and looked so invitingly soft. Her hair hung over her shoulders, revealing a smattering of freckles that ran down her arms. She had sensual breasts that looked like they would fill his hand with extra to spare. He had been privileged to see this much of her so far, and had to fight to control himself and his body, including his lesser-controllable appendages.

He placed a hand on her shoulder, wanting so badly to touch her again. He leaned over to her and kissed her other bare shoulder. Swishing her hair out of the way, he placed another kiss on her collarbone, then one at the base of her throat, and finally one on the side of her neck. She moaned softly and nuzzled her cheek against the side of his face as he gently kissed her neck. That was it for him and he lost any inch of self-control he had been holding onto. He grasped her face, cupped it in both of his hands and kissed her on the mouth. They fell back onto the bed and he came over her, kissing her with everything he had.

Ada ran her hand down Grant's back. Pausing briefly, she whispered, "Does it hurt you anymore?" Her hand hovered over his scars.

"No, but it will pain me if you dinna keep touching me." He laughed huskily at her snort in response.

Her hand kept up its torturous investigation. Upon reaching the bottom of his back, she slipped her hand into the top of his breeches, letting it glide over the muscular round of his arse. She gave a playful squeeze and Grant jolted from the kiss, startled by her playfulness.

"Oh, aye? It's like that, is it?" He bent his head down to her belly and bit her up the side of her rib cage. She giggled and squirmed, trying to escape the enchanting assault. Abruptly, the squirming stopped when he gently bit the side of her breast. He heard her gasp and taking that as a sign of willing participation, dragged his tongue in a hot line from the side of her breast to her nipple. He teased her slightly with flicks of his tongue before taking the tip into his mouth and sucking softly.

Releasing her from his mouth, he proceeded to administer the same treatment to the other breast.

Ada had never felt like this before. Her body had taken on a life of its own and damned her to the consequences of its actions. She glanced down to watch Grant's mouth on her breast and swore she had never seen anything so erotic in her life. She wanted to make him feel the way she did at this moment. In one fluid motion, her hand slid down his stomach and onto the front of his breeches. She could easily feel his manhood rigidly pressing against the fabric. She rubbed her hand over the area in small circular motions, cupping him gently.

"I think you might like this better if you take these off," she whispered into his ear and gently bit down on his earlobe.

He reached down to undo the laces but stopped midway. Instead, he placed his hand on the hips of the breeches she was wearing and dragged them down to her ankles, then off, one foot at a time. He ran his long hands up both her legs at the same time and ended by grabbing a handful of hips and planting a string of tiny kisses from her belly button downward. He stopped, looked up at Ada mischievously and got up onto his knees. With deliberate and painful slowness, he finished undoing the lacing on his breeches and pushed them down over his hips, his searing gaze never once leaving Ada's face.

Ada could feel a pool of heat growing like the flames of a forge deep in her belly. She had never felt desire with so much intensity before. She opened her arms for him to come back down to her and basked in the blazing heat as the skin of their bodies pressed together.

"Please, Grant. I need you," Ada moaned softly into his kiss. She could feel his erection pressing against her. She shifted under him, further parting her legs. She reached down and wrapped her hand around him and he froze as she guided him into her.

"Mother of God," is all he could manage as he felt himself slide into her slippery tightness.

He began to move slowly, tentatively as if he would break her. She wrapped her legs around his waist and pulled him deep into her.

"Oh, Lord. Ada, wait…"

She bit his chiseled shoulder and clenched her sex around him. He was lost, he cried out and came into her, crushing her to the bed with his weight and losing himself inside her.

She put her fingers in his hair as he pulled her into a kiss.

"I'm sorry, Ada. It's just, I couldna stop. It's that…" He tripped over his words.

"I wanted you very badly too, Grant. There is no need to apologize to me." Ada smiled.

"It's no' that." He saw her raise an eyebrow questioningly. "I mean, of course, I wanted ye badly. I wanted ye more than I've wanted anything in my life, but that's not what I was meaning. I meant I dinna know it would feel quite so good so fast." She thought he was blushing but it was too hard to tell in the darkness of the room. He looked down.

Confused, Ada asked, "What do you mean, you did not know? Do you mean it didn't feel as pleasurable other times?"

"There has only been one other time!" Grant blurted a little louder than necessary. "I've been close enough a time or two more but no, there has only been one other." He took one of Ada's hands in his own.

"Why didn't you tell me?" Ada stated accusingly.

"Well, it's no' the manliest thing, is it? Besides, I thought perhaps it did not need to be brought up. I assumed I had good enough self-control but I've learned I haven't any where yer concerned, lass." He stroked her cheek.

She smiled at him lying beside her on the bed and realized that despite the events of the past twenty-four hours, she was genuinely happy at this moment. She closed her eyes and went to snuggle against him for sleep.

"What are ye doing?" he asked her.

"Well, I was going to go to sleep, with you." She smiled sweetly.

"Spread your legs," he said as if he had just commented on the weather.

"What?" Not the least bit tired anymore, Ada's body obeyed before she could get her question answered.

"Ye'd no think I'd leave ye like that, do ye? Taking my own pleasure and giving ye none?" He seemed honestly affronted that Ada would think such a thing.

"I'm sorry, I am just not used to anyone wanting to give me pleasure. Besides that, you already have!"

"Ah yes, in the moment I forgot where ye came from. Please, let me do this for ye. I might be newer to some things but I'm verra good at others." He winked at her.

He kissed her slowly, his tongue gently touching hers in soft flicking motions. He traced his hands down the outside of her body, his hands skimming the sides of her breast, her ribs, and her hips. He lifted one hand from her for a moment and placed it down between her legs.

She gasped. No one had ever touched her like that. She had occasionally, in the darkness of her room and under the cover of night, touched herself softly but never had a man do so. She felt him slide his finger deep into her, agonizingly slow. She arched her back. She wasn't sure what she wanted but her body seemed to know. She pressed down on his finger and he removed it just as slowly as he entered.

"Steady, lass," he murmured to her.

He repeated the same action over and over, stopping occasionally to slide his finger up and rub her gently higher on her sex before plunging back down. Before she understood what was happening, she felt herself begin to lose control. Her breath was coming in ragged gasps. She no longer cared where she was, who she was or what she had done. Her mind and body exploded around her leaving her in a blessed state of undisturbed bliss. A few moments later, she cracked one eye open to a face that was staring down at her like a fox that had just caught a chicken.

"Enjoyed yerself, did ye?" He laid down beside her and enveloped her in his massive arms. "Now ye may go to sleep wit' me."

She managed a, "Hmm…" and drifted off feeling safe for the first time in a long time.

Chapter 15

She woke up shortly before dawn. Glancing out of the tiny window, she could tell that the sky would soon change into various shades of pink and orange; but for now, it held the soft grey light that was only slightly brighter than the darkness of full night. She rolled over and snuggled closer to Grant, who she could tell by the light snores, was still asleep. His snores stopped as she snuggled into him and he sleepily raised his hand to touch her cheek.

"All right?" he asked, his voice still muffled by sleep.

"Honestly, I find it puzzling that on a morning where I should be feeling the worst I have ever felt, I feel contented and happy." She sighed and stretched slightly. "I have never woken up beside a man before, you know."

He opened his eyes to look at her. "Nay yer husband?"

She felt a flush rise in her cheeks. She felt silly for being embarrassed, she knew it wasn't her fault. "He did not once stay past the completion of his martial duties. Though in truth, I never wanted him too."

Grant felt anger rise into his throat but he swallowed down the growl he was about to voice and looked at Ada, who was looking over at him. He could clearly see her eyes were obviously still attempting to hide the pain caused by that miserable piece of human excrement.

"Did he no? Well it was his loss, ye ken? That is one of the best parts." Rising slightly, he grabbed a handful of Ada's backside and buried his face into her neck, nuzzling his way down to the cushion softness of her breasts. "See?"

She laughed, trying to push his dark brown hair away from her face. "Your hair is tickling me!"

"Oh, a thousand apologies, milady," Grant said mockingly. "Is this better?" He grabbed her by both of her hips and scraped his raspy unshaven face repeatedly across her belly.

"Agggghhhh," she managed hoarsely while trying to kick him off. Her attempts at dislodging him were clearly having little to no effect, so she decided on a different approach. She put her legs out straight and inch-wormed her way lower until she was almost face-to-face with him.

She watched Grant's playful face transform into something completely different. He looked down at her and lowered his mouth onto hers. Her skin immediately blazed with heat. He rested his weight softly on top of her and deepened the kiss. He opened her lips with his own and needing no encouragement, she responded by tracing the tip of her tongue softly along his bottom lip. She felt his hand sliding down to her breast. She could feel it tighten slightly in anticipation. His hand travelled over her breast softly and back onto her side. She ached for more than that. Until last night, she had no idea her body could respond in this way.

She could feel him in between her legs, rubbing his flatteringly excited member back and forth in the already slippery apex of her thighs. Without purposeful intention, she found herself grinding shamelessly against him, making small circles with her own hips.

Her body ached and her breathing was erratic, she wanted him so completely that she did not think she could bear another minute of not being completely joined with him.

"God, Grant. Please, now…" she whispered.

"Aye, now." He spread her legs deftly with his knee and sank himself into her, groaning softly as her molten heat enveloped him.

"Christ, Ada, yer like fire." He bent to kiss her neck.

They began to move together. Her meeting each thrust with as much vigor and emotion as he was giving her. The pressure had been building since he had first entered her, each penetration bringing her closer and closer to losing herself completely. Finally, she reached up and grabbed his shoulders, pulling him down hard into her, then pressed her lips against his mouth and called out his name before dissolving utterly into the explosion from within her.

"Jesus!" Grant uttered suddenly as he felt her repeatedly clench around him. He too let go of himself and rested a warm glistening forehead against her brow. Not speaking, he laid down beside her, held her hand and watched the sky change to morning, feeling different than he ever had before.

When it was full light, Grant rose and began to dress for his trip to Watershaw house.

"It is important that ye stay inside until we know for sure what the outcome of last night's events was. I think it's best if we leave Gypsy in the barn today as well. People will know it was her that ye fled on." Grant tried to keep his voice light but Ada sensed the serious undertones beneath it.

Ada nodded. "I don't know which is worse: my fear that I killed him or my fear that I did not." She had put back on the old clothes Grant had given her the night before. He knew she could still see Colin when she looked at her now-dry dress hanging on the hearth. She looked upset and Grant knew there was nothing he could do to ease her anxiety until they knew for a fact what the situation was. He only hoped he could then come up with some way to keep her safe.

"Well, there's nay we can do about it now. Try not to worry yerself over much while I'm gone." He crooked a smile at Ada over his shoulder.

Ada snorted, appreciating his attempt to make her smile. "Oh, to be sure. I will just sit here and mend your socks while you are out discovering whether I did in fact kill my husband." She looked down at her hands, the humor disappearing into anguish.

Grant crossed the room and touched a hand to her cheek, bringing her face back up to his. "I will be back here by noontime. There is cheese and bread in the box on the table if ye find yerself hungry. I'll give the beasts some grain before I depart so ye needn't worry about Gypsy."

Grant turned and walked toward the door. Ada grabbed his hand and pressed a kiss on his palm. "Thank you," she said simply.

It was a pleasant day for a ride, even if his errand had his belly clenched in hundreds of tiny knots. He let Duff slow down his pace to a walk, as he did not want him influenced by Grant's haste to get to Watershaw house.

He would not have hurried his horse there for a regular trim and that was exactly what he was trying to portray. He wished he could ride as fast as Duff would take him but discretion was his main agenda. Within an hour, he saw the long lane of Ada's house spread out before him. He straightened himself in the saddle and walked the horse down the lane to the barn. He dismounted and took his trimming tools out of the saddlebag. He looked around slowly; it was very quiet.

Casually, he walked up to the barn door and swung it open. "Hello!" he yelled in greeting. "It's Ross the smith." He waited but no one returned his greeting. Damn, he thought Henry might have been in the barn and could have saved him from going to the main house. "Aye, well, no help for it then," Grant mumbled and swung the heavy wooden door shut and made his way to the house.

He walked onto the large wooden porch. Holding his tools, he reached the door and knocked three times, then waited, but no one came. This was a noticeable change from the prompt service Robertson usually gave. He knocked again, slightly louder this time. Stepping back from the door he could finally hear footsteps coming, then the door swung open and a flushed Robertson stuck his head outside.

"Oh, it is you, Mr. Ross," he stated as if expecting someone of much more importance.

Grant wondered feverishly whether it was a doctor they were expecting or an undertaker. "Aye, Mr. Watershaw asked me to come by this morning to trim a horse he recently sold. There was no one down at the barn and I dinna know which horse Mr. Watershaw wanted done." He was sweating. "Would ye be so kind as to ask him for me, sir, and I'll be out of yer hair." Grant restrained from shooting a glance at Robertson's almost entirely bald head and smiling.

"I ... Mr. Watershaw..." Robertson looked flustered and Grant noticed he was sweating freely as well.

"He usually likes to speak to me himself, aye? Would ye consider fetching him?" Grant pressed Robertson gently. He needed answers.

As if making up his mind, Robertson stepped out onto the front porch and closed the door softly behind him. "I cannot do that, Mr. Ross. You see, Mr. Watershaw has had some form of unfortunate accident. He was found in the barn yesterday by the stable boy doing the night check."

"My God!" Crossing himself for good measure Grant continued. "Was he hurt bad then, sir?"

"I fear he is." Robertson nodded gravely. "He has been slipping in and out of consciousness all night. The physician says he will likely live but there is no way to know when he will be fully awake or if he will have maintained all of his sensibilities."

Grant shook his head. "That is terrible news. I certainly will pray for his full and speedy recovery." Instead, Grant was praying to portray a look of sincerity successfully.

"I fear you have wasted a trip today, Mr. Ross. I will let Mr. Watershaw know you sent him your kind messages and prayers."

"No!" Grant almost shouted. "Dinna trouble him with me at all. We do not want his mind on horses and sales when it should be focused solely on getting well."

Robertson nodded approvingly. "Of course, you are right, Mr. Ross. Good day to you."

"Good day, sir." Grant walked calmly down the front stairs as Robertson shut the front door with a click.

So, the bastard did not die after all. He felt an overwhelming sense of relief knowing Ada would not be strapped with the guilt of killing a man for the rest of her life. Grant knew that guilt all too well and he would not wish it on anyone. However, a new problem now reared its ugly head. How much would Colin Watershaw remember when he woke up? Even if he remembered nothing of the actual attack, the fact that Ada had fled remained. Grant was flying through options in his head as Duff ambled down the dirt road toward home. If Ada was to return home today, she could claim she had witnessed the attack and had fled in fear for her own life, only to return when she deemed it safe to do so. In normal circumstances, that would have been an excellent idea but in this case, that was simply not an option. He knew she would never return to that house, and if Colin did recall the events of last night, he would surely kill her at first glance. He needed to speak to Ada and let her know what he found out so they could work out a solution together. He dug his heels gently into Duff's side. Needing no further prompting and knowing he was returning to his hay and oats, the horse lurched into a jog and headed toward home.

Ada felt as though she had looked out the tiny window one hundred times already. She knew it would take roughly two hours for Grant to travel to and from Watershaw house. That did not include the time it would take for him to figure out what had become of Colin.

Moreover, if someone called his bluff, he would have to stay to trim some random horse to make his story believable. She sighed and sat down in the wooden chair at the table. She contemplated the ordeal in the barn with Colin. She asked herself repeatedly if she could have done anything differently. Did she truly need to do what she did? Each time, she came back to the same answer: yes. She had never seen Colin look at her the way he had as he stood over her with the knife. There was no doubt in her mind, even now, that he had meant to kill her, and had she not taken action, he would have done so. The thought sent a chill straight through her. She got up and added another log to the hearth just for the sake of doing something.

She was pacing a rut in the floor when finally, she heard a horse trotting up to the house. Cautiously, she peeked through the window and relaxed as she saw Grant's bulky form slide out of the saddle and walk Duff into the barn.

She went to the table and poured a glass of water from the wooden pitcher. She also sliced up the lone apple she had found in the wooden bowl with the bread and cheese. She sucked the sticky juice off her fingertips and sat down to wait. She figured Grant would be wanting lunch when he came in from brushing Duff. She took one of the apple slices and popped it into her mouth whole, when the door opened and Grant walked in and shed his cloak.

She had risen as he came in, trying desperately to industriously chew the piece of apple she had just put into her mouth. Cursing her unladylike habits once again, she tried to smile politely at him.

He strode directly over to her, grabbed her apple filled face in both hands and planted an enthusiastic kiss on her tightly closed lips.

"It's good news I bring ye, lass. The bastard is alive, although he is incapacitated in his bed. Ye dinna kill him, so ye needna feel guilty." He smiled broadly. "Ye taste bonny, like apples."

Ada had swallowed her piece of apple while he was talking and managed to recover herself. She had not killed him. Relief swam through her body. Although Colin's survival brought up an entirely new set of problems, his attempted murder by her hand was a problem she was not prepared to deal with. She looked up to find Grant watching her closely, studying her reaction to the news. She smiled reassuringly back at him. "I made you a snack." She gestured toward the apple and water. "Well, 'made' might have been the wrong word, I prepared you a snack if you can call cutting up an apple and pouring a glass of water preparing something."

"Seeing as that an apple canna cut itself up and serve itself to me, aye I'd say ye prepared a fine snack." He laughed at her.

"I can't even tell if you are mocking me, Mr. Ross. If you are, I would be happy to sit down and enjoy this food myself and you can *prepare* yourself some other snack." She settled herself back in the wooden chair at the table and took a sip from the glass of water.

"That suits me fine, lass. I already have another snack in mind." He walked up behind her at the table, bent down and put her earlobe gently between his teeth. "Mmm." He laughed through clenched teeth. He put his hands on her shoulders and bit her neck in three places. "Nay, I was wrong, I think I'll take the apple."

He ducked as she turned and swung a playful smack in his direction. Her mood was clearly lightened by the news of Colin.

"Well, sir, you better pull up a chair before I decide that I no longer want to share with you." She pushed the apple slices and water toward him once he sat down. He picked up a slice and began to munch amiably.

"Will you tell me everything that happened when you went over there today? We will need to discuss what my next step is," Ada said apprehensively. She was afraid of what that would be.

Grant swallowed the bite he was chewing and took a sip of water. "What *our* next step is, Ada. I'll not let ye be alone in this, or anything else, come to think of it." He slid his hand across the wooden surface of the table and covered her hand with his own.

"Thank you." Her eyes welled up as the safe feeling she had while sleeping in Grant's arms began to creep back over her.

Grant began the retelling of everything he had learned at Watershaw house, pausing occasionally to take bites of the apple.

"So, it seems that although yon skinny bastard dinna die, we will not know how he truly fares until he stops slipping in and out of consciousness," Grant said.

"Is it possible that when he wakes up, he will remember it was I who hit him and will send everyone, including the law, after me? Or… he will wake up and not remember much. And knowing that I'm gone, he will use all resources and stop at nothing to find me. He will want further information, which he will assume I will divulge. Either way, it looks like I will be hunted down." Ada sighed, pushed her chair out from the table and stood up.

Grant stayed seated and stared into the cup in his hands. The thought of people searching for Ada made him queasy. He knew what it felt like to be on the run, and he did not want that for her. He wanted her to feel safe when she walked outside. Hell, he wanted her to be able to walk outside in the daylight, by herself! If she stayed with him, she was not going to be able to do any of those things for the foreseeable future. His insides dropped onto the floor. He would have to take her to a city somewhere and see she had a safe place to stay, maybe somewhere like New York—a big city where it was easy to blend in. Then, he would have to return here, alone.

Chapter 16

Grant placed his cup down and scraped his chair back from the table and rose. "Ada?"

She turned from staring at the hearth and looked at him. He did not want to have this conversation. He inhaled deeply through his nose and let the breath out. He looked at her and spoke softly. "I think it may be best if ye stay here for a few weeks, but ye must stay hidden and only go outside after dark."

She nodded. He noticed that her face had lightened when she heard him speak of staying here, but a heavy fist clenched around his heart nonetheless.

"...but after the initial hunt has died down in a few weeks, I fear I must take ye to New York, or another big city of your choosing, and find ye a safe place to blend in." His eyes searched her face for any hint of how badly she might react to this statement.

"Oh, of course it will be harder to find me in a strange place with hordes of people. Where would you like to go? Do you like New York? Do they have much need for blacksmiths there? Well, I suppose where there are horses..."

Grant realized her mistake and closed his eyes for a moment, sending up a quick silent prayer. "Lass, I'll take ye to the city but I'll no be staying there with ye. I'll need to return here or people will start to wonder where I've gone. It will be too suspicious." He swallowed as he watched tears spill down her cheeks.

"But I want to be with you, Grant. I only have you." She did not care if she sounded desperate and needy, perhaps she was all those things at this present moment.

"Oh, God. Ada, I want nothing more in this world than to be with ye, always. I have wanted it for a long time but I'll not sacrifice yer safety for my passion." He turned away from her.

Ada realized, with awe, that he was just as upset as she was. She walked up to him and put her cheek flat against his back. He smelled like horses and dust from the road. She breathed in deeply. She ran her hand lightly down his arm.

"We still have about two weeks together here, let us not sully it with sorrow for something in the future." Even as she spoke, she knew that spending her life without Grant would haunt her every waking moment for the rest of her life. But if she wanted a chance at a livable future, she would have to use these two remaining weeks to be with him, making and storing memories of their time together in her mind.

"Aye. All we can do is try." Grant turned and brushed a stray hair from her forehead.

Ada awoke the next morning alone. She rolled over on the tiny mattress and looked around Grant's one room cabin. For a fleeting moment, she was worried that something had happened but as soon as she became fully awake, she remembered him telling her he had several horses to do today and that he most likely would not be back until supper. She laughed softly to herself as she recalled the stern speech he had given her about not setting foot outside until after dark when he was home, and how she could not be too careful to not answer the door if anyone should come calling for him. He was so serious and concerned for her that she had not dared to laugh at his parental demeanor in front of him. She simply nodded and promised to stay inside—like a good girl. She didn't bother telling him she would not have dared to go outside anyway—she feared Colin's wrath above all else, apart from losing Grant. She pushed that terrible thought firmly away, urging herself to enjoy the day.

   She enjoyed the coziness of Grant's home. Her childhood home had been large but comfortable, nowhere near the sheer size of Watershaw house. She had always felt uncomfortable there like a guest in one of the large English manor homes she had read about in a lady's periodical her grandmother used to receive. Even her grandmother's house seemed too big to maintain. She liked the intimate feeling of everything being in one room. She wondered what the other ladies' reactions would be to living in a one room home. In fact, she knew exactly what they would say and what they would think of her for desiring such a thing. Overall, she cared very little about the opinions of women whose husbands deemed Colin a friend. Ada sighed. That was not exactly fair. She liked Louise Davaneaux, and Colin could put on a very good act in public. Her own grandmother went to her grave believing Colin was a fine and upstanding gentleman. He had even been willing to marry an old maid like Ada, and as such, was a hero in her eyes.

    Ada looked around the little house, admiring the simplicity of it. When one entered the front door, the bed was directly to their left against the wall under the window. It was very simply built with a straw mattress and two plain woolen blankets. There was a small wooden table, no bigger than a stool, at the head of the bed that Grant put his personals on when he changed into his nightclothes. There was nothing on the table now save a piece of broken leather and a horseshoe nail. She smiled at the clutter as it reminded her implicitly of him. The trunk at the end of the bed had remained untouched since the night she arrived and Grant had given her a change of clothes. The hearth was lovely; it was on the north wall of the cabin. Grant's few cooking pots hung on hooks he had forged himself and his few dishes and cups sat on a makeshift mantle that looked as if he had added it after the hearth was already built. The small supper table with a wooden chair and a stool sat on the wall opposite the front door, and the wooden box holding bits of food sat in the centre of it. The remaining wall was bare except for hooks for clothing and places where Grant had obviously been storing his boots when he was not wearing them. Her favorite part of the house was the ancient armchair that sat on an even more ancient round rug in the middle of the room. It was close enough to the hearth to be warm and inviting but far enough away that someone could cook at the fire without disturbing the person in the chair. In the past few days, she had caught herself staring at the chair, wishing she could sit in it with Grant in front of the fire—with his large arms wrapped around her and his deep voice speaking huskily in her ear. That thought lit a fire in her belly that seemed to warm her body from her toes to the tips of her ears. She looked out the window to gauge the time and sighed as she realized it would be hours before Grant was home. She began to clean his house, careful to only open the door a crack and quickly sweep the dirt outside before closing and barring it again. She had always enjoyed cleaning; she had learned how to clean when she was very young from her mother who thought it was a useful skill for any young lady to have, regardless of whether she would grow up to have servants perform the task for her. Now, as she was cleaning Grant's house, it was the first time she had felt useful since she married Colin Watershaw. "Hmmph," she said aloud, then shook her bad feelings out the tiny window along with the dust from her rag.

It was beginning to be dark by the time Ada heard Duff's hoof beats coming up the driveway. She knew Grant would go into the barn and give the horses their oats before turning them outside. They had decided it would be safe enough for Gypsy to graze outside at night without being seen. He would be letting both horses out shortly, then would finally be back inside with her.

Ada had wanted to prepare supper for Grant for when he came home but the house had been emptied of all food except for the apple core from the night before and the small chunk of cheese that had been her lunch. She did, however, pour him a glass of the whisky he had sitting up on the mantle and had it waiting for him as he walked in.

She had unlatched the front door when she heard him ride up and now the door quietly opened and Grant stepped in. His hair was dripping onto the wooden boards and his face had the ruddy tinge of being freshly scrubbed in very cold water.

"This is the best thing I've come home to for as long as I can remember." Grant slicked back his sopping hair and walked over to the cup of whisky on the table. "Oh, and yer all right too, I guess." He laughed and swung her into his arms.

She laughed with him. He seemed to be in quite the jovial mood. She hoped the news of no dinner would not dampen his high spirits. "I'm so glad you're home. It seemed you were gone an awfully long time."

She wiped water drops from his forehead.

"Aye, I was and I'm sorry for it. Surely this will make up for my absence?" He overturned the small cloth sack he had been carrying onto the table. Beans, bread, cheese and some sort of cloth wrapped meat that smelled like bacon rolled out onto the table.

"Oh wonderful!" Ada remarked smiling. "I was hoping you would not be too upset that there wasn't any food ready when you returned tonight. I'll start cooking right this minute."

"Why would I be angry wit' ye? I'm the one who told ye to stay in the house all day and there was no food in here to cook with." He looked suspiciously at her.

"I know, I just assumed you would be hungry and well, I..." Ada trailed off, feeling embarrassed. When would she finally realize this man was not Colin? She began to unwrap the bacon and took a knife from the mantle to slice up the meat.

"To tell you the truth, it's nay just the food I'm hungry for, aye?" He put down the empty whisky glass and came to stand behind her while she cut the meat, wrapping his arms around her waist.

"Grant Ross, I will not waste the perfectly good food you brought home for us by not serving it to you as fresh as I possibly can." Grant unhooked his hands and began to take a step back at her tone. "Besides," she turned and gave him a wink, "for what I have planned, we will both need the energy from full bellies and good drink." She laughed as he attempted to look aghast.

"Well, if I had ever heard of a reason to eat a good plate, that one would top it. If that is truly the case, lass, ye better give me two helpings."

Chapter 17

They finished their dinner of bacon and toast, which Ada had fried in the bacon grease, and sat back amiably sharing a glass of whisky.

"It's very rare that I have any company for dinner. It was wonderful. Thank ye." Grant lifted the glass in Ada's direction.

Surprised, she laughed softly. "I was actually thinking almost the same thought. Although, I've often had company at dinner, I've hardly ever had dinner conversation. I agree it was wonderful. I should be thanking you for letting me stay here and feeding me." She smiled at Grant.

"I was going to check on the horses in the field, just to make sure they are getting on as it is their first time turned out together. Perhaps ye'd rather go? Ye have not been outside all day long, and I know ye'll be missing your furry lassie." Grant quirked his eyebrow at her.

"Oh, yes please! I have been dying to see Gypsy all day. Let me grab my cloak." Ada already had her cloak in hand and was scurrying out the door before Grant could laugh silently at her enthusiasm. "I'll be back directly!"

"Aye, take yer time, I'll be right here. Call if you need anything and I'll come right away." He spoke the last words to the back of the door as Ada was already outside. A gust of air from the door blew out the candle on the table, making him laugh harder.

Grant moved to the middle of the floor, pulled the armchair back and spread one of the quilts from the bed on top of the old rug in front of the hearth. He moved quickly, wanting to finish his surprise before Ada came back from the field. He poured another glass of whisky for them to share. He walked quietly around the cabin and blew out all the remaining candles, allowing the soft orange glow of the hearth fire to cast the room in an enchanting haze of shadows.

Ada stood at the paddock fence with her hands tucked into her cloak against the chill of the night air. She could see Gypsy and Duff eating like old friends, side by side. She had thought it strange that Grant wanted to check on the horses. They had been together in the barn before and neither horse had a mean bone in their bodies. He had never expressed concern about putting them out together. Still, he was the expert not her and as the fresh breeze swirled around her cheeks, she was happy for the brief escape outside the cabin.

She told herself that all of this was temporary, and that one day, she would have her life back and be able to go outside and be seen in public. Yet, there was a fear deep down that kept gnawing away at her, like a small fish nibbling the bait on a hook it couldn't swallow whole. She thought back to the night in the barn with Colin. She could not have ever imagined the bizarre and frightening series of events that had unfolded recently in her life. However, this predicament resulted in her now being with Grant, who was the shining ray of light that arose from this dark and terrible situation. She shook her head to clear her melancholy. She should head back; otherwise Grant would wonder what was taking her so long. She gave a cheery goodnight wave to the horses and walked back toward the little house.

Opening the front door, she immediately saw the blanket laid out in front of the fire. Saying nothing, Grant walked up to her and unbuttoned the front of her cloak. He pulled the cloak off her and walked over to hang it on the wall. Whether from his touch or the warm glow of the fire, the night chill immediately left her body and was replaced by the feelings inside her that she was becoming accustomed to experiencing whenever Grant was close to her. He gestured to the blanket on the floor.

"Would ye care to sit wit' me awhile?"

"Of course, I would love to." She took Grant's hand and let him lead her closer to the warmth of the hearth.

Grant sat down with his long legs outstretched and his back resting against the bottom of the armchair. He patted the blanket and invited Ada to sit down with him. He watched her closely as she stepped onto the blanket and sat down between his legs, scooting her bum back against his crotch. She leaned back against his chest and sighed deeply as his arms came around her middle. He kissed the shoulder of her gown.

"The firelight makes ye look like a fairy. Yer eyes and hair twinkle in the light and ye have a glow all around ye." He breathed in the scent of her hair.

"This is the first time in my life that I have felt like I am where I should be. I'm not being pulled in any direction; I have nothing in the world to do but sit here and be with you. It's wonderful." Ada squeezed his forearms softly.

"I still cannot believe that ye have chosen to be with me. I know it was dire circumstances that brought ye here but I thank God that ye chose to run to me."

"I knew where I was going from the moment I mounted Gypsy." Ada smiled into the fire.

They were silent for a while, letting the fire flicker and crack while they relaxed in each other's company. It was full dark outside now and Ada shifted slightly and turned to look at Grant.

"Will you tell me about yourself? I mean, you already know how I grew up from when we traveled to my grandmother's estate but I hardly know anything about you." Ada hoped she hadn't overstepped. She was dying to know more about the man she was falling for but was scared her questions would bring up ghosts that were better left buried.

"I guess that it's only fair; although, I'll warn ye in advance there is nothing heroic or overly exciting about my life. Before I start, would ye mind grabbing the whisky from the table? We can share a drink during the telling." He hoped tonight's volume of drink would allow his memories to come easy.

When Ada had returned with the cup, Grant took a long sip and began to speak.

"I was actually born in Ireland. My mother was Irish and my father was a merchant who often brought goods across the Irish Sea between the Highlands and Ireland.

He was originally a Scot, and although I'm nay exactly sure how they met, they ended up marrying in Ireland. My mother died not long after I was born—a matter of days, and my father brought me and my older brother back to Scotland and brought us up near the coast and on the water."

"I'm sorry about your mother. It is terrible for children to lose their parents." Ada spoke quietly, reminded of her own mother's passing.

"I did miss her from time to time, and my father spoke of her often but I never knew her so it was not as hard for me as for some." He gave Ada's thigh a gentle squeeze in reassurance.

"In terms of growing up, my life was common. I sailed with my father and brother and helped them in their work but I seemed to know from a young age that I dinna want to be a merchant, so when I was three and ten, I asked my father if I could be apprenticed to a smith who worked in town. My father was happy to oblige me." Grant laughed out loud. "I wasna much of a merchant, no mind at all for the business. I think my father was more worried about me becoming a merchant. He was right pleased when I announced I had other plans."

Ada laughed too. The sound gave Grant an odd sense of encouragement. He was not one to talk about his life but he felt so at ease with Ada sitting in front of the fire, smelling the wood smoke in Ada's hair and feeling the warmth of her body seeping through his clothing. He wanted her to know him—to know all of him. He wanted to give her something of himself that he had not given to many people.

Perth, Scotland, August, 1745

"It's a wonder how I get any work done at all—stopping every few minutes to answer a question, or to help ye wi' the forge, or stoke up the fire ye have left to smolder. Christ, Ewan. Ye'll give me grey hair before I'm thirty." Grant ran a hand through his dark sweat drenched hair.

Ewan Sinclair was at least smart enough to avoid eye contact with Grant and stare at the dirt he was kicking with his leather shoe.

"I am sorry, sir. Truly. I only wished to know what it was that was causing that delicious smell, so when I went to take a peek I guess that is when the fire must have died down because when I came back, it was already in a poor state." Ewan wiped a thick wrist across his sweating brow. He then seemed to remember something and added, "Also, sir, the smell turned out to be oatcakes made by Miss Morgan, just three shops down. That's when I decided I would come back and ask ye when we were stopping for a meal. My wame is rumbling something fierce." Ewan peeked up from under his mop of blonde hair to see Grant staring down at him and quickly averted his eyes back down to the shop floor.

"Is there ever a time when yer not hungry, Ewan? I mean, if it were up to you, we would be stopping every hour to partake in a wee bite." Grant put down the hammer he was holding. "Git down to Miss Morgan and make sure ye bring back enough oatcakes for the both of us. There's coin on the table by the back door. Oh, and Ewan, see if ye can't find us some reasonably cooler water, the drinking bucket was left too close to the forge and is now more suitable for boiling laundry than drinking. Ye wouldna happen to know anything about that would ye?"

Ewan took his cue and in response to the question, grabbed the coins and ran out the back door.

"I'll be back before ye know it, sir!" he yelled from behind the house.

When Grant was sure Ewan was out of earshot, he sat down on a wooden stump and laughed aloud. As much as he highly doubted that Ewan Sinclair would ever become a master blacksmith, he had truly grown to love him as a younger brother. He had apprenticed him roughly a year ago when the lad was only about twelve years old. His parents had both died of fever and the poor lad had nowhere else to go. The past year had seen Ewan grow into an adolescent that was prone to distraction and accidents, often simultaneously, but he was as loyal as anyone could ever want. Grant now felt like he was raising someone as well as apprenticing them. Someone needed to teach Ewan the ways of the world and if his behavior of late was an indication of Grant's leadership and masculine brotherly advice, then perhaps he would have to enlist someone else to aide him in the cause.

The following afternoon, Grant had ridden out to look in on Conner Dundas. The elderly man had arrived at Grant's shop that same morning on a horse that looked almost as old as the man himself. He had never seen Conner come into town riding; rather, he always drove his horse and his ancient cart to do his errands. Everyone in town knew the older man's joints hurt him terribly and in the damp weather of fall or early spring, he could scarcely get to town at all. Even though today was fine and sunny, Grant still had to help Conner off his horse when he arrived at his shop. Using two stumps of wood as stools, Grant sat outside his front door while Conner explained that some English soldiers had come by demanding a meal and a drink. Living alone, Conner had limited stores but knowing the English would not leave without something, he offered them a small bag of leftover flour he had sitting in the back of his cart. They scoffed at the size and quality of the bag and taking offence, they demanded he give them food that was already prepared, adding that it was Conner's duty as a citizen of the English crown to aide his majesty's army in any way he could. Stating once again that he had nothing other than the unused flour, Connor was then pushed into a wooden chair in his kitchen and watched helplessly as the soldiers rummaged through his home, searching for any food they could find. Finding nothing, they marched out to his cart, took the flour and for good measure, lifted his cart slightly and kicked a wheel off the axle, knowing fair well that Conner would not be able to mend the cart himself. Grant had shaken his head apologetically at the old man's story. He had heard countless stories of the English mistreating the Scottish people, but he also knew that the conflict went both ways. As his father used to tell him, there are always two sides of a coin. Regardless of politics, Conner Dundas needed his cart and Grant said he would be happy to ride out this afternoon and help him get the wheel back on its axle. He sent Ewan to fetch a horse and hook it to a cart to drive Mr. Dundas back home. Shortly, Ewan watched as Grant drove the cart down the main road, with Conner's old gelding lagging behind them.

When Grant arrived at Conner's house, he was very glad to see that the wheel had not been damaged, nor the axle itself. It had been removed and left beside the wagon so simply that it was mocking Conner for his inability to re-attach the wheel. Grant maneuvered the wheel so it lined up with the axle, and all it needed was to be pushed on once the cart was lifted. Conner claimed he could manage to push the wheel slightly once Grant wrenched the heavy cart off the ground. Surprisingly, the wheel slid right into place and Grant set the cart down and hammered the wheel in for a tighter fit.

Sitting down on the grass, he accepted the glass of whisky from the elderly man. He sipped and wondered with a smile, where Conner had hidden this bottle when the English had come. The two men talked companionably for about an hour or so, then grudgingly, Grant rose from the ground and stretched pleasurably.

"I'll need to be getting back, Conner. God only knows what Ewan has done to the shop in my absence." Grant laughed, swallowed the last of his whisky and handed the glass back to Conner.

Conner chuckled. "The lad seems very eager, but last week I watched him trip ore' his own feet twice in the street on his way to your shop. Perhaps a smith's shop is nay the best place for such a clumsy wee man."

"Aye, trust me, Conner, I know it. The lad tries his best but I am not sure I could think of any trade that he would be truly suited to. I try to keep my eye on him and besides, he's more like a stubborn brother than an apprentice to me now anyway."

The two men shook hands on a job well done and a drink well shared, and Grant climbed into the borrowed wagon and clucked the horse forward for the hot ride back into town. Unusually for Scotland, this summer had been quite dry and the air was hot and clear. The sun beat down on his back and he rolled his sleeves up as he shook the reins and encouraged the horse into a faster walk in the direction of town.

Chapter 18

Ewan walked around the shop with a feeling of self-importance. He always felt proud that Grant thought he was capable enough to leave the shop for an afternoon and trust him to manage things. Grant would most likely be back roughly at supper hour. It would only take him a few hours to travel to Mr. Dundas' and fix the wheel that those damn soldiers had wickedly removed. Ewan smiled to himself. It also gave him a feeling of importance to curse, even if it was only in his head. Grant said that it was ungentlemanly to curse for no reason and that he should never ever do it in front of a lady but in his head, he thought Grant would allow it. Besides, he was practically a man now.

    He had just finished taking an order for a man who needed the hilt mended on his sword. Ewan had asked the man all the same questions he had heard Grant ask a thousand times and promised the man a price that he hoped wouldn't be too high or too low for a job this simple. He also managed to throw in a few questions he knew Grant would not exactly be keen on him asking, like whether the man planned on using the sword soon and whether the repair had anything to do with the Stuart Cause. Ewan often heard the men in town talking about the "Bonnie Prince" and the rightful king of Scotland. From what his young mind could pertain, he thought a Scottish king sounded a hell of a lot better than an English one and words like freedom, oppression, and rebellion often flitted through his head like sparks from the forge.

He had spoken to Grant about his thoughts once. They were sitting at the wooden table in the small room they shared off the back of the shop.

"Do ye think there will be a Scottish king again, Grant? Will the rebellion that Prince Charlie is forming be a success? Will ye fight? Can I?" Ewan blurted out between mouthfuls of soup that Miss Morgan had given them for their supper.

"First lad, clear yer mouth before ye speak. Have I not told ye that hundreds of times before?" Grant narrowed his eyes as he watched Ewan swallow. "To answer your questions, I am sure that one day there will be a Scottish king on the throne again but when that day is, I canna say. I also canna speak as to whether the rebellion will be a success or failure because I am neither a seer nor a gypsy. In terms of you fighting, nay that willna be happening and I am not a wee bit sorry either, so you can kindly wipe that sullen look of yer face and finish your soup." Grant finished by shoveling a spoonful of lukewarm beef soup into his mouth.

Ewan looked as if he was about to speak but swallowed theatrically so Grant could be sure his mouth was empty. Grant laughed in spite of himself. Ewan always seemed to make him laugh unexpectedly.

"Ye never answered the question about you, sir. Will ye fight for the prince?" Ewan asked curiously.

As Grant looked over the table at Ewan with his blond hair a ragged mess as always and his face smudged with dirt around the sides of his cheeks, which he had obviously neglected in his before dinner wash, he pictured leaving Ewan behind and marching to fight for a cause he was not sure he fully believed in.

"Nay, Ewan. I dinna think I will be fighting for the prince. Sometimes I believe we would be just as unhappy under Scottish rule as we are under English. I'll admit freely that the English do terrible things around Scotland these days but I am not sure that we Scots are completely innocent in all this mess either. I have a shop to care for and an apprentice to train." He looked directly at Ewan and added, "Besides, who will mend the weapons and reshape the armour if there is to be a rebellion? They will need me; rather, they will need the both of us. We willna be speaking anymore of this, do ye hear me, Ewan? The topic is verra dangerous and ye never know when the wrong ears will hear ye." As a signal of finality, Grant stood up and pushed his bowl to the middle of the table. "It's your night to clean the bowls." He smiled down at Ewan, walked outside and closed the door.

Ewan had thought of that night often when he heard people speaking about the rebellion or when he found himself thinking on it. He was always curious to know who the ears belonged to that Grant had spoken about. Who among the townspeople were with the rebellion and who were not?

Thinking about that conversation also brought him back to the fact that it would be dinner time in a little over an hour and Grant would be coming back around then. He needed to make sure the fire was still burning in the forge—God knows he had let it go out too many times already—and that was just counting this week. He was turned toward the forge in the back corner of the shop when he heard the tiny bell *tink* above the door.

Finishing quickly with the fire, he spoke whilst turning around. "Good Afternoon to ye, what can I help..." His voice caught in his throat once he had fully turned around to face the door. He coughed to clear it and carried on, standing taller. "What can I help you gentlemen with today?" Ewan asked professionally.

Four English soldiers stood elbow to elbow in the narrow confines at the front of the shop. They all stared down at Ewan with the same mocking, amused expression.

"Well, now. Look at this young sprite, James." The tallest of the men spoke first. He towered over Ewan by at least a foot and it seemed his red coat made him appear even larger.

"I told you Scotland was going to pot, Sam," the shorter man, whom Ewan could only assume was James, retorted laughingly. "They have young boys running their smith shops! Why, this young buck cannot be more than a month or two off his mother's milk."

The four men laughed rowdily. Ewan had half a mind to tell these English pigs where to go but he could hear Grant's ever-present voice in the back of his head chiding him about being respectful to whoever enters the shop no matter how much of a—Ewan searched his memory for Grant's words, then finding them he almost smirked—*filthy wee heathen bugger* they might be.

"Is there something ye need assistance with, sirs?" Ewan tried again. He sounded calmer than he expected to and gave himself a mental pat on the back. *So far so good.*

"We have business to discuss with the owner of this," he looked disapprovingly around the shop, "establishment…" he finished cruelly. It was James who had spoken again. Ewan really started to dislike this fellow.

"I am afraid, gentlemen, that the master smith is out on a call right now. He should be back this evening if ye are still in town, or I can give him a message if ye'd like to tell me." Ewan's shoulders ached from standing so tense, his fingernails—although short—were digging into the palm of his clenched fist. He hoped they would just leave after finding out Grant was unavailable.

The men looked at each other and Sam raised an eyebrow to James as if in silent question. The other two men, who seemed to be the muscle of the group, just shifted uncomfortably back and forth in the smoldering, tight confines of the shop.

This time, Sam spoke. "How long have you been an apprentice, son?" He looked curiously at Ewan.

"A little over a year now," Ewan responded.

"Well then, perhaps you do know enough for our needs," Sam said calmly.

"Enough of this shit! It's hotter than a burning witch in here, Sam. Just get on with the business so we can be on our way," one of the large squatty men said. Ewan glanced at his arms and realized they were about the same size as one of his own legs. He swallowed hard.

"Percy! We need to be sure that this boy is appropriate." James scowled at his friend's outburst and gestured for Sam to continue.

"Terribly sorry, my boy." Sam nodded his head toward Ewan. "So, over this past year, you have worked fairly closely with your master smith? Learned a sizable amount about your trade?"

"Aye, I am sure I can assist you if ye'll just tell me what it is ye need."

"Well, what we need is to know how much you are aware of the events happening right now. There are whispers of a rebellion against our Majesty the King. Do you know anything about this? Are you perhaps getting a little extra business in the making and repairing of weapons?"

Ewan's eyes glanced indirectly to the few swords that were on the work table by the forge.

"All I know, sir, is that people bring us business and we do our best to please them. I know little of rebellions or politics." Ewan hoped he looked calmer than he felt. Normally, his body was accustomed to the heat of the shop but he could feel sweat trickling down his back under his light shirt.

"So, you are saying that you have no leanings toward this Jacobite cause then?" Sam looked seriously down at Ewan, his eyes daring the boy to lie to him.

"As I told ye, sir, I just mend and build what people request. I have no political leanings either way." Ewan hoped that his true feelings did not show. He tried to think of what Grant would say to these men.

Surprisingly, the atmosphere in the room relaxed slightly and the four men smiled and nodded to each other. Ewan let out a breath he didn't realize he had been holding.

"Excellent!" Sam took a step toward Ewan and stuck out his hand. "What is your full name, son?"

Ewan was startled by the abrupt movement but stood his ground.

"Ewan Sinclair, sir." He shook the soldier's hand curiously.

"Well, Ewan Sinclair, congratulations! Your apprenticeship is over; you are now a blacksmith for His Majesty's army. You'll need a few minutes to collect your things I am sure. You can meet us outside."

Ewan's stomach hit the floor and he found it hard to draw a breath. He glanced from one man to the next, hoping to catch some sort of glint of amusement in their eyes to tell him that this was all a horrible joke. However, they all remained stoic, looking down at him. *Well, to hell with being respectful to your customers*, he thought wildly. Surely Grant would understand this was a very different situation.

"Like bloody hell I am!" Ewan yelled sharply at Sam.

Sam looked mildly surprised but this was soon replaced with a look of anger and warning.

"It was not a question of whether you wanted to or not, boy. It was a simple fact. You are now impressed into the English army and you will damn well accept it. We need smiths to aid us in quelling this damned uprising that your people have started."

Ewan took a step back but his calves came up hard against the edge of the stone forge. He was literally in the farthest back corner of the shop. He could see the side door but doubted he could make it there before the men noticed what was happening, and the front door was obviously out of the question with those four bastards standing in front of it. He glanced around quickly. He saw the pail for coal sitting about a foot away from where he stood. There was no help for it. He took a deep breath of the hot, dry air and quickly crouched down to grab the pail. He did not have time to form any thought other than the desperate need to get out of there.

He came up screaming and hurled the pail of coal at the four men. The sudden action surprised them and Ewan made a dash for the side door. It looked like he was going to make it when he felt his foot catch on the leg of a stool that sat near the wooden table Grant used as a desk. He fell flat on the dirt floor and Percy appeared at his side immediately, yanking him up by the arms. He was pulled to his feet and found himself face-to-face with Percy's greasy, sweating face. He spat at the soldier and a glob of spittle and dirt from his fall landed on the man's barrel of a chest. "I'll never go with you, you English Swine!" He kicked wildly and twisted, trying to escape the big man's iron grasp.

"Oh, but you will," James said, peering over Percy's massive shoulder at the goings on.

Ewan cleared his throat quickly to hock spit at James as well, but Percy saw this coming and his fist smashed Ewan across the face. Ewan's face felt like it was broken in two as he fell to the dirt floor for the second time in minutes.

James watched with a shoulder shrug as Ewan's head cracked against one of the many anvils left around the shop before he hit the floor in a puddle of blood from his bleeding nose and head.

Sam clicked his tongue. "*Tsk*, he should have just collected his things when I asked politely," Sam said, shaking his head.

The other soldiers laughed and began to make their way around the shop looking for things of value. If the neighbours heard the ransacking of the shop or the commotion that was now quiet, they knew better then to try and intervene. With sadness, guilt and fear, they turned the other cheek.

Chapter 19

Grant drove contently down the road toward town. With Conner being able to help lift the wheel into place, the job went quicker than Grant had expected. He would arrive in time for supper now and knew Ewan would have gotten hungry and probably arranged for some dinner for them at the tavern down the street. His stomach growled at the thought of dinner. Working outside always seemed to make him hungrier. Christ, he was turning into Ewan, with his mind always on food. He chuckled and urged the horse into a faster walk, anticipating a full belly.

Nearing the outskirts of the town, Grant saw two riders leaving almost at a full run. Thinking this was an odd occurrence, he moved his own wagon to the side of the road to allow them to pass. It was obvious their business had to be important or they would have no need for such speed. Surprisingly, he saw them slow as they approached. Grant waved them a greeting and waited for them to calm their dancing mounts.

"Mr. Ross, ye must come! It's your shop," John, the butcher, said. Grant recognized the man's son, Kirk, who rode with him.

"What about the shop?" Grant asked already reining up his horse.

"The English…" John's son yelled as Grant took off down the road, with the two men right on his tail.

"Oh, no, Ewan…" Grant said to both himself and God. He knew how Ewan felt about the English and he prayed with all he was worth that the lad had kept his wits about him and his mouth shut.

As the wagon thundered down the road to his shop, Grant knew Ewan was gone. Neighboring shopkeepers and townspeople crowded around the entrance to his place and a few of the women averted their gaze, tears running down their cheeks. He launched himself off the cart, leaving the reins dangling and ran into the shop. He instantly felt his stomach drop.

His shop was completely disheveled. It was clear the English had taken anything they deemed valuable. The swords he was mending were gone and the small wooden cup of coin was taken. Tables and chairs were tipped over and coal from the forge was spilled all over the floor with obvious malice. He took a few steps toward the forge and dropped to his knees. The dirt covering the floor by one of the larger anvils was soaked with blood. Turning his head slowly toward the door, he saw various people standing by the doorway, including John and Kirk.

"Where is he?" he asked numbly. "Is he dead?" He felt as though his stomach would empty its contents onto the floor at any second. He sat down abruptly off his knees.

John stepped into the shop and walked over to him. "He's nay dead that we know of Grant, but the English have taken him." John put a hand on Grant's head in comfort.

"Taken him? Taken him where? What could they possibly want with a young lad?" Grant placed his head in his hands. He knew the answer before John told him. They'd taken him into the army. They needed trades people to travel with the army, and it was only a bonus to deprive the enemy of a skilled apprentice. "Would ye all leave me, please?" Grant looked solemnly up at the surrounding people.

They began to file out of the shop and John, with a final apologetic nod to Grant, pulled the door to the shop shut, which now hung half off its hinges.

Looking up to make sure everyone was indeed gone, Grant laid his head on his bent knees and for his own sake as much as Ewan's, sobbed until he had no more tears.

Chapter 20

Late September, 1745

It had been a little over a month since Grant had joined the Jacobites to fight against the English. Overall, he was uninterested in the politics of the rebellion and more so driven by hatred and revenge against the English for what they had done to Ewan.

He had been looking for Ewan for weeks, asking around while he served with the army, trying to find out any information about what camp he might be living in, or where the army had moved him to. It was a dead trail—no one was talking and Grant was becoming increasingly blinded by rage.

When the Jacobites sacked Edinburgh in early September, Grant fought with a fury that shocked even himself. He seemed to burn with vengeance he was unaware he possessed. During the dull moments in camp, he often thought back to the day he had joined the army. He had walked through his workshop to his little room, just off the back that he had shared with Ewan. He stepped over the blood stain as he went. He picked up things he thought he might need as well as a few sentimental items to take with him. He shut the front door of the smith shop and walked away, never looking back. Grant no longer wanted to just mend swords and fix wagons for the Jacobites, he wanted to fight. He wanted blood and he wanted to cause the English the same pain he was feeling. Before this, he had never killed a man. He had seen men killed when he was working as a merchant with his father but he had never caused death by his own hand. The first night after the sack of Edinburgh, he was sick to his wame all night and was woken several times by the tortured faces of the men he had killed.

He was becoming someone he never wanted to become—someone he could not have ever pictured himself being.

Nearing the end of September, the Jacobite army won a battle near Prestonpans that greatly boosted the moral of the rebellion. There was an influx of new soldiers eager and fresh-faced to join the cause. These new men were sorely needed because for the next few months, the Stuart Army would be marching into England to fight on English soil.

Grant could not stomach the new soldiers' enthusiasm for adventure and excitement. He could, however, share their eagerness to spill English blood on English land. Moving into England meant that perhaps Grant would be one step closer to finding Ewan, or even gaining a tiny slice of information on the lad's whereabouts. The marching was long and exhausting and by the time the army made camp for the night, Grant could hardly keep his eyes open long enough to eat his dinner and find a space to lie down. Sitting at the fire one night, he scowled at the other men playing cards and dice. They seemed like they would be up for hours. *God only knew where they got the energy,* he thought. He stalked off a good distance away from the rowdy games and laid down on the damp grass, wrapping his blanket around himself to cut out as much of the chill as he could. He knew that the other men mocked him for his sour disposition and his "hermitish" ways, as one lad had put it. At one time, their opinions would have bothered him but in his present state of mind, he could think of nothing but Ewan and his own efforts. He suddenly felt very old, as if these past few months had aged him. He pressed his eyes closed, tried to clear the thoughts from his head and promptly drifted into a chilly sleep.

He did not think he had been asleep very long when he was awoken to a shuffling beside him. Instantly alert, he froze, trying to make out the origin of the noise in the pitch black. It sounded like footsteps muffled by the moist grass but no one had any reason to be walking toward him at this hour. As the sound drew closer, he realized he was right about the footsteps. He watched a woman walk toward him, with her wool skirt swishing the grass almost silently as she approached him. She seemed intent on her destination, which to his bewilderment, seemed to be his sleeping site. Her pale skin and light-coloured hair were the only parts visible on a night with no moon, giving her a ghostly appearance.

She whispered a soft greeting into the darkness.

"I think ye may be lost, lass, or mistaken. I am nay the man ye seek." Grant whispered quietly as she got closer, fearing his deep voice might startle her in the darkness. "Can I be of any help in finding someone for ye? Yer husband, perhaps? Or a father or brother?"

It was not uncommon for women to follow the armies so they could feed and care for their men back at camp. It was most likely she had turned the wrong way in the darkness and thought she was heading back to her own shelter.

"If ye are Grant Ross, then ye are the man I seek," she said in a quiet whisper. Her voice was soft and carried a small highland lilt that made her speech sound like a poem or a song.

"I am Grant Ross, but I fear that I have no knowledge as to why ye would seek me out, miss…" Grant shifted his blanket around his shoulders to keep out the chill.

The woman sat down on the grass beside him. She smelled of fresh air and a faint floral scent he could not place. She was sitting close to him, which seemed slightly odd but it was a cold night and it was dark. Maybe she had not realized how close she was when she sat down. Seeing her up close, she looked a few years younger than him. She had very light hair and a small oval-shaped face, which was mostly shadowed and hard to make out.

"I know ye, Mr. Ross, from Perth. I know ye own the smith shop and I know what the English did to it… and to young Ewan," she finished quietly.

The mention of Ewan's name was like a punch to the stomach. He swallowed hard.

The soft voice continued. "I used to listen to Ewan talk when he came into the tavern to get yer food. He spoke so highly of you, and himself." She paused briefly and laughed gently at the memory. "I ate there every day after finishing my night's work. I used to look forward to watching him come in and listening to him chatter like a hen to anyone who would listen. I saw you come from time to time as well. You are much less entertaining to listen to but much better to look at. My name is Tilly; I am one of Miss Rose's girls. Well, I was, until I followed the army.

"It is nice to officially meet ye then, Tilly, and thank ye for speaking highly of Ewan." Grant was beginning to wonder the real reason Tilly had sought him out. Miss Rose was a caretaker for many of the prostitutes in Perth. Grant had never partaken in Miss Rose's or her girls' services himself but he knew well enough what they did for a living, as did every other man in town.

"Do not think on it, Mr. Ross. Ewan made me laugh and in my line of work, laughter is a welcome break. I never told him that, so I thought I might tell you."

She fidgeted slightly and a pale hand came out from under her shawl and came to rest on Grant's leg.

His body warmed so suddenly he barely needed the protection of his blanket. He slowly inhaled and exhaled. He had never been with a whore before; in fact, it was a recurring joke with his closer friends. He had no moral obligations against it, he just never found himself in need of their services. He was a handsome, healthy man with a flourishing shop. He had kissed many girls when their fathers were not looking and even sinfully rolled around in the stables with one specific girl on a few separate occasions.

Now, sleeping alone and cold each night and feeling nothing but rage and sadness, he felt the warmth of

Tilly's hand on his leg ignite his most carnal senses and slightly pull him out of the fog he had been existing in.

"Why did ye seek me out tonight, lass? Ye have clearly been with the army for a while now if ye have travelled from Perth?" He sat barely moving, afraid that the slightest movement might dislodge her hand.

"I watch people, aye?" she responded and gently squeezed the leg under her hand. "Ye always look so sad and so empty. I thought maybe I could help ye feel a bit more alive, at least for tonight." He knew she was asking a question without fully stating one.

Grant was moved by her offer and for a moment, thought of rejecting her gently and returning to sleep, but loneliness and sadness were hard emotions to constantly carry and he wanted to feel nothing, if only for a short time.

"Aye, lass. I suppose ye can." He sat forward and pressed his lips against hers. Her face felt cold against his skin. He threw his blanket around her shoulders so they were cocooned together against the chill and deepened the kiss.

There was nothing romantic in the way Tilly moved. She was as straightforward and matter of fact as her profession demanded her to be. Grant was as thankful for this fact as he was for the small moment of respite he was about to receive from his own mind. When Grant began kissing Tilly, she had immediately slid her hand from its inviting place just above his knee to the inside of his thigh, and from there it was a short journey to the crotch of his breeches. She rubbed him briefly over the rough material and he felt himself harden instantly. It had been a long while since his hay loft rendezvous with Edith, and where she had been gentle and exploratory, Tilly was confident and skillful.

Grant barely had time to hiss a startled breath as her freezing hand wrapped around his heated skin. She began to move her hand and the frigid temperature did not seem to matter. As far as Grant was concerned, his balls could freeze off right then as long as Tilly kept up with her practiced ministrations.

He could feel his breath start to come in short gasps. He needed to touch her, he needed to feel her under his hand. He groped through the darkness for the bottom of her skirt. Finding her boot, he slid his hand up and under the hem of her skirts. He could feel her woolen stockings prickle his hand as he moved upwards. The stockings ended just above the knee and his hand traced along the soft skin of her inner thighs.

"Ross, Ross!" A hushed voice came from the direction of the campfire accompanied by unsteady footsteps making their way toward Grant.

Grant withdrew his hand swiftly and cursed under his breath.

"ROSS! It's Evan. Christ, man, its dark as all feck over here. Why ye do not just sleep nearer to the fire w' the rest of us I will never know." Evan slurred, he had obviously given up all attempts at trying to keep his voice down.

Tilly startled at the sound of footsteps and had scuttled back into the shadows.

"Evan, I'm over here, ye drunk bastard. Ye better have something of importance to tell me and not have just staggered away for a wee chat."

Grant turned his head and squinted in the shadows to see if he could make out Tilly's shielded form. Evan was right, it was black as coal tonight.

"I have no wish to be waking yer moody arse up unless it was important. Yer disposition dampers the effect of my drink." Evan laughed contagiously at his own joke.

Grant laughed in response and stood. Evan was one of the few people he had become close to during these past few months. Evan often teased Grant about being sour and antisocial but he seemed to understand the emotions Grant carried around with him.

"Well, I'm nay getting any younger, man. Piss or get off the pot," Grant urged Evan. He was secretly hoping Evan was not too drunk to forget what brought him over.

"Well, a group of us were wandering around after dinner looking for anyone who was willing to play dice with us," Evan started.

"You mean looking for someone whose money ye could take? Aye, continue," Grant cut in.

"Not take, win… ye make it sound so sinister, but that's nay the point right now. We came to the campfire of a few sergeants who seemed right eager to play dice against us. So, we played and we drank and before ye have time to spit, they had taken all our money."

"So, you woke me up to tell me ye lost at dice." Grant began to seriously doubt the importance of his mate's story.

"Will ye give me a chance to finish, Jesus Christ! I've never seen a man so eager to get back to his cold bed in all my life. It was not the fact that we lost that brings me here. It is the fact that Graham took offense to losing and started accusing the sergeants of cheating him. Needless to say, he was a bit gone wi' drink," Evan added.

"I gathered." Grant rolled his eyes. Although darkness made the gesture useless, it made Grant feel a little better.

"Aye," Evan continued unaffected by Grant's dry tone. "Well, then one of the younger sergeants and Graham started having words and before any of us knew what was happening, Graham punched him right in the eye and jumped on top of him when he fell down." Evan stopped to clear his throat, his voice slightly hoarse from the night's events. "So, to make a long story short, Graham is being flogged at sunrise today and I thought ye might like to be there as a show of support," Evan concluded.

Grant felt bad for Graham. He knew he had a temper when he drank. He knew the flogging would end up hurting his pride more than anything else.

"Aye, Evan. I'll be there." He clapped his friend on the shoulder in dismissal.

While Evan lurched back toward the campfire, Grant reached into the shadows for Tilly's hand but found empty space. He waved with outstretched arms briefly and feeling nothingness, quietly whispered her name several times. She was gone—no doubt spooked by Evan's intrusion as well as his story.

"God damn it to hell. I will flog Graham myself if I get the chance." Grant adjusted his increasingly uncomfortable trousers and lay down to sleep.

Chapter 21

As it turns out, Graham was not the only man to be flogged in the winter months. Aside from a few skirmishes here and there, the Scottish army seemed to be mainly doing a lot of marching and a lot of freezing. This was according to most of the conversation around the campfires in the evenings. Often, when men are put together in confined areas, are bored, uncomfortable, and drink that mischief ensues. The winter of 1745 was no different. Grant witnessed at least two or three men being punished every few weeks for doing something admittedly stupid to someone they should have steered clear from.

Other than Evan and a few other closer acquaintances, Grant continued to keep mainly to himself. For the sake of warmth, he had had to start sleeping close to the fire with all the other men but he missed the privacy and peacefulness of his secluded sleeping spots where he had liked to sleep in the slightly warmer fall weather. It was not uncommon for him to wake up to the lad beside him, sleeping pressed against his side. He often just closed his eyes and went back to sleep, thankful for the small patch of warmth.

By the end of December, the Jacobite army had travelled into England and managed to end up only one hundred and fifty miles from London. Grant stood in a grassy field, with his cloak pulled as high around his ears as it would go. Often, when he found a moment of solitude, he said a quick prayer for Ewan's safety as well as his own. He was in the middle of such a prayer when Evan and Robbie came walking over to him, with their own plaids pulled tight around them. The wind whipped their hair over their eyes as they approached.

"Fine day, is it no?" Grant said dryly.

"Oh, Aye, but just wait till ye hear the news we just heard. It's nay going to get any better." Robbie scowled against the wind.

"We are to march back to Scotland. Can ye believe that?" Evan took over, angrily shoving hair behind his ears. "We march our freezing carcasses almost all the way to bloody London and then they turn us around and march us right back from whence we came!"

"Did ye find out why?" Grant groaned internally. He could think of countless things he would rather be doing then turning around and going back home to Scotland. He was no closer to finding Ewan than when he started, and he was quickly falling victim to the melancholy of the camp around him.

"Well, some of the men are saying it is because we are waiting for support from the damn Frenchies," Evan replied.

"Aye. Well, we better march all the way home then because I think we can all guess how that will turn out," Grant added angrily.

Robbie was buried in his plaid up to his nose. "It is Lord George Murray and the other chiefs that are to blame. If it was up to the stuart, we'd be staying put."

Grant sighed. He knew that no matter what the Bonnie Prince did or thought, most of this army thought the sun shone out of his arse. So obviously, the men would blame the other chiefs for everything negative.

"Well, I dinna know about the two of ye but I'm going back to the fire to warm myself before my balls fall off from the cold. Besides, if I'm going to be marching back to Scotland, I may as well sit down while I can, aye?" Grant began to walk purposefully back toward the camp. Evan and Robbie fell instep beside him, complaining about everything from uncomfortable boots to how long it had been since they had lain with a woman. Grant thought of the distance back to Scotland and wondered whether these two would complain the whole way or eventually run out of things to be griping about.

January, 1746

Grant was not entirely wrong; Robbie and Evan had complained most of the march back to Scotland. However, in their defense, so had the rest of the men— himself included. They had left England in December, and the journey back to Scotland had been uneventful— unless one counted 'miserable cold weather' and 'more than occasional fights within your own ranks' as events.

After crossing into Scotland, to the surprise of the men, they were soon joined by fresh troops mostly from the north. These additions to the army boosted morale and eased the overall feeling of boredom and discontent the soldiers had been experiencing—at least for the short term.

"At least we are finally doing something more useful than wearing out the soles of our shoes," Grant said loudly to Robbie so he could be heard above the wind.

"Oh, aye. Standing around waiting for something to happen with this castle is much better," Robbie sarcastically replied, waving in the direction of the castle.

Not long after the augmentation of the Jacobite army, the troops had begun a siege on Stirling Castle. So far, it had been unsuccessful and tedious.

Grant still found it unnerving that he yearned for fighting. Not only did the marching and skirmishing not help him find Ewan, the lack of proper revenge against the English was building up in him and was boiling like hot water.

Before Grant could formulate his own sarcastic reply, a group of riders came over the field toward the section of the army in which Grant and his friends were serving. Robbie looked at Grant and shrugged one of his shoulders.

Grant raised his eyebrows. "I guess we'll soon see…" he said quietly to Robbie.

The party stopped a short distance from where Grant and Robbie were standing but did not dismount. Grant recognized one of the chiefs with some of his lower ranking officers. One of the officers commanded loudly to have the men gather closer together so they could hear what was about to be said. He silenced them by raising his gloved hand.

It was the chiefs turn to speak. "As many of ye may already know, the English forces have been following us since we left England. Well, it seems that the crafty wee bastards have managed to catch up with us. They have made a camp in Falkirk with their commander General Hawley and a force of about 9000 soldiers." He paused to clear his throat. Obviously, the man had given this speech several times today and his voice was becoming raspy. "In light of this fact, Lord Murray has decided that we shall gain the upper hand by abandoning our siege on Stirling Castle and dispatching an attack on the English forces at Falkirk."

A cheer went up from the men. Grant clapped Robbie hard on the back, smiling broadly.

The officer put his hand up again, asking for silence. The chief continued. "Ye will receive further directions from your commanding officers later this evening. May God bless and protect you all." The group of men pulled their horse's heads around and kicked them into a trot, off toward the next station of men.

Chapter 22

The snow was heavy and wet. Overall, it was a foul day. Grant scratched at his beard. Although it itched terribly, he was thankful for the bit of extra warmth it provided him on days like this. He hoped the bad weather was not an omen for the outcome of the day. He shifted his weight onto his right foot. His boots were beginning to let the coldness seep in. He needed to start moving.

"I'll be bloody frozen to death soon. It will save the English some trouble, aye?" Grant joked to the young soldier next to him. The boy nodded and managed a smile. He looked to be only about sixteen and he looked terrified.

Grant's stomach dropped, thinking of Ewan. He was probably as scared as this young man.

"Chin up, lad. All will be well. We have 8000 in our own army and cavalry as well. Plus, we have the higher ground. It will be over before ye know it and ye will be sitting around a campfire, thanking God for the experience." Grant nudged the boy's arm in reassurance. Trying to look calm and collected, he said a quick prayer that what he had promised the lad would come to pass.

It was about half an hour more before they started to move. Marching forward, Grant could feel the blood pumping through his body. He did not feel the cold any longer. His heartbeat was louder than the drummer in his ear. His breath came quick. It was easy to tell because each exhale produced a cloud of steam in front of him. He could hear the English lines approaching as the ground vibrated with the tremors of thousands of feet.

Grant heard the cry for muskets. He was suddenly very calm. He raised his musket and braced it against his shoulder. He was aware that his hands did not shake like they had in the first skirmish he had fought in. He looked up and saw them. The English lines were moving close enough to fire on.

The order was given and the musket volley plowed into the English army. A heavy scent of black powder hung in the air already. Before he had any conscious thought, Grant was dropping his musket and drawing his pistol, running at full speed with the rest of the Jacobites down the hill toward the enemy, screaming like berserkers. He took a moment to nod at the lad he had spoken to earlier, before they ran directly into chaos.

The English had sent the cavalry. Their artillery was too mired down in the mud to be any good. The Scots met this charge by dropping to the ground and killing the horses and resultantly, the riders as well.

Grant crouched at an approaching horse and braced his pistol on his arm. He shot the rider and once he was sure the man was off his horse, he kept running forward. With no time to reload his pistol, he slashed an oncoming horse down the side with his dirk and the rider was thrown as the horse reared and screamed. Grant jumped onto the man and slit his throat with his dirk before moving onto the next one.

He could hear men and horses screaming. Most of the men were far too close together to be using their swords. Many were using their pistols and dirks like him. His eyes found Evan who was clubbing a man with the end of his pistol. He looked the other way and realized the English were starting to run. It was common knowledge that the English were frightened by the Scottish tactic of a charging attack but he had expected the English dragoons to fare a little better. A young English rider started toward him. Grant raised his pistol and screamed loudly as he ran at the man and his horse. The inexperienced soldier thought better of his intentions, turned his horse hard and galloped in the opposite direction.

Realizing that it was safe, Grant sat down on the frigid ground. His body was giving off steam and his hair stuck to his head and face. He wondered whether it was sweat or blood that held it there, but it did not matter right now. Both armies were in states of confusion. The English were retreating but the Scots had separated greatly during the short battle and he could still hear fighting down near where their left flank had been. He was sure they had won, judging by the retreat and the number of dead Englishmen laying all around him, but the sense of disorientation and confusion seemed to hang heavily over the field.

Inverness, Late March, 1746

"I'll wipe the bloody floor with yer face if ye try that shite again."

"Try what? Winning? Maybe ye should concern yerself less with accusing me of cheating and more with working on yer game."

"I'll show ye my skill, ye thieving bastard!"

Grant stepped neatly to the side as the pair of bodies threw themselves onto the frozen muddy street in front of him and Evan. The army seemed to have been on a high after the victory at Falkirk. As they marched north and captured Inverness, the morale seemed to maintain a forward momentum. Now, after two months of waiting in the cold with improper rations and poor winter supplies, desertion was rife and the general discontent was more prevalent than ever. It did not help that most of the camp followers, apart from a few wives, had returned to their homes as well. This meant there were no whores for the men to entertain themselves with. It seemed that everyone around Grant was fighting, leaving, or cursing the rebellion for the situation they were now in. From time to time, Grant even considered going home, except he had no home to go back to. He was determined not to return to his shop in Perth without Ewan. He simply could not bring himself to go back there and work and live as if nothing had happened.

No one had been given any new information on the state of the rebellion. Grant's evenings were spent with Robbie, Evan and the young lad he had befriended at Falkirk called Charlie. They sat in the tent that Evan and Robbie shared either talking, playing cards, or on particularly cold evenings, huddled together under blankets talking about all the things they missed from home, such as hot stew and warm beds.

"The English are so close, why do they have us sitting here with our heads up our arses?" Robbie was sharpening his dirk for what seemed like the twentieth time that day.

"I still dinna ken, Robbie. Ye asked me that earlier this morning as well." Charlie laid on his back atop his blanket on the ground with his arms folded behind his head.

"I was no asking *ye* in particular! I was asking in general," Robbie snapped.

"Maybe now that it is slightly warmer than it was last month, the lords and the Stuart will decide to make a move?" Charlie purposed, sounding hopeful.

"Oh, aye, and we have only been waiting on that for two months. Sitting here freezing in a tent, that stinks like shite by the way, sleeping on frozen ground, not being given proper food to calm our bellies..."

"Christ, Robbie, enough! Do ye not think I know these things? I've been here too, aye? Suffering the same as ye—we all have," Charlie finished angrily.

Grant and Evan pulled back the flap of the tent, ducking their heads and stepping inside. Grant flopped down on a blanket by the door, rubbing his hands together against the chill.

"It smells terrible in here," Grant commented mildly, his nose scrunched up in displeasure.

Robbie raised his eyebrows and shot an angry glance at Charlie. "Oh, I hadna noticed, thank ye kindly for the reminder." He continued to sharpen his dirk, muttering under his breath in Gaelic.

"Perhaps this might cheer ye up, ye cantankerous auld bastard." Evan looked at Robbie. "Grant and I just heard that wee Prince Charlie wants the army to take position against the English. We are not running anymore, lads, nor waiting either!"

"They also said that the other lords were cautioning the prince to wait and not mount an attack just yet," Grant added from his perch by the door.

"Wait? All we have been bloody doing is waiting," Robbie sneered.

"I just thought ye might want to hear the whole story, aye? Grant responded.

"So, what is to happen then, lads?" Charlie asked.

"The word is they are going to tell us sometime tomorrow. I dinna know whether they actually will, but that's the word," Evan concluded.

Chapter 23

Early Morning, April 16, 1746

He had never felt this drained in his life. It was a tiredness that ached all the way to his bones. He wanted to lie down. However, if he were to lie down, he feared he would never rise again. He was fairly certain the only thing keeping him awake was the shooting pain in his feet and calves from walking that had merged with the pain in his stomach from starvation. He gave up and dropped unceremoniously to a sitting position on the wet ground.

It was odd that no one was talking. Stranger still was the absence of complaints. As he glanced around, he saw men laying down, leaning against whatever they could find or, like him, sitting in cold wetness. Everyone looked the same. Grant searched his mind for a word to describe it. Everyone just looked… overcome. He was sure he appeared much the same—pale with dark smudges under his eyes, chapped lips from the harsh wind and lack of water, slightly gaunt from improper and scarce food. If he could just close his eyes for a minute or two maybe he would feel slightly better.

They had received their orders yesterday morning as promised. The prince had decided that due to the relatively close proximity of the British army, a surprise assault on the duke's troops under the cover of night would be the most successful option. The Jacobite army was to march ten miles to Nairn where the English camp was and take them unawares. After leaving in the early evening, the Scottish soldiers attempted to make the grueling march. The ground was boggy and uneven, and many of the men fell behind due to the poor conditions of the terrain as well as their own poor physical conditions. Finally, upon coming within a few miles from the camp, the army was halted. The Jacobite scouts had discovered that the English camp was still quite awake with activity. With the night turning into day, the decision was made that to attack the camp now, would not be conducive to a Scottish victory and thus, the army was ordered to march the ten miles back to their original position on Drumossie Moor. Arriving several hours later, many of the men could barely stand, feeling weak from physical exhaustion and malnutrition.

"Where is Evan?" Robbie inquired from his position on the ground, lying wrapped in his plaid.

"He said he was going to the woods to try and find something to eat," Charlie responded, his voice sounded raspy and discouraged.

Grant must have fallen asleep where he sat because the next thing he heard was someone screaming and the rumble of hoof beats as a soldier quickly rode past on his horse.

"What...?" Grant struggled to ask Robbie who lay beside him.

"Get up!" yelled Charlie. "He said to form up, the English are fast approaching!"

Robbie, Grant and Charlie scrambled to their feet and grabbed their weapons. Immediately upon standing, Grant shut his eyes as a wave of dizziness swam over him. He took a deep slow breath and cold air flooded his lungs. He could smell the scent of marshy ground and allowed himself one moment to pretend he was elsewhere.

"Grant, are ye coming, man?" Robbie yelled from several paces ahead.

"Aye," Grant replied, opening his eyes. He shook his head to clear it and ran, limping slightly, to join his friends in the lines for battle.

They did not need to wait long before they began to feel the English cannon. The boggy ground vibrated as shots were fired and hit the ground with waves of flying mud and water.

"Why have they got us standing here, holding like targets for the sassanachs to shoot at?" Grant shouted over the noise.

"I think they are waiting for the English to advance," yelled Robbie. "Much longer though and there will be no need for them to advance because there will be no army left to face them."

A cannonball whizzed into the column that Grant was standing in. Men a few feet down from him screamed as the ball ripped through them and carried on into the column behind. Grant turned his head from the carnage. On his left, Charlie was throwing up in the grass. Grant smelled smoke, vomit and fear.

After what seemed like an eternity, the order was given for the Jacobites to charge. Glad to be doing anything other than standing where a cannonball could take his legs, Grant ran as fast as his tired body would allow. Although adrenaline pushed him forward, the terrain was boggy and unstable. It was like trying to run through a swamp. Grant picked up his feet but his progress was slowed as he tried to pull his right foot from the muddy, wet ground. He saw a small grouping of trees out of the corner of his eye and decided to move toward them. Perhaps he would be able to use the trunks to propel himself forward through the mud and give himself some better balance. Musket balls hissed in the air around him. He felt something burn across his arm but kept moving toward the trees. People were falling around him. He could hear them moaning, wounded, dying in the mud. There was so much destruction and they had not even reached the English lines yet. Grant spared a quick glance at his arm where the burning sensation was accompanied by a warm feeling; it felt odd against the cold temperature of the rest of his body. He was bleeding down his shirt, with blood running red against the dirty, once-white linen.

He arrived at the outskirts of the wooded area. The trees loomed over him and he reached out to grab the nearest one to pull himself along when he heard it. It was an odd sound—a reverberating thud, followed by an unrealistically slow, crunching crack. A shower of splinters fell onto Grant's shoulders. Realization ripped through him as he looked up. The side of the tree was shattered by an English cannon and a large branch was plummeting toward him. He lunged forward, trying vainly to move clear. The impact of the branch into his skull knocked him flat into the ground. He tried to reach his hands up to his head to feel the damage but he could not move. His head felt hot, he was dizzy and lights danced over his vision. He attempted to roll over but could not make his limbs move. His vision began to diminish, he could hear a strange whooshing sound in his ears, then the rest of his body went numb and he sunk down face first into the mud completely unconscious.

Chapter 24

Evan had been looking for food in the woods when his tiredness finally overcame him and he had laid down for a quick nap. He was woken up by the sound of cannon fire. Other soldiers, who had also found a secluded part of the woods to sleep in, were springing up around him. They too had obviously been awakened by the sounds of the battle. He had clearly missed the call to formation, and from the looks of it, many others had too. He wondered whether the rest of the army was in this much confusion and disarray. He hoped not, or else they would not have a prayer of victory.

He picked up his sword and ran toward where he would have been formed up had he heard the call. The Scots had already started the charge and he watched in dread as the English guns cut them down in massive numbers. Very few had managed to get to the English lines, and already so many lay dead on the moor. He decided that his best tactic was to stay close to the edge of the field and try to reach the English lines from a flank position. It was obvious that running straight over the open field was suicide. He crossed himself for the dead and dying and began to jog.

By the time he caught up to the battle, the English lines had advanced and the hand to hand combat was already brutal. He blocked out the screams of the wounded and concentrated on cutting down any Englishman he could find. In the back of his mind, he wondered about the safety of his friends. With so many dead already from the initial charge, he felt a lump of guilt swell in his throat. Had he been asleep while they were dying?

It was clear that the battle would be over in a matter of minutes. Scottish soldiers were yelling that Prince Charlie had already fled the field. He watched many of the men turn to run, to only be cut down by English soldiers from behind. They did not have a hope in hell as they ran back across the boggy field, with the English rifles shooting them like geese on a pond. Quickly, Evan backed into the trees, hoping he might find somewhere to hide for a while. Tears streamed down his face and he slashed them away angrily with his sleeve.

"Evan?" a startled whisper called from somewhere near the bottom of a tree. Charlie's head popped up from inside a circle of large rocks near the trunk.

"Christ, Charlie! I am so very glad to see ye, lad. I did not know whether ye were alive or dead." Evan ran toward the shelter.

Charlie had managed to dig a small hole in the dirt in the middle of the rock circle. Unless someone looked directly down from on top of the rocks, they could possibly manage to keep hidden until dusk.

"Ye crafty wee bastard, this might actually keep us alive," Evan whispered, his admiration apparent.

Charlie looked over at Evan and gave a small nod. His face was pale and bloodstained. He seemed to look even younger than he normally did.

"Robbie is dead." It was such a plain statement that Evan was not sure whether Charlie was trying to tell him the news or convince himself of it.

Evan punched the dirt with the side of his fist, wiped his nose again on his sleeve and asked softly, "Do ye know how?"

"Aye, I saw it…" Charlie stopped to take a breath and steady himself. "We were all running, Grant, Robbie and I. The ground was so wet and boggy we were all tripping and stumbling about like drunkards. A man fell beside Grant and he stopped to help him up. Robbie and I kept moving forward as fast as we were able. One minute he was running beside me and the next he was down. I stopped to see what had happened. An English shot had hit him in the neck. He was gone before I could pull his hands off the wound." Charlie looked as though he might be sick.

"And Grant?" Evan asked, although he was not sure he wanted to know.

"After I knew Robbie was gone, I looked around and started to crawl forward through the mud," Charlie sniffed. "I could not see Grant anywhere through the smoke from the guns."

"He might not be dead, then. I mean, we are no', so there's hope." Evan was trying to take Charlie's mind off Robbie so the lad would not be sick.

"Begging your pardon, Evan, but hope is not a word I put a lot of faith in right now." Charlie laid his head back against the rock wall and closed his eyes.

"Try to rest a bit, lad. I will take the first watch. I'll wake ye if I feel I need to sleep."

Evan watched as Charlie's breathing became regular and slow. He nudged the boy softly to make sure he was asleep. Receiving no response, Evan bowed his head and went entirely to pieces.

It was early evening when Evan gently shook Charlie awake. He had let him sleep all afternoon, not waking him to switch watch. In the aftermath of the day's events, Evan was sure he could not have slept, regardless of how desperately tired he was.

Charlie rubbed his hands on his face, then looked around. Obviously, the sleep had done him some good. He felt less likely to heave or faint now.

"Christ, Evan. What is that smell?" Charlie put his hand back up to his face.

"They are burning the bodies." Evan had his face crumpled up against the wind, which carried the scent of burnt flesh over the moor. "That's why I woke ye. The rest of the English will move on soon to chase down the rest of our army."

"Will we look for Grant?" Charlie gestured at the fire closest to where they were hiding.

"Aye, but I pray that we dinna find him. I hope he fled the field or found a place to hide."

"Where are all the wounded?"

"Dead." While Charlie slept, Evan had watched the English soldiers walk around the field methodically picking their way through the wounded and dead Scottish soldiers. Anyone who was moaning, moving or begging for aid or mercy was immediately bayoneted. The men who were not moving and most likely already dead were kicked savagely in the ribs a few times just to be sure. Evan was not going to share the details with Charlie. He wished he had not seen it himself.

The two men sat quietly until the last streaks of daylight vanished. The English were gone, and under the cover of semi-darkness, they would be able to quickly walk around the various fires and see whether there were any recognizable remains. They knew Robbie was dead so it would be an unnecessary risk to look for his body. Grant was probably dead too but they needed to be sure.

The fires had been started at the opposite end of the moor from where Evan and Charlie hid. Those bodies would be almost impossible to distinguish at this point, as the flames had been burning the longest there. They began to quickly check the piles closest to them which had been lit last. They found nothing in the first pile. The pop and hiss of burning skin had caused both Charlie and Evan to be violently sick in the wet grass. They had split up to circle the next two fire pits, hoping to finish the task as quickly as possible.

Charlie walked around the fire, while keeping a distance from the immense heat. He could see some of the men's faces through the flames. He stopped for a moment and stared into the fire. He was sure he could see his own face… burning into ashes like everyone else. He was still staring when he felt a hand on his arm. He jumped as if the devil himself were grabbing him.

"Easy, lad. It is only me," Evan whispered beside his ear. "I dinna want to call ye because I am not certain if any English are still about."

Charlie turned to look at Evan, his gut fell at the expression he saw on his friend's face.

"I found Grant." Evan shook his head and looked down at the ground.

Charlie crossed himself and dropped to one knee. The coolness of the marshy ground on his leg fought against the heat from the huge fire beside him. He looked up at Evan. "Such a bloody waste, all of this." He made a sweeping gesture of the moor around him.

"Aye." Evan put a hand down on Charlie's head. "Help me bring his body back to the hole, we can bury him proper."

Charlie rose from his knee and made his way weakly to the other fire, following Evan quietly through the darkness.

Chapter 25

Grant's body lay on the edge of the fire. He was face down in the mud and wet grass with one of his arms under his chest and his hips turned slightly to the side. He was covered in blood, ash and filth. His clothing had been so burned and damaged that his friends could not tell whether his skin was black from soot or black from lying wounded on the ground covered in drying blood. It was obvious from the amount of blood, he had been wounded badly. Evan hoped it was not a wound that had kept him alive only to be bayoneted by the English later in the afternoon. Whatever it was, he hoped that it had taken him quickly.

"The poor bastard," breathed Charlie, wanting to look away. "Are ye sure it's truly him, Evan?" There was a sad note of disbelief in his voice.

"Aye, I turned his head slightly to look upon his face, it's Grant."

Charlie straightened his shoulders and bravely tucked his hair behind his ears. "Well, would it be best to roll him over so one of us can take hold of his feet and one of us can take hold under his arms?"

"I'll lay my plaid on the ground and we can roll his body onto that. It will be easier for us to carry him that way." Evan shook his plaid onto the ground and Charlie helped him spread it out beside Grant.

With one pulling his upper body and the other pulling his legs, they managed to get Grant rolled onto his back atop Evan's plaid. They stepped back breathing hard and let the fire cast its eerie orange glow over his body.

"Mary Mother of God," choked Evan, as he backed up a step and crossed himself.

Grant's body had obviously been one of the last ones added to the already-lit fire. From their hiding place, Evan had watched how the English grabbed the hands and feet of the dead soldiers and swung them like a sack of grain, heaving them as high onto the pile as they could. Grant had clearly been thrown near the top of the pile and must not have landed soundly because the entire left side of his body was burned into broken blisters and bloody skin that was visible even in the dim light of the fire. The right side and his neck and head appeared to have escaped the flames almost altogether.

"How…?" Charlie asked staring at Grant's face, then looking at the rest of his body.

"His body must have rolled down the pile and landed like we found him. The fire must have only truly caught his left side before his body dislodged from where he was thrown by the soldiers."

"Christ," Charlie knelt and put a hand on Grant's cheek. "His hair is covered in dried blood; it looks as though his face was too before it hit the wet ground. Do ye think it's possible the blood and wetness stopped the fire from ravaging his face?"

"I couldna tell ye, lad. Let's carry him away before trouble finds us and we end up like poor Robbie and Grant."

The walk back to the hole beneath the tree seemed to take forever. As hard as they tried to keep the plaid-wrapped passenger off the ground, he outweighed them both and the boggy ground and cold wind made it even harder to carry a man of his size. Stumbling, they finally reached the hiding spot they had set out from. Having had to drag Grant's body the last few steps, they slid down to the ground, trying to catch their breath.

"Will we bury him now, then?" Evan asked, turning to look at Charlie who despite the cold, had droplets of sweat running down his face.

"I dinna think I can, Evan. I can barely lift my arms," Charlie replied wearily.

"Aye. Well, we can wrap the plaid around him and leave him just behind the rocks. He will not be seen in the darkness and we can rest a bit and bury him before first light," Evan panted.

They crawled back into the hole and huddled together for warmth, trying to forget the hunger in their bellies and the pain in their hearts.

A few hours later, both men were startled awake by a very quiet sound.

Evan froze and put a hand on Charlie's arm. "Stay quiet and completely still, if it's the English searching, maybe they will pass over us." His whisper was barely audible over the sounds of the night around them.

Charlie barely breathed and listened carefully for the sound to come again. He clasped Evan's hand on his arm, scared that any movement might give them away.

The sound came again. The sound was very close to them, it sounded like a slight rustling on the grass, too quiet to be footsteps. Perhaps an animal had come to investigate the aftermath of the battle. Charlie's hand relaxed and Evan removed his biting grip from Charlie's arm.

"It's no' but an animal… too quiet to be a soldier," Charlie said warily into Evan's ear.

"Aye, I think yer right. I'll take a quick look to be sure."

No sooner had Evan began to stand up quietly that the sound came again. This time, it was accompanied by a low haunting moan, which would have camouflaged with the wind had Evan not had his head so close to the source.

"Holy fucking Christ!" Evan grabbed the collar of Charlie's coat and hauled him up to where he was positioned. "Look…"

Charlie could feel Evan shaking beside him, watching and waiting quietly in terror for whatever it was that had spooked him.

"Christ, what is it, man?" Charlie breathed, unable to stand the waiting any longer.

"Shhh… Look!" Evan pointed a trembling finger at the plaid-wrapped shape in front of him. As if on cue, the rustling noise began again and the plaid moved ever so slightly back and forth where Grant's foot was resting beneath it. The low groan came again but this time, slightly longer.

"My God!" Charlie jumped up beside where Grant's body lay. "He's alive! Evan, for God's sake, man, get up here and help me."

Evan stood frozen where he was, finger still pointing at the plaid that Charlie was trying desperately to pull off Grant's face. "No... he's... dead... I..."

Charlie looked desperately at Evan who had started mumbling something incoherent about ghosts and the like, with his hand still suspended midair and his pointed finger now slightly sagging. He let go of the plaid for a moment and punched Evan hard in the jaw.

Evan stumbled and fell against the side of the rock. He put a hand to his face, looking dumbfounded at Charlie who sat perched in a squat position, looking down at him from the top of the hole.

"He's nay a ghost because he's nay bloody dead!" Charlie said sternly to Evan. "Now, get yer arse up here and help me, before I hit ye again."

Evan shook his head slightly and stood up to help Charlie, wondering to himself why his hands had suddenly stopped shaking.

They had no idea what to do for Grant. He remained unconscious except for the odd strangled moan and twitching of a limb. Having no clean water, they rubbed moisture over his lips from the ground, then ripped up the remains of Grant's shirt, dipped them in the freezing puddles and laid them over the fresh burns that covered his entire left side. He could obviously feel some pain because he seemed to fight against his unconscious state when a fresh frigid cloth was laid atop a burned area. Finally, when they finished tending to him as much as they could, they laid the plaid back over him, this time leaving his face exposed.

"What do we do with him? We need to get him clear of this place," Charlie said, thinking aloud.

"He spoke of his late father being a fairly notable merchant, correct?" Evan suggested.

"Aye, I seem to recall him saying something of the sort."

"Well, the only thing I can think of is to take him to the sea, explain who his father was and hope to God someone respected his father enough to take him aboard their boat and drop him in France, or the colonies—anywhere but here." Evan shrugged his shoulders helplessly. "I dinna think we have another option."

"I am not sure that he will make it much longer, Evan. I mean, look at him. He's so badly damaged and who knows whether he will ever wake up again." Charlie squatted down and gently patted Grant's shoulder.

"All we can do is try our best to give him a chance, lad," Evan squatted down across from Charlie, over Grants body, "and pray that's enough."

Chapter 26

He was being rocked. Side to side. Side to side. He was warm and oddly comforted by the motion. He felt like an infant swaddled tightly and pressed to his mother's chest as she rocked him softly to sleep. How did he know what that felt like? Did his mother have the chance to rock him? Or had she been too ill to cradle him after his birth before succumbing to the fever that took her? No, somehow, he knew she had held him, had stroked his soft fat cheek, examined his fine features, and saw a little of herself and his father. He felt his mother with him now, comforting, loving. He must be dead, then. Surely, he would fully awaken in heaven soon and see his mother again, embracing her and showing her the man he had become. He relaxed his body thinking of what he would tell her and what she would think of him. He embraced the darkness and no longer felt the rocking.

The swaying feeling was back. This time, it did not feel like a gentle mother's rocking but a sickening agitation that made him feel dizzy and nauseous. It suddenly struck him that if he was nauseous and dizzy, then he could not be dead, could he? Surely, once in heaven one does not feel earthly illnesses. No, he was definitely not dead. The more he started to realize his reality, the more pain he began to appreciate. Every struggled breath seemed to bring the pain on more intensely. He did not dare try and open his eyes. He scrunched up his face against the intense agony of his body. It seems that his head was aching as well but that was manageable compared to the fiery raw pain of his body. He groaned, he was not sure whether he had made a noise or whether it was only in his head. He felt something touch his chin, then a metal object thrust past his lips with some sort of bitter liquid on it. Weak and confused, he could not decide whether he should object to the random ministrations—he doubted he could have, even if he wanted to. On the third time, the liquid entered his mouth. His head began to spin once more, and he felt like he was sinking and floating at the same time. *Strange*, he thought before fading away once again.

Acadia, Late June, 1746

The slamming of the kitchen door and the pounding of footsteps in the kitchen woke Simon Cassidy with a start and had him pouncing out of bed quicker than he thought his old bones were capable of. His wife, Meghan, sat bolt upright and clung to the bedclothes, looking around violently in the dim moonlight of their small bedroom, and confirming his suspicions that he had not been hearing things. He put a slightly shaking hand up to shush her before she spoke and grabbed the small but reassuring fire iron from the hearth. Silently and quickly, he reached the bedroom door and whipped it open, surging to the top of the stairs. As he stopped at the top of the staircase, with the fire iron raised into striking position, his two oldest sons appeared at the bottom of the steps, their sweat a visible sheen in the darkness. Lowering the makeshift weapon, he hurried down the stairs, realizing that his wife was tentatively following behind him.

"What in God's name...? When did you dock? Why did you not send word?" Simon roared, surprising even himself. Obviously, the mix of sleep and adrenaline was wearing off. "Is this any way to enter the house? At this hour?" He had reached the foot of the stairs where his two sons stood. He reached out to hug them both.

"Father, Mother, you'll need to come. Please, we need your help," their eldest, Simon, said firmly. Simon Cassidy II had always been the calm child. He was sweet, with a nature to please everyone. Even in adulthood, he rarely caused controversy and was always especially polite and respectful to his parents. Hearing his tone, his parents hurried to follow him.

Their second son, Sean, was already striding back to the front door. As they hurried outside, Meghan saw them coming down the path leading to the house as she folded her arms against the cool spring night. It was little wonder that Simon and Sean were able to reach the house first to wake her and their father. The men coming down the path seemed to be carrying something large, awkward and heavy, judging by the sounds of their grunts and curses. The package swung only slightly above the ground in what she assumed to be a hammock. Something between a groan and a bellow split through the night air, seeming to silence anything else that might have been making a noise. Her hand shot out for her husband's arm, and her fingers squeezed it tightly. Whatever the noise was, it had encouraged the men to move quicker, and they swiftly but clumsily approached the front door of the house.

Simon Sr. had, with Sean, already run out to help the men maneuver into the house. Hearing a quieter whimper emerge from the hammock as it was hauled passed her into the kitchen, Meghan turned to Sean. "Ride for the healer." His mother touched his unshaven face with the palm of her hand. Sean turned on his heel and took off to the barn at a jog.

She turned and hurried through the front door of her house, with her nightgown swishing the dirt path.

Chapter 27

Young Simon was quickly stoking the fire and lighting the lamps. The small house was now bright compared to the dark night outside. The men had already placed their cargo on the kitchen table. The hammock had been opened like a fresh pea pod revealing a thin and badly injured man. It seemed as if the bodies in the kitchen had all taken a breath of air as the hammock was spread open and no one had seemed to let the breath back out. One man, whom Meghan did not recognize, was standing holding her wooden vase of wild flowers that had been sitting on the table and was staring pityingly at the prone body splayed in front of him.

"Well, you can put those down over there," she said sternly into the silence, pointing her finger toward the vase, then at the windowsill behind the flower man. Her statement seemed to break the trance and all at once, people were explaining, questioning, fetching water, ripping clean replacement bandages, and creating a crowded chaos.

Looking around to fully take in the scene of bustling bodies in her small kitchen, she knew where she needed to be and walked over to the man on her table. Having no healing skills other than removing splinters and kissing scrapes and bruises, she said a quick prayer of thanks that she had sent Sean for the healer. She pulled a wooden stool up to the side of the table, grabbed a hold of the man's very large, seemingly unhurt right hand, and squeezed. He turned his head toward her and blinked painfully. His dirty brown hair fell into his face. She smoothed it back gently.

"Hello," she whispered. "You are safe, the healer is coming and I am here with you."

The man closed his eyes tight and a single tear slid down his cheek onto the wooden boards of the old table. She wiped it away inconspicuously with the sleeve of her nightclothes and moved her other hand to the man's good hand, which twitched inside her grasp.

The Following Morning

He cracked one of his eyes open. The world around him seemed to be still—this was a start. A momentary sense of panic swept over him as he looked around and recognized nothing. He could not remember where he was nor how he got there. Where were his friends? He remembered a round face in front of him, with wrinkles, a sweet smile, and wisps of grey hair straying from a braid. He remembered the braid swinging when the face left his vision. It was then he closed his eyes.

His body felt surreal. It did not feel like it belonged to him. He was weak. He tried lifting his arms but could not manage to do so. The sense of panic was rising. He managed to lift his head a few inches and glance down at his body. It was covered by a clean white sheet pulled up to his chin. He could feel the left side of his body was somehow different to the right. It felt tight, itchy in a few places and very painful in a few others. He did not need to move to feel these sensations. *Odd*, he thought. His head felt cloudy. He had a throbbing ache behind his eyes, and his mind seemed clouded with a dense fog he was unable to lift. He remembered being very cold and very hungry, waiting in the snow with Charlie and Robbie. Evan had gone somewhere...

"Oh! You're awake. Good morning, you look..." The lady with the braid had come back, startling him. Now, her braid was tied into a tight bun on the back of her head. She wore a dark grey dress and smiled sweetly at him. She had dark smudges under her eyes. She looked weary.

"Who..." Grant tried to speak but it came out as a soft crackling whisper. He coughed and drank some water, which the braided woman was gently pressing to his lips. His throat hurt. He tried again. "Who..."

"Hush," she silenced him by pouring more water into his mouth, almost making him choke further. "I am Mrs. Meghan Cassidy. We met last night but I fear we did not get to exchange names or pleasantries." She smiled again.

Grant opened his mouth to ask another question but was silenced by a hand raised in the air by Mrs. Cassidy.

"I do not doubt that you have a lot of questions, and I will do my best to answer what I can, but it is probably best you let your voice rest and just sip the water that I give you." She was firm but sweet, in a mothering kind of way.

Grant nodded and took another sip as the cup was moved toward his mouth.

"You were brought here last night, well, I should say in the early hours of this morning, by my two oldest boys, Simon and Sean. It seems you were aboard a ship with them for almost two months' time. My son, Simon, is the captain of his father's old merchant boat *The Cassidy*. That is what you safely sailed on from Scotland to the colonies. You are in New France now— Acadia to be more precise."

Grant choked, coughed and wheezed. Tears rolled down his cheeks, his lungs burned, and his head throbbed. He closed his eyes in surrender. Two months? The colonies? He tried to quell the increasing panic.

"Goodness me, do you want me to continue?" Meghan Cassidy was helpfully wiping his streaming eyes and offering more sips of water. Her voice sounded nervous.

"I canna... remember... ship," Grant choked out. He opened his eyes and looked directly into the concerned but caring brown eyes of the elderly woman staring down at him. She nodded knowingly.

"You wouldn't, my dear. From what my sons have told me, you were consistently given doses of something every time you awoke, likely laudanum but I do not know for certain. It was for the pain, you see," she waved a hand gesturing at the sheet covering his body. "You were kept unconscious for the entire voyage."

A man who looked to be about twenty knocked twice and poked his head into the door. His dark hair was loose and hung around his shoulders.

"Did you want help sitting him up now, Mom, seeing as he's awake?" the head asked.

"Not just at this moment, Sean. I have not told him everything yet. I will call you back soon enough." She smiled at her son and back at Grant, as the head disappeared back through the crack and shut the door.

"That was my son, Sean. I am sorry for not making proper introductions but I figured you would be overwhelmed at the moment." She watched the man nod his head slightly and try to smile at her. "Well, where were we? Oh, yes! The fact that you were drugged for so long explains why you cannot move your limbs or body yet. You have not had to use any muscle for weeks. Now, in terms of your wounds..." She trailed off and scowled slightly.

"Please... it's alright," Grant whispered badly. A cup was once again pressed to his mouth. He swallowed and tried to prepare himself for whatever he was about to hear. By the pitying look he saw on Mrs. Cassidy's face, it was nay going to be pleasant.

Meghan took his hand in her own. "The men who brought you to safety—Simon can tell you what he knows of them later—said that you had quite a terrible wound on your head. Also, you have severe burns to the entire left side of your body. Apparently, everyone thought you were going to die. The ship's surgeon gave you the drugs so you would not die in pain, but you kept breathing. Each time they would check, you were still alive. Finally, after about a week of you continuing to live—thank the Lord—the ship's surgeon tried to do what he could for your burns." Meghan took a sip of the water herself and watched Grant's face worriedly for any reaction. "It might be a small comfort for you to know that your face did not seem to obtain any real damage. The boys said you had no hair at all on your face when they first saw you but it is not overtly marked, like the rest of you," she added and patted his hand softly.

Grant's face had remained unchanged through her telling. The fog he thought was lifting earlier seemed to have settled into an ominous haze inside his head. He did not know what to make of this news and right now, he was not sure he cared. He began to retreat to the safety of sleep. He felt the old woman rise and heard her walk to the door. He should have said something but instead, kept his eyes tightly closed and let the strange, frightening and harsh reality of wakefulness fade into sleep.

Chapter 28

Sean came into the room a few days later to help Grant sit up. His mother came fluttering through the door after him, carrying a tray with buttered biscuits and a jar of red jam. Sean exchanged a few polite words as he hoisted him into a sitting position. Surprisingly, Grant was able to wiggle his legs a tiny bit to aid in the process this time. Sean seemed slightly uneasy and left with a nod of the head in both Grant's and his mother's direction. Grant gave Meghan a confused and slightly concerned look.

"I will just give you some privacy." Meghan placed the tray on the dresser. "I will be back shortly and can help you with the food." She walked over to the bed and nonchalantly pulled the sheet all the way off him. "If it were me, I would be wanting to see the full extent of it." She turned and walked out of the room, with the wooden door silently clunking shut behind her.

Grant looked down at his body. This was the first time he could see what was under the white bed sheet. He had not a stitch of clothing on, except for the sheet which had now been removed and a small cloth laid across his crotch. *For dignity*, he imagined. He briefly wondered whether this is what he had arrived wearing but quickly pushed that thought out of his head to deal with more pressing matters. He tucked his chin down and began to scan his naked scar-ravaged body. His left foot and leg were completely devoid of the brown hair that was usually present there. Both the foot and the leg bore an assortment of colours ranging from flesh tones and white to pinks and reds, even dark purples in some areas. His skin was no longer flat and smooth as it had been. Instead, it was raised in some parts and pulled tight in others. The skin on his foot was puckered in various places and looked a bit like the wrinkles of a much older man or that of a dried fruit. Grant scowled. His gaze followed the mangled skin all the way up to his hip. A large herb smelling bandage covered the area between his hips and his oxter. He was not brave enough to find out what was beneath that bandage at the moment. He could feel pain when he breathed in and looking at the rest of the damage, it would not be anything positive under there, so best to leave it till later. His arm was next. There was also an absence of hair on it. It would be safe to assume that underneath the rib bandages, most—if not all—of his chest hair would be gone as well. His arm and hand looked much the same as his feet and leg. The skin was pulled in various directions, and valleys and caverns were present where previously there were none. Colours ranging from pale to fiery red were all over his body. He seemed to be missing the fingernail on his smallest finger completely, with an empty white patch standing out against the dark purple of the rest of his finger. He would have to ask Mrs. Cassidy about his neck as he had no way of examining it, although she had said his face fared well. How could this be, he could not fathom. Perhaps his neck was also better than the rest of his body. He did not dare ask anyone to remove the cloth from his loins. He would wait as he was not sure he could handle anymore stark reality right now anyway. He sighed. He could smell a bird cooking from somewhere close by. He imagined a big, brown, crispy chicken being set on a table before him and smiled. He looked down at his own skin, then thought of the chicken roasting away peacefully in the fire, and started to laugh.

"Christ!" His side hurt when he inhaled but he was unable to stop. He howled with laughter. His eyes filled with tears and his side burned like fire. The ridiculous comparison made the hilarity continue to spill out of him in a series of snorts and whoops, and what could be embarrassingly described as giggles.

Meghan Cassidy poked her head into the door, with her eyes wide and her mouth pursed together like she was certain the man had gone completely mad with shock. "Are you quite alright?" she ventured the question toward the chuckling on the bed.

"Oh, aye," Grant managed to whisper. "I guess ye could say I'm only half as well done as that hen out there!" He barely got the words out before amusement bubbled up again and Grant was laughing and cursing his pain, between hiccups.

Her dark grey eyebrows shot up to her hairline. "Indeed... I'll just leave you a bit then..." Meghan closed the door tightly on the gasps and snickers from inside the room.

After two fortnights had passed, Grant regained some of his strength. He could walk around the small home and often tried to do increasing numbers of laps around the outside, where he could use the wall for stability if he needed to. He had become closer to the Cassidy family and tried to help in any way he could. This 'help' usually consisted of peeling vegetables or husking corn while sitting at the kitchen table. He was still too weak to join the men of the family in the outside work. Meghan Cassidy remained as jovial as ever, telling Grant daily that he did not need to help her and he should be putting his energy into healing. However, that did not seem to stop her, on several occasions, from plunking down a bowl of peas for him to shuck from their pods.

It had been about a week and a half after his arrival that Grant had had the opportunity to speak with Simon. There had been a brief knock on the door and Simon had come into the room at Grant's invitation and sat down on the wooden chair that sat next to Grant. Simon looked different than the rest of the Cassidy family. His hair was dark blonde and had a slight curl to it, and the curls touched his shoulders as he wore his hair loose. His skin was tan and dark brown—no doubt from his occupation. He looked aged and wrinkled, though he was most likely around Grant's age.

"Are you feeling somewhat improved, Mr. Ross?" Simon inquired politely, looking at Grant with a slight tilt to his head. "If I may be bold, you seem to look a mite better than when we carried you onto my boat."

Grant snorted amused at the comment. "Please, call me Grant. I feel myself healing daily with the tender care of yer gracious mother and the generosity of yer father and this family." Grant scanned Simon's face gratefully. "Although, I dinna yet ken the circumstances that brought us together. I have no doubt that ye saved my life, Mr. Cassidy, and I would like to formally thank ye for that."

Simon smiled, leaned forward and putting his elbows on his knees, reached out and gently squeezed Grant's uninjured arm. "It's Simon. Please, think no more on the matter. I acted out of human decency and respect for the brotherhood that we share in the merchant trade."

Grant raised an eyebrow.

"Do you feel well enough today to hear the telling of it or would you rather wait until you have more strength and more rest?" Simon looked down at his hands which were clasped together. His elbows were still on his knees. "It would be amiss for me to tell you that the tale is a happy one."

Grant felt the ball of hope he had been holding onto since he became conscious, drop. He needed to know, regardless. "Aye, I'm well enough, if ye please, Simon. I imagine what ye have to tell me will not get any better with time."

Young Simon sat up in the chair and stretched his legs out in front of him and crossed them at the ankles. He reached into the inside pocket of the brown vest he was wearing and pulled out a flask. He took a long drink of whatever was inside and offered a sip to Grant. At Grant's nod and thanks, he helped pour a sip into the big man's mouth and set the flask down on the small table beside the bed. Raising a darkly tanned arm, he tucked his disheveled curls behind his ears and began to talk.

"My ship, well, she had been docked in Scotland all winter. A fault of my own and a harsh trick played by Mother Nature. We did not manage to beat the winter storms that came early this year and after attempting the trip home in November, we were forced to turn back and winter in a Scottish port at Nairn aboard *The Cassidy*. By God's grace we had a load of cargo that was free of any goods that would spoil, minus of course the food for the crew on our voyage back home." He crossed himself briefly before continuing. "Once the worst of winter had lifted and we could start preparation for our return home, it was already mid-April. We were finally finished loading the stores we had managed to replenish when our paths—yours and mine, that is—crossed.

Scottish Coast, Late April, 1746
Simon sat on a crate wrapped in his cloak. He watched his crew walk up and down the gangplank, rolling barrels and hefting wooden boxes up the ramp and onto the ship. He wondered whether it would be warmer if he just helped them but aware of his station as captain, he remained sitting and continued to supervise the loading from his chilly spot atop the crate. They had been hard pressed to obtain the meager supplies they had gathered and he had hoped it would be enough to last the crew the voyage back home to the colonies. With the Scottish rebels in Nairn until early April, only to then be chased out by the English forces, the town was understandably pillaged of most of its food and supplies. For a few

nights before the English had left town, he heard them speak of a large battle that was to take place not far from their current location. Having been an observer of the condition of both armies as they passed through, he felt a sense of hopelessness for the Scots, who looked like they would not fare well at all.

A few days later, his observations proved correct as English soldiers appeared back in town, hunting Scotsmen and questioning their involvement with the Jacobites, the recent battle and something they referred to as 'the rising'. The town had become quiet. People did not venture out and his own crew only left the ship to visit the local taverns in the evening or warily during the day if they were commanded to scavenge for supplies. Even upon presenting their merchant papers and being clearly from the colonies, his men were questioned by the English soldiers on more than one occasion.

So, as he sat on his increasingly chilly wooden crate, Simon briefly paused to thank God that he was to set sail in the morning. Although the English had only been in town for one or two days, he could only imagine things would be getting a lot worse before they got better, and he did not want his ship, his cargo, his crew, or even himself for that matter to be privy to miseries unveiling.

Chapter 29

The evening prior to embarking on the journey home, the crew of *The Cassidy* visited the local taverns. As always, the men needed drinks and whores before setting sail. Simon laughed heartily at his first mate, Thomas, who was imitating a newer crew member's inability to keep his rations down the first week or so at sea. The poor lad had puked his guts over the side for days while continuing to work, all the while being mercilessly teased by the crew. Simon clapped Thomas on the back who was now bent over theatrically clutching his stomach and bulging his cheeks out, spurred on by gales of laughter from around the room. He moved around the men and out the door to quickly relieve himself behind the tavern and possibly have a brief drag on his pipe before returning to the merrymaking inside.

  He leaned against a wooden fence. The night air was a cool and refreshing change in comparison to the less desirable smells from inside the tavern. He could smell the sea, wood smoke and brief wafts of the soup he had eaten for dinner that must have been mingled in with his cloak. He inhaled deeply on his pipe and closed his eyes, thinking of home.

"Sir! Sir, please. I am begging yer pardon!" a sharp whisper nearly made him jump out of his skin. His hand instinctively went to his knife at his hip. He stood very still.

The owner of the voice must have seen Simon's hand move toward his belt, as a young man quickly stepped out of the shadows beside the tavern wall.

"Please, sir. I mean no harm. None. Please..." The young man was barely visible in the moonless evening. Simon could tell he had his hands stretched out in front of him, showing no weapon. He could also see the outline of a kilt blowing in the cool air under the boy's cloak. He had spoken with a weary desperation.

"If it is not theft, what is it that brings you creeping around in the dark, then?" Simon stepped closer to the back door of the tavern.

"I only need to speak to someone in authority of the ship that's docked in the harbour. I know there are sailors in there," he gestured briefly to the tavern, "I have seen them myself. It's a matter of life and death, sir. I beg ye." The boy took a step closer to Simon and dropped to his knees. "Are ye a man of God, sir?"

"Most fortunately for you, I seem to be." Sensing nothing hostile, Simon removed his hand from his belt and took a few puffs on his pipe, trying to ensure it did not go out. "Why are you inquiring about the ship?"

"I need transport sir... not for myself though, I'd never be so bold as to ask for that. My friend is injured sir... might not make it... we thought he was dead... but he isna. We need help, we being my friend Evan and I...

This may seem a rare request, sir, and I'm doing a piss poor job of explaining, but would ye be able to accompany me to the shed on the other side of the yard?"

The young man was still on his knees in the dark. He had managed to move closer to Simon as he talked, probably unintentionally.

"So, you want me to follow a somewhat nonsensical stranger into a shed, in the dark?" Simon puffed his pipe.

"My name is Charlie, sir. With the almighty God as my witness, no harm will come to ye. Please." The last word came out almost as a whisper.

Simon felt himself believing the man. He did not sense a threat and was slightly curious about this poorly-described injured friend that awaited in the shed.

"Better be quick about it; otherwise, my crew will notice if I am not back soon enough." Simon began to walk toward the unstable looking shed, doubting his sanity with each step.

"Thank you! God bless you!... your crew, sir?" His young shadowy acquaintance was following quickly behind through the grass.

"Yes, Simon Cassidy, captain of the merchant ship *The Cassidy*. It seems that you accosted the right person in the dark, son. Maybe God is on your side after all."

The light inside the shed was nonexistent; unfortunately, the same could not be said for the smell. Simon walked into the small shack behind Charlie and was immediately overcome with a smell he couldn't quite place. It was a sweet, acrid, meaty scent mixed with the smell of cooking coals from a hearth. A thick odour hung in the air and remained in his nostrils.

The young man and another man—whom he assumed to be Evan—were talking quickly and quietly to each other. However, all of Simon's attention was on the black mass that laid on the floor a few feet in front of him. As his eyes became accustomed to the pitch black, the shape became slightly clearer.

"I thank ye kindly for coming, Captain Cassidy."

This voice was different. Lower than Charlie's but filled with the same sense of panic and grief mingled together with exhaustion.

"What has happened to him?" Cassidy gestured to the dark mass on the ground. As if on cue, it gave an unearthly moan.

"Christ Almighty!" Simon stepped back.

Evan and Charlie began to tell Grant's story as much as they could, with the little information they knew. They could only speak to where they found him and how he obtained the burns. They did not need to tell the captain that they were escaped Jacobites as he had almost certainly figured that out on his own by now.

"So, we are asking ye, sir, will ye take him aboard your ship and take him with ye? He has no one here in Scotland and I willna have him die in the hands of the English that have already taken so much from him." Evan finished speaking. His tone was bitter, as the battle was still so fresh.

"Please, believe me when I say that I truly feel terrible that this man has suffered so, but you know as well as I that he probably will not last the night, let alone survive two months at sea." Simon felt his words add to the hopelessness that was already cocooned in the shed.

"It is true that he will likely die, but at least he will die peacefully aboard a ship and not on the run in some godforsaken hideout," Charlie added. "His father was a merchant as well, maybe the feel of the sea once again beneath him will give him fond memories in his passing.

"His father was a merchant? What is this man's name?" Simon had sailed with his own father for many years until his father had retired the captaincy to him, so he knew of all the merchants that sailed similar routes to his own.

"His name is Grant Ross, sir, but I dinna know his sire's given name. All Grant ever said was that his father was a Scot. He knew his father had business in Ireland but also traded as far as the colonies before he died." Evan hoped that he had remembered correctly.

Simon removed his hat and ran a hand through his hair. "His given name was Calder. Calder Ross was an acquaintance of my father, Simon," Simon said quietly to honour the fallen.

There was silence in the scanty shed. The only sound was the laboured, irregular breaths from the floor.

A drunken call from the back door of the tavern pierced the silence like a dagger, making all three men jump.

"Capt'n? Are you there? Are you all right?"

Simon quietly opened the door to the shed and called back loudly. "I am fine, can a man not shit in peace?"

"Oh, yes sir, certainly." The tavern door closed and Simon turned his head back to the two men in the shadows.

"I'll take him aboard. I will meet you back here in an hour's time." He strode out of the shed, carefully closing the decrepit door behind him.

Evan grasped Charlie's hand in the dark shed and they sat down beside their friend. They were too tired to feel the small wave of relief wash over the shed.

Chapter 30

In a little over an hour, a soft *rap* sounded on the door of the shed, followed by a whispered voice. "It is Simon."

Charlie rubbed his eyes wearily, he must have been dozing. He stood up as the shed door creaked open. Simon and a burly man that was slightly shorter than Simon, entered.

"This is my first mate, Weaver, he will be helping us this evening. I would trust him with my life and you are both going to have to trust me." Weaver nodded his head in acknowledgment to both Charlie and Evan.

There was no time to waste with mistrust. "We thank ye both kindly." Evan returned Weaver's nod of greeting.

Dismissing the thanks with a wave and intent on the task at hand, Simon began to explain the method in which they would get Grant aboard *The Cassidy*. He had considered a few options while mulling over ale in the tavern waiting for more citizens to go home to their beds and more of his crew to head either back to the ship or find a woman to pass the evening with. The less distractions, the better. Charlie, Evan and Grant were being hunted by the English soldiers, so he had to take that into consideration with his plan.

"I have brought an old blanket from the tavern. That cloth he is wrapped in is a target for the English," pointing to the plaid. "We will need to transfer him onto the woolen blanket and if anyone stops us, we will tell them a crew member was injured recently and has been convalescing at a town person's home but since we set sail with the dawn tomorrow, he is being moved back to the ship." Simon pulled a large chunk of bread and a small piece of cheese from his pocket.

"I managed to obtain this for you. It is not much but I did not want to look suspicious." He handed the cheese and bread to Charlie and Evan.

"We've brought this too." Weaver removed his canteen and set it on the floor at Evan's feet.

"May God bless you both," Charlie whispered, "for everything."

Simon took Charlie's outstretched hand and shook it firmly.

"Shall we roll him onto the blanket then?" Evan laid the blanket Simon had brought out on the floor beside Grant. It took all four men to roll Grant over as delicately as possible, trying not to touch the worst of his wounds. Although he moaned with each movement, he did not wake. With the grey woolen blanket wrapped around him, Weaver hoisted the side by his feet while Simon hoisted the side by Grant's head so he swung between them like a hammock. Both men were already grunting and swearing softly with the effort of lifting Grant's unconscious weight.

"He's a big'un," Weaver's voice grunted as he strained.

"Charlie and I are able to carry him, if ye'll just lead the way to the ship, sir." Evan stepped forward, moving to take the burden from Simon.

"You two need to stay here for a few more hours and leave shortly before dawn. The city is crawling with Englishmen as you probably well know," Simon said directly to Evan.

"We'll no be leaving him! I canna until I've seen him safely aboard the ship." Charlie looked at Evan, his eyes wide.

"You can and you must. Would he want you both risking your lives on his behalf more than you have already? We will get him to the ship." Simon's tone was final and somehow believable.

Evan thought it was easy to picture this man as a leader. He trusted him to keep his word. Charlie looked at Evan and seeing his gentle nod, watched the two men walk out the shed door laden with the weight of his friend.

Acadia, June, 1746

"So, I am sad to have to tell you that after I left that shed, I have no idea as to the whereabouts or well-being of your friends. I took what I still believe to have been the proper action and left them in the safety of the shed after Weaver and I took you." Simon finished the story and took a long swig from the flask sitting on the table at Grant's bedside.

Grant raised his eyes to meet Simon's. "I owe ye my life and I have nothing I can give ye that would ever be good enough. I swear to ye though, I will try and pay ye back."

Simon smiled, it softened his hard features considerably. He got up from the chair and arched his back with a groan. "I'll give you some time to absorb all you have learned. Everything seems to feel a bit clearer after a rest."

"Aye, I think I might need one." Grant shimmied his body down as Simon helped adjust the pillow behind him.

Grabbing his flask from the table, Simon turned to walk out of the room. His step was light on the wooden floor boards. Grant spoke from the bed.

"You're sure there were only the two men in the shed with me? Nay a third? A man named Robbie?" Grant knew the answer to the question before Simon had time to turn around.

"It was only the two of them, Evan and Charlie. I am sorry, Grant." Simon left the room, closing the door behind him. Grant heard him speak quietly to his mother about leaving Grant to himself for a while. Grant, relieved no one else would be coming in for a bit, let a tear slide down his cheek. He closed his eyes, said a prayer for Charlie and Evan and said goodbye to Robbie.

"Rest in peace, lad. May yer soul not wander or tarry on this earthly plain but may the angels carry ye home." He smiled. His father had said that at a friend's funeral when he was a little child. He did not think he had paid enough attention to have committed it to memory. He drifted to sleep thinking about family, thankfulness and loss.

It was not until the second month of being at the Cassidy's home that Grant felt he had almost regained most of his former strength and ability. By this time, it was already the end of August and while young Simon and Sean were gone working before the winter kept them docked, Grant was able to help the older Simon with the outside chores. It seemed he improved a little bit more with every passing day. He was sitting with Meghan and Simon for a late dinner after hauling rocks to repair a hole the Cassidy's boar had made in its enclosure, when he first told them of his plan to work as a blacksmith in the colonies.

"We will be sad to see you go when you decide it's time, Grant." Meghan put her hand on his and squeezed tightly. "I've grown a bit fond of you over the months," she laughed.

"You are in no rush to leave, I hope? There is no reason not to stay the winter here with us," Simon added, wiping his upper lip on his sleeve, and thus earning him an irritated scowl from Meghan.

"I think I will be leaving as soon as I might find some steady work. I have long overstayed my welcome, seeing as I am an uninvited occupant that was thrust into your laps." Grant smiled at Meghan who had begun to open her mouth to object. "I know you two do not see me that way, and I am grateful for it. All of ye have treated me as a dear friend and I will be thankful for your friendship every single day for the rest of my life."

"Well, if you are intent on going, I will make some inquiries for you with some friends of mine to see if they have heard of what the blacksmith situation is in neighbouring towns." Simon said as he cut into his potato and forked a big spoonful into his mouth.

"That would be very kind of ye," Grant said after swallowing his own mouthful.

"Of course, we will expect to have you come back and see us every now and then." Meghan's chair scraped as she stood up to bring over the biscuits with honey, she had made fresh for dessert.

"Oh, aye, to be sure." Grant nodded enthusiastically. He chuckled internally at the motherly tone in which she had made that last statement seem like a question; when in reality, she left no question about it.

They spent the rest of the dinner discussing the contents of a letter from Meghan's sister that had arrived earlier that day. Grant listened politely and watched the couple bicker playfully about one thing or another. He would truly miss this when it came time to move on.

Chapter 31

"So, I left there about a month later and made my way down here. Simon had found out that the man who had been working in this area moved south with his family and the next closest blacksmith was a full day's ride away and understandably, not that reliable." He shifted his back against the armchair. "I had done the odd job for a few neighboring farms after I recovered and earned enough money to pay for a room until I could work enough to obtain somewhere permanent." He gestured with one hand to the walls around him.

"Do you see them often?" Ada turned her head backwards to look at Grant.

"Oh, aye. I try to go back at least twice a year. Three times if I'm lucky. It's only a three-day ride in good weather, so it's none too bad to travel." Grant kissed Ada gently on the cheek. He shifted uncomfortably.

"I dinna ken if it is the same for you, lass, but my arse is completely numb from sitting so long on this floor. Shift over so I can get up, aye?" Grant laughed as Ada scooted her bum forward and closer to the fire. He rose, stretched his clasped hands over his head, with his arms unable to fully stretch because of the ceiling.

Several knuckles popped as he pressed his hands out in front of him instead.

Ada stood up and brushed her skirt down. She wished she had more to wear then this one gown or Grant's old breeches.

"Grant?" Ada looked at him as he took another swig from his cup. He was imposingly handsome. She watched as his large hand set the cup down on the table and rubbed his chin. She heard the faint scraping of unshaven whiskers. His hair was untied and hung messily above his shoulders. He noticed her watching him and smiled broadly. Had she been a younger, giddier woman, her knees might have felt weak.

"Aye, my wee fairy?" He stepped toward her.

"Thank you for telling me." She put her hand on his cheek.

Grant put his hand over her own and turning his face slightly, gave her a kiss on the palm.

Her palm tingled from his raspy cheek. Ada regarded his soft and gentle expression. She was not used to a man eyeing her with anything but contempt. She felt able to be herself, to be more like she used to be. She felt more confident. She moved her hand from his cheek and placed it on his chest where he had left the neck of his shirt open. She caressed his skin with her fingertip.

"I think I'd like it very much if you would take me to bed, Mr. Ross." She lifted her eyes from the opening of his shirt and raised an eyebrow.

Grant said nothing. His masculine fingers went to the laces on the front of her dress. He held her gaze trance-like as he skillfully undid her gown. He moved his hands to the sides of her neck, slid them down to her collarbone and onto her shoulders, then pushed the sleeves of her dress down her arms as his hands traveled the same path. The top half of her dress slid down to her waist where it stopped, hanging off her hips and behind. Still holding her eyes with his own, he slid his hand up her body from her waist and paused to cup her full breast. She gasped and caught her bottom lip in her teeth as he kneaded her breast in his hand.

He watched her teeth release the shiny pink lip from their grasp. He wanted to feel her against him, feel that same lip drag along his skin. Liberating her breast from his hand, he stepped back and pulled his shirt over his head, throwing it onto the armchair by the fire. Then, she was on him, her arms thrown around his neck and her soft chest crushed hard against his own. She kissed him generously, exploring his mouth with the tip of her tongue. He made a masculine urging sound with his throat and met his tongue with hers. His hands slid down her back and under her dress. She felt him cup her backside and squeeze thoroughly with both hands. The feeling was a mixture of a stinging pinching pain and a glorious wave of pleasure. She tipped her pelvis forward against him and felt his solid manhood rubbing against her belly through his pants. She ground herself wantonly against him. Encouraged by his sharp inhale, she kissed the side of his neck, and standing on her toes, bit his earlobe.

His hands shot immediately to her waist, he spun her away so her back was facing his body. He licked up the back of her neck and underneath her hair while he quickly undid the top of her skirt. She felt her nipples go hard and her body ripple with goose flesh as he continued to softly kiss her nape. With one quick jerk, Grant pulled her skirt over her hips and left it in a heap around her ankles. He pulled her immediately back against him and ran his right hand down the front of her stomach, over her pelvis and into the slippery crevice between her legs. His other hand slid up her body in the opposite direction onto her breast, grasping soundly. By reaction, she thrust back against him, forcing her warm softness further into his hand.

She titled her head back to look at him. He smirked roguishly and bent to kiss her.

"Please, Lord, yes... yes." She could feel her cheeks starting to burn. She had no coherent thought other than the wonderful things Grant was doing between her legs.

"I need ye very badly, Ada," Grant whispered exquisitely in her ear as his hand retreated from her.

She turned around to face him. He was already undoing the lace fly of his breeches. Feeling reckless and empowered, she stepped out of the dress around her ankles. She took a step back. Grant watched her, his large fingers still working his laces. She slowly bent over and pulled her woolen stockings as far up as they could go, which ended up being slightly above her knees. She stood upright.

Grant froze, his thumbs inside the waist of his breeches, ready to pull them down. He watched her with an expression of admiration and surprise.

Ada stepped back again, slowly making her way to the bed. She sat down on the edge of the bedclothes and scooted herself back. Supporting herself upright on her arms and bending her knees up in front of her, she slowly separated her legs.

"Fucking hell," Grant managed to emit as he released the breath he was not aware he was holding. He shoved his breeches violently down his legs and kicked them off. His body could not move fast enough as his eyes traced every very visible inch of Ada's seductive form.

"You can have me, Grant." Ada smiled at his look of hunger.

He closed the few steps between them and was quickly on her, with her legs wrapped around his back. He slowly entered her, listening to her gasp his name and feeling her pleasing tightness. As he began to move within her, his world moved around him and he knew that nothing could ever be the same.

They had fallen asleep late, lying on their backs side by side. Just as Ada felt herself on the brink of sleep, Grant's hand slid over and intertwined his fingers with her own. There was no sexual implication in his gesture, he was merely assuring her he was there.

A few short hours later, they were startled out of sleep by the sound of purposeful knocking on the door.

Grant rolled himself onto one elbow, scrubbing a hand over his face. "What in Christ?"

The knocking sounded again, starting to sound more like thumping than polite knocking.

"Mr. Ross, we would like to speak with you," a voice appealed from the other side of the wooden door. "It is a matter of some importance."

Ada stared wide-eyed at Grant, the blanket pulled up to her chin. "They know, Grant. They know!" Ada's frantic whispers were making Grant's stomach clench.

"MR. ROSS!" The pounding continued.

"Aye, I am just now out of bed. Ye'll give me a blessed minute to put on some clothes!" Grant yelled back at the wooden door. The hammering ceased.

Grant pointed to Ada and then gestured to the corner behind the front door. Swinging the front door open would hide her from sight as long as they did not come inside and close the door. She quickly gathered one of the blankets around her and tiptoed to the corner. Grant grabbed her arm on her way past.

He put his mouth up to her ear. "I'll not let them near ye, I swear to God almighty, Ada. Trust me and keep quiet."

It was all Ada could do to keep her hands from shaking as she huddled quietly in her corner behind the door. She barely dared to breathe as Grant finished tying his breeches and strode to the door. He grasped the handle and glanced at Ada, his face was unreadable. He swung the door open.

"Can a man no even have a lie in on the day of the Lord? It's barely dawn!" Grant spoke to the gentlemen accusingly. The sky had just started to streak pink and orange playing contrast with the greyish brown frost-hardened muddy ground.

"We are sorry to interrupt you on a Sunday, Mr. Ross, but we are here on important business to be sure." The two men were obviously servants from the look of their dress. They also looked cold and tired, like they had been working all night. They probably expected

Grant to invite them inside while they talked. *They had a better chance of the ground catching fire where they stood,* Grant thought impatiently.

The two stood there staring at Grant. Grant stared back. Finally, deducing they were not gaining an invitation into the smoky warmth of the cottage, the shorter fellow sighed and began to speak.

"We have been hired on behalf of the Watershaw house to inquire with every homestead we come across as to whether anyone has seen or heard anything about Mrs. Watershaw's whereabouts."

"I have heard about Mr. Watershaw's recent accident. I assumed Mrs. Watershaw would be at home at her husband's side, is she no?" Grant asked keeping his face neutral.

"It seems that the night of the accident she vanished, and a horse was gone from the stable as well."

Grant swallowed, his stomach tightened and his hand gripped the door, praying no one noticed the white knuckles grasping the handle. He had forgotten about the bloody horse. Ada's mare was still outside, not yet put away in the barn from her night turn out. Grant said a quick prayer that they would not think twice about the extra horse in his field, let alone recognize Gypsy.

"I had not heard. I am immensely sorry for the whole situation. Shall I come with you gentlemen and aid in the search? I just need to grab my cloak." Grant gestured to the coat hooks on the wall.

"Oh no, Mr. Ross. Thank you kindly but Mr. Watershaw's man, Robertson, has hired us personally and we will be continuing on our own." One of the men tucked his neck farther into his coat.

"As long as yer sure. I wish ye all the luck finding her. I hope nothing amiss has happened to the lady." Grant furrowed his brow in concern.

"Oh yes, to be sure. Good day, Mr. Ross, sorry to have bothered you." The men moved to their horses standing out front.

"No bother at all. Godspeed!" Grant waved confidently as the men mounted, then he shut and locked the door behind him.

"Holy Christ," he sighed as he leaned his back against the large wooden door and turned toward Ada.

Chapter 32

The incident at the door had once again sobered both Ada and Grant to the situation they were in. The pleasing haze of last night's love-making had been overtaken by a worm of fear that had inched its way into Grant's brain and chilled his body as much as the morning ride should have. As soon as the two men had ridden away, Grant ran outside and put Gypsy into the stall in the barn. He threw her some hay and as he leaned briefly on the stall door watching the dust and bits of hay float in the streams of sunlight, he pondered the impossibility of what he had to do. It was now clearer than ever that it was unsafe for Ada to stay with him. But each time they made love and every time she looked at him with such trust in her eyes, his heart grew fuller and he prayed he would have the strength to part with her when the time came.

   He had needed to ride to the coast to pick up some iron bar stock. He was running low on thicker sizes that made shoes for the heavy farming horses. He had been told that a merchant ship had just docked a few nights prior and he figured this might be his last chance to stock up before winter. The day was chilly but the sun was promising a warmer afternoon. He thought he would partake in some lunch at a local tavern after purchasing his supplies and maybe enjoy the ride back home in the warmer afternoon. He also needed to think and clear his head. When had his life become so complicated? He slapped Duff softly on the side of his neck as they ambled along, the horse twitched his furry ears in response. For as long as he could remember, he loved the feel of a horse under him. The methodical swaying soothed him as his horse sauntered along a smooth dirt path. He had no need for haste. Ada had insisted she would be fine and planned to read by the fire, even though the only books Grant owned were a tiny weathered bible, which had been his mother's, and a copy of *A Farriers New Guide,* a book on anatomy, illness and disease in horses—quality reading material to be sure. Grant was certain she would have selected the horse guide. She was probably reading about the various diseases while yearning to run back and forth to the barn to make sure Gypsy was not exhibiting any of the symptoms.

The pair ambled into town shortly before midday. Grant rode directly to the front of the small hardware and ironmonger shop and dismounted smoothly, his boots crunching the newly thawed dirt as he landed. He looped Duff's reins over the hitching post, for formality more than anything as Duff would not stray without him. He gave the geldings neck a scratch under his mane and set off into the shop. A small bell clinked above his head as he ducked to enter the shop.

"Good day to you, can I help you with anything?" With the sound of the bell, the shopkeeper popped out from behind the counter where he was obviously crouching down to attend to something.

"Aye, I certainly hope so. I am here for some iron bars. I am low on the thicker ones and with the winter coming, I'll need to replenish my stock. I had word that a merchant ship arrived from England not a few days past?" Grant tilted his head, watching the man as he nodded along to his words.

"Right you are, son, it came in..." The man rolled his eyes to the ceiling, considering, "...came in, just three days ago, in the evening. I got my merchandise from the ship just yesterday afternoon. So, you came at the right time." The man walked out from behind the counter and gestured for Grant to follow him. They walked to the back of the shop where there were many different sizes of iron bars tied in bundles, bound with leather straps and leaning against the back wall.

As Grant selected what he needed, the shopkeeper wandered back to his counter.

"If you need any assistance, just give a call."

"I will do that, thank you." Grant had gathered up the iron he needed and carried it over to the counter a few minutes later.

"Would it be too much of a bother to pick this up on my way out of town? I plan on grabbing a wee bite at the tavern and I have a bit more shopping to attend to." Grant held the bars as the shopkeeper tied a new strip of leather around them.

"Certainly, I will keep them behind the counter for you. Please take your time. What do you do with the iron, if you don't mind me asking?"

"Not at all, I am a blacksmith. It's for shoes and the like." Grant smiled.

"Ah, a useful profession indeed." Will you be needing anything else?" The gentlemen leaned the iron bundle against the wall behind the counter.

"As a matter of fact, yes. With my home and business not close to here, I fear I have poor knowledge of this port. Would you be able to direct me to a shop where I might be able to purchase some material for sewing?" Grant looked sheepishly at the shopkeeper who had raised one eyebrow in a questioning look. "It is for my mother; she is confined to bed and cannot get out to buy her own necessities."

"Of course, how terrible it must be for her." The shopkeeper clicked his tongue and shook his head briefly in sympathy. "If you go down the main street in town and take a left, there is a trading post that sells quite a few different fabrics. I am sure they will have what your mother requires."

"Thank ye kindly, ye have been most helpful." Grant payed the shopkeeper, shook his hand firmly and walked out squinting as the sun shone into his eyes, which were now accustomed to the dimness of the shop. He started his walk in the direction he had been told.

Grant had other reasons for riding to this specific port town, which was much further from the town from which he usually purchased iron bar stock: he did not want people to recognize him. He had planned on surprising Ada with some material so she could do some sewing while he was away during the days. Perhaps she could make herself some new clothes, seeing how she only had the one gown. He had thought about going to

Mr. Sims shop in town but had realized it would only raise suspicions as people knew he had no female relatives. Here, however, was safe to do so. He was not relishing the thought of buying fabric and not knowing what type to buy, what colours, or how much he needed, but there was nothing to be done about that.

Less than half of an hour later, Grant headed back toward Duff, his arms wrapped around three different types of material, each prettier than the last. He smiled as he pictured them against Ada's skin. The woman selling the fabrics also managed to sell him one length of blue ribbon and two lengths of lace. She had certainly seen him coming. He chuckled to himself, excited with his purchase and looking forward to returning home and watching Ada open it. When he reached Duff, he tucked the surprise into his saddle bags and buckled them up. His stomach gave an offensively loud growl. He smacked Duff on the rump, told him he would be back soon and turned back up the street toward the tavern for some food.

The tavern was nearly empty apart from a few blokes who, from what Grant could assume, probably rarely left. The place seemed pleasant enough. It was overfilled with chairs, stools and tables and Grant had a hard time imagining if the place was ever full. The place had the typical odour one would associate with a tavern—a mix of old and new food, ale, and unwashed humans. Busy port towns always seemed worse because of the people arriving from months at sea and making the tavern their first stop. It always seemed to take a bit of time to acclimatize his nose to the smell of a tavern, and if not a bit of time than a bit of drink. Grant sat down on one of the higher stools by the bar. A plump older woman with very few teeth plunked his requested ale down in front of him and smiled brightly as she went to grab his plate of lunch, which today happened to be a fish chowder with bread for dipping.

His food had just been delivered when the tavern door lurched open and a group of men, about six or seven, strolled into the room and sat down. Some sat at a table together, some by the fireplace and one on a stool at the bar beside Grant. From the salt stains on their clothes, these men were clearly sailors. Their faces were burned to a dark brown colour by the sun, leaving them with calloused skin that was aged and worn, like leather. The older man beside him scratched at the back of his head absentmindedly.

"I was wondering when I would see anyone off that ship. You have been docked for three days, and not one of you has come in!" the barwoman said.

"Well, trust me, missus," the man beside Grant replied in an untraceable British accent, "we'd a been on land the first night had we been allowed. Some of the crew have took feverish just before we docked and the captain ordered everyone to stay aboard." He swigged his ale purposefully and wiped his mouth on his sleeve. "Bloody hogwash if yer asking me... most of us are fit as a fiddle. Right lads?"

The group of sailors gave a cheer and pounded the wooden tables, relieved to have been released from the confines of the ship that Grant overheard was called *The Mary Victoria.*

"Well, if they let you out, where are all the rest of you?" The woman questioned as she ladled out bowls of chowder, giving one to the man at the bar and tucking his coin into her apron.

"Oh, Christ, missus, we'd all still be on that boat had we not taken matters into our own hands. The captain is in his cabin all day working on some correspondence or the like. We just walked right down the gangplank and strolled over here, quick as you like." He smiled brightly, revealing several black rimmed teeth and took a large sniff of the bowl in front of him. He shut his eyes and smiled dreamily. "We will have a few drinks, eat our fill and be back on the boat before anyone notices we left. It happens all the time, missus," he nodded assuredly. He took another large sniff of his soup. This time sneezing explosively into his hands. He turned to look at Grant.

"Pardon me, mate," he said politely, referring to the sneeze. "Jesus, you're a big lad, aren't you? What ship are you on?" He spooned a bite of chowder into his mouth.

"I'm only in town for the day, actually, nay from a ship at all," Grant replied, sipping his own ale.

"Ah, a Scot! What is it that you do then? The name's Clive." He stuck out his hand to Grant.

"It is good to meet ye, Clive. I am Grant Ross. I am a blacksmith by trade." He took the man's extended hand and shook it firmly. Picking up his bread, he swirled it in the chowder to soften the crust and took a large salty bite.

"A blacksmith, you say? I never had the skill for working with my hands. I reckon that the only thing I was ever good at was ship work." Clive shrugged his shoulders and downed the last swig of his ale. "It never bothered me none, I can't imagine living my life on dry land. I love the feel of the ocean under my feet, I do." He coughed into a dirty handkerchief and shoved it back in his trousers.

Grant laughed ironically. "My father was a merchant and I had no desire for that line of work, it is a good thing some like it and some dinna, I suppose."

"Amen to that, mate." Clive clapped Grant on the shoulder. He picked up his chowder bowl in both hands like a cup and drank the rest of his meal hurriedly. He stood up, the stool legs scraping the wooden floor.

"Are you off then?" The barwoman had reappeared with the sound of moving furniture. "Make sure you tell the others to come down for a drink once you lot get excused from the ship!" She waved and bustled back into the back room.

"It was nice to meet ye." Grant shook Clive's hand again in farewell.

"And yourself. Enjoy the day." Clive turned and joined the other crew from the ship, who now began to all stand and stretch after finishing their meals in haste to get back to the boat unnoticed.

Grant returned home that evening just as the sun had begun its descent into a purple and red sky. He called out to make sure Ada knew it was him and took Duff into the barn. He unsaddled him and brushed him down before letting both him and Gypsy out to graze in the pen behind the cabin. Gypsy had whinnied happily at Duff's return, no doubt being bored alone in the barn all day. Grant had brushed her quickly as well before she went out, feeling slightly silly for wanting her to feel special too. His feelings for Ada were obviously projecting onto her horse.

He washed briefly in the trough, shivering as the water trickled down his back. The air was turning colder again. He let himself in the back door. Ada was setting some of the smoked beef he had purchased the day before, along with the carrots and beets she had boiled, on the table. She turned when the door opened and smiled warmly at him. His stomach fluttered and he thought himself childish for the notion. She walked over to him, placed a hand on each of his reddened cheeks and kissed him softly on his lips. She then put her hands around his waist in a hug and laid her cheek on his chest, sighing.

"I missed you." She said it so simply and matter of fact he knew it had to be true.

He put a large hand on the back of her head and kissed the top of her hair. "I missed ye too." He suddenly felt warm.

Chapter 33

The first week Ada had stayed with Grant flew by. She had thanked him so appreciatively for the material he had purchased her that one would have thought it was made of solid gold. He was glad to know she spent her days sewing her new dress instead of being bored nearly to tears waiting around his one room house and unable to go outside while he was gone all day working, often returning past sunset. Their evenings were spent learning about each other, telling stories, sitting by the hearth and more often than not, making love.

They had discussed the plan for when they would leave: in one week's time, on Sunday morning when most of the townspeople would be in church. They would pack up and ride out to a port three days from Grant's house. That way, Ada could get on a ship for the South and Grant could begin the three-day journey back home, which would undoubtedly be the most miserable ride of his life. As necessary as they both knew it was, Ada had cried during their conversation and as Grant had held her against his chest, he felt tears slide down his own cheeks and land in the softness of her hair.

It was near the end of the second week when Ada woke Grant up in the middle of the night with her hand moving slowly down his chest. He stirred awake, nuzzling her neck. She giggled. He liked it when she allowed her playfulness to emerge. Her hand slid lower, he moaned into the darkness. She wrapped her hand around his already very alert cock and began a slow torturous assault of sensations. Now, fully awake, he slid his own hand down to join hers. He covered her hand with his and ceasing the motion, rolled over and skillfully flattened Ada to her back and positioned himself on top of her.

"Unnngghh..." Grant's eyes scrunched shut, pain etched into his features.

"What's happening? Are you all right?" Ada sat up as Grant rolled off her, worry flooding her body.

Grant had flopped back down on the bed with his hands up and the heels of his palms pressed onto his temples.

"Christ, this headache. I had it all day today but it wasna as bad while I was working but now, it hurts something fierce. It goes all the way down to my neck and back."

"You didn't tell me you felt unwell! What can I do?" Ada was already climbing out of bed. "I am going to get you a cold cloth to place over your eyes." Ada felt her way through the darkness to the table. She lit a candle from the embers of the fire and poured water into a bowl from the wooden ewer. She took a scrap of material from the dress she was sewing and placed it in the bowl of water. Wringing all the water out of it, she walked hastily back to Grant and placed it over his closed eyes.

"I dinna eat lunch today," Grant said through clenched teeth. Exhaling deeply, he continued, "I most likely just worked too hard and dinna take proper care of myself. It would no' be the first time." He raised a hand to put pressure on the cloth over his eye sockets.

"Would you like something now? A piece of bread perhaps? Some whisky?" Ada was sitting on the side of the bed, softly stroking Grant's hair.

"Thank you, but God, no. I couldna eat a bite. I feel as my head might roll off my shoulders if I move a muscle." Grant shifted slightly. He let out another groan.

"Perhaps it would feel better if it did?" Ada was trying to lighten the mood. She was worried. In the time she had known Grant, he had never complained about pain, and she had seen him with sizeable cuts and bruises from his work.

"Aye, perhaps. Ye may as well just come back to bed lass, no sense us both being awake. I think this cool cloth is helping. No doubt I will be back to sleep in no time as well." Grant hoped Ada could not tell he was lying through his teeth. There was no way he was going to sleep with this pain tonight. However, he did not want Ada to stay up worrying about him. But the sheer act of talking was making him worse.

As she climbed in beside him, she tried not to jostle the bed any more than necessary. She placed a kiss on Grant's chest and lay back on her pillow.

"You will feel better tomorrow, Grant. I am sure of it." It was not long before Ada had drifted back to sleep.

Ada woke again in the darkness of predawn. She could tell by Grant's breathing that he was not asleep. She stirred gently.

"Ada, would ye please get me some water?" Grant whispered, feeling her wake beside him.

"Of course." She slid out of the bottom of the bed and filled a cup with water from the ewer and came back over to Grant's side. He lifted his head slightly and she helped him take a sip.

Grant slowly laid his head back on the pillow. He was pale and he had dark smudges under his eyes. He obviously had not slept.

"Why did you not wake me? You clearly have had a terrible night." Ada put a hand on his cheek. He was warm to the touch—too warm.

"Aye, well, there is nothing to be done but wait it out. I must have an ague. My head is aching slightly less but my back and joints have replaced the pain in my head. I only felt myself getting chilled not too long ago. I would have woken ye had I have had need of ye. Dinna fash, lass, I'll be right soon enough. I just need to let it run its course." He smiled at her, his eyes scanned up and down her body from his place on the bed. "There is one more thing ye could do though..."

"Anything." She smiled back.

"Put something else on... I can see right through that old shirt of mine and I really dinna have the energy for that kind of excitement right now." He winked at her with smiling eyes, which he promptly shut.

She snorted with mirth. "Well, that is your own fault for looking. Why don't you concentrate on feeling better instead of feeling me?" She blushed as she looked down at the shirt she had been sleeping in. "I was getting dressed anyway, I will have you know. I am going out to tend the horses." She saw him open his eyes and held up a hand to stop him. "... and yes, I will be careful and keep in the barn."

"They can wait until this evening, I'm sure to feel better by then." Grant did not want her outside at all without him there.

"No, they cannot." Ada was slipping his cloak around her. She pulled up the hood, walked over to the bed, and kissed his forehead. "I'll be back as soon as I'm finished. Try to get some sleep." She squeezed his hand and he shut his eyes again. He heard the back door click closed and Duff give a high-pitched whinny from the field at the appearance of life from the cabin.

Ada led the horses into the barn. She had already pitchforked out the stalls from the day before and filled their mangers with hay and their wooden pails with water. Thankfully, Grant had two stalls in his small barn, one for Duff and the other in case he needed it for a customer's horse. The second stall was now occupied by Gypsy. Ada scratched her on the forehead, ruffling her forelock. Duff, with a piece of hay hanging from his mouth, thrust his body against his stall door, craning his head toward Ada. He was jealous of the attention Gypsy was getting.

Ada laughed out loud. "Listen, you two, I need to go back inside and make sure Grant is doing okay. As much as we would all love for me to stand here and dote on you all day, I fear I cannot." Duff neighed in her hand with his velvety lips. She bent her cheek to his head, "I love you too," she whispered and with a final pat on both their necks, she exited the barn ensuring to pull up her hood and check her surroundings before walking the few steps to the back door of the house.

    She creaked the back door open quietly, and upon hearing a gentle snore, closed the door softly behind her, placed the latch across and hung the cloak on one of the iron hooks along the back wall. Taking advantage of the light from the fire, she tiptoed to the big armchair and picked up her sewing basket. She was adding a bit of lace to the sleeves of one of the new dresses she was sewing. She thought about the wonderful surprise this material had been from Grant. She gazed over at him, he seemed to be sleeping soundly. Although she noticed that he had the blankets pulled right up to his chin and the fire was burning high, no sweat shone on his face—that worried her. She hoped he would wake up feeling much better but her gut was telling her the opposite. She shoved that thought to the very back of her head and angrily stabbed at the sleeve of her sewing, accidentally poking her finger. She hissed under her breath and brought the offended digit to her mouth. Sucking the metallic taste of her own blood and cursing her carelessness, she closed her eyes and leaned her head back against the big chair. "Please, just let him be fine." She took a few deep breaths and went back to her sewing, thankful for the constant snoring.

    Grant slept long past the evening meal. Ada had eaten some porridge; she did not want to prepare anything that made a lot of noise while cooking. She had been checking on Grant from time to time throughout the day. He seemed to be getting hotter to the touch. He was fretfully waking now, making small groaning noises and thrashing his feet under the blanket. Ada had little skill in healing as she had never had reason to learn anything but the basic healing arts. She sat down on the bed beside Grant. She put a hand on his shoulder and shook him gently.

"Grant, you need to take some water, you are burning with fever." She shook him a little harder.

He cracked open his eyes. They were bleary and not focusing on her face. She held the cup to his lips and tipped some liquid in. He coughed but managed to swallow it with only a small amount spilling on his shirt. The blankets had slipped down with his thrashing and he began to shake uncontrollably. The house itself was overly hot. Ada had stoked the fire hoping the heat would help Grant break his fever but watching his teeth chatter and his body tremble, she could tell this was clearly not working. Ada wrung her hands as she looked at Grant. He was getting worse.

"You are far worse. I am scared, Grant. I do not know what to do, how to help you. I fear I need to go fetch a healer." Ada was looking down into Grant's pale and ailing face.

With her decision made, she was about to rise but a hand shot out from under the blanket, gripping her forearm like an iron clamp.

"No, Ada," Grant whispered very hoarsely. She poured a little more water past his lips.

"Grant, you have to see a doctor. I cannot let you get any worse... nothing is worth that." Ada put her other hand over his.

"No. You are worth that. Promise me ye will stay in this house no matter how long it takes me to feel well again. Promise me." Grant's grasp on her arm was weakening.

"I need help, Grant."

"Promise me, Ada." Grant continued to tremble.

Ada looked down at him. Maybe he was right. It was probably just an ague and he would be better in a few days' time. This would most likely be the worst of it.

"I promise," she said quietly, a tear sliding down onto her dress. She watched his body relax. The tremors continued but the angst was disappearing.

"Well, let me see what we can do to get you warm then." Ada took off her dress and slid under the covers beside him, pressing herself against his fiery hot skin. She wrapped her arms around him and even threw her leg over his legs. He groaned as the pressure of her body hurt him and made his joints and back ache. She ignored it, whispering softly, "You will be just fine, we will get you warmer, hush now, hush." At this point, her whispered musings were an attempt to comfort herself as well as Grant.

They had stayed like that until the next morning. When Ada awoke, she had to peel her sweat dried skin off Grant's. She was excited momentarily until she realized it had been only her who was sweating. As she held a hand to his forehead, Grant's fever remained unbroken.

"Fucking Christ." Ada cursed the blasted illness under her breath.

"...and a fine good morning to ye too..." Grant turned his head slightly to look at Ada's face. Her brow was furrowed with worry and frustration. He wished he was not the cause.

"I'm sorry, I had thought perhaps your fever had broken but I was mistaken." She took a deep breath through her nose and exhaled.

"Truly, I do not feel as terrible as I did last evening. I am sure that I am on my way to being back to my old self again." Grant fumbled for Ada's hand. "I'm sorry ye are worried, but I wish ye wouldna. All will be well, I promise." He squeezed her hand, intertwining his fingers in hers.

She took the cup from the table beside the bed and offered it to him. As he took three large sips of water, she felt mildly encouraged.

Around midday, Grant had woken up from a nap while Ada was reading his book on horse illness. Upon seeing him wake up, she rose from the armchair and grabbed a wooden chair from the table and brought it to the bedside.

"How do you feel? Because you look awful," Ada inquired jokingly.

"Aye, thank ye kindly. I feel about the same, no better but no worse." Grant scratched his chin, his stubble was beginning to itch him.

"I took care of the horses while you slept. I did not make you anything to eat, I doubted you would feel like anything. I can make you something now if you want."

"No, I have no appetite." Grant looked at Ada. "Would ye mind just stepping out the back door for a moment please, lass. I need a minute of privacy."

Ada nodded, got up and went to the back door. She stepped outside and closed it behind her, letting the chill of the air refresh her from the smell of illness inside. She leaned on the wall of the cabin. She could smell the wood behind her back. She knew Grant was using the chamber pot. He had refused to let her help him at all, and even refused to let her empty it for him. She should have persisted but seeing his embarrassment, she had relented and now just stepped outside whenever he needed a break. As it had been the past few days, she would go back in to find him weakened and lying limp and dizzy on the bed but the chamber pot would be emptied and his dignity would be intact. She heard the front door click closed. She would give him a few minutes to return to bed and then she would re-enter. She shook out her skirts in the cool air. They were meant to be leaving in the next two days. She couldn't see how Grant would be fit to ride a long journey by then. Her heart gave a little jump at the thought of getting to spend a little more time with him. Holding that positive thought close to her chest, she smoothed her hair and tucked wisps behind her ears that the wind had blown. She opened the door and walked back in, feeling refreshed.

Chapter 34

After a fairly good day, Grant began to feel terrible again in the evening. Every position he laid in made him ache and waves of nausea broke over him like a coming storm. His skin felt hot and tingly and even the inside of his mouth seemed to burn with fever. Ada had insisted on sitting in the arm chair and keeping a watchful eye on him. She refused to get into the bed and try to sleep. Deep down, he was thankful for her insistence. The thought of the bed jostling in any fashion made him wretch. As the cabin grew darker, he lay alone in bed—alone with his pain and alone with his thoughts. He could feel the stinging on his arms and legs; it was similar to the sensation he felt on his hands and face. His torso seemed to be the only part of him that was unreceptive to this irritating, painful sensation. It seems that all his other senses were heightened in the dark. It seemed odd that his skin could burn while he lay there freezing. He closed his eyes, trying to ignore the fact that this fever might be negatively influencing his thinking as well. He heard Ada breathing rhythmically from the armchair, occasionally giving a small snore in her sleep. Grant needed to concentrate on that sound to still his mind. Count her breaths, drift off to sleep and heal. One breath... two... three breaths... snore... four breaths... he began to drift and let the tides of fever take him down.

Ada woke up in the big chair in front of a fire that had long since been extinguished. Her head was turned at an awkward angle against the side of the chair. Wincing, she shut her eyes again and tried to massage the knots out of the back of her protesting neck. She stretched her head gingerly up and down and side to side, then finally allowed herself to open her eyes again and kneaded her shoulders gently. She turned her head slowly toward the bed, afraid that quick movement might jar the pain back into her muscles. She hoped Grant was faring better this morning then he was when she had fallen asleep last night. She could see the back of his head. His face was turned on the pillow against the wall, his dark hair spilling over the cloth. He was not trembling anymore. *That's a reassuring sign*, she thought. Her eyes scanned down his body to his hand which was sticking out of the blankets and hanging eerily over the edge of the bed. She closed her eyes and opened them again, squinting in the morning light at Grant's motionless hand. Small raised bumps were scattered over his skin. They were pinkish and white.

Reckoning dawned on Ada and she shot from her chair. "Oh, God! Please, no!" She ran to the bed and threw off the blanket covering Grant's frame. Her eyes went immediately to his feet; the same offending rash was present there, continuing with a few spots on both legs. She could feel tears welling up in her eyes. She forced herself to roll his head over and look at his face.

His face seemed less affected then his limbs at this point, but still a rash was present there as well. The roughness with which Ada rolled him must have startled Grant into alertness. He groaned and tried to open his eyes. Ada hastily threw the blanket back up over his body.

"Ada? What?" He was in pain; she could tell from the lines on his face as he spoke.

"Grant, can you hear what I am saying to you?" Ada needed to be sure. She swiped at her eyes and sniffed into her sleeve, but the tears just resurfaced and leaked down her face.

"Aye, I can," Grant said calmly. Although feeling terrible, he had obviously sensed Ada's emotional state.

"You, I am fairly certain..." Ada was sobbing in earnest now, choking on words, because there was no easy way to tell someone what she needed to tell him.

"It is bad then, is it?" Grant sounded resigned as if he had already known.

Ada nodded but seeing how Grant's eyes were still closed, this was a useless and foolish gesture. "Pox." Ada choked. "Grant, I am sure it is smallpox." Her legs would not hold her and she slipped down to the floor in a whoosh of skirts. "What do I do? God, please tell me what can I do?"

She looked up, Grant had remained as still as when he'd woken. Not moving, he absorbed the news. The minutes ticked by. Ada continued to sit on the floor beside the bed. Her crying seemed under control now and her occasional hiccups were the only thing to break the silence.

"Ada," Grant finally spoke. She winced as even his whispers sounded gravelly and painful. He coughed with difficulty to clear his throat. "I need you to go to the port as planned, lass. Ye canna stay here, and I canna go with ye."

The tears began to renew themselves in Ada's eyes. "How can you ask that of me? I will not go without you. I have already had smallpox, so I'll be fine here!"

"God, Ada. It is tearing my heart into pieces. I can barely think it let alone say it aloud. Ye will go, ye will ride to the port and be safe, and ye will do it for me because I love ye."

Ada stood up shakily from the wooden floor and reached for him. He put his hand up to stop her. His eyes pleaded with her.

There was nothing to say. What could she possibly say? Not wanting to upset him, she took a small step back from the bed. "I love you too." Ada breathed sadly. "You should sleep, you look exhausted and we can speak more later when you feel more rested."

Grant knew Ada was trying to ignore his request in hopes he would go to sleep and change his mind or simply forget what they had spoken of. "Yes, I am tired, and I feel verra ill, but I need you to please listen for a minute." Seeing Ada's nod of acknowledgment, he continued. "Tomorrow morning, ye need to leave while it is still dark. We missed the window of time that Sunday's service would have granted us." Grant was getting chilled again. "Ye will take what food is left in the house and ye will ride Gypsy and pony Duff to her saddle."

"Duff?" Ada's eyes went wide. "Why would I take Duff with me? How will I get him back to you...?" She trailed off as realization struck her. "Listen to me, Grant Ross, you are not going to die! Don't you even consider that as an option!"

"Well, truly, I am not hoping for that myself." Grant began to cough. Ada helped him sip some water and tucked his blankets higher. "Thank you." He tried to smile reassuringly at her. "Ada, think about it. Even if I dinna die, which I promise is what I am trying to do, I willna be able to care for him for weeks or months even." Grant closed his eyes.

Ada stood in silence. Looking down at him, she felt every emotion she had ever felt wash over her. The underlying devastation was breaking her heart. This man had made her feel worthy, valuable, useful, loved... she could never repay that, and only hoped she gave him some of the same happiness.

"Grant?" Ada whispered in case he had already fallen asleep.

"Aye?" His voice was barely audible.

"If I leave tomorrow, will I ever see you again?" Ada did not want to know his answer. She was afraid of the truth; she was afraid of fate.

"WHEN ye leave tomorrow, ye will ride to a port, board a ship and sail somewhere safe. Wait for a time and then write me a letter telling me that yer safe." He sighed deeply. "Hopefully, ye will think of me often, as I will continuously be thinking about you." He drifted off to sleep.

Ada felt cold. Her hands and knees shook. She made it to the armchair in front of the fire and sat down hard.

She took some material that was hanging over the arm of the chair, held it against her face and sobbed silently, letting the material muffle her sobs until she felt she had no breath left. Swiping the back of her hand roughly across her eyes, she got up to stoke the fire. The warmth of the flames did little to warm her bone-deep chill. She took down the whisky flask and drank deeply again and again, hoping to melt the ice inside her. Finally, she sat back in the chair, pulled Grant's cloak around her and stared into the flames.

She awoke in the middle of the night with the smell of Grant's cloak surrounding her body. The cabin was pitch black; she had fallen asleep watching the shapes in the flames and had not banked the fire like she normally would have. Grant would be cold. She could hear him breathing and thanked the Lord for that small mercy. She bent to stoke the fire. Grabbing the iron fire poker, she pushed the larger log to the rear of the hearth. The kindling still shone orange under a blanket of grey ash. She took some of the wood shavings and bits of straw that Grant left in a small box beside the hearth and placed them atop the dying kindling. She blew gently, and tiny flames erupted. The smell of wood smoke began to permeate the cabin. Dusting her hands on her skirt, she got off her knees and went to check on Grant. She figured the only way she would get through what she needed to do today was to take everything task by task, and not think about saddling Gypsy and riding away.

She moved to the back door to grab the candle so she could better assess Grant's condition. She quietly unlatched the back door and peered outside to help gauge the time. It looked to be a few hours past midnight. If her instinct was correct, that would give her roughly three to four hours before dawn. Re-latching the door, she lit the candle from the hearth and approached Grant's bedside. She held the candle close to his face. More of the papules had erupted around his cheeks and forehead. Lifting the blanket softly, she moved the candle close to his hands and feet and saw that much more of his limbs were covered with the expanding rash. The rash did not seem to be filled with fluid yet. She recalled that this made him slightly less contagious to others. Although she was immune to the illness because of her childhood infection, she did not want to carry it to others after she left the house. The thought of leaving created a wave of sadness she had a hard time pushing back.

"There is too much to do, Ada. Get control and get moving," she told herself aloud. Looking down, Grant had not stirred at all by the sound of her voice. No time to waste. She grabbed his cloak off the armchair and went out the back door into the night to ready the horses.

Both horses were grazing happily but raised their heads and began to amble toward the fence when they saw her approach.

"Bit of a change of plans tonight, my friends. I doubt either of you will mind as long as there is food involved." Duff reached the gate first, nodding his heavy head up and down in anticipation of being fed.

"I will be back in a moment." Ada disappeared into the small barn. She re-emerged pushing the wooden wheelbarrow filled with hay. The pitchfork Grant had forged sat on the top and a rope halter for Gypsy hung around her neck. She parked the wheelbarrow off to the side of the gate and slid Gypsy's halter over her ears. She opened the gate and led Gypsy out of the pasture and into the stall in the barn, throwing her some hay to keep her occupied.

"One happy, one to go..." Ada was getting used to talking to herself. Having spent so much time alone in the house, she did not have time to wonder whether this was worrisome. She went back out to the pasture and saw Duff. His head was stretched over the fence and he was happily munching on hay from the wheelbarrow. Ada laughed and lifted the gate to the pasture. She did not worry about closing it behind her as she knew Duff would follow the hay. She drove the hay out to the middle of the pasture and dumped it into a big pile on the ground. She repeated, filling and dumping the wheelbarrow until there were four very large piles of hay in varying places in the field. Ada was sweating despite the cold frosted air.

"Well that takes care of food then..."

Ada moved to the trough that was used for water in the outside pen. As she peered inside, the water was slushy but not frozen. She went into the barn and grabbed the wooden bucket from Duff's stall and began the exhausting task of filling up the trough with water from the well. She stopped counting after seven buckets, and pulled the wisps of sweaty hair away from her face. Heave... carry... dump... she kept telling herself there was only a few more to go. Finally, after what seemed like two hundred trips to the well, the trough was full. Ada leaned on the fence for a moment to catch her breath. Duff had been periodically switching between hay piles as Ada had been filling the water trough, obviously tasting the hay in each pile to ensure that it met his high standards. He stopped to stare at Ada against the fence, perhaps ensuring she had not made an error and that all this hay was still his to eat.

"Try not to eat it all in one sitting!" she called to him. He simply dropped his head back down and continued to chew.

Her sweat was beginning to dry in the wind, making her shiver. She grabbed the wooden bucket full of water and closed the gate tightly, ensuring it was secured, then walked back into the barn. Although the barn was cool, it felt warm without the cold wind blowing. She dumped the water into Gypsy's pail and hung the bucket back in Duff's stall where it belonged. Ada stood still for a moment, the barn always calmed her. Although it was dark outside, the light of the moon allowed her to see her surroundings. She listened to the crunching, grinding noise of Gypsy eating her hay. She could smell the pleasant smell of horses mixed with the familiar earthy smell of the hay. Even the pungent smell of recent manure calmed her spirit.

She needed to return to the house. She had made two dresses out of the material Grant had brought her home. She had been wearing one and saved the other—it was going to be a surprise for Grant. She had put it in the barn under a woolen blanket that Grant covered her saddle with. With no ability to ride anywhere since she had fled to Grant's, she thought it would be a safe place to hide the dress until she could surprise him by wearing it one day when he returned from work. Sadly, the dress now held another purpose. Having kept the dress out of the house, it was most likely safe from the pox. Ada had remembered people burning their clothes and bedding during the smallpox outbreak in her childhood, and assumed clothes could carry the illness as well. If she was going to leave, she would have to wear this dress to avoid spreading the disease. She felt her face warm with the tears that made tracks down her cold cheeks. How could she leave him? Her outside work had taken a bit longer than an hour and she needed to return inside to finish the rest of her preparations. She let the tears run and walked slowly back inside, carrying her dress over her shoulder.

She left the dress on the floor at the back door and picked up the burning candlestick she had left on the table. She grabbed the small wooden bowl from the shelf above the table and put an apple and a heel of bread into it. She brought the bowl quietly to the small wooden table by the head of the bed. She placed the bowl down gently and poured a large cup of fresh water from the ewer and placed the full glass beside the bowl. She knew Grant was too poorly to eat but she felt better leaving food and drink beside him, just in case. Next, she moved to the fire in the hearth. She would need to add a few more good-sized logs to ensure it kept burning but did not burn the cabin down in the process. She pushed the logs back against the stone and watched the sparks fly softly like fireflies in the dark. As she looked around the room and realized she was almost finished her preparations, her stomach knotted up. She soundlessly made a circuit of the cabin. She picked up her old dress from when she first arrived, her newly-sewn dress she had been wearing, her underclothes, and the scraps from her sewing. She sat down in the armchair in front of the fire and dumped the pile on the floor in front of her. She placed each piece into the hearth one at a time. As smoke and ash blew up the chimney from the burning clothing so did pieces of Ada's soul. She would never be the same, and she knew that. She would leave herself behind with Grant and carry with her just a shell of who she once was. It did not matter anymore. Nothing mattered right now but him.

Chapter 35

She stood beside a saddled Gypsy who was tied to the hitching post at the front of the cabin. She had walked over to Grant to say goodbye. She had tried to rouse him gently, and he had awoken slightly but spoke words she did not understand. His fever was too high; he was not aware any longer. She told him she loved him and walked purposely to the hearth, stripped naked, threw the old shirt and breeches she was wearing into the fire and walked to the back door to put on her dress. A new sense of urgency guided her step. He was far worse. Shivering from the cold as well as the hasty wash down she had given herself in the barn, she mounted Gypsy wearing the woolen blanket from the barn as a cloak. Having not been ridden for over a fortnight, Gypsy tossed her head and side-stepped while Ada got her stirrups.

"I know, love, easy now." She patted her neck softly.

She urged Gypsy forward lightly with her heels, preparing for the surge of energy beneath her. The horse began down the path at a quick trot but stopped at the end of the lane. She gave a high pitch mare-ish squeal and seemed to wait. Sure enough, a whinny of what could only be goodbye came from the fence behind her as Duff trotted over to the rail. Ada looked at Duff and reached up to scratch Gypsy between her ears. Sharing the mutual feeling of loss, she touched the mare's sides again with her heels and they were off down the road.

The signs of dawn were already beginning to emerge. The sun would be fully up within twenty minutes. She had left later then she intended too. Having not been worked, Gypsy puffed a bit and Ada slowed her to a walk. Ada's own body tingled with the urge to move faster but pushing her horse would get her nowhere. She spoke to Gypsy as they walked along, telling her what was in her heart—the things she could only tell Grant. The weather was warmer today than it had recently been. She was quite snug under her woolen blanket and the riding had loosened her muscles and warmed up her body. Gypsy was as toasty as a bonfire underneath Ada's legs. The last time Ada rode around these parts was the night she had fled; she obviously had not been able to admire the beauty of the landscape then. Even though most of the trees had already lost their leaves, the bare trees stood beautiful and simplistic, their branches reaching for each other like lover's hands. As she rode farther, things began to appear familiar to her. A large rock that stood on top of a small hill was so completely out of place it seemed like magical intervention that the rock could be there at all. As she rode, the sun emerged, changing the colour of the sky and brightening the road in front of them. Soon, she would start seeing scattered houses, and people would be tending their livestock, waking their children and cooking breakfast. She had taken an apple and some cheese from Grant's house and nibbled it gingerly. The cheese was old and had a musty taste but she was hungry and it was nourishment. By the time she had finished her wedge of cheese, Gypsy was rested enough and Ada's sense of urgency was back, gnawing at her belly like her earlier hunger. She loosened the reins, giving Gypsy her head and shot down the road, leaving a trail of dust floating in the air behind her.

They rode another half hour until they approached the location she had been heading to. She passed through the white wooden fence line onto the lane leading to the house. She took a deep breath of morning air. Gypsy walked down the lane and Ada stopped her outside the front door. She dismounted and climbed the four squeaking wooden steps to the porch of Louise Davaneaux's home. She straightened her woolen blanket and knocked loudly. Any attempt to tame her hair would have been futile as she had ridden away from Grant's with it wet and the blankets pulled up like a hood. Impatiently, she knocked again louder. She heard muffled footsteps and a bolt slide across the door as it unlatched.

Louise's butler, Hughes, appeared in the doorway. He frowned as he took in her appearance, then gasped as he realized who she was. As quickly as it had changed, his expression went back to neutral and he cleared his throat.

"May I help you?" He was cool and indifferent. She had no time for this.

"Get me Louise. Quickly, please," Ada said shortly.

"Madam, Mistress Davaneaux is busy entertaining her breakfast guests at the moment, I will let her know that you..." Hughes caught the look in Ada's eye and ceased his practice speech.

"You will get her and you will get her now." Ada was losing patience and Grant was losing time.

"This is highly irregular!" Hughes' cheeks were blotching red with anger.

"NOW!" Ada stomped her foot as she spoke. "Or I swear to you, I will damn decorum to hell and go inside and find her myself, loudly."

Hughes scowled at Ada but nodded and shut the door, leaving her standing on the front porch. If he was not back with Louise in the next five minutes, she was going in there. So, she stood wringing her hands with restlessness. She exhaled deeply and approached the door to bang loudly again when it opened. A very confused Louise stepped onto the front porch. Louise saw Ada's face and screamed.

"ADA! Thank God in heaven, I had thought you dead. I am thrilled to have you returned to us, but where?" She looked over Ada from shoes to disheveled hair. She was clasping both her hands and shaking them enthusiastically.

Ada took a step past Louise quickly and pulled shut the front door of the house.

It was no doubt that people inside had heard Louise scream, which now gave her less than a minute to speak.

"Louise, I need help. Please, you must listen. Tell no one. I need you to send Martha to Grant Ross's cabin. He has smallpox and he is very badly. She needs to help him."

Louise was staring at her with her brown eyes wide open. Ada was fairly certain she hadn't blinked yet. "Grant Ross? But how...?"

"Send her, please, as quickly as you can. I have no right to ask but I could not think of anywhere else to go." Ada felt the tears forming in her eyes again.

"Ada, I..." Louise was clearly torn. She looked at Ada's pained face and the decision was made. "Of course, I will."

Ada melted in relief, "Oh, God, thank you, thank you." Ada was clasping Louise's hands tightly. She began to shake, "I need to explain to you..." Ada was cut off by the door swinging open and Allain Davaneaux bursting onto the front porch with a concerned look on his face.

"Louise, you screamed, whatever is the matter?" He looked past Louise, and upon seeing Ada, he turned as pale as the ghost he thought she was.

Ada looked up at him and her face dropped in fear and defeat as she saw the man who had followed Allain onto the porch. Colin Watershaw stood at Allain's shoulder, his face the same shade of white as Allain's. His look of shocked uncertainty was soon replaced by vindictive triumph. He had a bandage wrapped around his head and his eyes were still tinged with bruises.

"Ada?" Colin's voice cracked as he said her name.

"Colin. I am glad you are not dead," Ada said coldly. She stared boldly into his face.

"Where the hell have you been?" His tone was harsh and accusing. Louise and Allain had stepped back to let them speak.

Louise spoke softly, "Perhaps Allain and I will just pop inside and give you two a moment together." Colin was already nodding politely in approval.

"No, stay." Ada did not take her eyes off Colin. "You asked where I have been, I have been somewhere safe. Safe from you."

Colin stiffened. "Safe from me? As I recall it—and I do recall it, wife, have no doubt—you are the one who viciously attacked me with a horseshoe. You nearly killed me." Colin spat the words at her.

"I am certain that you did not tell our friends," Ada gestured a hand to the Davaneauxs, "that you came at me with a knife, only after beating me with a riding crop. My choices were to hit you with that horseshoe, or die. I chose wisely," Ada seethed. She thought she had heard Louise gasp.

Colin turned to the couple quietly watching this scene unfold with uncertain eyes. "It is obvious that Ada has been through some trauma and is quite incapacitated right now. I am so terribly sorry for this dreadfully rude scene. I will take my wife home now and make sure she gets some proper rest and medical attention." Colin attempted to grab Ada's hand but she pulled away from him swiftly.

"I'll not go anywhere with you, you lying bastard." Louise's eyebrows shot up at Ada's tone.

"Well, you will, you are my wife, and I only want to get you help. If I need to call the authorities to help me force you to return home, I will. Please do not make me do that, Ada." Colin feigned friendly concern while Ada looked at him disgusted. He grabbed her arm above the elbow. "Come, Ada."

Ada attempted to shake him off but his grip held tight. "No." Ada did not have time for this, Grant needed help. She wanted to be with him, to feel safe.

"Ada..." A soft hand grasped her other arm. Louise pulled her in close for a hug. Colin let go of her arm while Allain patted Colin's shoulder in a consolatory fashion, speaking quietly to him. Ada squeezed Louise hard and she squeezed back. Nestling her mouth close to Ada's ear, she whispered, "Go with him, Ada. Do not make it worse for yourself. I will send help to Mr. Ross and I will try to aid you in any way I can. I believe you." Louise grabbed both of Ada's cheeks with her hands and kissed her on the forehead. "She was merely overwhelmed, Colin. She's been through so much. I am sure you are right and her own bed and some rest will do her a world of good." Louise turned to Ada. "I will call on you tomorrow afternoon, to ensure you are improving." Louise smiled at Ada and she tried to smile back, but failed. She turned toward Colin.

"Fine." She started walking down the stairs before he could say anything more.

Watershaw House

Ada sat in her bedroom in a tub of very hot water, crying silently. The reality of what had happened and what she had lost was now truly hitting her. The ride to Louise's house, the adrenaline and anger of seeing Colin again had all kept her sadness and realization at bay. Now, sitting in her bath back in this house, *his* house, fear, loneliness and worry overtook her.

The carriage ride home had been thankfully uneventful. She had quietly stared out the window. Colin was sitting across from her obviously too shocked to be as repugnant as usual. He had glared at her for a while, but seeing it gaining no response, he made a disgusted grunt and looked away. She predicted he must still be in a fragile enough state that a physical altercation would be unwise and she thanked God for that. Oddly, the fear of him beating her was less than it had been before she left. She could not imagine that the physical pain inflicted by Colin could be worse than the pain her heart was feeling right now. She had not been prepared to go home. She was planning on secretly staying at Louise's for a few days, then returning to Grant. The realization that this would not be the case was the most devastatingly painful blow she could have ever received.

She slept restless the first night. Colin had not spoken one word to her and after Marie had stopped fussing around her, she climbed into her old bed. She was uneasy. She expected Colin to come into her room and be unrelentingly brutal and angry for what she had said in front of Louise and Allain. She jumped at every creak she heard outside her door, but he never came. When she closed her eyes, she tried to picture Grant and his heavy warmth in the bed beside her but when she opened her eyes, the cool white bed linens greeted her with loneliness.

Marie came in the next morning and found Ada already awake, standing at the windowsill.

"Madam! Are you well? Did you sleep comfortably?" Marie waited politely for Ada to turn from the window.

The maid's voice had startled Ada out of a trance. She had been staring at the frost that covered the white and grey ground. Her mind had been on Grant. She wanted desperately to know how he was faring. Had

Martha been able to ease his suffering? Get his fever down? She turned to face Marie.

"I did not sleep well at all, but that was expected. I am well, thank you, Marie. I'm just tired," Ada pulled her robe closer around her, "and cold."

"Well, I should think so, standing with your bare feet on the cold floor, right over by the frosted window. Please, get back into your bed and I will put a bed warmer down by your feet and fetch your breakfast up here. I will let everyone know you are not feeling strong enough to come downstairs at the moment." Marie was already guiding Ada back to her bed. She did not resist it; the bed looked wonderfully warm and comfortable and she honestly felt she did not have the energy to resist anything right now.

"Marie? Was Colin home last night?" Ada inquired softly.

"Oui, madam. Why do you ask?" Marie's small pleasant face looked uncomfortable.

"I said some..." she paused to think of an appropriate word, "dangerous... things in front of the Davaneauxs. He was angry. I thought he would come up here."

"Oh," Marie shifted a little on her feet, "he was entertaining someone last evening." She looked down.

"Oh?" Ada felt nothing. "Who is she?"

Marie's eyes shot up to Ada's face, she had clearly assumed Ada would have guessed the visitor was a male friend. "I do not know her name, madam. I believe she works in town." Marie stopped and looked as if she was deciding whether to say more. "She has spent most nights here recently. I am sorry, madam. I should not have said that so bluntly, please forgive me." This situation had obviously made Marie very nervous.

"It is truly no matter. I hope he spends all his time with her and leaves me to myself. Frankly, I want nothing at all to do with my husband." Ada shrugged her shoulders. Oddly, Marie did not look shocked at all by this revelation. "Marie? I hope you know that I value our conversations. In this house I have no one, but I hope I have you."

Marie smiled at Ada genuinely and Ada thought she saw a whisper of a blush creep into the young woman's pretty face. "You will always have me, madam."

Tears stung Ada's eyes. She could not seem to control her emotions as of late. "Thank you, Marie, truly." Ada sniffed and gratefully climbed back under her blankets, propping herself up against the pillows Marie had set up for her.

"De rien." Marie exited the room and closed the door behind her.

Chapter 36

After eating her breakfast in bed and taking a brief nap, Ada had only agreed to emerge from her room with the announcement that Louise Davaneaux had come to pay her a visit. She received her in the front room with the large windows. The natural light coming in lifted her spirits. Louise had embraced her tightly. Her look of concern and pity should have made Ada feel something, anything at all but instead, the dark cloud of sadness just hovered over her like a rainstorm. When the tea had been served and they were sure they were alone, Ada asked in an urgent whisper whether there was any news. Louise had stated that Martha had not come home after she left yesterday and she had received no news of any kind. Ada had nodded politely and looked inside her teacup. Louise had slid closer to Ada on the sofa and put her hand on Ada's back.

"Have you been at Mr. Ross' this whole time, Ada?" Louise asked softly.

Ada nodded. She did not trust herself to speak. She feared she would feel Louise stiffen, utter a gasp or a *tsk* of disapproval.

"You are very fond of him?" Louise looked at Ada's face, with her dark hair piled neatly on her head. Ada moved her eyes from her teacup to a face free from judgment. She looked at her friend sorrowfully.

"Louise, I love him with every single part of my soul." Ada searched Louise's face. There was no sense in lying to Louise, and she did not want to.

"Oh, my poor dear." Louise pulled Ada close to her and the two friends hung onto one another. Ada cried into Louise's dress as her friend cooed calming words to her.

After they had finally released each other, Ada wiped her red eyes. "I would like to speak privately, even more privately than this." Ada gestured to the empty front room. "Would you walk outside with me?"

The two women walked, wrapped in their cloaks, scarves and woolen muffs and while they walked, Ada told Louise everything—everything about Colin, her marriage, the night in the barn, her sudden departure, Grant's cabin and lastly, Grant himself. They walked until their noses and cheeks were bright red and their toes ached with cold. Only then did they find themselves back on the front porch of Watershaw house.

Louise pulled a warm hand out of her muff and held it out for Ada to grasp. "I wish I had known sooner, about Colin I mean... there is nothing I could have done. You know as well as I do that there is still nothing I can do except share the burden now and ensure you know that you are not alone."

"I know there is nothing for me to do but exist now and turn to my friends and faith. I will also need to attempt to be as agreeable and invisible as possible.

Many people live their lives in worse circumstances than mine." Ada shivered. "Shall we go inside and warm up with another cup of tea?"

"I would like that." Louise squeezed Ada's hand tighter for emphasis. "I promise I will not breathe a word of this, Ada, and anything I find out from Martha, I will get word to you with most haste."

"Thank you so much." Ada felt her eyes well up once again.

After Louise left, Ada retired to her room. She did not want to read right now. She picked up the needlepoint she had started months ago, then put it back down in its place. She paced around aimlessly picking up objects, moving things around and even sorting through her drawer full of ribbons. She tried to think what she had normally done in her free time at Watershaw house but those memories seemed lifetimes away. She wondered how a few weeks of difference could change your entire existence. She missed tidying up around Grant's small cabin. She missed cleaning the fireplace, she even missed trying to cook small meals and, my God, did she ever miss him. She sat down on the end of her bed trying to feel anything but numb. Perhaps it was better that she felt nothing—nothingness had to be better than heart-breaking pain and worry.

She flopped backwards onto her mattress with her knees bent and her feet dangling above the floor. She sighed, Colin would undoubtedly be home for dinner tonight. She could not hope to avoid him forever. It was strange. Before she left, the thought of being subservient and neutral toward Colin made her feel physically ill, as if she was letting him win somehow.

Now, as she thought about the rest of her life, she finally accepted that being unobtrusive and invisible were her only chances of winning—her victory being in making it through life as numbly and unharmed as possible. She closed her eyes and tried to picture Duff and Gypsy running around the small pen behind Grant's cabin, tossing their heads in the wind and nickering to each other amiably, with Gypsy pinning her ears and squealing as Duff got too friendly. Grant had laughed at the mare's reaction. He had shouted at Duff from the backdoor where he was standing, "Aye, well, that's what ye get, lad, for not listening to 'no' the first time!" Ada smiled and relaxed into sleep.

Ada breathed deeply. Hot air filled her lungs. It was sticky today and the breeze was turning the day into a beautiful summer afternoon. She could smell wildflowers and took another long breath. She could also smell the water. She was sitting in long grass. She glanced around and smiled when she saw Gypsy munching happily in the shade of a large willow tree, the leaves dancing and twirling like ribbons in the slow breeze. She began to realize that she had been in this field before, plenty of times in fact. This was her favorite spot to go when she was younger. She spent entire summers lying on her back and watching the clouds under her large straw hat. If she remembered correctly, she would have packed a... her hand went to the pocket of her dress and felt the familiar bulge of an oatcake wrapped in a cloth handkerchief. She could not understand why Gypsy and her childhood were existing at the same time but she had the common sense not to complain. She was at peace and felt relaxed. She reached her hand deep into the other pocket. The flask she always filled with raspberry cordial felt warm under her fingertips and she smiled. A butterfly fluttered toward her, it's orange and black colouring vivid against the light blue of the sky. It flew past her and over her shoulder and she turned to watch it fly out of sight. A movement on the hill in front of her pulled her eyes from the butterfly's waltz and focused her gaze on a woman walking up the hill toward her. The woman was beautiful; her long pale-yellow dress was set off by the grass around her knees. She also wore a straw bonnet, which covered a mass of dark red hair. She waved. Ada was walking toward her before she had any conscious thought of doing so. She walked closer, her gait so elegant she appeared to be floating through the long grass. As the two approached each other, Ada saw a smattering of freckles stippled across her nose and cheeks. She stopped, frozen to the spot, as she watched the woman take the final steps that would bring them together.

"Mother?" Ada exclaimed incredibly, her voice escaping as a whisper. She closed her eyes tightly and opened them again to see a young version of her mother still standing before her, smiling gently.

"Hello, Ladybug." Her mom reached a practiced hand up and cupped her cheek softly. "Just look how beautiful you are."

"How? You are not real. I am dreaming. I must be." Ada tilted her head and pressed her cheek into her mother's hand. She breathed in. Her mother smelled of baking and herbs. She sighed.

"*I do not know how, love. And yes, you are dreaming, but I am very real.*" *He mother reached for both Ada's hands as her brown eyes looked over Ada's features, so similar to her own.*

"*Mother, I...*" *Ada stood holding her mother's hands as birds carried on with their normal existence.*

"*Ada, I need to tell you that I am aware of what has happened to you. Your life has been everything but perfect. Yes, you have had wonderful moments but those wonderful moments seem like pearls in an ocean of sorrowful, hateful things. I am so sorry, love. I am sorry for not being there. I am sorry for leaving you.*"

Ada shook her head. "*You had no choice, you were so sick. You do not need to apologize. I always knew you wanted to stay with me.*"

"*I know you knew I loved you and never wanted to leave you, but the fact remains, love, that I did leave you. A mother feels guilty always, even for things she cannot help or change.*"

A tear glided down Ada's cheek. Her mother's thumb wiped it away.

"*Listen to me, Ada. As you already know, life is not always kind. It is not a pretty story written to put children to sleep at night. Life hurts. It gives things and it takes them away without remorse. Life makes you cry, it makes you bleed but you also rejoice and you love. You need to do whatever you can in this life to survive. If you must endure, then endure but do not lose yourself in the process. Remember, pet, no one can decide your life for you. They can impact your existence but they cannot decide who you are, what you dream, what you remember, and what you wish for. Even if everything you touch seems to fall apart, remember that you are the only one who can rebuild it."* Her mother pulled her into an embrace. She felt so warm and smelled like home and safety. Ada wanted to stay there forever. She closed her eyes. *"I miss you every day, but I am so very proud of you, my strong beautiful daughter."* The lights behind Ada's closed eyes shone bright yellow.

She opened her eyes to see the ceiling beams of her bedroom in Watershaw house. With her heart pounding, she sat up slowly. She blinked and ran a hand through her hair. She took a deep breath and swore she could smell baking and herbs.

"I miss you too," she said to the room around her. Her numbness lifted slightly. She still felt the deep pangs of devastation but she also felt a tiny pin prick of light seeping into her fortress of darkness—hope.

Less than an hour later, Marie had finished helping Ada get ready for dinner. She walked down the staircase gripping the rail so tightly she thought her fingernails would indent the wood. She felt the overwhelming urge to return to her room and avoid Colin for a little while longer; however, she knew that making him angrier would not benefit her situation, so she used the railing for support and forced her feet to pad down the carpeted steps. She stood straight and walked toward the double French doors of the dining room. From the hall, she could see Colin was seated at the head of the table. His head was turned to the side, addressing someone else. As Ada turned the corner through the doors, she saw a small slip of a woman seated in the seat to the left of Colin at the table. The woman's eyes went wide as Ada walked into the room. She ceased speaking immediately and stared down at her lap and a red blush crept up her chest. The girl looked to be barely sixteen. Ada said nothing, pulled out her own chair at the end of the table and sat down.

"Colin, I was not aware we were having company for dinner. I am sorry for my rudeness but I was not informed of a guest. Of course, you are most welcome." Ada smiled at the girl whose mouth was very inelegantly hanging open as she stared, shocked at Ada's words. Ada turned her gaze to Colin and met him with a very neutral look. "I am afraid I have yet to learn your name?" Ada continued sweetly.

"Mary Ellen Scott, ma'am, but I am called Ellen." The girl glanced at Colin. The poor creature looked so awkward. It was clear Colin had not mentioned that his recently-returned wife would be joining them for dinner.

"Ellen works in town, Ada. She has been spending a lot of time here in your absence. I was just distraught, and she has such a calming presence. We have actually become quite good friends." The word friends made his lip curl in a vindictive smile. "Have we not, Elle?" He reached for the girl's hand.

Ada thought for sure the girl would faint. Ada took a sip of her wine. "Well, it is wonderful to have friends. Shall we toast to friendship?" Ada raised her glass and took another sip. She was careful to keep sarcasm and anything but polite attentiveness out of her tone. She began to eat the food that Robertson had placed before her. The room was silent except for the sounds of cutlery scraping and wine glasses being set down on the table.

"Well, this is delicious, is it not, Ellen? May I call you Ellen?" Ada addressed the girl as she was taking a large bite off her spoon. She nodded shyly while chewing.

Colin put his silverware on top of his plate and signaled to Robertson to take it. He wiped his face with the corner of the dinner napkin and placed it on the table.

"Elle, my dear, would you excuse my wife and I for a moment of private conversation? I will have Robertson bring your plate upstairs and I will join you presently." The girl basically jumped off her chair and muttering a brief farewell to Ada, was out of the room like a shot. It was easy to see why Colin liked this small mouse-like submissive girl. She was as big around as Ada's dinner knife and the opposite of Ada in every way which—no doubt the reason Colin found her so appealing.

Ada continued to cut her meat daintily and chew softly, looking at Colin.

"I must confess, Ada, I thought you would be slightly more upset about being made a fool of, within your own home." Colin was concentrating on his wine. He swirled the cup in a circular motion in his hand.

Ada tilted her head slightly to the side, "Well, my getting upset will not change your mind, Colin. Besides, it is your right as my husband to do as you wish. I am in no position to stop you." She nearly choked on the words.

Colin set down his glass and fixed her with an angry suspicious stare. "Where have you been, Ada?" His tone was firm.

"I was scared, so I left. I felt I had to." She took another bite calmly.

"Where did you go?" Colin was growing more irritated. Ada could see the tenseness in his shoulders.

"I will not tell you that. I am sorry." Ada braced herself.

"Oh, you will not tell me? Well, maybe not right now, Ada, but mark my words, wife, you will tell me whether you like it or not and my guess is on the latter." Colin pushed his chair out and walked toward her end of the table. Ada closed her eyes and pulled her shoulders up, bracing for the worst. Nothing came. She opened her eyes cautiously and Colin was gone—no doubt upstairs *entertaining* Ellen.

That was interesting, Ada thought to herself as she ate her last spoonful of peas. Perhaps she could handle this after all.

Two Weeks Later

Ada sat in the carriage holding onto the seat as it bumped down the snow-covered road. There was not enough snow to require the cutter yet, but the carriage was having trouble skidding and bumping over ice on the dirt road. A few of the ladies had organized a women's luncheon to welcome Ada home, most likely to hear her side of the story. Ada had been dreading this event since she had received the invitation a week ago. She just hoped the ladies would be tactful enough to leave well enough alone if she pretended that it was still just too terrifying to discuss. Her one saving grace was that Louise would be there and she could possibly redirect the conversation. Also, this would give Ada another chance to ask Louise if she had heard anything about Grant.

By the end of the tea, Ada had still not managed to speak to Louise alone and thought she might literally burst with anticipation. As the ladies were departing, she hugged everyone and thanked them for their kindness. Louise appeared at her side.

"Ada, dearest, it appears my carriage horse has broken one of his harness lines. Would it be such an inconvenience to ask you and your carriage to take me home?" Louise squeezed Ada's elbow discreetly.

"Goodness, that is bad luck. Of course, we will take you home." Ada smiled genuinely at Louise. "I shall be glad of the company."

After a lengthy goodbye and heartfelt thanks, the two ladies bundled themselves up and climbed in the back of Ada's carriage, immediately pulling the fur blanket over their knees against the chill.

"I truly hate the winter." Louise shoved her hands under the fur.

"Louise, please..." Ada asked pleadingly.

"I am so sorry I could not talk to you earlier today; you were quite the hot commodity at that luncheon and I could hardly steal you away without someone following us or borrowing you back." Louise shifted slightly. "Ada, Martha came back two days ago to gather some more things she needed."

Ada's mind raced. If she came back for supplies, that means he's still alive. She thanked God and crossed herself.

"He is very poorly, Ada. I am so truly sorry." Louise's eyes scanned Ada's face. Seeing that she had only shut her eyes, she decided it was safe to continue. "Martha said that the blisters themselves are not as bad as she has seen, but it is his fever that is worrying her. It has been too high for too long and he is not taking any nourishment. She can only dribble spoonfuls of tea into his mouth but most of the time, he spits those back out. She does not think he can swallow properly because of the swelling."

Ada's mouth went dry. She tried to take a deep breath but could not.

"I need to do something. I need to go to him." Ada felt herself getting frantic.

"Ada, there is nothing you can do. You have sent Martha, that is all that can be done. You cannot leave Colin again. It will do Mr. Ross no good to have people looking for you and heaven forbid, finding you there."

Ada opened her mouth to argue but she knew Louise was right. She laid her head on her friend's shoulders, cursed and cried as the carriage bumped over the road to home.

After that carriage ride, Ada had not seen or heard from Louise for a few days. She prayed each morning to both God and her mother to deliver Grant from this. She may not have a life with him, but she needed him to be alive. All this enduring could not be in vain.

That evening, she stayed up late reading a book in front of the fireplace in her bedroom. Her mind had kept her awake. She heard footsteps in the hall outside her room. They were too heavy to be Marie's, so she thought Robertson must be turning down the lamps before retiring. Colin had not come to her bed in the time she had been home, which was a little over a fortnight. She prayed that this was because of Ellen and she hoped the girl would stay forever if it meant she was left safe and unmolested. As the footsteps approached her door, she knew her luck had run dry. Before she could finish that thought, Colin opened the door and walked inside, swaying slightly. He was clearly very drunk. His normally clear and penetrating eyes were glassed-over and bloodshot. He scanned the room, blinking slowly before his eyes fixed on Ada in the armchair.

"Ada, come with me." He gestured with his hand toward the door, half turning and expecting her to follow.

Ada looked suspiciously at him, "Where?"

"To my room..." He was standing in the doorway waiting for her to rise. Seeing her remain still, he slammed the door into the wall with such force that the iron handle gouged the wooden wall and sent small splinters flying. "NOW!" He bellowed and took a step toward her.

She jumped up from her chair. Out of fear of angering him further, she followed him silently to his room.

Ada had only been in Colin's room twice and both times, it had been somewhat disheveled and smelled faintly of spirits and tobacco. It was larger than her own room and included a small table in the corner which always had papers spread all over it—most likely where Colin prepared his documentation for his horse sales and breeding. He had not liked to use the downstairs office since his father's passing, very shortly after the wedding. She stepped guardedly into his room and stopped dead, then turned to look at him with her mouth open.

Ellen, who lay nude on the bed, uttered a shrill squeak and grabbed at the bedclothes and pulled them up to her chin. Her face was turning the colour of an overly ripe strawberry.

"Ada, you remember Ellen?" Colin spoke slowly.

"Colin, what is the meaning of this?" Ada snapped, her cautious tone disappearing.

"I, Colin!" Ellen's eyes were as big as dinner plates, she looked pleadingly at him.

"Both of you, shut up." Colin dragged a wooden chair from the table in the corner to the end of the bed, ignoring both women.

"Sit." He pointed to the chair and looked at Ada.

"Colin, what is going on?" Ada tried to sound composed and calmer than before.

Colin closed the space between them in three steps. He quickly slapped her across the face and grabbed her hair, dragging her to the chair. "I said, sit." He thrust her into the wooden chair.

She thought she had heard Ellen utter a short scream and suddenly wondered if Ellen had never seen this side of him. She brought her palm up to her burning cheek and looked directly at Ellen in the bed. The girl had tears streaming down her face and she was looking at the door. Ada shook her head ever so slightly, warning the girl to stay where she was. She would fare much worse if Colin had to catch her.

"Now," Colin slurred, "I have a predicament that the two of you will help me solve. As you know, Ada, I can barely stand being in your presence, let alone having to copulate with you. Unfortunately, in the eyes of the law, you are my wife and are therefore required to carry my heir." He turned his eyes to Ellen, "You, my dear, could never carry my heir because of your low social standing, and let us be honest, shall we? I would not want a child who could inherit any of your terribly dull personality traits or conversational abilities. However, you are pleasing to my eyes and I do enjoy the way you feel under me."

Ellen looked at Colin with shock and total betrayal.

"Ah, come now, pet," he reached down and put his hand on her cheek, "you did not think it was more than that, did you?"

Ellen cast her eyes down into her lap.

Ada bit the inside of her cheek to keep from saying anything. Instead, she sat silently and waited for Colin to finish.

"Well, then, here is what is going to happen. Ellen and I will begin the proceedings and Ada will sit in that chair and wait until I am almost ready. When I tell you to," Colin was now addressing Ada, "you will bend over the chair and lift your skirts and I will spill my seed inside you. This way, I will diminish the time you and I need to be 'together' but will still yield the same results. Clever, is it not?"

Ada thought she might vomit on the carpet by his feet. She looked directly at him, and did not dare glance at Ellen. She braced herself.

"Do I look like one of your fucking broodmares, you filthy bastard?" She fumed as she stared at his drunken face.

Colin began to laugh, surprising everyone. "Now that you mention it, Ada, I have often felt like I would rather fornicate with one of them instead of you."

"I will not do this, Colin." Ada attempted to stand up from the chair.

He was chillingly calm. "Yes, you will." Colin grabbed a rope from the dresser and was already on her before she could move toward the door. He shoved her hard into the bed. She pushed up on her arms and attempted to stand back up. He grabbed the back of her head by her hair and slammed her forehead into the post of his four-post bed. She blinked hard to clear her swimming vision. She could hear Ellen screaming in earnest now. Too scared to run, she had wrapped herself into a ball, screaming and crying. Ada felt the rope tying one of her legs to the bottom of the bedpost. The rope bit hard into her stinging ankle. She stopped struggling, afraid of losing consciousness. Colin grabbed her hands and tied her wrists together, pulling both arms above her head and attaching them to the other bedpost so her face was pressed into the mattress and her behind was presented in the air. She was tied at the foot of the bed, unable to look away from the proceedings about to happen. She closed her eyes and prayed for strength. She thought about other things, trying to block out Ellen's protests and her increasing sobs. She could feel the bed rhythmically moving beneath her and she could hear Colin's grunting breaths. She waited with her eyes tightly closed, her head throbbing and her ears ringing. The sounds grew less and less. She finally heard silence and felt the bed shift under Colin's weight. Hands gripped her hips and she tried to recoil as Colin entered her, the ropes digging into her skin. She counted four thrusts and it was over. She did not open her eyes. She did nothing but remained still, and waited. She could hear Colin getting dressed. She could hear him pick something up from the dresser. He came over to her, cut the rope binding her hands and threw the knife on the bed beside her.

"Free yourself and get out." He was breathing heavily and looked almost shaken, more sober than before. He left the room after leaving her the knife.

Ada quickly turned her head to look at Ellen. She hoped the girl was not too badly hurt. She would undoubtedly be shaken. Ellen lay on the bed, her arms and legs splayed to either side. Ada panicked. She quickly hacked her feet free and crawled up the bed to the young girl's face. Her mouth was open and her eyes were slightly bulging. Ada looked at her throat and saw harsh red fingermarks around her tiny neck. Desperately, Ada placed her ear to the girl's chest. When she heard nothing, she shook her violently by the shoulders and called her name but the girl did not move. She was dead. Ada sat up slowly. She felt very cold. She pulled the sheet over the girl and left the room. She walked back to her own bedroom and threw up in the chamber pot. She stood up, thought of the young girl's fearful expression and threw up once again.

"God, please deliver me from evil." She knelt on the carpet, with the chamber pot in her hands and continued to pray repeatedly.

At some point, she must have gotten up and gone to bed. She did not remember doing so but as she forced her eyes open, she could see that light was fusing in the window and she was in her own room, in her bed, under a blanket. Her head throbbed mercilessly. She felt as though she had been kicked in the face by a horse. She reached a hand up to her forehead and felt a massive raised knot. It was hot to the touch. She carefully traced a finger along the bump and realized that it went from her brows to slightly higher than her hair line. She pushed herself up on her elbows and dizziness enveloped her. She squinted and pushed a pillow up behind her to prop herself into a somewhat seated position.

The door opened after two soft quiet knocks and Marie quietly padded in, carrying a tray laden with various items. She placed the tray down on the small table and sat down in Ada's reading chair and turned to smile softly at Ada.

She spoke in a whisper. "I am glad you have awoken. The doctor will be coming shortly and I have brought you a cold cloth for your head and a small bit of toasted bread for your breakfast."

Marie must have already been in this morning and emptied the chamber pot where Ada had thrown up. The room was straightened and her gown from yesterday was put away.

"Marie, tell me what is going on?" Ada wondered if anyone had found poor Ellen yet. She hoped the authorities had talked to Colin and that he had been taken away already. "Can I please have some butter for the toast? I feel dreadful." Ada looked at Marie, who was looking at her with a confused and worried expression on her small face.

"You are safe now, madam, do not fret. I cannot imagine what you went through last evening." Marie took a small dish with fresh butter in it and started to spread it on Ada's toast.

Ada shook her head slowly. It hurt, so she stopped. "Colin told you what happened?" Ada's voice gave away her surprise.

"Oui, madam. Such a terrible thing. He has told everyone; the proper authorities have been notified. Everything is fine now." Marie looked at Ada and held the plate out for Ada to grab. Ada stared at the plate, waited for about thirty seconds, then lifted her hand toward it. She looked down at the brownish crispy toast, with the butter glistening on the still-warm surface.

"Marie, can I please have some butter for my toast?" Ada asked, continuing to look at the plate.

Marie looked at Ada worriedly, "Of course you can, I'll fetch some soon." She looked at the freshly buttered toast and back at Ada's bruised and swollen face.

"Whenever you get time is fine. So, what is going to happen with Colin? Did they take him already?" Ada inquired, as she took a small bite of toast despite not feeling hungry.

"Did they take him where?" Marie's brows pulled together, as if she was trying to follow a very confusing story.

Ada took her time answering. "Why, to jail of course!"

Marie sat on the bed beside Ada and put a hand on her leg. "Madam, you are worrying me. Mr. Watershaw saved your life last night. Why would he be in jail?"

Ada choked explosively on her bite of toast. Marie handed her a glass of water and smacked her on the back. Each smack reverberated in her head.

"He did what?" Ada was trying to remember. She thought everything was crystal clear but now her head felt so muddled. What was happening to her? She closed her eyes and laid her head back on her feather pillow.

Another knock sounded at her door but she did not bother opening her eyes. Marie jumped up to answer it. She could hear more footsteps enter her room. She heard two male voices speaking. She recognized one as Colin's and she shuddered involuntarily. *The other must be the doctor*, she thought.

"As I was saying, a family friend was staying with us. Unbeknownst to me, she must have been harboring some inappropriate feelings for me because I left the women—both Ellen and my wife—alone in my room for a moment to fetch a cigar and when I returned to finish discussing the next day's activities, I found Ellen on top of my poor wife, bashing her head against the bed post. I was terrified and ran over to help but she came at me as well, as though she was possessed. I tried to hold her back and tried to stop her, but I guess my strength was too much in that moment. The poor girl. I was just overcome with worry for my wife." Colin finished and walked over to the bed to look down at Ada. "Please sir, make her well again."

Ada's eyes opened and stared at Colin looking down at her. His dead eyes gave no hint to the others of the true events of last evening.

Marie was speaking with the doctor now. Ada could only hear snippets of the conversation as Marie was much quieter and more reserved then Colin. "Yes, she has been acting oddly this morning. She takes a long time to answer questions and repeats herself often. I am very worried."

The doctor strode over to the beside and placed his brown leather bag on the small round table beside Ada's bed. He was a younger man, maybe ten years older than Ada. His once-black hair had streaks of grey and white. His eyes were kind and only showed the faintest of lines around them. "Good morning, my dear. You have been through so much but you are safe now. I am here to help you." The doctor turned to Marie and Colin. "I would like to speak to Mrs. Watershaw alone, if that is agreeable with her. I find it often makes the patient calmer." He saw Ada try to nod politely.

Colin and Marie left and closed the door behind them. Ada looked pleadingly at the doctor.

"Please sir, you need to listen to me. My husband killed that girl on purpose." Ada searched the doctors face for a shocked reaction.

"I know, I know, Mrs. Watershaw," he said as he patted her arm. "It was a terrible thing he had to do to save your life." He turned his attention back to the leather bag and retrieved some instruments.

"He did not do it to save my life, he did it because he wanted to. He is the one who cracked my head against the bedpost, not Ellen!" Ada was starting to become frantic. She sat up and put her hands on the man's shoulders. "Please! You must believe me! He murdered her in cold blood."

The doctor grasped Ada's arms and pulled her hands off his shoulders. "My dear, you have had a trauma and the inner working of your head has been injured. You need rest. These delusions and fears will all fade away as soon as you become yourself again. I promise you that."

Ada shook her head and dizziness hit her like a wave. "No! Listen to me... Please!" She looked around vainly wishing for something to materialize that might help her prove her claim. The doctor grasped her chin with one hand and pressed a tiny glass to her lips.

"Just a little drink, Mrs. Watershaw. You need to sleep." Ada tried to turn her head but his grasp was too strong. She opened her mouth and swallowed as the small amount of bitter liquid ran down her throat. She laid back down.

"I'm telling you ... truth..." She started to lose her faculties as she slipped into an opium-induced sleep.

The doctor packed up his leather bag, rose from the bed and left the vial of laudanum on the bedside table. When he walked into the hall, he was met with Mr. Watershaw, who was sitting on a bench further down the hall, and Robertson, who was standing beside him. Colin rose as he strode over.

"Your wife has suffered a very serious injury to her head. I believe that her brain has been grievously affected and it will be more than a week until she recovers all her faculties. It will be even more time before the swelling and the bruising disappear from her face. I have given her a sedative. It's just a sleeping aid. It would be best to keep her sleeping for a least four or five days until some of the swelling has gone down. I have left a vial of medicine at her bedside. She was raving unseemly accusations that she will no doubt regret terribly when she wakes up but just reassure her that it is not her fault and the guilt will subside."

Colin shook the doctor's hand. "Thank you so much, sir. Robertson will pay your fee and see you out. I would like to go check on my wife now."

"Very good, sir." Robertson gestured to the stairs and the two men retreated from view.

Colin walked toward Ada's door and once he was sure the men were out of sight and earshot, he turned on his heel and walked the other way toward his bedroom. "Sleep well, wife." Colin sneered at his own joke and closed the door behind him.

Chapter 37

It had been over a week before Ada had begun to feel well again. She had soon realized that the only way she was going to stop being force-fed laudanum was to act calm and mention nothing about the night of Ellen's death, unless directly asked a question. In that case, she would refer to the story Colin told the doctor and that was all. She knew Marie had believed her accusations but with a young girl found strangled in Colin's bedroom, Marie had wisely kept her beliefs to herself and Ada did not blame her one bit. Colin had apparently turned Louise, who had written one message and showed up at the door twice to try and see Ada, away. Marie recounted that Colin had stated she was too ill and needed complete rest and silence as per the doctor's orders. Ada was miserable. Her facial swelling had gone down considerably and the dark black bruising under both her eyes had faded into a yellowish green. She was still experiencing mild headaches and one of her eyes was red on the inside and made Ada shiver when she looked in the mirror. Overall, she felt physically decent but mentally, she was in agony. She longed for Grant. She missed him so completely that is was almost overwhelming. She kept hearing the words her mother said to her in her dream, *"Remember, pet, no one can decide your life for you. They can impact your existence but they cannot decide who you are, what you dream, what you remember, and what you wish for. Even if everything you touch seems to fall apart, remember you are the only one who can rebuild it."* She took strength and solace in the fact that her dreams and memories were always her own and they were always of Grant. Had it only been two months since she had been forced to say goodbye to him and ride away? Time had passed so slowly and it seemed as she had been apart from him much longer than she actually had. While she was lost in memories, Marie came silently into her room.

"Madam, do you feel well enough for a visit at Lady Davaneaux's home today?" Before she could even venture an answer, Marie was already pulling a gown out for her.

"I would love to Marie but Colin will not allow it. I feel like I am a prisoner in this room." Ada sighed. She felt very down today.

Marie basically skipped over to where Ada was sitting. "You have forgotten! Mr. Watershaw is away today and is staying overnight at the large horse auction in Annapolis Royal. He will not know you have gone. I think you need to get out of this house. Louise sent a message. Her husband is also away at the sale and she would be glad for your company." Marie beamed at Ada. She was happy to have been able to deliver good news for once.

"Thank you, Marie. I will go. I will tell Robertson I will be needing the carriage."

"Madam, Mr. Watershaw has taken the carriage, the groom and most of the horses with him to the auction. Perhaps you would like to take Gypsy?" Marie lit up like a candlestick. She knew what effect this suggestion would have on Ada.

A wide smile spread across Ada's face.

"It is a lovely day. It is very snowy but there is a large warming sun. I will fetch your heavy cloak."

Ada walked over to the garment Marie had pulled out for her. It was her dark blue riding habit. She laughed to herself. Marie had obviously thought this through.

The ride to the Davaneaux house was brisk but wonderful. Gypsy was feeling fresh in the chilly weather and with her lack of exercise lately, the little horse ate up the ground between Ada and Louise's house in no time. Ada had to hold her back to stop her from plowing through snowbanks with unsure footing but by the time she arrived on Louise's front porch, she was red cheeked, utterly refreshed and cautiously optimistic. She prayed that Louise would have news of Grant and she hoped against hope that the news would be good.

She knocked on the large front door, her leather riding gloves muffling the sound slightly. Louise's butler appeared and ushered her inside. Louise floated down the stairs in a heavy cloak with a scarf and muff. When she saw Ada, she ran over and flung her arms around her friend's neck. She pulled back and looked at Ada's face. Tears formed in her eyes.

"I am so sorry for this." She touched the bruising on Ada's forehead. "I suspected Colin's story was false but I could do nothing about it. I feel so helpless."

Ada smiled at her friend's kindness and shrugged. "Thank you, believing me is the best gift you could give me."

Louise hugged her hard again. "I would like for us to chat in private. It is a chilly day for a walk but..."

"It is not terrible outside. I rode Gypsy here this morning. Colin had taken the horses and Henry to the sale with him."

"Well, that explains why your cheeks are like ice. Shall we walk Gypsy down to the barn? We can give her a small snack, and the barn will be warmer as it will cut the wind. Most of the horses and people, save trainer John, are also gone. I gave John the day off because his mother is ailing, so we will have privacy there." Louise pulled her scarf over her head and led the way onto the front porch. Ada grabbed Gypsy's reins and led her toward the barn, walking companionably beside Louise.

Louise yanked at the barn door and it finally swung open. Ada laughed to herself, Louise always looked so out of place in anywhere other than a garden party or her parlor. *God bless her,* Ada thought.

"Oh, could you tie her over there?" Louise pointed to Gypsy and then to an outside rail. "I want to make sure there is some hay in a stall for her before we bring her in." Ada smiled again. Louise had no idea what she was doing.

Ada walked into the barn behind Louise, leaving the door open. Gypsy whinnied in protest of being left outside. "Louise, I can get the hay, please... there is no need for you to get dirty for my horse..." The word stuck in her throat.

Louise was standing in the aisle of the barn beaming and basically floating off the ground with excitement. Ada looked past her farther down the aisle.

"Oh, God, oh, my God..." Ada's voice was a whisper.

Grant stood in the aisle looking at her. She could see his chest moving with heavy breaths.

"Oh, God..." She wanted to run to him but she felt her legs weaken and she went to her knees and began to sob hysterically.

He moved instinctively, running to her and dropping to his knees in front of her. He gathered her to his chest and squeezed her against him, trying to melt her into him. "Thank you, God, thank you..." he was muttering to himself as they swayed back and forth on their knees, not moving from their embrace and crying together.

"I'll leave you, then. You will be alone for at least an hour. I'll see you at the house later, Ada." Louise smiled and wiped her eyes. She closed the barn door behind her and left the pair in weeping silence.

With her head tucked solidly against his chest, she could smell him and feel his skin through his shirt. She felt like she was home. No matter where she ended up in this life, this was always where her true home would be. Grant reached down and tucked a finger under her chin, turning her face up to look at his.

"Jesus, what has he done to you? Your beautiful face." Grant's eyes were surveying what was left of her bruising and the redness of her eye. He did not have a look of pity; his face held a mixture of concern and anger. He stroked one cheek with his thumb softly. "He'll not get away with this." Grant's tone was final.

Ada took his hand in hers. "Please, Grant. I just got you back. I cannot lose you to jail or the gallows. Promise me you will do nothing." When Grant's face looked as if he would refuse, Ada said softer, "Please, love, promise me."

Grant closed his eyes and exhaled deeply, then opened them to find Ada's wide eyes staring at him. He nodded softly. "I'll bide." He stood up and reached for Ada's hands, hauling her up and against him. He pulled her close to him and bent his head toward hers. He nuzzled his nose briefly against hers and bent his lips to her.

She felt his lips close on hers and they instantly warmed to the fire that was started between them. She held onto him with her arms around his neck and enjoyed the sensuous feeling of slow kissing in the cool air. She finally pulled back and surveyed his face. "I thought you were going to die," she spoke softly.

"Aye, so did I." Grant smiled lazily. "I told ye to leave this place, Ada. I told ye to go to the port, to safety."

"I know. I couldn't." Ada reached up and touched his cheek. "You would not have left me," she said simply.

"Well, then, I guess I owe ye my life. I will never be able to thank ye, ye brave wee thing."

A loud whinny screamed outside the door, interrupting their reunion. Gypsy was growing very impatient of waiting in the cold and had decided to make her needs known again. Ada went out to grab her while Grant pitched some hay in a stall. As Ada led her down the short hallway, she could see Grant spreading out a carriage blanket on a mound of straw in a clean empty stall. He looked at her, and their eyes locked as the door swung closed on Gypsy's stall.

"Milady? Would you care to repose with me awhile?" Grant offered his hand to Ada as he bowed, mocking gentlemanly manners.

"Why sir, this is very forward of you." Ada laughed and took his hand.

She reclined onto the soft fur carriage blanket that indented with a crunching noise as she laid down. Grant laid beside her. He had removed his cloak and now proceeded to cover them both with it. The smell of the straw warmed her soul as much as the big arms wrapped around her. Grant placed a small chaste kiss on her cheek, which led to less innocent kisses on her mouth. He stopped breathlessly. He looked at her. His face seemed full of wonderment. It was as if his feelings for her had grown during their separation. Before she left, he was certain he could not feel more for her, but as he laid with her in his arms once again, it seemed he could.

"I love ye so much, Ada. I have never been happier in this life than when I am in your arms." He spoke quietly, his emotions present on his face.

She looked at him. He was still so beautiful. She could see a few extra scars marring his neck and hands from his recent illness but it somehow created a paradox that made him look both fierce and vulnerable. "I love you too, Grant," she said, unable to say anything else as her eyes welled with tears. Grant cupped the back of her head. When his hand met her hair, a loosely placed hair pin fell onto the blanket, causing a resulting sequence of hair pins to shake loose and her hair to cascade around her face. The mood instantly changed. She looked up from her fallen hair pins and saw Grant's face. His eyes burned into her with lustful intensity. She felt every nerve in her body jump to attention and the softness of her own hair on her cheek brought its own sense of arousal.

"Would it be terribly vulgar to ask ye to make love to me on this blanket, in this freezing barn, with only half of an hour's time left before ye must go back to Louise?" Grant said, searching her face. His hand, however, was already searching other parts of her, sliding down the outside of her skirt.

"Let me see if I remember how." Ada wrapped her arms around Grant's neck and pulled him in. She needed him. She needed to be whole again.

He kissed her wildly, covering her mouth and neck with fevered kisses. He felt her hands slide down the outside of his body and fumble with the laces of his breeches. He lifted his body up with his arms as she tugged the material over his arse and down to the middle of his thighs. He was already hard and his cock had sprung from the front of his pants as she pulled them down. He leaned in to kiss her again and grabbing the bottom of her skirt, he hiked it up on both sides, leaving her open to him. There was no time for foreplay and neither of them wanted any. Their lust had become a need. Spreading her legs, she expected him to enter her fiercely, driving away the feelings of loneliness, fear and sadness. Instead, she felt him slide into her inch by inch, her emotions melting from her body into the straw pile beneath. Her whole body seemed to meld around him. He came down to her, kissing her lips with the gentleness of the wind carrying a leaf. His hands were on either side of her body. She reached her arms under his armpits and grabbed his shoulders, pulling him deeper into her body. He bent his elbows with a low groan and she felt his weight upon her. He was sweaty in the coolness of the barn. He wiped his brow briefly with the sleeve of his shirt. His speed was increasing and she felt herself begin to lose reality. She sank her teeth into his shoulder and let go.

He felt her tighten around him and could hear her panting breath in his ear. He went with her, because he knew he always would.

He shifted his weight from her body onto his side and quickly huddled her against his chest. He felt a chill where his sweat-dampened face cooled in the winter air.

"I willna live my life without ye," he said into the top of her head.

"There is nothing..." she started to speak but thought about her words, "I am not sure what to do." She spoke with a sigh, the glow of the recent wearing off to the dimness of the present.

"Just let me hold ye for one more moment, I will think on it later," he said as he squeezed her tightly.

Chapter 38

They had kissed goodbye behind the closed door of the barn, knowing they would see each other soon but not knowing when. He had told her she was stronger than anyone could ever hope to be. She walked the path back to Louise's house feeling the cool wind disguise her flushed face and wet eyes. Louise unlocked the front door and immediately opened her arms. Ada walked into them without hesitation.

"Thank you so much, Louise. You have truly given me something I have been finding myself in short supply of lately: kindness." She hugged her friend fiercely.

"We will fix this, Ada. I promise you. There has to be something we can do." Louise released Ada from the hug. "Let us retire to my sewing room upstairs and you can tell me all about the... horses." She laughed teasingly.

The pair had spent the entire evening eating, laughing and generally behaving in the most undignified manner. Ada thought that other than her time with Grant, this was the best she had felt in a long time. She knew that upon Colin's return late tomorrow, her giddiness would be doused again in misery but she refused to let that quell her enjoyment of a dear friend and the knowledge that her love was waiting, always behind her. She pushed negativity aside and had another glass of wine. Louise had invited her to stay the night, not wanting her to ride Gypsy home in the dark, cold dusk. She accepted the offer immediately and was now laying back on a feather mattress, slightly gone with drink, snorting in a most unrefined manner between gales of laughter at Louise's impression of various acquaintances of theirs. It was very late when they finally went to sleep.

Chapter 39

Colin and Bernard walked around the outdoor pens at the equine auction in Annapolis Royal. Colin tried to shrug his shoulders higher to push his wool coat up to cover more of his ears. It was frigid. The temperature had dropped suddenly and the light foggy drizzle of the morning had become freezing and windy misery by the afternoon. The main auction was at three. Colin pulled out his pocket watch, it had to be getting close to that time. It was held inside and would offer at least a brief reprieve from the wind and the slushy ground. This was the most important auction of the year. Because the sale was held in the winter, many people depended on the extra income to get them through to the following year, when farming and livestock were more profitable during other seasons. Colin and Bernard both had some horses in the sale, and having perused the pens, Colin had his eye on a few worth bidding on—should they go for the right price.

"How do you think ours look in comparison this year, Watershaw?" Bernard asked, with his eyes squinted and his face slightly scrunched from the wind.

"Well, if they can manage to not bloody freeze to death before the auction begins, I think we stand to make quite a profit today. I overheard positive talk around our broodmares earlier this morning."

"If the horses do not freeze to death, I am sure that I will. Shall we go inside and find a decent seat for the sale? I would take a cold bench with a draft over this wind any day." Not waiting for Colin to agree, Bernard turned toward the sale barn and starting sloshing his way to the entry. Colin followed behind him.

The auction began about ten minutes after the pair sat down. In the meantime, they had chatted casually with some other breeders they had not seen since last year's sale. The younger horses and the ponies were auctioned off first. One of the stallions that Colin was interested in was up next. He nudged Bernard in the ribs with his elbow and pointed to the sale program. Bernard politely ended his conversation and waited. The stallion walked onto the sale floor with his neck arched high and his nostrils flared in alertness. He was not a horse of huge size but his breeding was impeccable and his confirmation was perfection. The horse stomped, pawed the ground and let out a loud squeal when the handler pulled on his lead rope. He was still black, but his coat was giving way to the dapple grey that would become lighter and more beautiful as he aged. The auctioneer began the bidding and Colin put his hand up to start it off.

Bernard clapped Colin on the shoulder, "Good day today, good day. A little extra coin in our purse to spend on some well-deserved luxuries tonight." The smile on

Bernard's face told Colin exactly what sort of luxuries he had in mind.

Colin smiled broadly. Having paid the bill for the horses he purchased, including the new stallion, he collected the money from his sales and was quite happy with the business of the day. "I am inclined to agree with you, Bernard. The luxury of a warm place to thaw my bones sounds ideal."

"Warm place for your bones?" Bernard laughed. "There are other parts of my body that I am more eager to unfreeze."

Colin laughed as they walked down the path toward the inn and tavern which also played host to a bawdy house for paying customers. The inn would be packed to its rafters tonight because of the sale. The rooms would be scarce and the women outnumbered ten to one. Colin and Bernard had paid for their rooms a day early, having sent a groom of Bernard's to ride ahead and ensure that both would obtain private quarters. As for the women, Colin would have one regardless of circumstances.

The tavern was cramped, but the warmth from the many patrons in close quarters was welcoming. The smell, however, was not. Colin wrinkled his aristocratic nose, "Christ, it smells like a horse's ass in here." He spoke harshly to Bernard, trying to breathe only through his mouth.

"Let's just eat and retire to our rooms quickly. Hopefully, this stench will not carry upstairs as well." Bernard shuffled in the direction of the bar, nudging people and pushing his way through.

"There are two getting up over there." Bernard pointed to a table in the centre of the room, where two men were putting their cloaks and hats back on.

Colin shoved his way unceremoniously to the centre of the room, bumping people's arms, spilling drinks, and pushing bodies out of his way. He put his hand on the back of one of the chairs and nodded at the man who had just stood up, who nodded back to him curtly. Colin took off his coat and threw it on the empty chair beside him to hold the place for Bernard who was getting whisky for them both. Colin scanned the room. He recognized many of the men from the auction and a few others who must be grooms or servants the business men had travelled with. Everyone seemed relaxed and happy to be out of the cold. Two younger men who looked about eighteen and twenty sat looking at the fire. The blond man with long, curly hair occasionally rose to survey the crowd, while the dark-haired boy seemed to keep an eye on the other side of the room. Colin wondered how they had managed to obtain the best seats in the establishment, close to the fire and away from the crowd. As he was pondering the situation, Bernard sat down with the whisky while a serving woman trailed behind him with a fresh smelling chicken dish. Bernard mumbled something about preferring to have the young serving girl instead of the supper and Colin's attentions were brought back to the table. The pair ate companionably. When Bernard finished, he excused himself for the evening, stating he was off to have an "after dinner sweet" as he called it. The young woman came back to clear the plates shortly after Bernard had retired.

"Can I get you another drink, sir?" she asked loudly over the roar of the full room.

Colin grabbed her sleeve and pulled her face closer to his, "You can send my drink to my room with a pretty young woman carrying it. Someone who has your looks will do, but hopefully cleaner." He released her sleeve with a flick of his hand as he stood up, draining his cup. "The sooner the better." He strode past her and made his way pompously up the stairs.

It took less than a quarter of an hour for a timid knock to sound outside Colin's door. He bade the person to enter from his reclined position on the bed. A small sparrow of a woman entered the room. Her delicate face was personable but professional.

"Well, now, you will do nicely... Miss...?" Colin raised his eyebrows in inquiry.

"Elise, just Elise is fine." She walked further into the room with delicate footsteps.

"How old are you, Elise?" Colin asked from his place on the bed, his hands clasped behind his head.

"I am four and twenty," she answered simply. She was obviously used to polite conversation with clients.

"That will do just fine. Now, take off your dress, Elise, and slowly."

She undid the lacing of her loose-fitting gown and let it fall to the floor in a whoosh of worn fabric. She bent and removed each shoe one by one and stood back up to face Colin. He patted the bed beside him.

"Come here."

She walked over to him in a matter of fact way. She put one knee on the bed and instead of lying beside him, she straddled him, putting her legs on either side of his hips. Colin twitched slightly.

"I said beside me, not on top of me."

"Well, most men like the view from down there, are you sure you don't want to give it a try, love?" She reached to stroke his cheek placatingly.

"Do you think you are in control here, whore?" Colin sat up abruptly, grabbed her by her upper arms and threw her onto her back. She quickly scooted into a seated position on the bed beside him, looking shocked and afraid.

"If you want to be rough, sir, it will cost extra and you cannot leave marks." Elise had collected herself again and her neutral face was back in place.

Colin began to laugh. "How much extra, then?" He slapped her hard across the face. "Oh, my dear. How much for that? I do hope that does not leave a mark."

Her hand went to her stinging face and she attempted to leave. Colin pushed her roughly back down on the bed. She screamed loudly but his hand quickly covered her mouth to stifle her. She could feel his other hand trying to pry her tightly clenched legs apart, so she bit his hand, savagely tasting blood.

"You little bitch!" Colin pulled his damaged hand back from Elise's mouth. She screamed again. His hand shot out to the dresser beside the bed and grabbed a clay cup, unintentionally knocking the matching clay pitcher onto the wooden floor and smashing it into a thousand pieces. He brought the cup down hard and smashed it against the woman's temple. Feeling her relax in unconsciousness beneath him, he began to stand up when the door flung open.

"Is everything all right in here? I heard a crash." A man who looked to be in his late fifties stood at the door. His robe hung askew, it had obviously been thrown on in haste. Another man in similar disarray entered after him, looking wildly around.

"My, God, man! What have you done?" The first man's eyes took in the scene of the shattered pottery, the bloody and unconscious woman, and Colin's bleeding hand.

"This bitch attacked me!" Colin rose completely from the bed. His shirtfront was covered in blood from where he had been cradling his bleeding hand.

The second man, whose face was practically white with shock, took another step inside the room. "It looks quite different from where we are standing, Mr. Watershaw."

Colin recognized him from earlier today at the auction house.

"Call for the authorities, this is simply outrageous!" the first man yelled. He was mopping his head with the belt of his robe. "Also, can someone fetch some help for this poor girl?"

Footsteps were coming up the hall outside the room. Colin was breathing hard. He looked at the unconscious woman beside him, the half-dressed and half-panicked men at the door, and reached his hand quietly under the pillow of his bed.

"You will not be calling the authorities," Colin said coldly with an eerie calm. With a resigned sigh, he pulled a large pistol from underneath the pillow and aimed it at the first gentlemen who had come through the door. There was a moment of shocked silence as the gun went off and the ball hit its mark, crumpling the first man on the floor, dead. His chest leaking blood onto the dirty floorboards beneath.

Chaos ensued. The second man fell to the ground, covering his head, and some women were heard screaming from nearby rooms. Another man launched himself into the room. Colin recognized him as the young blonde man who had been sitting by the fire. Quickly making sense of the scene, the young man pulled a knife from his belt and threw it across the room.

Colin felt the impact before the pain. He looked down at the knife buried in his chest, then sat down abruptly on the floor beside the bed, and fell onto his side. He coughed and foamy blood bubbled from his mouth. The blonde man strode to the bed, stepped over Colin and picked up Elise's lifeless form and quickly carried her out of the room, pausing briefly at the door to converse with the other young man in the hall.

"I've got her. See to the bodies and the other guests, aye?" He walked briskly down the hall with his delicate burden.

Chapter 40

Watershaw House

As Ada wandered around the large home she shared with Colin she could not help but notice that her situation already felt better knowing Grant was alive and that she was loved. Even knowing that Colin was to return today could not quell the small bursts of excitement she felt when she thought about running into Grant in town, or catching glimpses of him while he worked on Colin's horses. She knew those simple things would not be enough forever but for right now, she was more content than she had been in a while. She entered Colin's office. She was only permitted in there to use the library, so once inside, she made her way to the shelves of books. Her finger trailed along the spines of the books as she tried to choose something new, something to keep her busy for a few hours. She had finally selected a book that promised a story about a murder within a royal family when she heard commotion in the front hall. She grabbed her book and walked briskly toward the ongoing noise. She could hear footsteps coming toward her as well and as she opened the door to Colin's office, Robertson nearly toppled into the room on top of her.

"Robertson, whatever is this? Are you quite alright?" He was clearly upset about something. In all her time at the house, she had never seen his demeanor to be anything but composed and serious.

"Ma'am, a rider has come from Annapolis Royal. There has been a terrible tragedy," Robertson's eyes were beginning to tear up. Ada's stomach clenched involuntarily.

"Speak, Robertson," Ada said roughly. "If you please," she added after seeing the pain in his face.

"It is Mr. Watershaw, ma'am. He's dead." He hung his head and sniffed as he looked at the carpet under his feet.

Ada had a hard time processing this. "What did you say?" She asked in a curious voice.

"I am so sorry, Mrs. Watershaw, he is dead. The rider said something about being stabbed in the chest... God save us what a tragedy, such a young man." Robertson looked somewhat uncomfortable, either with his own grief or the fact that he expected unrelenting female grief from her and he was unsure how to handle it.

"Get me Marie." It was all Ada could manage. She needed to talk to someone trustworthy, someone who was not loyal to Colin. Robertson was no doubt relieved to get out of her presence and sped off to do her bidding. He was almost out of view when she added, "Robertson! Also, send someone for Grant Ross."

The butler turned back around with a questioning look on his face. "Do it now!" Ada was more aggressive than assertive but she did not care, she had no time for his loyalty bullshit. The man nodded, turned and scurried away. Ada sat down abruptly on the wooden stool that Colin kept by the door of his office and tried to calm her breathing... "Jesus Christ," she whispered. "Freedom."

Ada stopped at the window in the office. She had been pacing back and forth waiting for Grant to arrive. Marie had burst into Colin's office almost immediately after being summoned and she had stared at Ada with wide eyes, unsure of how to behave. She tentatively grabbed Ada's hand and made the customary condolences before asking whether there was anything she could fetch for her. Ada had squeezed Marie's hand tight and spoke in a low quiet tone.

"Let us speak and act freely with each other. I mourn him no more than you do, but we must put on a show." Ada's eyes searched Marie's face. She saw her let out a sigh as a wave of tension seemed to flow out of her features.

"*Oui*, madam, we will do what is proper but I will grieve him how he truly deserves." Marie led Ada by the hand to the parlour. "Let us wait elsewhere, away from his belongings so we are not reminded of bitter memories."

When Grant arrived at Watershaw house, he had not known what to expect. A small feeling of dread had made a nest in the bottom of his belly and stayed there until he reached the front door. When he knocked, the butler had not opened the door but instead, a young tiny girl who had introduced herself as Marie bade him to follow her. He saw Ada standing in the living room. Her hands were clasped together and she was squeezing them tightly. He had immediately asked what was wrong and was promptly filled in on the entire situation. He felt it would be un-Christian of him to rejoice in a man's death but if there was anyone who deserved to die for the way he lived, it was Colin Watershaw. The two women and Grant sat close together and discussed the next steps. Ada seemed to be understandably shocked at the situation and trying to process her own feelings, which were no doubt very similar to his own. Together, the trio decided that Marie would stay at Watershaw house and handle the bureaucratic tasks that needed to be taken care of, such as writing the death notice, starting funeral plans, setting the house to rights for visitors wishing to pay respects and the like. Ada and Grant would travel to Annapolis Royal to meet with the law regarding Colin's death and arrange to have his body transported back home for burial.

Annapolis Royal, Two Days Later

Grant and Ada were waiting in a clean white room inside the office of a governing official in Annapolis Royal. Ada sat in a large wooden chair adorned with a lace knitted pillow. A large wooden desk sat in front of her. Grant sat slightly behind her in a smaller wooden chair that had been brought in from the hallway upon their arrival. They had been waiting less than ten minutes when the door opened and a tall white-haired gentleman walked into the room and introduced himself as Matthew Stuart Cumberland. His voice was calm and quiet for such a tall man and his British accent suited both his clothing and his demeanor.

"Mistress Watershaw, please allow me to give you my heartfelt condolences on the most tragic and untimely passing of your husband." He grasped her hand tightly and looked sincerely into her face.

"Thank you kindly for your sympathies. I must admit, his death is... shocking to me." Ada smiled softly at him. "Please, allow me to introduce my travelling companion and dear friend, Mr. Grant Ross."

Grant stepped forward and shook Mr. Cumberland's hand strongly. "It is a pleasure, sir."

"Very good to meet you, Mr. Ross. Shall we all take a seat?" Ada and Grant had risen when he entered the room and upon his gesturing, sat back down in their seats as Mr. Cumberland took the spot behind his large desk. He opened his top drawer and took out a few sheets of paper with writing covering both sides.

"As you likely know, I work closely under the governor and I am sure that you have plenty of questions regarding your husband's passing, the repercussions resulting from his death, and basically the story in its entirety. So, I thought perhaps it would be best to tell you the details from start to finish."

"Please do, Mr. Cumberland, thank you so much." Ada smiled reassuringly.

"I do have to forewarn you, Mrs. Watershaw, that some of the details are not fit for a lady's ears and I hesitate to share them with you." Mr. Cumberland looked at Grant hoping for back up in this matter.

Grant spoke before Ada could. "Mrs. Watershaw has prepared herself to know the entire truth. She feels it will help with the healing process." Grant smiled sweetly as Ada looked back at him with a look of gratitude.

"Very well, then." Mr. Cumberland's face did not look like it agreed with his words but he began the retelling regardless. "It seems that following the auction, where he had a very successful day, Mr. Watershaw found himself in a house of... a... somewhere that men..." He looked to Grant pleadingly.

"A brothel. Yes, continue..." Ada chimed in helpfully.

Mr. Cumberland's mouth remained slightly ajar and he promptly closed it as soon as he realized. "Um, yes, yes, quite so, a brothel." He proceeded to tell the story, in its entirety, to Ada and Grant.

Ada chose various moments to gasp and utter, "Dear, God." She hoped it sounded authentic. Truthfully, she was surprised that Colin had not done more to the poor woman.

"I can assure you that the entire incident was looked into and Mr. Watershaw's death was found to be a faultless act by the young man due to the nature of the event and his concern for the safety of others around him. I am very sorry, Mrs. Watershaw."

Ada blinked tears back. It was all so unnecessary. "I appreciate you sharing the story with me, I am so sorry for the pain and suffering my husband has caused." Ada felt sick to her stomach.

Grant, who had been entirely silent said quietly, "Did the young woman live, sir?"

"Oh, yes! Oh, yes, she is recovering nicely. I believe someone said her name was Elise." Mr. Cumberland added.

"I would very much like to meet her and apologize." Ada felt she needed to try and make this right, however she could. She could clearly not help the gentleman Colin killed but she might be able to offer a small token and her apologies to Miss Elise.

"Mrs. Watershaw, that is really not necessary. I applaud your sensitive nature but it would be most irregular for you to visit her, considering."

"I will go with her. What is the location, please?" Grant was very courteous but his tone was firm and Mr. Cumberland realized there was no sense in objecting any further. He told them the location of the brothel and saw them out the front door.

The brothel was only a ten-minute walk from Mr. Cumberland's office. They opted to stroll through the cold winter air instead of hiring a coach to drive them. Ada had hoped the cool air would calm her head.

Surprisingly, the building was very tidy and looked new. Its wood was clean and the area around it was well maintained. Grant opened the door and gestured for Ada to enter before him. The downstairs of the establishment seemed to be just a quaint tavern with a fireplace and some tables set up for food, drink and gaming. A few people were playing cards around one of the tables and barely looked up when Ada and Grant entered. Grant strode to the bar and asked the woman working there for the owner of the establishment.

"I am his wife. He is not in right now. Can I help you with anything?" She was not much to look at but she seemed personable and direct.

Grant briefly explained the situation and made the proper introductions. When the woman heard Ada had come to offer her apologies to Elise, she offered them both a drink and bade them to sit down while she went and spoke to Elise.

"Do you think she will see us?" Ada sipped her ale and asked Grant hopefully.

"Aye, I think so. Well, I hope she does," Grant replied most unhelpfully.

Five minutes later, the woman reappeared on the staircase and beckoned Ada and Grant to follow her upstairs. The table of men below watched as they ascended the stairs and elbowed each other laughing and mumbling something under their breath about a two-for-one price. Grant shot them an angry look and then shook his head, following Ada up the stairs. There were several rooms on the second level of the building. The pair were led to the third door on the left-hand side. The woman had knocked softly and walked away after a faint voice came from the inside, bidding them to enter.

"Hello," a soft voice from the bed said. The woman sitting up in bed was classically pretty, even with all the bruising and abrasions marring her face. She was dainty, like a small finch with expressive eyes that were now rimmed with red and blue marks.

"Hello. My name is Ada Watershaw. I have come on my own behalf to offer you my heartfelt apologies for the terrible suffering my hus... late husband has inflicted on you." Ada stayed where she was standing, not wanting to get too close in case she was not a welcome visitor.

"You can sit if you like, Mrs. Watershaw." The girl looked at the chair by the bedside.

Ada moved to the chair, sat down, and looked at the woman. "Are you truly all right?"

"I will heal, ma'am, thank you. I appreciate you coming all the way down here to apologize. I am sorry about your loss."

Ada leaned closer to the girl. "To tell you the truth, I have looked like you look now and even worse more than a few times because of Mr. Watershaw, and a part of me is happy he can never do this to another person again. I suppose that makes me wicked but I thought you should know."

Elise looked at Ada straight in the eyes, "You are not wicked, Mrs. Watershaw. From my experience, men like that do not ever change, they just get worse. You are lucky to be able to get out now before you end up deader than him."

Ada's eyes teared slightly. She did not think she needed to hear someone say they understood but it certainly felt nice to have a stranger tell her she was going to be okay. "I would like to offer you some money. I hope you will not take any offense. I simply want to help you and ensure that you get proper remuneration for what you have had to endure." The girl started to shake her head. "Please." Ada asked sincerely.

Elise's hand rose from the blankets and clasped Ada's. "Thank you, Mrs. Watershaw." The two women smiled knowingly at each other for a moment.

Ada sat back and swiped at her eyes with the back of her hand. "I do have a question for you. Does the man who killed Mr. Watershaw still work here? I would like to tell him not to feel guilty on my account and that I believe he acted rightly."

"He does, ma'am, and he is the type that would feel guilty about making someone a widow. I am sure he will be very pleased to speak with you." Elise breathed through her nose in what might have been a laugh. "In fact, Mrs. Watershaw, he has been feeling so awful about what happened, and that it happened under his watch, that he gave me this cow bell to ring whenever I need anything. When I ring it, he comes running." This time, Elise laughed. "The owners, Mr. and Mrs. Morton, hate it but they feel bad for me too and let me use it." Her face broke into a wide grin. "Shall we?" She held up the cow bell and rang it loudly in the air.

Ada turned her head to the side against the clanging metal and could not help but laugh at the look of power on Elise's face. She could also hear Grant laughing from behind her. He had taken up a seat on a small bench in the corner of the room, trying to seem as unobtrusive as possible for a large man.

The staircase creaked and footsteps sounded down the hallway. "See?" Elise remarked. "Works like a charm!" She set the bell back down on the small shelf beside her bed. A moment later, three knocks echoed on the door.

"Come in," Elise called from the bed.

The door opened and a young man, who looked just under twenty, stepped inside. "I should never have given ye that..." His Scottish voice had started laughingly but choked off.

The wooden bench Grant was sitting on screeched against the floor. He stared disbelievingly at the young man. "Mary Mother of God..." Grant muttered and sat down hard on the bench.

"Grant?" the boy asked incredibly.

Grant shot off the bench once more and crashed into the boy who was moving toward him at the same speed. "Ewan! Jesus Christ, lad. I thought ye were dead. I looked for ye, I looked everywhere." Grant and Ewan were clasped together with their arms around each other in an unending hug. Tears streamed down Grant's cheeks and although Ada could not see Ewan's face, she knew he was crying as well.

Both her and Elise sat in stunned confusion and watched the men embrace, let go and embrace again, thumping each other on the back between snorts and laughter.

Chapter 41

Ada had given money to Elise, wished her well and was now following the two men, who were chatting like young girls, downstairs. They had decided to sit at a table in the tavern and catch up. Brief introductions had been made upstairs after the initial shock had worn off and Ada made it clear to Ewan that she did not blame him for his actions at all. Ewan had looked slightly surprised at this but politely said nothing. Grant had clapped him on the shoulder and suggested they all have a few drinks together and could perhaps clear some things up for him.

More than a few hours later, the three of them had more than a few ales inside them and Grant and Ewan had mostly filled each other in on each other's lives for the past five years.

"So, I get how ye came to be here, I know how ye were injured but I dinna think I understand how ye know the delightful Mrs. Watershaw here..." Ewan gestured for more drinks, giddy from both drunkenness and seeing Grant again.

"I told ye, her husband was one of my clients," Grant answered, finishing the last of his ale with one large swig.

"Oh aye, and ye always find yourself travelling companions of your client's wives, do ye?" Ewan was sharp and it was becoming clear just how much he had seen in his short life.

"Ewan!" Grant spoke sharply, "Christ, ye'll not be making such implications about Ad... Mrs. Watershaw." Grant was more than a little drunk.

"Begging your pardon, ma'am." Ewan turned to Ada who was contently sipping her drink, her cheeks flushed with merriment and alcohol.

"Of course," she replied politely, then began to giggle. She suddenly found the conversation hilarious but was not exactly sure why.

Both Grant and Ewan eyed her suspiciously, which made her laugh even harder. They continued with their conversation, tactfully ignoring her.

"I dinna work in an establishment such as this without learning a thing or two about men and women, Grant." Ewan gestured around him with a wave of his hand.

"Well, whatever ye think ye have learned, young Ewan, ye dinna need to be making accusations about Ada or myself." Grant's accent was thicker when he was drinking.

"Ada? What a pretty name." Ewan looked at Ada.

"Damn, obviously, I have had too many." Grant looked at Ada with apologetic eyes.

Ada walked over to Grant's chair and put her hands on his cheeks. She placed a small kiss on his lips and looked at his shocked face. This was the first time they had made any kind of physical contact in public. "It is okay, love." She turned and looked at Ewan whose ale was frozen, midair, in his hand. "You are right," she said simply, "I love him."

Ewan's mouth curved up on one side of his face in an endearing smirk. "Well, I am glad of it because the way he has been looking at ye these past couple of drinks, I was beginning to worry for yer safety..." Ewan laughed and ducked as Grant tried to cuff him in the back of his head.

Ada stood there laughing with both men and realized she was happy. She was free and happy. She never wanted to stop feeling the way she did right now. "Ewan?"

"Aye?" His face turned upwards to look at her, his blond locks falling back off his face.

"You will come stay with us, won't you? I do not think Grant will leave this town without taking you with him." Ada looked at his shocked blue eyes.

Ewan looked from Ada to Grant. "I cannot do that, ma'am, I have steady work here..."

"I could really use a hand with business, Ewan," Grant added.

"Christ, Grant. I am a shite blacksmith and ye ken that well enough," Ewan retorted.

Grant chuckled, "Aye, but ye belong with me, lad. We are family."

Ada's eyes teared up and Ewan looked down into his mug of ale. Ada saw him swallow hard. That was all it took. "I would like very much to come with ye both, thank ye." Ewan's eyes were rimmed red.

They had taken a room in the brothel, too drunk to go elsewhere in the cold and too drunk to care about the impropriety of it. Ewan had gone to his own bed and Grant and Ada had made their way upstairs. They lay in bed, staring at the ceiling and talking in low quiet voices.

"There is so much to do when I get back. I have a funeral to plan, estates to handle, livestock to ship..." Ada sighed heavily. The carefree haze of the evening was wearing off.

"Aye, and I will be there to help ye in whatever way I can." Grant sounded sleepy. "Plus, we also have Ewan now. However helpful he may be, is yet to be decided." Grant smiled broadly.

Ada rolled and kissed him gently. "For as long as I have known you, you have made me feel like everything with be all right, thank you for that."

Grant rolled to face Ada, smiled, and kissed her forehead. "Things willna always be easy, lass, but I am here with ye and you with me. That is more than I have had for most of my days, so whatever else comes flying at us from the darkness, we will handle it together."

They fell asleep facing each other, blissfully unaware of the turbulence the future would bring, because at this present moment, they were safe, content and loved.

Author Biography

The past has bewitched Emma Stack for as long as she can remember. Some of her most treasured childhood memories consist of cannons, musket demonstrations, and standing on various fort ramparts, imagining what it was like hundreds of years ago.

The adventures of her childhood led her to obtain a degree in history and eventually, a degree in education to teach history at the high school level. It is also not surprising, but somewhat coincidental that she ended up marrying an artillery soldier and presently lives in Northern Ontario on a military base.

For Emma, writing allows her to blend historical accuracy with her creativity and imagination. Canadian history has always been her constant source of inspiration, with its enthralling and exciting history just waiting to make it into the genre of historical romance. When she is not writing, Emma can be found re-enacting at a heritage village with her son or singing and dancing around her living room.

Emma completed her debut novel *Better Than This* and is currently working on a new series of books set in the War of 1812.

Manufactured by Amazon.ca
Bolton, ON